THE WORKS OF
ROBERT LOUIS STEVENSON
TUSITALA EDITION
VOL. XVI

WEIR OF HERMISTON
SOME UNFINISHED STORIES

BY

ROBERT LOUIS STEVENSON

LONDON: WILLIAM HEINEMANN, Ltd:
IN ASSOCIATION WITH CHATTO & WINDUS:
CASSELL & COMPANY, LTD: AND LONGMANS,
GREEN & COMPANY.

First published, TUSITALA EDITION, May, 1924.
Second Impression . . . . July, 1924.

CONTENTS

A*

THE DEATH OF STEVENSON *

By LLOYD OSBOURNE

STEVENSON had never appeared so well as during the months preceding his death, and there was about him a strange serenity which it is hard to describe, for in quoting from his talks I might easily convey a sense of depression and disillusionment that would read like a contradiction. I think he must have had some premonition of his end ; at least, he spoke often of his past as though he were reviewing it, and with a curious detachment as though it no longer greatly concerned him.

" I am the last of Scotland's three Robbies," he said once. " Robbie Burns, Robbie Fergusson, and Robbie Stevenson—and how hardly life treated them all, poor devils ! If ever I go back I shall put up a stone to poor Fergusson on that forgotten grave of his."

Then he repeated the words in broad Scots as though their cadence pleased him :

" Scotland's three Robbies ! "

On another occasion he said to me : " I am not a man of any unusual talent, Lloyd ; I started out with very moderate abilities ; my success has been due to my really remarkable industry—to developing what I had in me to the extreme limit. When a man begins to sharpen one faculty, and keeps on sharpening it with tireless perseverance, he can achieve wonders. Everybody knows it ; it's a commonplace ; and yet how rare it is to find anybody

* This is one of thirteen papers on Stevenson at different ages by Lloyd Osbourne, his stepson and collaborator, who shared his life from 1876 until its end in 1894. They have been specially written for this Edition of the Works of Robert Louis Stevenson.

doing it—I mean to the uttermost as I did. What genius I had was for *work !* "

Another observation of his comes back to me : " A writer who amounts to anything is constantly dying and being re-born. I was reading *Virginibus* the other day, and it seemed to me extraordinarily good, but in a vein I could no more do now than I could fly. My work is profounder than it was ; I can touch emotions that I then scarcely knew existed ; but the Stevenson who wrote *Virginibus* is dead and buried, and has been for many a year."

Another : " How the French misuse their freedom ; see nothing worth writing about save the eternal triangle ; while we, who are muzzled like dogs, but who are infinitely wider in our outlook, are condemned to avoid half the life that passes us by. What books Dickens could have written had he been permitted ! Think of Thackeray as unfettered as Flaubert or Balzac ! What books I might have written myself ! But they give us a little box of toys, and say to us, ' You mustn't play with anything but these.' "

Another : " The *bourgeoisie's* weapon is starvation. If as a writer or artist you run counter to their narrow notions they simply and silently withdraw your means of subsistence. I sometimes wonder how many people of talent are executed in this way every year."

Another : " We don't live for the necessities of life ; in reality no one cares a damn for them ; what we live for are its superfluities."

Another : " The saddest object in civilisation, and to my mind the greatest confession of its failure, is the man who can work, who wants work, and who is not allowed to work."

Several times he referred to his wish to be buried on the peak of Mount Vaea. Although it was on our property and was always conspicuously in our view, Stevenson was the only one of us who had ever scaled its precipitous slopes. But in spite of his request I never could bring myself to cut a path to the summit. I knew it would be a terrific task, but this was not my real objection. I shrank, as may be imagined, from the association with his death that it involved. What was it but the path to his grave ? And to work on it was unutterably repugnant to me. Thus, in spite of his vexation, I always contrived to evade his request.

In the late afternoon, as some of us played tennis in front of the house, he would walk up and down the veranda, and I began to notice how often he stopped to gaze at the peak. It was specially beautiful at dusk with the evening star shining above it, and it was then he would pause the longest in an abstraction that disturbed me. I always tried to interrupt such reveries ; would call to him ; ask him the score ; would often drop out of a game in order to join him and distract his attention. It is a curious thing that his previous illnesses, which might so easily have concluded in his death, caused me less anguish than the look on his face as he now stared up at Vaea. I think it was the realization that he meant to fight no longer ; that his unconquerable spirit was breaking ; that he was not unwilling to lie on the spot he had chosen and close his eyes for ever.

Yet life for us all had never been more pleasant ; Samoa was enjoying one of its rare spells of peace ; the English man-of-war *Curaçoa* had lain so long in port that her officers had become very much our friends, and were constantly staying with us. There were about sixteen of them, and they made a delightful addition to our society ; and with several R. L. S. was really intimate. He was working hard on *Weir of Hermiston*, and was more than pleased with his progress. He was well. Why, then, should his glance linger so persistently on the peak of Vaea, and always in that musing way ?

It troubled me.

One evening, after dinner, he read the first chapters of *Weir* aloud. I had my usual pencil and paper for the notes I always took on such occasions, but that night I made none. It was so superbly written that I listened to it in a sort of spell. It seemed absolutely beyond criticism ; seemed the very zenith of anything he had ever accomplished ; it flowed with such an inevitability and emotion, such a sureness and perfection, that the words seemed to strike against my heart. When he had finished I sat dumb. I knew I should have spoken, but I could not. The others praised it ; lauded it to the skies ; but I was in a dream from which I could not awake. I poured out a whisky and soda for myself, and sat there like a clod, looking at the ceiling.

Then the party broke up, and we dispersed on our different ways to bed ; I out of doors, to go to my own cottage a few hundred yards away. I had hardly passed the threshold of the door, however, when I heard Stevenson behind me. He was in a state of frightful agitation ; was trembling, breathless, almost beside himself.

" My God, you shall not go like that ! " he cried out, seizing me by the arm, and his thin fingers closing on it like a vice. " What ! Not a single note, not a single word, not even the courtesy of a lie ! You, the only one whose opinion I depend on, and all you can say is ' Good-night, Louis ' ! So that is your decision, is it ? Just ' Good-night, Louis '—like a blow in the face ! "

The bitterness and passion he put into these words is beyond any power of mine to describe.

Then he went on in the same appalling key of reproach while I listened like the criminal I felt I was. Never had he been so humiliated ; never had he been so intolerably insulted. He was no child who had always to have his lollipops ; he could brace himself for any criticism, no matter how damning. But the contempt of silence ! That sitting there and saying nothing ! The implication that it was too bad even to discuss. All that preparation to take notes, and then not a damned word ! Unworthy even of notes, was it ? Good God, it was more than he could bear !

Put yourself in my place ; try to imagine my feelings ; I who had been so carried away by *Weir* that this was the ironical climax ! Oh, that idiotic silence ! What had possessed me ? I had known all the while it was inexcusable

—yet I had sat there looking at the ceiling, oblivious of the author and thinking only of the book.

Then I tried to tell him the truth, but with difficulty, realising how unpardonably I had hurt his pride, which was really much more concerned than the question of my judgment. That it was a masterpiece ; that never before had he written anything comparable with *Weir*, that it promised to be the greatest novel in the English language.

We were in the dark. I could not see his face. But I believe he listened with stupefaction. The reaction when it came was too great for his sorely strained nerves ; tears rained from his eyes—and mine, too, streamed. Never had I known him to be so moved ; never had I been so moved myself ; and in the all-pervading darkness we were for once free to be ourselves, unashamed. Thus we sat, with our arms about each other, talking far into the night. Even after thirty years I should not care to divulge anything so sacred as those confidences ; the revelation of that tortured soul ; the falterings of its Calvary. Until then I had never conceived the degree of his daily suffering ; the petty, miserable dragging ailments that kept him in a " perpetual discomfort." He spoke of the " physical dishonour " ; of the " degradation " of it ; of moments when he had longed for death. To me his heroism took on new proportions, and I was thankful I had refused an important post in order to stay with him. " It will not be for long," he said.

At parting he told me to remind him of this talk if we should ever have the slightest misunderstanding again ; but while such was its meaning no words can convey the tenderness of its expression—the softened voices, the eyes suffusing in the starlight, the lingering clasp of the hand. That night of *Weir* evokes the most affecting of all my recollections.

H.M.S. *Curaçoa*, with all those good friends on board, left us in November, and the weather, as though in mourning, broke in deluges of rain. The wet season, as it is called, begins in November ; and with it a heat and stickiness, an oppressiveness, lifelessness, and debilitation that makes this period of the year something to dread. But we were fortunate in having a pleasant intermission for the thirteenth —R. L. S.'s birthday—when we gave a great Samoan party, which, including the retainers and hangers-on—an inseparable part of such an entertainment—brought up over a hundred people. Then the rain poured again, and kept pouring until the beginning of December, when there was another sunny interval. After dinner on the evening of the second, R. L. S., who was in excellent spirits, surprised us by proposing we should play some games.

" We are getting horribly dull up here," he said. " Everybody sticks round a lamp with a book, and it is about as gay as a Presbyterian mission for seamen. Let's play a game I have just thought of."

The game consisted of each in turn entering the room, and in pantomime, with any accessories we could lay our hands on, portraying one of our friends or acquaintances for the others to guess at. We started a little self-consciously, none but R. L. S. was very eager about it ; but in a short time we were wildly hilarious and continued the pastime with shouts of laughter. R. L. S. excelled everyone ; there was a touch of Harry Lauder in his broad, rich characterisations, and in the exuberance of his own pleasure in them. We kept at it long after our usual bedtime, and our good-nights were said amid giggles of recollection. It was one of the most amusing evenings we had ever spent in Vailima—and was Stevenson's last.

The next day I had some business in Apia, and did not return until late in the afternoon. The weather had been so good that I left word to have one of the tennis-courts mown and re-marked ; but as we no longer needed two since the *Curaçoa* had gone, I had told my men to ignore the second except to cut the grass. I regretted my decision when I saw what they had done, which had been to inscribe the unused lawn with my Samoan name L O I A in gigantic white letters, covering the entire court ! It had the silliest look. What a spectacle for any supercilious German officers paying a formal call ! But there it was, flattering and absurd, and supposed to be a pleasant surprise for me !

R. L. S. was dictating some of *Weir* to my sister, and they both seemed glad to stop and listen to the budget of news I had brought up. But first I led them to the window and showed them the lawn, the sight of which—and of my annoyance—sent them off into peals of laughter. Then, after a little talk, which looking back on it I recall as even gayer than usual, I went over to the cottage to change and have a plunge in the pool. I was away perhaps an hour or more, when I heard a curious stir in the house and a voice calling my name. Tragedy always has its own note. The intonation was sufficient to send me in startled haste across the way.

Stevenson was lying back in an arm-chair, unconscious, breathing stertorously and with his unseeing eyes wide open ; and on either side of him were my mother and sister, pale and apprehensive. They told me in whispers that he had suddenly cried out : " My head—oh, my head ! " and then had fallen insensible. For a while we fanned him ; put brandy to his lips, strove in vain to rouse him by speaking. We could not bring ourselves to believe he was dying. Then we had a cot brought down, and taking him in my arms—it was pitiable how light he was—I carried him to it and extended him at length. By this time the truth was evident to us—that he had had an apoplectic stroke. His reddened face and that terrible breathing were only too conclusive.

I had our fastest horse saddled and brought to the door —" Saumaiafe," a blood-mare that had won several races— and off I went at breakneck speed for the doctor in Apia. I was lucky in finding him—a short, thick-set, rather portly German, with most of his face hidden in grey whiskers and not unlike the portraits of von Tirpitz. At my urging—I simply would not tolerate any denial—he timidly mounted my horse, giving me the little black bag he dared not carry himself. With this in my hand I ran after him through the town, hoping to find a tethered horse on the way. Sure enough there was one, and in an instant I was on it and galloping off, while its astonished owner, emerging from a bar, gazed after me with amazement. Soon overtaking the doctor, we went on together at a speed miserably disproportionate to the suspense I was in, while he gravely questioned me, and muttered " Ach, ach ! " in none too hopeful a tone.

Stevenson, where I left him on the cot, was still breathing in that dreadful way. The doctor looked down at him long and earnestly and then almost imperceptibly shook his head.

" A blood-clot on the brain," he said. " He is dying."

In half an hour, at about eight in the evening, Stevenson was dead.

On leaving the doctor said to me in a low and significant voice : " You must bury him before three to-morrow."

Misunderstanding my look of horror, he murmured something more in the way of explanation. But I was thinking of that path to Vaea ; that path I had never made ; of Stevenson's wish which I had always thwarted. Were he to be buried on the summit that path had to be made between dawn and three o'clock the next day. It seemed impossible, but I said to myself, " It has to be done ! It has to be done ! " I had failed the living, but I would not fail the dead. In desperation I sent out messengers to several of my closest friends—chiefs whom I relied on like brothers. I needed two hundred men at dawn, and explained the urgency. But the axes, the bush-knives, the mattocks, picks, spades and crowbars ? Vailima had no more than sufficient for thirty, and I doubted if the chiefs could equip as many more. In bitter perplexity I went back to consult my mother, who reminded me we should also need some kind of mourning for these men.

By this time the news of R. L. S.'s death had spread far and wide, and Samoan messengers were beginning to arrive from every direction, facilitating our task. The upshot of it was that we had one of the shops opened in the town, and arrangements made to bring up the necessary tools as well as hundreds of white vests, and dozens of bolts of black cotton cloth. Two yards of this wide, black cotton would suffice to make a *lavalava*, as the kilt-like Samoan garment is called ; and in these and white undershirts our Vailima retainers could make a creditable appearance, and one which they would consider appropriate.

Mr. Clarke, one of our missionary friends, arrived to volunteer his invaluable services, and to him was confided the duty of finding a coffin and having it sent up at dawn ; he was also given a list of those who were to be specially invited for the funeral next day at two o'clock. The suddenness of this planning was almost overwhelming ; we were half distracted by it ; the only serene and untroubled face was that of Tusitala, lying there at peace.

Late that night we washed his body and dressed it in a soft white linen shirt and black evening trousers girded with a dark-blue silk sash. A white tie, dark-blue silk socks and patent-leather shoes completed the costume. The sash may sound extraordinary, but it was the custom to wear sashes in Samoa. Indeed, the whole costume seems to call for some explanation. Except for the short white mess-jacket, which was omitted, it was our usual evening-dress ; though it is impossible to recollect why this was chosen in preference to the white clothes ordinarily worn in the daytime. Possibly it was decided by those patent-leather shoes which R. L. S. had always liked so much and which showed off his slender and shapely feet to such perfection.

Stevenson had never cared for jewellery of any kind ; except for his studs and sleeve-links he had nothing but a plain silver ring, which we left on his finger. This was the ring with which he had plighted his troth with my mother so many years before, and which was similar to the one she always wore herself ; perhaps they had not been able to afford gold in those early days, or may have preferred the homely peasant silver from some association connected with it. I gazed at it with moistened eyes, this symbol of bygone romance which had come so far to lie at last on Vaea.

Placing the body on our big table we drew over it the red English ensign, twelve feet long and proportionately broad, that we habitually flew over the house. Then candles were lit, and a little party of our Samoans, begging us to retire, took on themselves the self-appointed duty of spending the night beside the bier. They were all Roman Catholics, and at intervals intoned Latin prayers in unison. There was a wonderful beauty in the cadence of that old, old tongue, so sonorous, so impressive, and so strange to hear on such lips. All that night as I tried to sleep the murmur of it was in my ears.

Before dawn Vailima began to seethe with men, one little army after another marching up with its chiefs. I went out and greeted them, and then we had a little council together—these tall, grave men, so understanding and so used to command, who quietly apportioned the work between themselves and lost no time in fruitless discussion. Tusitala's wish would be obeyed; it was as sacred to them as it was to me. In turn they volunteered their assurance that by two o'clock the path would be ready and the grave dug on the summit of Vaea.

All that morning the still air was broken by the crash of trees; the ringing sound of axes, the hoarser thud of mattocks and crowbars pounding on rocks. But the men themselves had been warned to make no sound; there was none of the singing and laughter that was such an inseparable part of concerted work. Silent, glistening with sweat and in a fury of effort each strove with axe or bushknife, with mattock, spade or pick to pay his last tribute to Tusitala. I made my way through them to the summit, my heart swelling at such determination, and chose the spot for the grave. The view from it was incomparable; the rim of the sea, risen to the height of one's eyes, gave a sense of infinite vastness; and it was all so lonely, so wild, so incredibly beautiful that one stood there awe-stricken.

All that morning Stevenson's body lay in state, and in succession chief after chief arrived to pay his last homage. Each carried an *ie tonga*, one of those priceless old mats which are so finely woven that they are as soft and pliable as a piece of silk, and which are valued in the degree of their antiquity. With an *ie tonga* in his hand each chief advanced alone and, stopping within a dozen feet of the body, addressed it as though it were alive. It was a touching rite, and some of the speeches were exceedingly eloquent. One old chief whom I had never seen before, and whose harsh features and sullen expression impressed me at first very unfavourably, brought the finest mat of all, and made a speech that moved everyone to tears. He had a voice of magnificent range ; the diction of a most accomplished orator, a power of pathos I have never heard equalled.

"Samoa ends with you, Tusitala," he concluded in a peroration of tragic intensity. "When death closed the eyes of our best and greatest friend, we knew as a race that our own day was done."

An unexampled number of fine mats were brought and laid on Stevenson's body ; so many that the flag was entirely heaped with them ; and amongst them some so ancient that they were almost black and needed care in handling them. Samoans have nothing more precious. *Ie tonga* represent jewellery, riches, social position ; some specially famous have individual names ; some in conferring exalted rank are an inseparable part of native nobility ; murders have been committed for them ; families squabble furiously over their disposition, beginning feuds that last for generations. Yet the irony is that they are of no practical worth whatever, and are never so coveted as when almost falling to pieces with age. Ours we returned afterwards to all the various donors. Knowing their value we had not the heart to retain them when we left Samoa.

At two o'clock the coffin was brought out, and borne by a dozen powerful Samoans led the way up the mountain. Directly behind were thirty or forty more men who at intervals changed places with the bearers. It was a point of honour with them all to keep their heavy burden shoulder-high, though how they contrived to do so on that precipitous path was a seeming impossibility. A party of a score or more white people followed interspersed with chiefs of high rank. Behind these again were perhaps two hundred Samoans, all in the white undershirts and black *lavalavas* which had been given them for that day of mourning.

The sun shone mercilessly; the heat was stifling; but of course our own feeling was one of thankfulness that rain had not intervened. A heavy rain in Samoa is a veritable cloud-burst. We should never have been able to make the path had it rained, and the whole interment would have been robbed of its dignity and beauty. But the heat made it a terrible climb for some of our guests. There was one elderly white man who I thought would never reach the summit alive. We knew him but slightly; were surprised, indeed, to see him; I doubt if Stevenson had ever spoken to him more than half a dozen times.

" I am going on if it kills me," he said, deaf to all our entreaties to turn back. " I venerated Stevenson; he shall not be laid in his grave without my last tribute of respect."

With mottled face, shirt half open, gasping for breath and occasionally lying down while we fanned him, he persevered with an almost irritating obstinacy. But I really believe it did kill him, for the poor fellow was ill for a month afterwards and then died. There were others who looked almost as spent, but who were animated by a similar resolution. The photographs of Mount Vaea, like all photographs of mountains, diminish its height; it would be easy for one who has seen it only in pictures to get a very mistaken impression. From Vailima to the summit is a most formidable ascent for sedentary people, unaccustomed to exercise.

We gathered about the grave, and no cathedral could have seemed nobler nor more hallowed than the grandeur of Nature that encompassed us. The sea in front, the primeval forest behind, crags, precipices, and distant cataracts gleaming in an untrodden wilderness. The words of the Church of England service, movingly delivered, broke the silence in which we stood. The coffin was lowered, flowers were strewn on it, and then the hurrying spades began to throw back the earth.

> " Under the wide and starry sky,
> Dig the grave and let me lie,
> Glad did I live and gladly die,
>   And I laid me down with a will.

> " This be the verse you grave for me :
> *Here he lies where he longed to be;*
> *Home is the sailor, home from sea,*
>   *And the hunter home from the hill."*

TO
MY WIFE

I saw rain falling and the rainbow drawn
On Lammermuir.   Hearkening I heard again
In my precipitous city beaten bells
Winnow the keen sea wind.   And here afar,
Intent on my own race and place, I wrote.
    Take thou the writing : thine it is.   For who
Burnished the sword, blew on the drowsy coal,
Held still the target higher, chary of praise
And prodigal of counsel—who but thou?
So now, in the end, if this the least be good,
If any deed be done, if any fire
Burn in the imperfect page, the praise be thine.

                                    R. L. S.

WEIR OF HERMISTON
A FRAGMENT

WEIR OF HERMISTON

INTRODUCTORY

IN the wild end of a moorland parish, far out of the sight of any house, there stands a cairn among the heather, and a little by east of it, in the going down of the braeside, a monument with some verses half defaced. It was here that Claverhouse shot with his own hand the Praying Weaver of Balweary, and the chisel of Old Mortality has clinked on that lonely gravestone. Public and domestic history have thus marked with a bloody finger this hollow among the hills ; and since the Cameronian gave his life there, two hundred years ago, in a glorious folly, and without comprehension or regret, the silence of the moss has been broken once again by the report of firearms and the cry of the dying.

The Deil's Hags was the old name. But the place is now called Francie's Cairn. For a while it was told that Francie walked. Aggie Hogg met him in the gloaming by the cairnside, and he spoke to her, with chattering teeth, so that his words were lost. He pursued Rob Todd (if any one could have believed Robbie) for the space of half a mile with pitiful entreaties. But the age is one of incredulity ; these superstitious decorations speedily fell off ; and the facts of the story itself, like the bones of a giant buried there and half dug up, survived, naked and imperfect, in the memory of the scattered neighbours. To this day, of winter nights, when the sleet is on the window and the cattle are quiet in the byre, there will be told again, amid the silence of the young and the additions and corrections of the old, the tale of the Justice-Clerk and of his son, young Hermiston, that vanished from men's knowledge ; of the Two Kirsties and the Four Black Brothers of the Cauldstaneslap ; and of Frank Innes, " the young fool advocate," that came into these moorland parts to find his destiny.

CHAPTER I

LIFE AND DEATH OF MRS. WEIR

THE Lord Justice-Clerk was a stranger in that part of the country ; but his lady wife was known there from a child, as her race had been before her. The old " riding Rutherfords of Hermiston," of whom she was the last descendant, had been famous men of yore, ill neighbours, ill subjects, and ill husbands to their wives though not their properties. Tales of them were rife for twenty miles about ; and their name was even printed in the page of our Scots histories, not always to their credit. One bit the dust at Flodden ; one was hanged at his peel door by James the Fifth ; another fell dead in a carouse with Tom Dalyell ; while a fourth (and that was Jean's own father) died presiding at a Hell-Fire Club, of which he was the founder. There were many heads shaken in Crossmichael at that judgment ; the more so as the man had a villainous reputation among high and low, and both with the godly and the worldly. At that very hour of his demise, he had ten going pleas before the session, eight of them oppressive. And the same doom extended even to his agents ; his grieve, that had been his right hand in many a left-hand business, being cast from his horse one night and drowned in a peat-hag on the Kye-skairs ; and his very doer (although lawyers have long spoons) surviving him not long, and dying on a sudden in a bloody flux.

In all these generations, while a male Rutherford was in the saddle with his lads, or brawling in a change-house, there would be always a white-faced wife immured at home in the old peel or the later mansion-house. It seemed this succession of martyrs bided long, but took their vengeance in the end, and that was in the person of the last descendant, Jean. She bore the name of the Rutherfords, but she was the daughter of their trembling wives. At the first she was not wholly without charm. Neighbours recalled in her, as a child, a strain of elfin wilfulness, gentle little mutinies, sad little gaieties, even a morning gleam of beauty that was not to be fulfilled. She withered in the growing, and (whether it was the sins of her sires or the sorrows of her mothers) came to her maturity depressed, and, as it were, defaced; no blood of life in her, no grasp or gaiety; pious, anxious, tender, tearful, and incompetent.

It was a wonder to many that she had married—seeming so wholly of the stuff that makes old maids. But chance cast her in the path of Adam Weir, then the new Lord Advocate, a recognised, risen man, the conqueror of many obstacles, and thus late in the day beginning to think upon a wife. He was one who looked rather to obedience than beauty, yet it would seem he was struck with her at the first look. "Wha's she?" he said, turning to his host; and, when he had been told, "Ay," says he, "she looks menseful. She minds me——"; and then, after a pause (which some have been daring enough to set down to sentimental recollections), "Is she releegious?" he asked, and was shortly after, at his own request, presented. The acquaintance, which it seems profane to call a courtship, was pursued with Mr. Weir's accustomed industry, and was long a legend, or rather a source of legends, in the Parliament House. He was described coming, rosy with much port, into the drawing-room, walking direct up to the lady, and assailing her with pleasantries, to which the embarrassed fair one responded, in what seemed a kind of agony, "Eh, Mr. Weir!" or "O, Mr. Weir!" or "Keep me, Mr. Weir!" On the very eve of their engagement it was related that one had drawn near to the tender couple, and had overheard the lady cry out, with the tones of one who talked for the sake of talking, "Keep me, Mr. Weir, and what became of him?" and the profound accents of the suitor's reply, "Haangit, mem, haangit." The motives upon either side were much debated. Mr. Weir must have supposed his bride to be somehow suitable ; perhaps he belonged to that class of men who think a weak head the ornament of women—an opinion invariably punished in this life. Her descent and her estate were beyond question. Her wayfaring ancestors and her litigious father had done well by Jean. There was ready money and there were broad acres, ready to fall wholly to the husband, to lend dignity to his descendants, and to himself a title, when he should be called upon the Bench. On the side of Jean, there was perhaps some fascination of curiosity as to this unknown male animal that approached her with the roughness of a ploughman and the *aplomb* of an advocate. Being so trenchantly opposed to all she knew, loved, or understood, he may well have seemed to her the extreme, if scarcely the ideal, of his sex. And besides, he was an ill man to refuse. A little over forty at the period of his marriage, he looked already older, and to the force of manhood added the senatorial dignity of years ; it was, perhaps, with an unreverend awe, but he was awful. The Bench, the Bar, and the most experienced and reluctant witness, bowed to his authority—and why not Jeannie Rutherford ?

The heresy about foolish women is always punished, I have said, and Lord Hermiston began to pay the penalty at once. His house in George Square was wretchedly ill-guided ; nothing answerable to the expense of maintenance but the cellar, which was his own private care. When things went wrong at dinner, as they continually did, my lord would look up the table at his wife : " I think these broth would be better to sweem in than to sup." Or else to the butler : " Here, M'Killop, awa' wi' this Raadical gigot—tak' it to the French, man, and bring me some puddocks ! It seems rather a sore kind of business that I should be all day in Court haanging Raadicals, and get nawthing to my denner." Of course this was but a manner of speaking, and he had never hanged a man for being a Radical in his life ; the law, of which he was the faithful minister, directing otherwise. And of course these growls were in the nature of pleasantry, but it was of a recondite sort; and uttered as they were in his resounding voice, and commented on by that expression which they called in the Parliament House " Hermiston's hanging face "— they struck mere dismay into the wife. She sat before him speechless and fluttering; at each dish, as at a fresh ordeal, her eye hovered toward my lord's countenance and fell again; if he but ate in silence, unspeakable relief was her portion; if there were complaint, the world was darkened. She would seek out the cook, who was always her *sister in the Lord*. " O my dear, this is the most dreidful thing that my lord can never be contented in his own house ! " she would begin; and weep and pray with the cook; and then the cook would pray with Mrs. Weir; and the next day's meal would never be a penny the better—and the next cook (when she came) would be worse, if anything, but just as pious. It was often wondered that Lord Hermiston bore it as he did; indeed he was a stoical old voluptuary, contented with sound wine and plenty of it. But there were moments when he overflowed. Perhaps half a dozen times in the history of his married life— " Here ! tak' it awa', and bring me a piece of bread and kebbuck ! " he had exclaimed, with an appalling explosion of his voice and rare gestures. None thought to dispute or to make excuses; the service was arrested; Mrs. Weir sat at the head of the table whimpering without disguise; and his lordship opposite munched his bread and cheese in ostentatious disregard. Once only Mrs. Weir had ventured to appeal. He was passing her chair on his way into the study.

" O, Edom ! " she wailed, in a voice tragic with tears, and reaching out to him both hands, in one of which she held a sopping pocket-handkerchief.

He paused and looked upon her with a face of wrath, into which there stole, as he looked, a twinkle of humour.

" Noansense ! " he said. " You and your noansense ! What do I want with a Christian faim'ly ? I want Christian broth ! Get me a lass that can plain-boil a potato, if she was a whüre off the streets." And with these words, which echoed in her tender ears like blasphemy, he had passed on to his study and shut the door behind him.

Such was the housewifery in George Square. It was better at Hermiston, where Kirstie Elliot, the sister of a neighbouring bonnet-laird, and an eighteenth cousin of the lady's, bore the charge of all, and kept a trim house and a good country table. Kirstie was a woman in a thousand, clean, capable, notable ; once a moorland Helen, and still comely as a blood horse and healthy as the hill wind. High in flesh and voice and colour, she ran the house with her whole intemperate soul, in a bustle, not without buffets. Scarce more pious than decency in those days required, she was the cause of many an anxious thought and many a tearful prayer to Mrs. Weir. Housekeeper and mistress renewed the parts of Martha and Mary ; and though with a pricking conscience Mary reposed on Martha's strength as on a rock. Even Lord Hermiston held Kirstie in a particular regard. There were few with whom he unbent so gladly, few whom he favoured with so many pleasantries. " Kirstie and me maun have our joke," he would declare, in high good-humour, as he buttered Kirstie's scones and she waited at table. A man who had no need either of love or of popularity, a keen reader of men and of events, there was perhaps only one truth for which he was quite unprepared : he would have been quite unprepared to learn that Kirstie hated him. He thought maid and master were well matched ; hard, handy, healthy, broad Scots folk, without a hair of nonsense to the pair of them. And the fact was that she made a goddess and an only child of the effete and tearful lady ; and even as she waited at table her hands would sometimes itch for my lord's ears.

Thus, at least, when the family were at Hermiston, not only my lord, but Mrs. Weir too, enjoyed a holiday. Free from the dreadful looking-for of the miscarried dinner, she would mind her seam, read her piety books, and take her walk (which was my lord's orders), sometimes by herself, sometimes with Archie, the only child of that scarce natural union. The child was her next bond to

life. Her frosted sentiment bloomed again, she breathed
deep of life, she let loose her heart, in that society. The
miracle of her motherhood was ever new to her. The
sight of the little man at her skirt intoxicated her with
the sense of power, and froze her with the consciousness
of her responsibility. She looked forward, and, seeing
him in fancy grow up and play his diverse part on the
world's theatre, caught in her breath and lifted up her
courage with a lively effort. It was only with the child
that she forgot herself and was at moments natural ; yet
it was only with the child that she had conceived and
managed to pursue a scheme of conduct. Archie was to
be a great man and a good ; a minister if possible, a saint
for certain. She tried to engage his mind upon her favourite books, Rutherford's " *Letters*," Scougal's " *Grace
Abounding*," and the like. It was a common practice of
hers (and strange to remember now) that she would carry
the child to the Deil's Hags, sit with him on the Praying
Weaver's stone and talk of the Covenanters till their tears
ran down. Her view of history was wholly artless, a
design in snow and ink ; upon the one side, tender innocents with psalms upon their lips ; upon the other the
persecutors, booted, bloody-minded, flushed with wine :
a suffering Christ, a raging Beelzebub. *Persecutor* was a
word that knocked upon the woman's heart ; it was her
highest thought of wickedness, and the mark of it was
on her house. Her great-great-grandfather had drawn the
sword against the Lord's anointed on the field of Rullion
Green, and breathed his last (tradition said) in the arms
of the detestable Dalyell. Nor could she blind herself to
this, that had they lived in those old days, Hermiston
himself would have been numbered alongside of Bloody
Mackenzie and the politic Lauderdale and Rothes, in
the band of God's immediate enemies. The sense of this
moved her to the more fervour ; she had a voice for that
name of *persecutor* that thrilled in the child's marrow ;
and when one day the mob hooted and hissed them all
in my lord's travelling carriage, and cried, " Down with
the persecutor ! down with Hanging Hermiston ! " and

mamma covered her eyes and wept, and papa let down the glass and looked out upon the rabble with his droll formidable face, bitter and smiling, as they said he sometimes looked when he gave sentence, Archie was for the moment too much amazed to be alarmed, but he had scarce got his mother by herself before his shrill voice was raised demanding an explanation : Why had they called papa a persecutor ?

" Keep me, my precious ! " she exclaimed. " Keep me, my dear ! this is poleetical. Ye must never ask me anything poleetical, Erchie. Your faither is a great man, my dear, and it's no for me or you to be judging him. It would be telling us all, if we behaved ourselves in our several stations the way your faither does in his high office ; and let me hear no more of any such disrespectful and undutiful questions ! No that you meant to be undutiful, my lamb ; your mother kens that—she kens it well, dearie ! " and so slid off to safer topics, and left on the mind of the child an obscure but ineradicable sense of something wrong.

Mrs. Weir's philosophy of life was summed in one expression—tenderness. In her view of the universe, which was all lighted up with a glow out of the doors of hell, good people must walk there in a kind of ecstasy of tenderness. The beasts and plants had no souls ; they were here but for a day, and let their day pass gently ! And as for the immortal men, on what black, downward path were many of them wending, and to what a horror of an immortality ! " Are not two sparrows," " Whosoever shall smite thee," " God sendeth His rain," " Judge not that ye be not judged "—these texts made her body of divinity ; she put them on in the morning with her clothes and lay down to sleep with them at night ; they haunted her like a favourite air, they clung about her like a favourite perfume. Their minister was a marrowy expounder of the law, and my lord sat under him with relish ; but Mrs. Weir respected him from afar off ; heard him (like the cannon of a beleaguered city) usefully booming outside on the dogmatic ramparts ; and meanwhile, within and out of shot, dwelt in her private garden, which she watered with grateful tears. It seems strange to say of this colourless and ineffectual woman, but she was a true enthusiast, and might have made the sunshine and the glory of a cloister. Perhaps none but Archie knew she could be eloquent ; perhaps none but he had seen her—her colour raised, her hands clasped or quivering—glow with gentle ardour. There is a corner of the policy of Hermiston, where you come suddenly in view of the summit of Black Fell, some-times like the mere grass top of a hill, sometimes (and this is her own expression) like a precious jewel in the heavens. On such days, upon the sudden view of it, her hand would tighten on the child's fingers, her voice rise like a song. " I to the hills ! " she would repeat. " And O, Erchie, arena these like the hills of Naphtali ? " and her easy tears would flow.

Upon an impressionable child the effect of this con-tinual and pretty accompaniment to life was deep. The woman's quietism and piety passed on to his different nature undiminished ; but whereas in her it was a native sentiment, in him it was only an implanted dogma. Nature and the child's pugnacity at times revolted. A cad from the Potterrow once struck him in the mouth ; he struck back, the pair fought it out in the back stable lane towards the Meadows, and Archie returned with a con-siderable decline in the number of his front teeth, and unregenerately boasting of the losses of the foe. It was a sore day for Mrs. Weir ; she wept and prayed over the infant backslider until my lord was due from Court, and she must resume that air of tremulous composure with which she always greeted him. The judge was that day in an observant mood, and remarked upon the absent teeth.

" I am afraid Erchie will have been fechting with some of they blagyard lads," said Mrs. Weir.

My lord's voice rang out as it did seldom in the privacy of his own house. " I'll have nonn of that, sir ! " he cried. " Do you hear me ?—nonn of that ! No son of mine shall be speldering in the glaur with any dirty raibble."

The anxious mother was grateful for so much support; she had even feared the contrary. And that night when she put the child to bed—" Now, my dear, ye see ! " she said, " I told you what your faither would think of it, if he heard ye had fallen into this dreidful sin ; and let you and me pray to God that ye may be keepit from the like temptation or stren'thened to resist it ! "

The womanly falsity of this was thrown away. Ice and iron cannot be welded ; and the points of view of the Justice-Clerk and Mrs. Weir were not less unassimilable. The character and position of his father had long been a stumbling-block to Archie, and with every year of his age the difficulty grew more instant. The man was mostly silent ; when he spoke at all, it was to speak of the things of the world, always in a worldly spirit, often in language that the child had been schooled to think coarse, and sometimes with words that he knew to be sins in themselves. Tenderness was the first duty, and my lord was invariably harsh. God was love ; the name of my lord (to all who knew him) was fear. In the world, as schematised for Archie by his mother, the place was marked for such a creature. There were some whom it was good to pity and well (though very likely useless) to pray for ; they were named reprobates, goats, God's enemies, brands for the burning ; and Archie tallied every mark of identification, and drew the inevitable private inference that the Lord Justice-Clerk was the chief of sinners.

The mother's honesty was scarce complete. There was one influence she feared for the child and still secretly combated ; that was my lord's ; and half unconsciously, half in a wilful blindness, she continued to undermine her husband with his son. As long as Archie remained silent, she did so ruthlessly, with a single eye to heaven and the child's salvation ; but the day came when Archie spoke. It was 1801, and Archie was seven, and beyond his years for curiosity and logic, when he brought the case up openly. If judging were sinful and forbidden, how came papa to be a judge ? to have that sin for a trade ? to bear the name of it for a distinction ?

"I can't see it," said the little Rabbi, and wagged his head.

Mrs. Weir abounded in commonplace replies.

"No, I canna see it," reiterated Archie. "And I'll tell you what, mamma, I don't think you and me's justifeed in staying with him."

The woman awoke to remorse; she saw herself disloyal to her man, her sovereign and bread-winner, in whom (with what she had of worldliness) she took a certain subdued pride. She expatiated in reply on my lord's honour and greatness; his useful services in this world of sorrow and wrong, and the place in which he stood, far above where babes and innocents could hope to see or criticise. But she had builded too well—Archie had his answers pat: Were not babes and innocents the type of the kingdom of heaven? Were not honour and greatness the badges of the world? And at any rate, how about the mob that had once seethed about the carriage?

"It's all very fine," he concluded, "but in my opinion, papa has no right to be it. And it seems that's not the worst yet of it. It seems he's called 'the Hanging Judge' —it seems he's crooool. I'll tell you what it is, mamma, there's a tex' borne in upon me: It were better for that man if a mile-stone were bound upon his back and him flung into the deepestmost pairts of the sea."

"O my lamb, ye must never say the like of that!" she cried. "Ye're to honour faither and mother, dear, that your days may be long in the land. It's Atheists that cry out against him—French Atheists, Erchie! Ye would never surely even yourself down to be saying the same thing as French Atheists? It would break my heart to think that of you. And O, Erchie, here arena *you* setting up to *judge?* And have ye no' forgot God's plain com-mand—the First with Promise, dear? Mind you upon the beam and the mote!"

Having thus carried the war into the enemy's camp, the terrified lady breathed again. And no doubt it is easy thus to circumvent a child with catchwords, but it may be questioned how far it is effectual. An instinct in his breast detects the quibble, and a voice condemns it. He will instantly submit, privately hold the same opinion. For even in this simple and antique relation of the mother and the child, hypocrisies are multiplied.

When the Court rose that year and the family returned to Hermiston, it was a common remark in all the country that the lady was sore failed. She seemed to lose and seize again her touch with life, now sitting inert in a sort of durable bewilderment, anon waking to feverish and weak activity. She dawdled about the lasses at their work, looking stupidly on ; she fell to rummaging in old cabinets and presses, and desisted when half through ; she would begin remarks with an air of animation and drop them without a struggle. Her common appearance was of one who has forgotten something and is trying to remember ; and when she overhauled, one after another, the worthless and touching mementoes of her youth, she might have been seeking the clue to that lost thought. During this period she gave many gifts to the neighbours and house lassies, giving them with a manner of regret that embarrassed the recipients.

The last night of all she was busy on some female work, and toiled upon it with so manifest and painful a devotion that my lord (who was not often curious) inquired as to its nature.

She blushed to the eyes. " O, Edom, it's for you ! " she said. " It's slippers. I—I hae never made ye any."

" Ye daft auld wife ! " returned his lordship. " A bonny figure I would be, palmering about in bauchles ! "

The next day, at the hour of her walk, Kirstie interfered. Kirstie took this decay of her mistress very hard ; bore her a grudge, quarrelled with and railed upon her, the anxiety of a genuine love wearing the disguise of temper. This day of all days she insisted disrespectfully, with rustic fury, that Mrs. Weir should stay at home. But, " No, no," she said, " it's my lord's orders," and set forth as usual. Archie was visible in the acre bog, engaged upon some childish enterprise, the instrument of which was mire ; and she stood and looked at him a while like one about to call; then thought otherwise, sighed, and shook her head, and proceeded on her rounds alone. The house lasses were at the burnside washing, and saw her pass with her loose, weary, dowdy gait.

"She's a terrible feckless wife, the mistress!" said the one.

"Tut," said the other, "the wumman's seeck."

"Weel, I canna see nae differ in her," returned the first. "A füshionless quean, a feckless carline."

The poor creature thus discussed rambled a while in the grounds without a purpose. Tides in her mind ebbed and flowed, and carried her to and fro like seaweed. She tried a path, paused, returned, and tried another; questing, forgetting her quest; the spirit of choice extinct in her bosom, or devoid of sequency. On a sudden, it appeared as though she had remembered, or had formed a resolution, wheeled about, returned with hurried steps, and appeared in the dining-room, where Kirstie was at the cleaning, like one charged with an important errand.

"Kirstie!" she began, and paused; and then with conviction, "Mr. Weir isna speeritually minded, but he has been a good man to me."

It was perhaps the first time since her husband's elevation that she had forgotten the handle to his name, of which the tender, inconsistent woman was not a little proud. And when Kirstie looked up at the speaker's face, she was aware of a change.

"Godsake, what's the maitter wi' ye, mem?" cried the housekeeper, starting from the rug.

"I do not ken," answered her mistress, shaking her head. "But he is not speeritually minded, my dear."

"Here, sit down with ye! Godsake, what ails the wife?" cried Kirstie, and helped and forced her into my lord's own chair by the cheek of the hearth.

"Keep me, what's this?" she gasped. "Kirstie, what's this? I'm frich'ened."

They were her last words.

It was the lowering nightfall when my lord returned. He had the sunset in his back, all clouds and glory; and before him, by the wayside, spied Kirstie Elliott waiting. She was dissolved in tears, and addressed him in the high, false note of barbarous mourning, such as still lingers modified among Scots heather.

"The Lord peety ye, Hermiston! the Lord prepare ye!" she keened out. "Weary upon me, that I should have to tell it!"

He reined in his horse and looked upon her with the hanging face.

"Has the French landit?" cried he.

"Man, man," she said, "is that a' ye can think of? The Lord prepare ye, the Lord comfort and support ye!"

"Is onybody deid?" says his lordship. "It's no Erchie?"

"Bethankit, no!" exclaimed the woman, startled into a more natural tone. "Na, na, it's no sae bad as that. It's the mistress, my lord; she just fair flittit before my e'en. She just gi'ed a sab and was by wi' it. Eh, my bonny Miss Jeannie, that I mind sae weel!" And forth again upon that pouring tide of lamentation in which women of her class excel and over-abound.

Lord Hermiston sat in the saddle, beholding her. Then he seemed to recover command upon himself.

"Weel, it's something of the suddenest," said he. "But she was a dwaibly body from the first."

And he rode home at a precipitate amble with Kirstie at his horse's heels.

Dressed as she was for her last walk, they had laid the dead lady on her bed. She was never interesting in life; in death she was not impressive; and as her husband stood before her, with his hands crossed behind his powerful back, that which he looked upon was the very image of the insignificant.

"Her and me were never cut out for one another," he remarked at last. "It was a daft-like marriage." And then, with a most unusual gentleness of tone, "Puir bitch," said he, "puir bitch!" Then suddenly: "Where's Erchie?"

Kirstie had decoyed him to her room and given him "a jeely-piece."

"Ye have some kind of gumption, too," observed the Judge, and considered his housekeeper grimly. "When all's said," he added, "I micht have done waur—I micht have been marriet upon a skirling Jezebel like you!"

"There's naebody thinking of you, Hermiston!" cried the offended woman. "We think of her that's out of her sorrows. And could *she* have done waur? Tell me that, Hermiston—tell me that before her clay-cauld corp!"

"Weel, there's some of them gey an' ill to please," observed his lordship.

CHAPTER II

FATHER AND SON

MY Lord Justice-Clerk was known to many; the man Adam Weir perhaps to none. He had nothing to explain or to conceal; he sufficed wholly and silently to himself; and that part of our nature which goes out (too often with false coin) to acquire glory or love, seemed in him to be omitted. He did not try to be loved, he did not care to be; it is probable the very thought of it was a stranger to his mind. He was an admired lawyer, a highly unpopular judge; and he looked down upon those who were his inferiors in either distinction, who were lawyers of less grasp or judges not so much detested. In all the rest of his days and doings, not one trace of vanity appeared; and he went on through life with a mechanical movement, as of the unconscious, that was almost august.

He saw little of his son. In the childish maladies with which the boy was troubled, he would make daily inquiries and daily pay him a visit, entering the sick-room with a facetious and appalling countenance, letting off a few perfunctory jests, and going again swiftly, to the patient's relief. Once, a Court holiday falling opportunely, my lord had his carriage, and drove the child himself to Hermiston, the customary place of convalescence. It is conceivable he had been more than usually anxious, for that journey always remained in Archie's memory as a thing apart, his father having related to him from beginning to end, and with much detail, three authentic murder cases. Archie went the usual round of other Edinburgh boys, the high school and the college; and Hermiston looked on, or rather looked away, with scarce an affectation of interest in his progress. Daily, indeed, upon a signal after dinner, he was brought in, given nuts and a glass of port, regarded sardonically, sarcastically questioned. "Well, sir, and what have you donn with your book to-day?" my lord might begin, and set him posers in law Latin. To a child just stumbling into Corderius, Papinian and Paul proved quite invincible. But papa had memory of no other. He was not harsh to the little scholar, having a vast fund of patience learned upon the bench, and was at no pains whether to conceal or to express his disappointment. "Well, ye have a long jaunt before ye yet!" he might observe, yawning, and fall back on his own thoughts (as like as not) until the time came for separation, and my lord would take the decanter and the glass, and be off to the back chamber looking on the Meadows, where he toiled on his cases till the hours were small. There was no "fuller man" on the Bench; his memory was marvellous, though wholly legal; if he had to "advise" extempore, none did it better; yet there was none who more earnestly prepared. As he thus watched in the night, or sat at table and forgot the presence of his son, no doubt but he tasted deeply of recondite pleasures. To be wholly devoted to some intellectual exercise is to have succeeded in life; and perhaps only in law and the higher mathematics may this devotion be maintained, suffice to itself without reaction, and find continual rewards without excitement. This atmosphere of his father's sterling industry was the best of Archie's education. Assuredly it did not attract him; assuredly it rather rebutted and depressed. Yet it was still present, unobserved like the ticking of a clock, an arid ideal, a tasteless stimulant in the boy's life.

But Hermiston was not all of one piece. He was, besides, a mighty toper; he could sit at wine until the day dawned, and pass directly from the table to the Bench with a steady hand and a clear head. Beyond the third bottle, he showed the plebeian in a larger print; the low, gross accent, the low, foul mirth, grew broader and commoner; he became less formidable, and infinitely more

disgusting. Now, the boy had inherited from Jean
Rutherford a shivering delicacy, unequally mated with
potential violence. In the playing-fields, and amongst his
own companions, he repaid a coarse expression with a
blow ; at his father's table (when the time came for him
to join these revels) he turned pale and sickened in silence.
Of all the guests whom he there encountered, he had
toleration for only one : David Keith Carnegie, Lord
Glenalmond. Lord Glenalmond was tall and emaciated,
with long features and long delicate hands. He was often
compared with the statue of Forbes of Culloden in the
Parliament House ; and his blue eye, at more than sixty,
preserved some of the fire of youth. His exquisite dis-
parity with any of his fellow-guests, his appearance as of
an artist and an aristocrat stranded in rude company,
riveted the boy's attention ; and as curiosity and interest
are the things in the world that are the most immediately
and certainly rewarded, Lord Glenalmond was attracted
to the boy.

"And so this is your son, Hermiston ? " he asked,
laying his hand on Archie's shoulder. "He's getting a
big lad."

"Hout ! " said the gracious father, "just his mother
over again—daurna say boo to a goose ! "

But the stranger retained the boy, talked to him, drew
him out, found in him a taste for letters, and a fine, ardent,
modest, youthful soul ; and encouraged him to be a visitor
on Sunday evenings in his bare, cold, lonely dining-room,
where he sat and read in the isolation of a bachelor grown
old in refinement. The beautiful gentleness and grace of
the old Judge, and the delicacy of his person, thoughts,
and language, spoke to Archie's heart in its own tongue.
He conceived the ambition to be such another ; and, when
the day came for him to choose a profession, it was in
emulation of Lord Glenalmond, not of Lord Hermiston,
that he chose the Bar. Hermiston looked on at this
friendship with some secret pride, but openly with the
intolerance of scorn. He scarce lost an opportunity to
put them down with a rough jape ; and, to say truth,

it was not difficult, for they were neither of them quick. He had a word of contempt for the whole crowd of poets, painters, fiddlers, and their admirers, the bastard race of amateurs, which was continually on his lips. "Signor Feedle-eerie!" he would say. "Oh, for Goad's sake, no more of the Signor!"

"You and my father are great friends, are you not?" asked Archie once.

"There is no man that I more respect, Archie," replied Lord Glenalmond. "He is two things of price. He is a great lawyer, and he is upright as the day."

"You and he are so different," said the boy, his eyes dwelling on those of his old friend, like a lover's on his mistress's.

"Indeed so," replied the Judge; "very different. And so I fear are you and he. Yet I would like it very ill if my young friend were to misjudge his father. He has all the Roman virtues: Cato and Brutus were such; I think a son's heart might well be proud of such an ancestry of one."

"And I would sooner he were a plaided herd," cried Archie, with sudden bitterness.

"And that is neither very wise, nor I believe entirely true," returned Glenalmond. "Before you are done you will find some of these expressions rise on you like a remorse. They are merely literary and decorative; they do not aptly express your thought, nor is your thought clearly apprehended, and no doubt your father (if he were here) would say 'Signor Feedle-eerie!'"

With the infinitely delicate sense of youth, Archie avoided the subject from that hour. It was perhaps a pity. Had he but talked—talked freely—let himself gush out in words (the way youth loves to do and should), there might have been no tale to write upon the Weirs of Hermiston. But the shadow of a threat of ridicule sufficed; in the slight tartness of these words he read a prohibition; and it is likely that Glenalmond meant it so.

Besides the veteran, the boy was without confidant or friend   Serious and eager, he came through school and college, and moved among a crowd of the indifferent, in the seclusion of his shyness. He grew up handsome, with an open, speaking countenance, with graceful, youthful ways ; he was clever, he took prizes, he shone in the Speculative Society.[1] It should seem he must become the centre of a crowd of friends ; but something that was in part the delicacy of his mother, in part the austerity of his father, held him aloof from all. It is a fact, and a strange one, that among his contemporaries Hermiston's son was thought to be a chip of the old block. "You're a friend of Archie Weir's ? " said one to Frank Innes ; and Innes replied, with his usual flippancy and more than his usual insight : " I know Weir, but I never met Archie." No one had met Archie, a malady most incident to only sons. He flew his private signal, and none heeded it ; it seemed he was abroad in a world from which the very hope of intimacy was banished ; and he looked round about him on the concourse of his fellow-students, and forward to the trivial days and acquaintances that were to come, without hope or interest.

As time went on, the tough and rough old sinner felt himself drawn to the son of his loins and sole continuator of his new family, with softnesses of sentiment that he could hardly credit and was wholly impotent to express. With a face, voice, and manner trained through forty years to terrify and repel, Rhadamanthus may be great, but he will scarce be engaging. It is a fact that he tried to propitiate Archie, but a fact that cannot be too lightly taken ; the attempt was so unconspicuously made, the failure so stoically supported. Sympathy is not due to these steadfast iron natures. If he failed to gain his son's friendship, or even his son's toleration, on he went up the great, bare staircase of his duty, uncheered and unde- pressed. There might have been more pleasure in his relations with Archie, so much he may have recognised at moments ; but pleasure was a by-product of the singular chemistry of life, which only fools expected.

[1] A famous debating society of the students of Edinburgh University.

An idea of Archie's attitude, since we are all grown up and have forgotten the days of our youth, it is more difficult to convey. He made no attempt whatsoever to understand the man with whom he dined and breakfasted. Parsimony of pain, glut of pleasure, these are the two alternating ends of youth ; and Archie was of the parsimonious. The wind blew cold out of a certain quarter—he turned his back upon it ; stayed as little as was possible in his father's presence ; and when there, averted his eyes as much as was decent from his father's face. The lamp shone for many hundred days upon these two at table—my lord ruddy, gloomy, and unreverent ; Archie with a potential brightness that was always dimmed and veiled in that society ; and there were not, perhaps, in Christendom two men more radically strangers. The father, with a grand simplicity, either spoke of what interested himself, or maintained an unaffected silence. The son turned in his head for some topic that should be quite safe, that would spare him fresh evidences either of my lord's inherent grossness or of the innocence of his inhumanity ; treading gingerly the ways of intercourse, like a lady gathering up her skirts in a by-path. If he made a mistake, and my lord began to abound in matter of offence, Archie drew himself up, his brow grew dark, his share of the talk expired ; but my lord would faithfully and cheerfully continue to pour out the worst of himself before his silent and offended son.

"Well, it's a poor hert that never rejoices," he would say, at the conclusion of such a nightmare interview. "But I must get to my plew-stilts." And he would seclude himself as usual in the back room, and Archie go forth into the night and the city, quivering with animosity and scorn.

CHAPTER III

IN THE MATTER OF THE HANGING OF DUNCAN JOPP

IT chanced in the year 1813 that Archie strayed one day into the Judiciary Court. The macer made room for the son of the presiding judge. In the dock, the centre of men's eyes, there stood a whey-coloured, misbegotten caitiff, Duncan Jopp, on trial for his life. His story, as it was raked out before him in that public scene, was one of disgrace and vice and cowardice, the very nakedness of crime; and the creature heard and it seemed at times as though he understood—as if at times he forgot the horror of the place he stood in, and remembered the shame of what had brought him there. He kept his head bowed and his hands clutched upon the rail; his hair dropped in his eyes and at times he flung it back; and now he glanced about the audience in a sudden fellness of terror, and now looked in the face of his judge and gulped. There was pinned about his throat a piece of dingy flannel; and this it was perhaps that turned the scale in Archie's mind between disgust and pity. The creature stood in a vanishing point; yet a little while, and he was still a man, and had eyes and apprehension; yet a little longer, and with a last sordid piece of pageantry, he would cease to be. And here, in the meantime, with a trait of human nature that caught at the beholder's breath, he was tending a sore throat.

Over against him, my Lord Hermiston occupied the bench in the red robes of criminal jurisdiction, his face framed in the white wig. Honest all through, he did not affect the virtue of impartiality; this was no case for refinement; there was a man to be hanged, he would have said, and he was hanging him. Nor was it possible to see his lordship, and acquit him of gusto in the task. It was plain he gloried in the exercise of his trained faculties, in the clear sight which pierced at once into the joint of fact, in the rude, unvarnished gibes with which he demolished every figment of defence. He took his ease and jested, unbending in that solemn place with some of the freedom of the tavern; and the rag of man with the flannel round his neck was hunted gallowsward with jeers.

Duncan had a mistress, scarce less forlorn and greatly older than himself, who came up, whimpering and curtseying, to add the weight of her betrayal. My lord gave her the oath in his most roaring voice, and added an intolerant warning.

"Mind what ye say now, Janet," said he. "I have an e'e upon ye; I'm ill to jest with."

Presently, after she was tremblingly embarked on her story, "And what made ye do this, ye auld runt?" the Court interposed. "Do ye mean to tell me ye was the panel's mistress?"

"If you please, ma loard," whined the female.

"Godsake! ye made a bonny couple," observed his lordship; and there was something so formidable and ferocious in his scorn that not even the galleries thought to laugh.

The summing up contained some jewels. "These two peetiable creatures seem to have made up thegither, it's not for us to explain why."—"The panel, who (whatever else he may be) appears to be equally ill set-out in mind and boady."—"Neither the panel nor yet the old wife appears to have had so much common sense as even to tell a lie when it was necessary." And in the course of sentencing, my lord had this *obiter dictum* : "I have been the means, under God, of haanging a great number, but never just such a disjaskit rascal as yourself." The words were strong in themselves : the light and heat and detonation of their delivery, and the savage pleasure of the speaker in his task, made them tingle in the ears.

When all was over, Archie came forth again into a changed world. Had there been the least redeeming greatness in the crime, any obscurity, any dubiety, perhaps he might have understood. But the culprit stood, with his sore throat, in the sweat of his mortal agony, without defence or excuse ; a thing to cover up with blushes ; a being so much sunk beneath the zones of sympathy that pity might seem harmless. And the judge had pursued him with a monstrous, relishing gaiety, horrible to be conceived, a trait for nightmares. It is one thing to spear a tiger, another to crush a toad ; there are æsthetics even of the slaughter-house ; and the loathsomeness of Duncan Jopp enveloped and infected the image of his judge.

Archie passed by his friends in the High Street with incoherent words and gestures. He saw Holyrood in a dream, remembrance of its romance awoke in him and faded ; he had a vision of the old radiant stories, of Queen Mary and Prince Charlie, of the hooded stag, of the splendour and crime, the velvet and bright iron of the past ; and dismissed them with a cry of pain. He lay and moaned in the Hunter's Bog, and the heavens were dark above him and the grass of the field an offence. " This is my father," he said. " I draw my life from him ; the flesh upon my bones is his, the bread I am fed with is the wages of these horrors." He recalled his mother, and ground his forehead in the earth. He thought of flight, and where was he to flee to ? of other lives, but was there any life worth living in this den of savage and jeering animals ?

The interval before the execution was like a violent dream. He met his father ; he would not look at him, he could not speak to him. It seemed there was no living creature but must have been swift to recognise that imminent animosity ; but the hide of the Lord Justice-Clerk remained impenetrable. Had my lord been talkative, the truce could never have subsisted ; but he was by fortune in one of his humours of sour silence ; and under the very guns of his broadside Archie nursed the enthusiasm of rebellion. It seemed to him, from the top of his nineteen years' experience, as if he were marked at birth to be the perpetrator of some signal action, to set back fallen

Mercy, to overthrow the usurping devil that sat, horned and hoofed, on her throne. Seductive Jacobin figments, which he had often refuted at the Speculative, swam up in his mind and startled him as with voices ; and he seemed to himself to walk accompanied by an almost tangible presence of new beliefs and duties.

On the named morning he was at the place of execution. He saw the fleering rabble, the flinching wretch produced. He looked on for a while at a certain parody of devotion, which seemed to strip the wretch of his last claim to manhood. Then followed the brutal instant of extinction, and the paltry dangling of the remains like a broken jumping-jack. He had been prepared for something terrible, not for this tragic meanness. He stood a moment silent, and then—" I denounce this God-defying murder," he shouted ; and his father, if he must have disclaimed the sentiment, might have owned the stentorian voice with which it was uttered.

Frank Innes dragged him from the spot. The two handsome lads followed the same course of study and recreation, and felt a certain mutual attraction, founded mainly on good looks. It had never gone deep ; Frank was by nature a thin, jeering creature, not truly susceptible whether of feeling or inspiring friendship ; and the relation between the pair was altogether on the outside, a thing of common knowledge and the pleasantries that spring from a common acquaintance. The more credit to Frank that he was appalled by Archie's outburst, and at least conceived the design of keeping him in sight, and, if possible, in hand, for the day. But Archie, who had just defied—was it God or Satan ?—would not listen to the word of a college companion.

" I will not go with you," he said. " I do not desire your company, sir ; I would be alone."

" Here, Weir, man, don't be absurd," said Innes, keeping a tight hold upon his sleeve. " I will not let you go until I know what you mean to do with yourself ; it's no use brandishing that staff." For indeed at that moment Archie had made a sudden—perhaps a warlike—movement. "This has been the most insane affair; you know it has. You know very well that I'm playing the good Samaritan. All I wish is to keep you quiet."

"If quietness is what you wish, Mr. Innes," said Archie, "and you will promise to leave me entirely to myself, I will tell you so much, that I am going to walk in the country and admire the beauties of nature."

"Honour bright?" asked Frank.

"I am not in the habit of lying, Mr. Innes," retorted Archie. "I have the honour of wishing you good-day."

"You won't forget the Spec.?" asked Innes.

"The Spec.?" said Archie. "Oh no, I won't forget the Spec."

And the one young man carried his tortured spirit forth of the city and all the day long, by one road and another, in an endless pilgrimage of misery; while the other hastened smilingly to spread the news of Weir's access of insanity, and to drum up for that night a full attendance at the Speculative, where further eccentric developments might certainly be looked for. I doubt if Innes had the least belief in his prediction: I think it flowed rather from a wish to make the story as good and the scandal as great as possible; not from any ill-will to Archie—from the mere pleasure of beholding interested faces. But for all that his words were prophetic. Archie did not forget the Spec.; he put in an appearance there at the due time, and, before the evening was over, had dealt a memorable shock to his companions. It chanced he was the president of the night. He sat in the same room where the Society still meets—only the portraits were not there; the men who afterwards sat for them were then but beginning their career. The same lustre of many tapers shed its light over the meeting; the same chair, perhaps, supported him that so many of us have sat in since. At times he seemed to forget the business of the evening, but even in these periods he sat with a great air of energy and determination. At times he meddled bitterly and launched with defiance those fines which are the precious and rarely used artillery of the president. He little thought, as he did so, how he resembled his father, but his friends remarked upon it, chuckling. So far, in his high place above his fellow-students, he seemed set beyond the possibility of any scandal; but his mind was made up—he was deter-mind to fulfil the sphere of his offence. He signed to Innes (whom he had just fined, and who had just impeached his ruling) to succeed him in the chair, stepped down from the platform, and took his place by the chimney-piece, the shine of many wax tapers from above illumin-ating his pale face, the glow of the great red fire relieving from behind his slim figure. He had to propose, as an amendment to the next subject in the case-book, " Whether capital punishment be consistent with God's will or man's policy ? "

A breath of embarrassment, of something like alarm, passed round the room, so daring did these words appear upon the lips of Hermiston's only son. But the amend-ment was not seconded; the previous question was promptly moved and unanimously voted, and the momen-tary scandal smuggled by. Innes triumphed in the fulfil-ment of his prophecy. He and Archie were now become the heroes of the night; but whereas every one crowded about Innes, when the meeting broke up, but one of all his companions came to speak to Archie.

" Weir, man ! that was an extraordinary raid of yours ! " observed this courageous member, taking him confidentially by the arm as they went out.

" I don't think it a raid," said Archie grimly. " More like a war. I saw that poor brute hanged this morning, and my gorge rises at it yet."

" Hut-tut ! " returned his companion, and, dropping his arm like something hot, he sought the less tense society of others.

Archie found himself alone. The last of the faithful— or was it only the boldest of the curious ?—had fled. He watched the black huddle of his fellow-students draw off down and up the street, in whispering or boisterous gangs. And the isolation of the moment weighed upon him like an omen and an emblem of his destiny in life. Bred up in unbroken fear of himself, among trembling servants, and in a house which (at the least ruffle in the master's voice) shuddered into silence, he saw himself on the brink of the red valley of war, and measured the danger and length of it with awe. He made a détour in the glimmer and shadow of the streets, came into the back stable lane, and watched for a long while the light burn steady in the Judge's room. The longer he gazed upon that illuminated window-blind, the more blank became the picture of the man who sat behind it, endlessly turning over sheets of process, pausing to sip a glass of port, or rising and passing heavily about his book-lined walls to verify some reference. He could not combine the brutal judge and the industrious, dispassionate student ; the connecting link escaped him ; from such a dual nature, it was impossible he should predict behaviour ; and he asked himself if he had done well to plunge into a business of which the end could not be foreseen ; and presently after, with a sickening decline of confidence, if he had done loyally to strike his father. For he had struck him—defied him twice over and before a cloud of witnesses—struck him a public buffet before crowds. Who had called him to judge his father in these precarious and high questions ? The office was usurped. It might have become a stranger ; in a son—there was no blinking it—in a son, it was disloyal. And now, between these two natures so antipathetic, so hateful to each other, there was depending an unpardonable affront : and the providence of God alone might foresee the manner in which it would be resented by Lord Hermiston.

These misgivings tortured him all night and arose with him in the winter's morning ; they followed him from class to class, they made him shrinkingly sensitive to every shade of manner in his companions, they sounded in his ears through the current voice of the professor ; and he brought them home with him at night unabated and indeed increased. The cause of this increase lay in a chance encounter with the celebrated Dr. Gregory. Archie stood looking vaguely in the lighted window of a book shop, trying to nerve himself for the approaching ordeal. My lord and he had met and parted in the morning as they had now done for long, with scarcely the ordinary civilities of life ; and it was plain to the son that nothing had yet reached the father's ears. Indeed, when he recalled the awful countenance of my lord, a timid hope sprang up in him that perhaps there would be found no one bold enough to carry tales. If this were so, he asked himself, would he begin again ? and he found no answer. It was at this moment that a hand was laid upon his arm, and a voice said in his ear, " My dear Mr. Archie, you had better come and see me."

He started, turned around, and found himself face to face with Dr. Gregory. " And why should I come to see you ? " he asked, with the defiance of the miserable.

" Because you are looking exceeding ill," said the doctor, " and you very evidently want looking after, my young friend. Good folk are scarce, you know ; and it is not every one that would be quite so much missed as yourself. It is not every one that Hermiston would miss."

And with a nod and a smile, the doctor passed on.

A moment after, Archie was in pursuit, and had in turn, but more roughly, seized him by the arm.

" What do you mean ? what did you mean by saying that ? What makes you think that Hermis—my father would have missed me ? "

The doctor turned about and looked him all over with a clinical eye. A far more stupid man than Dr. Gregory might have guessed the truth ; but ninety-nine out of a hundred, even if they had been equally inclined to kindness, would have blundered by some touch of charitable exaggeration. The doctor was better inspired. He knew the father well ; in that white face of intelligence and suffering, he divined something of the son ; and he told, without apology or adornment, the plain truth.

" When you had the measles, Mr. Archibald, you had them gey and ill ; and I thought you were going to slip between my fingers," he said. " Well, your father was

anxious. How did I know it ? says you. Simply because
I am a trained observer. The sign that I saw him make
ten thousand would have missed ; and perhaps—*perhaps*,
I say, because he's a hard man to judge of—but perhaps
he never made another. A strange thing to consider !
It was this. One day I came to him : 'Hermiston,' said
I, 'there's a change.' He never said a word, just glowered
at me (if ye'll pardon the phrase) like a wild beast. ' A
change for the better,' said I. And I distinctly heard him
take his breath."

The doctor left no opportunity for anti-climax ; nodding
his cocked hat (a piece of antiquity to which he clung)
and repeating " Distinctly " with raised eyebrows, he took
his departure, and left Archie speechless in the street.

The anecdote might be called infinitely little, and yet
its meaning for Archie was immense. " I did not know
the old man had so much blood in him." He had never
dreamed this sire of his, this aboriginal antique, this
adamantine Adam, had even so much of a heart as to be
moved in the least degree for another—and that other
himself, who had insulted him ! With the generosity of
youth, Archie was instantly under arms upon the other
side : had instantly created a new image of Lord Hermiston,
that of a man who was all iron without and all sensibility
within. The mind of the vile jester, the tongue that
had pursued Duncan Jopp with unmanly insults, the
unbeloved countenance that he had known and feared
for so long, were all forgotten ; and he hastened home,
impatient to confess his misdeeds, impatient to throw
himself on the mercy of this imaginary character.

He was not to be long without a rude awakening. It
was in the gloaming when he drew near the doorstep of
the lighted house, and was aware of the figure of his
father approaching from the opposite side. Little daylight lingered ; but on the door being opened, the strong
yellow shine of the lamp gushed out upon the landing
and shone full on Archie, as he stood, in the old-fashioned
observance of respect, to yield precedence. The Judge
came without haste, stepping stately and firm ; his chin

raised, his face (as he entered the lamplight) strongly illumined, his mouth set hard. There was never a wink of change in his expression ; without looking to the right or left, he mounted the stair, passed close to Archie, and entered the house. Instinctively, the boy, upon his first coming, had made a movement to meet him ; instinctively, he recoiled against the railing, as the old man swept by him in a pomp of indignation. Words were needless ; he knew all—perhaps more than all—and the hour of judgment was at hand.

It is possible that, in this sudden revulsion of hope and before these symptoms of impending danger, Archie might have fled. But not even that was left to him. My lord, after hanging up his cloak and hat, turned round in the lighted entry, and made him an imperative and silent gesture with his thumb, and with the strange instinct of obedience, Archie followed him into the house.

All dinner time there reigned over the Judge's table a palpable silence, and as soon as the solids were despatched he rose to his feet.

" M'Killop, tak' the wine into my room," said he ; and then to his son : " Archie, you and me has to have a talk."

It was at this sickening moment that Archie's courage, for the first and last time, entirely deserted him. " I have an appointment," said he.

" It'll have to be broken, then," said Hermiston, and led the way into his study.

The lamp was shaded, the fire trimmed to a nicety, the table covered deep with orderly documents, the backs of law books made a frame upon all sides that was only broken by the window and the doors.

For a moment Hermiston warmed his hands at the fire, presenting his back to Archie ; then suddenly disclosed on him the terrors of the Hanging Face.

" What's this I hear of ye ? " he asked.

There was no answer possible to Archie.

" I'll have to tell ye, then," pursued Hermiston. " It seems ye've been skirling against the father that begot ye, and one of His Maijesty's Judges in this land ; and that in the public street, and while an order of the Court was being executit. Forbye which, it would appear that ye've been airing your opeenions in a Coallege Debatin' Society ; " he paused a moment : and, then, with extraordinary bitterness, added : " Ye damned eediot."

" I had meant to tell you," stammered Archie. " I see you are well informed."

" Muckle obleeged to ye," said his lordship, and took his usual seat. " And so you disapprove of Caapital Punishment ? " he added.

" I am sorry, sir, I do," said Archie.

" I am sorry, too," said his lordship. " And now, if you please, we shall approach this business with a little more parteecularity. I hear that at the hanging of Duncan Jopp—and, man ! ye had a fine client there—in the middle of all the riffraff of the ceety, ye thought fit to cry out, ' This is a damned murder, and my gorge rises at the man that haangit him.' "

" No, sir, these were not my words," cried Archie.

" What were yer words, then ? " asked the Judge.

" I believe I said, ' I denounce it as a murder ! ' " said the son, " I beg your pardon—a God-defying murder. I have no wish to conceal the truth," he added, and looked his father for a moment in the face.

" God, it would only need that of it next ! " cried Hermiston. " There was nothing about your gorge rising, then ? "

" That was afterwards, my lord, as I was leaving the Speculative. I said I had been to see the miserable creature hanged, and my gorge rose at it."

" Did ye, though ? " said Hermiston. " And I suppose ye knew who haangit him ? "

" I was present at the trial ; I ought to tell you that, I ought to explain. I ask your pardon beforehand for any expression that may seem undutiful. The position in which I stand is wretched," said the unhappy hero, now fairly face to face with the business he had chosen, " I have been reading some of your cases. I was present while Jopp was tried. It was a hideous business. Father, it was a hideous thing ! Grant he was vile, why should you hunt him with a vileness equal to his own ? It was done with glee—that is the word—you did it with glee, and I looked on, God help me ! with horror."

"You're a young gentleman that doesna approve of Caapital Punishment," said Hermiston. "Weel, I'm an auld man that does. I was glad to get Jopp haangit, and what for would I pretend I wasna ? You're all for honesty, it seems ; you couldna even steik your mouth on the public street. What for should I steik mines upon the bench, the King's officer, bearing the sword, a dreid to evil-doers, as I was from the beginning, and as I will be to the end ! Mair than enough of it ! Heedious ! I never gave twa thoughts to heediousness, I have no call to be bonny. I'm a man that gets through with my day's business, and let that suffice."

The ring of sarcasm had died out of his voice as he went on ; the plain words became invested with some of the dignity of the Justice-seat.

"It would be telling you if you could say as much," the speaker resumed. "But ye cannot. Ye've been reading some of my cases, ye say. But it was not for the law in them, it was to spy out your faither's nakedness, a fine employment in a son. You're splairging ; you're running at lairge in life like a wild nowt. It's impossible you should think any longer of coming to the Bar. You're not fit for it ; no splairger is. And another thing : son of mines or no son of mines, you have flung fylement in public on one of the Senators of the Coallege of Justice, and I would make it my business to see that ye were never admitted there yourself. There is a kind of a decency to be observit. Then comes the next of it—what am I to do with ye next ? Ye'll have to find some kind of a trade, for I'll never support ye in idleset. What do ye fancy ye'll be fit for ? The pulpit ? Na, they could never get diveenity into that bloackhead. Him that the law of man whammles is no' likely to do muckle better by the law of God. What would ye make of hell ? Wouldna your gorge rise at that ? Na, there's no room for splairgers under the fower quarters of John Calvin. What else is there? Speak up. Have ye got nothing of your own?"

"Father, let me go to the Peninsula," said Archie. "That's all I'm fit for—to fight."

"All? quo' he!" returned the Judge. "And it would be enough too, if I thought it. But I'll never trust ye so near the French, you that's so Frenchifeed."

"You do me injustice there, sir," said Archie. "I am loyal; I will not boast; but any interest I may have ever felt in the French——"

"Have ye been so loyal to me?" interrupted his father. There came no reply.

"I think not," continued Hermiston. "And I would send no man to be a servant of the King, God bless him! that has proved such a shauchling son to his own faither. You can splairge here on Edinburgh street, and where's the hairm? It doesna play buff on me! And if there were twenty thousand eediots like yourself, sorrow a Duncan Jopp would hang the fewer. But there's no splairging possible in a camp; and if you were to go to it, you would find out for yourself whether Lord Well'n'ton approves of caapital punishment or not. You a sodger!" he cried, with a sudden burst of scorn. "Ye auld wife, the sodgers would bray at ye like cuddies!"

As at the drawing of a curtain, Archie was aware of some illogicality in his position, and stood abashed. He had a strong impression, besides, of the essential valour of the old gentleman before him, how conveyed it would be hard to say.

"Well, have ye no other proposeetion?" said my lord again.

"You have taken this so calmly, sir, that I cannot but stand ashamed," began Archie.

"I'm nearer voamiting, though, than you would fancy," said my lord.

The blood rose to Archie's brow.

"I beg your pardon, I should have said that you had accepted my affront. . . . I admit it was an affront; I

did not think to apologise, but I do, I ask your pardon ;
it will not be so again, I pass you my word of honour. . . .
I should have said that I admired your magnanimity with
—this—offender," Archie concluded with a gulp.

" I have no other son, ye see," said Hermiston. " A
bonny one I have gotten ! But I must just do the best
I can wi' him, and what am I to do ? If ye had been
younger, I would have wheepit ye for this rideeculous
exhibeetion. The way it is, I have just to grin and bear.
But one thing is to be clearly understood. As a faither,
I must grin and bear it ; but if I had been the Lord
Advocate instead of the Lord Justice-Clerk, son or no
son, Mr. Erchibald Weir would have been in a jyle the
night."

Archie was now dominated. Lord Hermiston was coarse
and cruel ; and yet the son was aware of a bloomless
nobility, an ungracious abnegation of the man's self in
the man's office. At every word, this sense of the greatness of Lord Hermiston's spirit struck more home ; and
along with it that of his own impotence, who had struck
—and perhaps basely struck—at his own father, and not
reached so far as to have even nettled him.

" I place myself in your hands without reserve," he
said.

" That's the first sensible word I've had of ye the night,"
said Hermiston. " I can tell ye, that would have been
the end of it, the one way or the other ; but it's better ye
should come there yourself, than what I would have had
to hirstle ye. Weel, by my way of it—and my way is the
best—there's just the one thing it's possible that ye might be
with decency, and that's a laird. Ye'll be out of hairm's
way at the least of it. If ye have to rowt, ye can rowt
amang the kye ; and the maist feck of the caapital punishment ye're like to come across'll be guddling trouts. Now,
I'm for no idle lairdies ; every man has to work, if it's
only at peddling ballants ; to work, or to be wheepit, or
to be haangit. If I set ye down at Hermiston, I'll have
to see you work that place the way it has never been
workit yet ; ye must ken about the sheep like a herd ;

ye must be my grieve there, and I'll see that I gain by ye. Is that understood?"

"I will do my best," said Archie.

"Well, then, I'll send Kirstie word the morn, and ye can go yourself the day after," said Hermiston. "And just try to be less of an eediot!" he concluded, with a freezing smile, and turned immediately to the papers on his desk.

CHAPTER IV

OPINIONS OF THE BENCH

LATE the same night, after a disordered walk, Archie was admitted into Lord Glenalmond's dining-room where he sat, with a book upon his knee, beside three frugal coals of fire. In his robes upon the bench, Glenalmond had a certain air of burliness : plucked of these, it was a may-pole of a man that rose unsteadily from his chair to give his visitor welcome. Archie had suffered much in the last days, he had suffered again that evening ; his face was white and drawn, his eyes wild and dark. But Lord Glenalmond greeted him without the least mark of surprise or curiosity.

"Come in, come in," said he. "Come in and take a seat. Carstairs" (to his servant), "make up the fire, and then you can bring a bit of supper," and again to Archie, with a very trivial accent : "I was half expecting you," he added.

"No supper," said Archie. "It is impossible that I should eat."

"Not impossible," said the tall old man, laying his hand upon his shoulder, "and, if you will believe me, necessary."

"You know what brings me ?" said Archie, as soon as the servant had left the room.

"I have a guess, I have a guess," replied Glenalmond. "We will talk of it presently—when Carstairs has come and gone, and you have had a piece of my good Cheddar cheese and a pull at the porter tankard : not before."

"It is impossible I should eat," repeated Archie.

"Tut, tut !" said Lord Glenalmond. "You have eaten nothing to-day, and, I venture to add, nothing yesterday.

There is no case that may not be made worse; this may be a very disagreeable business, but if you were to fall sick and die, it would be still more so, and for all concerned —for all concerned."

" I see you must know all," said Archie. " Where did you hear it ? "

" In the mart of scandal, in the Parliament House," said Glenalmond. " It runs riot below among the bar and the public, but it sifts up to us upon the bench, and rumour has some of her voices even in the divisions."

Carstairs returned at this moment, and rapidly laid out a little supper; during which Lord Glenalmond spoke at large and a little vaguely on indifferent subjects, so that it might be rather said of him that he made a cheerful noise, than that he contributed to human conversation; and Archie sat upon the other side, not heeding him, brooding over his wrongs and errors.

But so soon as the servant was gone, he broke forth again at once. " Who told my father? Who dared to tell him ? Could it have been you ? "

" No, it was not me," said the Judge; " although—to be quite frank with you, and after I had seen and warned you—it might have been me. I believe it was Glenkindie."

" That shrimp ! " cried Archie.

" As you say, that shrimp," returned my lord; " although really it is scarce a fitting mode of expression for one of the Senators of the College of Justice. We were hearing the parties in a long, crucial case, before the fifteen; Creech was moving at some length for an infeftment; when I saw Glenkindie lean forward to Hermiston with his hand over his mouth and make him a secret communication. No one could have guessed its nature from your father; from Glenkindie, yes, his malice sparked out of him a little grossly. But your father, no. A man of granite. The next moment he pounced upon Creech. ' Mr. Creech,' says he, ' I'll take a look of that sasine,' and for thirty minutes after," said Glenalmond, with a smile, " Messrs. Creech and Co. were fighting a pretty uphill battle, which resulted, I need hardly add, in their total rout. The case was dismissed. No, I doubt if ever I heard Hermiston better inspired. He was literally rejoicing *in apicibus juris*."

Archie was able to endure no longer. He thrust his plate away and interrupted the deliberate and insignificant stream of talk. " Here," he said, " I have made a fool of myself, if I have not made something worse. Do you judge between us—judge between a father and a son. I can speak to you ; it is not like. . . . I will tell you what I feel and what I mean to do ; and you shall be the judge," he repeated.

" I decline jurisdiction," said Glenalmond, with extreme seriousness. " But, my dear boy, if it will do you any good to talk, and if it will interest you at all to hear what I may choose to say when I have heard you, I am quite at your command. Let an old man say it, for once, and not need to blush : I love you like a son."

There came a sudden sharp sound in Archie's throat. " Ay," he cried, " and there it is ! Love ! Like a son ! And how do you think I love my father ? "

" Quietly, quietly," says my lord.

" I will be very quiet," replied Archie. " And I will be baldly frank. I do not love my father ; I wonder sometimes if I do not hate him. There's my shame ; perhaps my sin ; at least, and in the sight of God, not my fault. How was I to love him ? He has never spoken to me, never smiled upon me ; I do not think he ever touched me. You know the way he talks ? You do not talk so, yet you can sit and hear him without shuddering, and I cannot. My soul is sick when he begins with it ; I could smite him in the mouth. And all that's nothing. I was at the trial of this Jopp. You were not there, but you must have heard him often ; the man's notorious for it, for being—look at my position ! he's my father and this is how I have to speak of him—notorious for being a brute and cruel and a coward. Lord Glenalmond, I give you my word, when I came out of that Court, I longed to die —the shame of it was beyond my strength : but I—I——"

he rose from his seat and began to pace the room in a disorder. "Well, who am I ? A boy, who have never been tried, have never done anything except this twopenny impotent folly with my father. But I tell you, my lord, and I know myself, I am at least that kind of a man—or that kind of a boy, if you prefer it—that I could die in torments rather than that any one should suffer as that scoundrel suffered. Well, and what have I done ? I see it now. I have made a fool of myself, as I said in the beginning ; and I have gone back, and asked my father's pardon, and placed myself wholly in his hands—and he has sent me to Hermiston," with a wretched smile, "for life, I suppose—and what can I say ? he strikes me as having done quite right, and let me off better than I had deserved."

"My poor, dear boy ! " observed Glenalmond. "My poor, dear and, if you will allow me to say so, very foolish boy ! You are only discovering where you are ; to one of your temperament, or of mine, a painful discovery. The world was not made for us ; it was made for ten hundred millions of men, all different from each other and from us ; there's no royal road there, we just have to sclamber and tumble. Don't think that I am at all disposed to be surprised ; don't suppose that I ever think of blaming you ; indeed I rather admire ! But there fall to be offered one or two observations on the case which occur to me and which (if you will listen to them dispassionately) may be the means of inducing you to view the matter more calmly. First of all, I cannot acquit you of a good deal of what is called intolerance. You seem to have been very much offended because your father talks a little sculduddery after dinner, which it is perfectly licit for him to do, and which (although I am not very fond of it myself) appears to be entirely an affair of taste. Your father, I scarcely like to remind you, since it is so trite a commonplace, is older than yourself. At least, he is *major* and *sui juris*, and may please himself in the matter of his conversation. And, do you know, I wonder if he might not have as good an answer against you and me ? We say we sometimes find him *coarse*, but I suspect he might retort that he finds us always dull. Perhaps a relevant exception."

He beamed on Archie, but no smile could be elicited.

"And now," proceeded the Judge, "for 'Archibald on Capital Punishment.' This is a very plausible academic opinion; of course I do not and I cannot hold it; but that's not to say that many able and excellent persons have not done so in the past. Possibly, in the past, also, I may have a little dipped myself in the same heresy. My third client, or possibly my fourth, was the means of a return in my opinions. I never saw the man I more believed in; I would have put my hand in the fire, I would have gone to the cross for him; and when it came to trial he was gradually pictured before me, by undeniable probation, in the light of so gross, so cold-blooded, and so black-hearted a villain, that I had a mind to have cast my brief upon the table. I was then boiling against the man with even a more tropical temperature than I had been boiling for him. But I said to myself: 'No, you have taken up his case; and because you have changed your mind it must not be suffered to let drop. All that rich tide of eloquence that you prepared last night with so much enthusiasm is out of place, and yet you must not desert him, you must say something.' So I said something, and I got him off. It made my reputation. But an experience of that kind is formative. A man must not bring his passions to the bar—or to the bench."

This story had slightly rekindled Archie's interest. "I could never deny," he began—"I mean I can conceive that some men would be better dead. But who are we to know all the springs of God's unfortunate creatures? Who are we to trust ourselves where it seems that God himself must think twice before He treads, and to do it with delight? Yes, with delight. *Tigris ut aspera.*"

"Perhaps not a pleasant spectacle," said Glenalmond. "And yet, do you know, I think somehow a great one."

"I've had a long talk with him to-night," said Archie.

"I was supposing so," said Glenalmond.

"And he struck me——I cannot deny that he struck

me as something very big," pursued the son. "Yes, he is big. He never spoke about himself; only about me. I suppose I admired him. The dreadful part——"

"Suppose we did not talk about that," interrupted Glenalmond. "You know it very well, it cannot in any way help that you should brood upon it, and I sometimes wonder whether you and I—who are a pair of sentiment-alists—are quite good judges of plain men."

"How do you mean?" asked Archie.

"*Fair* judges, I mean," replied Glenalmond. "Can we be just to them? Do we not ask too much? There was a word of yours just now that impressed me a little when you asked me who we were to know all the springs of God's unfortunate creatures. You applied that, as I understood, to capital cases only. But does it—I ask myself—does it not apply all through? Is it any less diffi-cult to judge of a good man or of a half-good man, than of the worst criminal at the bar? And may not each have relevant excuses?"

"Ah, but we do not talk of punishing the good," cried Archie.

"No, we do not talk of it," said Glenalmond. "But I think we do it. Your father, for instance."

"You think I have punished him?" cried Archie.

Lord Glenalmond bowed his head.

"I think I have," said Archie. "And the worst is, I think he feels it! How much, who can tell, with such a being? But I think he does."

"And I am sure of it," said Glenalmond.

"Has he spoken to you, then?" cried Archie.

"Oh, no," replied the Judge.

"I tell you honestly," said Archie, "I want to make it up to him. I will go, I have already pledged myself to go, to Hermiston. That was to him. And now I pledge myself to you, in the sight of God, that I will close my mouth on capital punishment and all other subjects where our views may clash, for—how long shall I say? when shall I have sense enough?—ten years. Is that well?"

"It is well," said my lord.

"As far as it goes," said Archie. "It is enough as regards myself, it is to lay down enough of my conceit. But as regards him, whom I have publicly insulted? What am I to do to him? How do you pay attentions to a—an Alp like that?"

"Only in one way," replied Glenalmond. "Only by obedience, punctual, prompt, and scrupulous."

"And I promise that he shall have it," answered Archie. "I offer you my hand in pledge of it."

"And I take your hand as a solemnity," replied the Judge. "God bless you, my dear, and enable you to keep your promise. God guide you in the true way, and spare your days, and preserve to you your honest heart." At that, he kissed the young man upon the forehead in a gracious, distant, antiquated way; and instantly launched, with a marked change of voice, into another subject. "And now, let us replenish the tankard; and I believe, if you will try my Cheddar again, you would find you had a better appetite. The Court has spoken, and the case is dismissed."

"No, there is one thing I must say," cried Archie. "I must say it in justice to himself. I know—I believe faithfully, slavishly, after our talk—he will never ask me anything unjust. I am proud to feel it, that we have that much in common, I am proud to say it to you."

The Judge, with shining eyes, raised his tankard. "And I think perhaps that we might permit ourselves a toast," said he. "I should like to propose the health of a man very different from me and very much my superior —a man from whom I have often differed, who has often (in the trivial expression) rubbed me the wrong way, but whom I have never ceased to respect and, I may add, to be not a little afraid of. Shall I give you his name?"

"The Lord Justice-Clerk, Lord Hermiston," said Archie, almost with gaiety; and the pair drank the toast deeply.

It was not precisely easy to re-establish, after these

emotional passages, the natural flow of conversation. But the Judge eked out what was wanting with kind looks, produced his snuff-box (which was very rarely seen) to fill in a pause, and at last, despairing of any further social success, was upon the point of getting down a book to read a favourite passage, when there came a rather startling summons at the front door, and Carstairs ushered in my Lord Glenkindie, hot from a midnight supper. I am not aware that Glenkindie was ever a beautiful object, being short, and gross-bodied, and with an expression of sensuality comparable to a bear's. At that moment, coming in hissing from many potations, with a flushed countenance and blurred eyes, he was strikingly contrasted with the tall, pale, kingly figure of Glenalmond. A rush of confused thought came over Archie—of shame that this was one of his father's elect friends ; of pride, that at the least of it Hermiston could carry his liquor ; and last of all, of rage, that he should have here under his eye the man that had betrayed him. And then that, too, passed away ; and he sat quiet, biding his opportunity.

The tipsy senator plunged at once into an explanation with Glenalmond. There was a point reserved yesterday, he had been able to make neither head nor tail of it, and seeing lights in the house, he had just dropped in for a glass of porter—and at this point he became aware of the third person. Archie saw the cod's mouth and the blunt lips of Glenkindie gape at him for a moment, and the recognition twinkle in his eyes.

" Who's this ? " said he. " What ? is this possibly you, Don Quickshot ? And how are ye ? And how's your father ? And what's all this we hear of you ? It seems you're a most extraordinary leveller, by all tales. No king, no parliaments, and your gorge rises at the macers, worthy men ! Hoot, toot ! Dear, dear me ! Your father's son, too ! Most rideeculous ! "

Archie was on his feet, flushing a little at the reappearance of his unhappy figure of speech, but perfectly self-possessed. " My lord—and you, Lord Glenalmond, my dear friend," he began, " this is a happy chance for me, that I can make my confession and offer my apologies to two of you at once."

"Ah, but I don't know about that. Confession? It'll be judeecial, my young friend," cried the jocular Glenkindie. "And I'm afraid to listen to ye. Think if ye were to make me a coanvert!"

"If you would allow me, my lord," returned Archie, "what I have to say is very serious to me; and be pleased to be humorous after I am gone!"

"Remember, I'll hear nothing against the macers!" put in the incorrigible Glenkindie.

But Archie continued as though he had not spoken. "I have played, both yesterday and to-day, a part for which I can only offer the excuse of youth. I was so unwise as to go to an execution; it seems I made a scene at the gallows; not content with which, I spoke the same night in a college society against capital punishment. This is the extent of what I have done, and in case you hear more alleged against me, I protest my innocence. I have expressed my regret already to my father, who is so good as to pass my conduct over—in a degree, and upon the condition that I am to leave my law studies." . . .

CHAPTER V

WINTER ON THE MOORS

1. At Hermiston

THE road to Hermiston runs for a great part of the way up the valley of a stream, a favourite with anglers and with midges, full of falls and pools, and shaded by willows and natural woods of birch. Here and there, but at great distances, a byway branches off, and a gaunt farmhouse may be descried above in a fold of the hill; but the more part of the time, the road would be quite empty of passage and the hills of habitation. Hermiston parish is one of the least populous in Scotland; and, by the time you came that length, you would scarce be surprised at the inimitable smallness of the kirk, a dwarfish, ancient place seated for fifty, and standing in a green by the burn-side among two-score gravestones. The manse close by, although no more than a cottage, is surrounded by the brightness of a flower-garden and the straw roofs of bees; and the whole colony, kirk and manse, garden and graveyard, finds harbourage in a grove of rowans, and is all the year round in a great silence broken only by the drone of the bees, the tinkle of the burn, and the bell on Sundays. A mile beyond the kirk the road leaves the valley by a precipitous ascent, and brings you a little after to the place of Hermiston, where it comes to an end in the back-yard before the coach-house. All beyond and about is the great field of the hills; the plover, the curlew, and the lark cry there; the wind blows as it blows in a ship's rigging, hard and cold and pure; and the hill-tops huddle one behind another like a herd of cattle into the sunset.

The house was sixty years old, unsightly, comfortable ; a farmyard and a kitchen-garden on the left, with a fruit wall where little hard green pears came to their maturity about the end of October.

The policy (as who should say the park) was of some extent, but very ill reclaimed ; heather and moorfowl had crossed the boundary wall and spread and roosted within ; and it would have tasked a landscape gardener to say where policy ended and unpolicied nature began. My lord had been led by the influence of Mr. Sheriff Scott into a considerable design of planting ; many acres were accordingly set out with fir, and the little feathery besoms gave a false scale and lent a strange air of a toy-shop to the moors. A great, rooty sweetness of bogs was in the air, and at all seasons an infinite melancholy piping of hill birds. Standing so high and with so little shelter, it was a cold, exposed house, splashed by showers, drenched by continuous rains that made the gutters to spout, beaten upon and buffeted by all the winds of heaven ; and the prospect would be often black with tempest, and often white with the snows of winter. But the house was wind and weather proof, the hearths were kept bright, and the rooms pleasant with live fires of peat ; and Archie might sit of an evening and hear the squalls bugle on the moorland, and watch the fire prosper in the earthy fuel, and the smoke winding up the chimney, and drink deep of the pleasures of shelter.

Solitary as the place was, Archie did not want neighbours. Every night, if he chose, he might go down to the manse and share a " brewst " of toddy with the minister —a hare-brained ancient gentleman, long and light and still active, though his knees were loosened with age, and his voice broke continually in childish trebles—and his lady wife, a heavy, comely dame, without a word to say for herself beyond good-even and good-day. Harum-scarum, clodpole young lairds of the neighbourhood paid him the compliment of a visit. Young Hay of Romanes rode down to call, on his crop-eared pony ; young Pringle of Drumanno came up on his bony grey. Hay remained on the hospitable field, and must be carried to bed ; Pringle got somehow to his saddle about 3 A.M., and (as Archie stood with the lamp on the upper doorstep) lurched, uttered a senseless view-holloa, and vanished out of the small circle of illumination like a wraith. Yet a minute or two longer the clatter of his break-neck flight was audible, then it was cut off by the intervening steepness of the hill ; and again, a great while after, the renewed beating of phantom horse-hoofs, far in the valley of the Hermiston, showed that the horse at least, if not his rider, was still on the homeward way.

There was a Tuesday Club at the " Cross-keys " in Crossmichael, where the young bloods of the country-side congregated and drank deep on a percentage of the expense, so that he was left gainer who should have drunk the most. Archie had no great mind to this diversion, but he took it like a duty laid upon him, went with a decent regularity, did his manfullest with the liquor, held up his head in the local jests, and got home again and was able to put up his horse, to the admiration of Kirstie and the lass that helped her. He dined at Driffel, supped at Windielaws. He went to the new year's ball at Hunts-field and was made welcome, and thereafter rode to hounds with my Lord Muirfell, upon whose name, as that of a legitimate Lord of Parliament, in a work so full of Lords of Session, my pen should pause reverently. Yet the same fate attended him here as in Edinburgh. The habit of solitude tends to perpetuate itself, and an austerity of which he was quite unconscious, and a pride which seemed arrogance, and perhaps was chiefly shyness, discouraged and offended his new companions. Hay did not return more than twice, Pringle never at all, and there came a time when Archie even desisted from the Tuesday Club, and became in all things—what he had had the name of almost from the first—the Recluse of Hermiston. High-nosed Miss Pringle of Drumanno and high-stepping Miss Marshall of the Mains were understood to have had a difference of opinion about him the day after the ball— he was none the wiser, he could not suppose himself to

E

be remarked by these entrancing ladies. At the ball itself my Lord Muirfell's daughter, the Lady Flora, spoke to him twice, and the second time with a touch of appeal, so that her colour rose and her voice trembled a little in his ear, like a passing grace in music. He stepped back with a heart on fire, coldly and not ungracefully excused himself, and a little after watched her dancing with young Drumanno of the empty laugh, and was harrowed at the sight, and raged to himself that this was a world in which it was given to Drumanno to please, and to himself only to stand aside and envy. He seemed excluded, as of right, from the favour of such society—seemed to extinguish mirth wherever he came, and was quick to feel the wound, and desist, and retire into solitude. If he had but understood the figure he presented, and the impression he made on these bright eyes and tender hearts; if he had but guessed that the Recluse of Hermiston, young, graceful, well spoken, but always cold, stirred the maidens of the county with the charm of Byronism when Byronism was new, it may be questioned whether his destiny might not even yet have been modified. It may be questioned, and I think it should be doubted. It was in his horoscope to be parsimonious of pain to himself, or of the chance of pain, even to the avoidance of any opportunity of pleasure; to have a Roman sense of duty, an instinctive aristocracy of manners and taste; to be the son of Adam Weir and Jean Rutherford.

2. *Kirstie*

Kirstie was now over fifty, and might have sat to a sculptor. Long of limb, and still light of foot, deep-breasted, robust-loined, her golden hair not yet mingled with any trace of silver, the years had but caressed and embellished her. By the lines of a rich and vigorous maternity, she seemed destined to be the bride of heroes and the mother of their children; and behold, by the iniquity of fate, she had passed through her youth alone, and drew near to the confines of age, a childless woman.

The tender ambitions that she had received at birth had been, by time and disappointment, diverted into a certain barren zeal of industry and fury of interference. She carried her thwarted ardours into housework, she washed floors with her empty heart. If she could not win the love of one with love, she must dominate all by her temper. Hasty, wordy, and wrathful, she had a drawn quarrel with most of her neighbours, and with the others not much more than armed neutrality. The grieve's wife had been "sneisty"; the sister of the gardener who kept house for him had shown herself "upsitten"; and she wrote to Lord Hermiston about once a year demanding the discharge of the offenders, and justifying the demand by much wealth of detail. For it must not be supposed that the quarrel rested with the wife and did not take in the husband also—or with the gardener's sister, and did not speedily include the gardener himself. As the upshot of all this petty quarrelling and intemperate speech, she was practically excluded (like a lightkeeper on his tower) from the comforts of human association; except with her own indoor drudge, who, being but a lassie and entirely at her mercy, must submit to the shifty weather of "the mistress's" moods without complaint, and be willing to take buffets or caresses according to the temper of the hour. To Kirstie, thus situate and in the Indian summer of her heart, which was slow to submit to age, the gods sent this equivocal good thing of Archie's presence. She had known him in the cradle and paddled him when he misbehaved; and yet, as she had not so much as set eyes on him since he was eleven and had his last serious illness, the tall, slender, refined, and rather melancholy young gentleman of twenty came upon her with the shock of a new acquaintance. He was "Young Hermiston," "the laird himsel'": he had an air of distinctive superiority, a cold straight glance of his black eyes, that abashed the woman's tantrums in the beginning, and therefore the possibility of any quarrel was excluded. He was new, and therefore immediately aroused her curiosity; he was reticent, and kept it awake. And lastly he was dark and she fair, and he was male and she female, the everlasting fountains of interest.

Her feeling partook of the loyalty of a clanswoman, the hero-worship of a maiden aunt, and the idolatry due to a god. No matter what he had asked of her, ridiculous or tragic, she would have done it and joyed to do it. Her passion, for it was nothing less, entirely filled her. It was a rich physical pleasure to make his bed or light his lamp for him when he was absent, to pull off his wet boots or wait on him at dinner when he returned. A young man who should have so doted on the idea, moral and physical, of any woman, might be properly described as being in love, head and heels, and would have behaved himself accordingly. But Kirstie—though her heart leaped at his coming footsteps—though, when he patted her shoulder, her face brightened for the day—had not a hope or thought beyond the present moment and its perpetuation to the end of time. Till the end of time she would have had nothing altered, but still continue delightedly to serve her idol, and be repaid (say twice in the month) with a clap on the shoulder.

I have said her heart leaped—it is the accepted phrase. But rather, when she was alone in any chamber of the house, and heard his foot passing on the corridors, something in her bosom rose slowly until her breath was suspended, and as slowly fell again with a deep sigh, when the steps had passed and she was disappointed of her eyes' desire. This perpetual hunger and thirst of his presence kept her all day on the alert. When he went forth at morning, she would stand and follow him with admiring looks. As it grew late and drew to the time of his return, she would steal forth to a corner of the policy wall and be seen standing there sometimes by the hour together, gazing with shaded eyes, waiting the exquisite and barren pleasure of his view a mile off on the mountains. When at night she had trimmed and gathered the fire, turned down his bed, and laid out his night-gear—when there was no more to be done for the king's pleasure, but to remember him fervently in her usually very tepid prayers, and go to bed brooding upon his perfections, his future career, and what she should give him the next day for dinner—there still remained before her one more opportunity ; she was still to take in the tray and say good-night. Sometimes Archie would glance up from his book with a preoccupied nod and a perfunctory salutation which was in truth a dismissal ; sometimes—and by degrees more often—the volume would be laid aside, he would meet her coming with a look of relief ; and the conversation would be engaged, last out the supper, and be prolonged till the small hours by the waning fire. It was no wonder that Archie was fond of company after his solitary days ; and Kirstie, upon her side, exerted all the arts of her vigorous nature to ensnare his attention. She would keep back some piece of news during dinner to be fired off with the entrance of the supper tray, and form as it were the *lever de rideau* of the evening's entertainment. Once he had heard her tongue wag, she made sure of the result. From one subject to another she moved by insidious transitions, fearing the least silence, fearing almost to give him time for an answer lest it should slip into a hint of separation. Like so many people of her class, she was a brave narrator ; her place was on the hearthrug and she made it a rostrum, mimeing her stories as she told them, fitting them with vital detail, spinning them out with endless " quo' he's " and " quo' she's," her voice sinking into a whisper over the supernatural or the horrific ; until she would suddenly spring up in affected surprise, and pointing to the clock, " Mercy, Mr. Archie ! " she would say, " whatten a time o' night is this of it ! God forgive me for a daft wife ! " So it befell, by good management, that she was not only the first to begin these nocturnal conversations, but invariably the first to break them off ; so she managed to retire and not to be dismissed.

3. *A Border Family*

Such an unequal intimacy has never been uncommon in Scotland, where the clan spirit survives ; where the

servant tends to spend her life in the same service, a
helpmeet at first, then a tyrant, and at last a pensioner ;
where, besides, she is not necessarily destitute of the pride
of birth, but is, perhaps, like Kirstie, a connection of her
master's, and at least knows the legend of her own family,
and may count kinship with some illustrious dead. For
that is the mark of the Scot of all classes : that he stands in
an attitude towards the past unthinkable to Englishmen,
and remembers and cherishes the memory of his fore-
bears, good or bad ; and there burns alive in him a sense
of identity with the dead even to the twentieth generation.
No more characteristic instance could be found than in
the family of Kirstie Elliott. They were all, and Kirstie
the first of all, ready and eager to pour forth the particulars
of their genealogy, embellished with every detail that
memory had handed down or fancy fabricated ; and, behold ! from every ramification of that tree there dangled
a halter. The Elliotts themselves have had a chequered
history ; but these Elliotts deduced, besides, from three
of the most unfortunate of the border clans—the Nicksons,
the Ellwalds, and the Crozers. One ancestor after another
might be seen appearing a moment out of the rain and
the hill mist upon his furtive business, speeding home,
perhaps, with a paltry booty of lame horses and lean kine,
or squealing and dealing death in some moorland feud
of the ferrets and the wild cats. One after another closed
his obscure adventures in mid-air, triced up to the arm
of the royal gibbet or the Baron's dule-tree. For the rusty
blunderbuss of Scots criminal justice, which usually hurt
nobody but jurymen, became a weapon of precision for
the Nicksons, the Ellwalds, and the Crozers. The exhilaration of their exploits seemed to haunt the memories
of their descendants alone, and the shame to be forgotten.
Pride glowed in their bosoms to publish their relationship
to " Andrew Ellwald of the Laverockstanes, called ' Unchancy Dand,' who was justifeed wi' seeven mair of the
same name at Jeddart in the days of King James the Sax."
In all this tissue of crime and misfortune, the Elliotts of
Cauldstaneslap had one boast which must appear legiti-

mate : the males were gallows-birds, born outlaws, petty thieves, and deadly brawlers ; but, according to the same tradition, the females were all chaste and faithful. The power of ancestry on the character is not limited to the inheritance of cells. If I buy ancestors by the gross from the benevolence of Lyon King of Arms, my grandson (if he is Scottish) will feel a quickening emulation of their deeds. The men of the Elliotts were proud, lawless, violent as of right, cherishing and prolonging a tradition. In like manner with the women. And the woman, essentially passionate and reckless, who crouched on the rug, in the shine of the peat fire, telling these tales, had cherished through life a wild integrity of virtue.

Her father Gilbert had been deeply pious, a savage disciplinarian in the antique style, and withal a notorious smuggler. " I mind when I was a bairn getting mony a skelp and being shoo'd to bed like pou'try," she would say. " That would be when the lads and their bit kegs were on the road. We've had the riffraff of two-three counties in our kitchen, mony's the time, betwix' the twelve and the three ; and their lanterns would be standing in the forecourt, ay, a score o' them at once. But there was nae ungodly talk permitted at Cauldstaneslap. My faither was a consistent man in walk and conversation ; just let slip an aith, and there was the door to ye ! He had that zeal for the Lord, it was a fair wonder to hear him pray, but the family has aye had a gift that way." This father was twice married, once to a dark woman of the old Ellwald stock, by whom he had Gilbert, presently of Cauldstaneslap ; and, secondly, to the mother of Kirstie. " He was an auld man when he married her, a fell auld man wi' a muckle voice—you could hear him rowting from the top o' the Kye-skairs," she said ; " but for her, it appears she was a perfit wonder. It was gentle blood she had, Mr. Archie, for it was your ain. The countryside gaed gyte about her and her gowden hair. Mines is no to be mentioned wi' it, and there's few weemen has mair hair than what I have, or yet a bonnier colour. Often would I tell my dear Miss Jeannie—that was your mother, dear, she was cruel ta'en up about her hair, it was unco' tender, ye see—'Houts, Miss Jeannie,' I would say, 'just fling your washes and your French dentifrishes in the back o' the fire, for that's the place for them ; and awa' down to a burn side, and wash yersel' in cauld hill water, and dry your bonny hair in the caller wind o' the muirs, the way that my mother aye washed hers, and that I have aye made it a practice to have wishen mines—just you do what I tell ye, my dear, and ye'll give me news of it ! Ye'll have hair, and routh of hair, a pigtail as thick's my arm,' I said, 'and the bonniest colour like the clear gowden guineas, so as the lads in kirk'll no can keep their eyes off it !' Weel, it lasted out her time, puir thing ! I cuttit a lock of it upon her corp that was lying there sae cauld. I'll show it ye some of thir days if ye're good. But, as I was sayin', my mither——"

On the death of the father there remained golden-haired Kirstie, who took service with her distant kinsfolk, the Rutherfords, and black-a-vised Gilbert, twenty years older, who farmed the Cauldstaneslap, married, and begot four sons between 1773 and 1784, and a daughter, like a postscript, in '97, the year of Camperdown and Cape St. Vincent. It seemed it was a tradition in the family to wind up with a belated girl. In 1804, at the age of sixty, Gilbert met an end that might be called heroic. He was due home from market any time from eight at night till five in the morning, and in any condition from the quarrel-some to the speechless, for he maintained to that age the goodly customs of the Scots farmer. It was known on this occasion that he had a good bit of money to bring home ; the word had gone round loosely. The laird had shown his guineas, and if anybody had but noticed it, there was an ill-looking, vagabond crew, the scum of Edinburgh, that drew out of the market long ere it was dusk and took the hill-road by Hermiston, where it was not to be believed that they had lawful business. One of the countryside, one Dickieson, they took with them to be their guide, and dear he paid for it ! Of a sudden in the ford of the Broken Dykes, this vermin clan fell on the laird, six to one, and

him three parts asleep, having drunk hard. But it is ill
to catch an Elliott. For a while, in the night and the
black water that was deep as to his saddle-girths, he
wrought with his staff like a smith at his stithy, and great
was the sound of oaths and blows. With that the ambuscade was burst, and he rode for home with a pistol-ball
in him, three knife wounds, the loss of his front teeth,
a broken rib and bridle, and a dying horse. That was
a race with death that the laird rode! In the mirk night,
with his broken bridle and his head swimming, he dug
his spurs to the rowels in the horse's side, and the horse,
that was even worse off than himself, the poor creature!
screamed out loud like a person as he went, so that the
hills echoed with it, and the folks at Cauldstaneslap got to
their feet about the table and looked at each other with
white faces. The horse fell dead at the yard gate, the
laird won the length of the house and fell there on the
threshold. To the son that raised him he gave the bag
of money. " Hae," said he. All the way up the thieves
had seemed to him to be at his heels, but now the hallu-
cination left him—he saw them again in the place of the
ambuscade—and the thirst of vengeance seized on his
dying mind. Raising himself and pointing with an
imperious finger into the black night from which he had
come, he uttered the single command, " Brocken Dykes,"
and fainted. He had never been loved, but he had been
feared in honour. At that sight, at that word, gasped out
at them from a toothless and bleeding mouth, the old
Elliott spirit awoke with a shout in the four sons. " Wanting the hat," continues my author, Kirstie, whom I but
haltingly follow, for she told this tale like one inspired,
" wanting guns, for there wasna twa grains o' pouder in
the house, wi' nae mair weepons than their sticks into
their hands, the fower o' them took the road. Only Hob,
and that was the eldest, hunkered at the doorsill where
the blood had rin, fyled his hand wi' it, and haddit it
up to Heeven in the way o' the auld Border aith. ' Hell
shall have her ain again this nicht! ' he raired, and rode
forth upon his earrand." It was three miles to Broken

Dykes, down hill, and a sore road. Kirstie has seen men from Edinburgh dismounting there in plain day to lead their horses. But the four brothers rode it as if Auld Hornie were behind and Heaven in front. Come to the ford, and there was Dickieson. By all tales, he was not dead, but breathed and reared upon his elbow, and cried out to them for help. It was at a graceless face that he asked mercy. As soon as Hob saw, by the glint of the lantern, the eyes shining and the whiteness of the teeth in the man's face, "Damn you!" says he; "ye hae your teeth, hae ye?" and rode his horse to and fro upon that human remnant. Beyond that, Dandie must dismount with the lantern to be their guide; he was the youngest son, scarce twenty at the time. "A' nicht long they gaed in the wet heath and jennipers, and whaur they gaed they neither knew nor cared, but just followed the bluid stains and the footprints o' their faither's murderers. And a' nicht Dandie had his nose to the grund like a tyke, and the ithers followed and spak' naething, neither black nor white. There was nae noise to be heard, but just the sough of the swalled burns, and Hob, the dour yin, risping his teeth as he gaed." With the first glint of the morning they saw they were on the drove road, and at that the four stopped and had a dram to their break-fasts, for they knew that Dand must have guided them right, and the rogues could be but little ahead, hot foot for Edinburgh by the way of the Pentland Hills. By eight o'clock they had word of them—a shepherd had seen four men "uncoly mishandled" go by in the last hour. "That's yin a piece," says Clem, and swung his cudgel. "Five o' them!" says Hob. "God's death, but the faither was a man! And him drunk!" And then there befell them what my author termed "a sair misbegowk," for they were overtaken by a posse of mounted neighbours come to aid in the pursuit. Four sour faces looked on the reinforcement. "The deil's broughten you!" said Clem, and they rode thenceforward in the rear of the party with hanging heads. Before ten they had found and secured the rogues, and by three of the afternoon, as they rode up the Vennel with their prisoners, they were aware of a concourse of people bearing in their midst something that dripped. "For the boady of the saxt," pursued Kirstie, "wi' his head smashed like a hazel-nit, had been a' that nicht in the chairge o' Hermiston Water, and it dunting it on the stanes, and grunding it on the shallows, and flinging the deid thing heels-ower-hurdie at the Fa's o' Spango ; and in the first o' the day Tweed had got a hold o' him and carried him off like a wind, for it was uncoly swalled, and raced wi' him, bobbing under brae-sides, and was long playing with the creature in the drumlie lynns under the castle, and at the hinder end of all cuist him up on the sterling of Crossmichael brig. Sae there they were a' thegither at last (for Dickieson had been brought in on a cart long syne), and folk could see what mainner o' man my brither had been that had held his head again' sax and saved the siller, and him drunk ! " Thus died of honourable injuries and in the savour of fame Gilbert Elliott of the Cauldstaneslap ; but his sons had scarce less glory out of the business. Their savage haste, the skill with which Dand had found and followed the trail, the barbarity to the wounded Dickieson (which was like an open secret in the county) and the doom which it was currently supposed they had intended for the others, struck and stirred popular imagination. Some century earlier the last of the minstrels might have fashioned the last of the ballads out of that Homeric fight and chase ; but the spirit was dead, or had been reincarnated already in Mr. Sheriff Scott, and the degenerate moorsmen must be content to tell the tale in prose and to make of the " Four Black Brothers " a unit after the fashion of the " Twelve Apostles " or the " Three Musketeers."

Robert, Gilbert, Clement, and Andrew—in the proper Border diminutives Hob, Gib, Clem, and Dand Elliott—these ballad heroes, had much in common ; in particular, their high sense of the family and the family honour ; but they went diverse ways, and prospered and failed in different businesses. According to Kirstie, " they had a' bees in their bonnets but Hob." Hob the laird was, indeed, essentially a decent man. An elder of the Kirk, nobody had heard an oath upon his lips, save, perhaps, thrice or so at the sheep-washing, since the chase of his father's murderers. The figure he had shown on that eventful night disappeared as if swallowed by a trap. He who had ecstatically dipped his hand in the red blood, he who had ridden down Dickieson, became, from that moment on, a stiff and rather graceless model of the rustic proprieties; cannily profiting by the high war prices, and yearly stowing away a little nest-egg in the bank against calamity; approved of and sometimes consulted by the greater lairds for the massive and placid sense of what he said, when he could be induced to say anything; and particularly valued by the minister, Mr. Torrance, as a right-hand man in the parish, and a model to parents. The transfiguration had been for the moment only; some Barbarossa, some old Adam of our ancestors, sleeps in all of us till the fit circumstance shall call it into action; and for as sober as he now seemed, Hob had given once for all the measure of the devil that haunted him. He was married, and, by reason of the effulgence of that legendary night, was adored by his wife. He had a mob of little lusty, barefoot children who marched in a caravan the long miles to school, the stages of whose pilgrimage were marked by acts of spoliation and mischief, and who were qualified in the countryside as " fair pests." But in the house, if " faither was in," they were quiet as mice. In short, Hob moved through life in a great peace—the reward of any one who shall have killed his man, with any formidable and figurative circumstance, in the midst of a country gagged and swaddled with civilisation."

It was a current remark that the Elliotts were " guid and bad, like sanguishes"; and certainly there was a curious distinction, the men of business coming alternately with the dreamers. The second brother, Gib, was a weaver by trade, had gone out early into the world to Edinburgh, and come home again with his wings singed. There was an exaltation in his nature which had led him to embrace with enthusiasm the principles of the French Revolution, and had ended by bringing him under the hawse of my Lord Hermiston in that furious onslaught of his upon the Liberals, which sent Muir and Palmer into exile and dashed the party into chaff. It was whispered that my lord, in his great scorn for the movement and prevailed upon a little by a sense of neighbourliness, had given Gib a hint. Meeting him one day in the Potterrow, my lord had stopped in front of him. " Gib, ye eediot," he had said, " what's this I hear of you ? Poalitics, poalitics, poalitics, weaver's poalitics, is the way of it, I hear. If ye arena a' thegither dozened with eediocy, ye'll gang your ways back to Cauldstaneslap, and ca' your loom, and ca' your loom, man ! " And Gilbert had taken him at the word and returned, with an expedition almost to be called flight, to the house of his father. The clearest of his inheritance was that family gift of prayer of which Kirstie had boasted ; and the baffled politician now turned his attention to religious matters—or, as others said, to heresy and schism. Every Sunday morning he was in Crossmichael, where he had gathered together, one by one, a sect of about a dozen persons, who called themselves " God's Remnant of the True Faithful," or, for short, " God's Remnant." To the profane, they were known as " Gib's Deils." Bailie Sweedie, a noted humorist in the town, vowed that the proceedings always opened to the tune of " The Deil Fly Away with the Exciseman," and that the sacrament was dispensed in the form of hot whisky-toddy ; both wicked hits at the evangelist, who had been suspected of smuggling in his youth, and had been overtaken (as the phrase went) on the streets of Crossmichael one Fair day. It was known that every Sunday they prayed for a blessing on the arms of Bonaparte. For this, " God's Remnant," as they were " skailing " from the cottage that did duty for a temple, had been repeatedly stoned by the bairns, and Gib himself hooted by a squadron of Border volunteers in which his own brother, Dand, rode in a uniform and with a drawn sword. The " Remnant " were believed, besides, to be " anti-

nomian in principle," which might otherwise have been
a serious charge, but the way public opinion then blew
it was quite swallowed up and forgotten in the scandal
about Bonaparte. For the rest, Gilbert had set up his
loom in an outhouse at Cauldstaneslap, where he laboured
assiduously six days of the week. His brothers, appalled
by his political opinions, and willing to avoid dissension
in the household, spoke but little to him; he less to them,
remaining absorbed in the study of the Bible and almost
constant prayer. The gaunt weaver was dry-nurse at
Cauldstaneslap, and the bairns loved him dearly. Except
when he was carrying an infant in his arms, he was rarely
seen to smile—as, indeed, there were few smilers in that
family. When his sister-in-law rallied him, and proposed
that he should get a wife and bairns of his own, since he
was so fond of them, " I have no clearness of mind upon
that point," he would reply. If nobody called him in
to dinner, he stayed out. Mrs. Hob, a hard, unsym-
pathetic woman, once tried the experiment. He went
without food all day, but at dusk, as the light began
to fail him, he came into the house of his own accord,
looking puzzled. " I've had a great gale of prayer upon
my speerit," said he. " I canna mind sae muckle's what
I had for denner." The creed of God's Remnant was
justified in the life of its founder. " And yet I dinna
ken," said Kirstie. " He's maybe no more stockfish than
his neeghbours! He rode wi' the rest o' them, and had
a good stamach to the work, by a' that I hear! God's
Remnant! The deil's clavers! There wasna muckle
Christianity in the way Hob guided Johnny Dickieson, at
the least of it; but Guid kens! Is he a Christian even?
He might be a Mahommedan or a Deevil or a Fire-
worshipper, for what I ken."

The third brother had his name on a doorplate, no
less, in the city of Glasgow. " Mr. Clement Elliott," as
long as your arm. In his case, that spirit of innovation
which had shown itself timidly in the case of Hob by the
admission of new manures, and which had run to waste
with Gilbert in subversive politics and heretical religions,

bore useful fruit in many ingenious mechanical improvements. In boyhood, from his addiction to strange devices of sticks and string, he had been counted the most eccentric of the family. But that was all by now; and he was a partner of his firm, and looked to die a bailie. He too had married, and was rearing a plentiful family in the smoke and din of Glasgow; he was wealthy, and could have bought out his brother, the cock-laird, six times over, it was whispered; and when he slipped away to Cauldstaneslap for a well-earned holiday, which he did as often as he was able, he astonished the neighbours with his broadcloth, his beaver hat, and the ample plies of his neck-cloth. Though an eminently solid man at bottom, after the pattern of Hob, he had contracted a certain Glasgow briskness and *aplomb* which set him off. All the other Elliotts were as lean as a rake, but Clement was laying on fat, and he panted sorely when he must get into his boots. Dand said, chuckling: " Ay, Clem has the elements of a corporation." " A provost and corporation," returned Clem. And his readiness was much admired.

The fourth brother, Dand, was a shepherd to his trade, and by starts, when he could bring his mind to it, excelled in the business. Nobody could train a dog like Dandie; nobody, through the peril of great storms in the winter time, could do more gallantly. But if his dexterity were exquisite, his diligence was but fitful; and he served his brother for bed and board, and a trifle of pocket-money when he asked for it. He loved money well enough, knew very well how to spend it, and could make a shrewd bargain when he liked. But he preferred a vague knowledge that he was well to windward to any counted coins in the pocket; he felt himself richer so. Hob would expostulate: " I'm an amature herd," Dand would reply: " I'll keep your sheep to you when I'm so minded, but I'll keep my liberty, too. Thir's no man can coandescend on what I'm worth." Clem would expound to him the miraculous results of compound interest, and recommend investments. " Ay, man? " Dand would say, " and do you think, if I took Hob's siller, that I wouldna drink it

or wear it on the lassies ? And, anyway, my kingdom is
no' of this world. Either I'm a poet or else I'm nothing."
Clem would remind him of old age. "I'll die young,
like Robbie Burns," he would say stoutly. No question
but he had a certain accomplishment in minor verse. His
"Hermiston Burn," with its pretty refrain—

> "I love to gang thinking whaur ye gang linking
>   Hermiston burn, in the howe ; "

his "Auld, auld Elliotts, clay-cauld Elliotts, dour, bauld
Elliotts of auld," and his really fascinating piece about
the Praying Weaver's Stone, had gained him in the neighbourhood the reputation, still possible in Scotland, of a
local bard ; and, though not printed himself, he was recognised by others who were and who had become famous.
Walter Scott owed to Dandie the text of the "Raid of
Wearie" in the *Minstrelsy* and made him welcome at his
house, and appreciated his talents, such as they were,
with all his usual generosity. The Ettrick Shepherd was
his sworn crony ; they would meet, drink to excess, roar
out their lyrics in each other's faces, and quarrel and
make it up again till bedtime. And besides these recog-
nitions, almost to be called official, Dandie was made welcome for the sake of his gift through the farmhouses of
several contiguous dales, and was thus exposed to mani-
fold temptations which he rather sought than fled. He
had figured on the stool of repentance, for once fulfilling
to the letter the tradition of his hero and model. His
humorous verses to Mr. Torrance on that occasion—
"Kenspeckle here my lane I stand "—unfortunately too
indelicate for further citation, ran through the country
like a fiery cross ; they were recited, quoted, paraphrased
and laughed over as far away as Dumfries on the one
hand and Dunbar on the other.

These four brothers were united by a close bond, the
bond of that mutual admiration—or rather mutual hero-
worship—which is so strong among the members of
secluded families who have much ability and little culture.
Even the extremes admired each other. Hob, who had

as much poetry as the tongs, professed to find pleasure in Dand's verses; Clem, who had no more religion than Claverhouse, nourished a heartfelt, at least an open-mouthed, admiration of Gib's prayers; and Dandie followed with relish the rise of Clem's fortunes. Indulgence followed hard on the heels of admiration. The laird, Clem, and Dand, who were Tories and patriots of the hottest quality, excused to themselves, with a certain bashfulness, the radical and revolutionary heresies of Gib. By another division of the family, the laird, Clem, and Gib, who were men exactly virtuous, swallowed the dose of Dand's irregularities as a kind of clog or drawback in the mysterious providence of God affixed to bards, and distinctly probative of poetical genius. To appreciate the simplicity of their mutual admiration, it was necessary to hear Clem, arrived upon one of his visits, and dealing in a spirit of continuous irony with the affairs and personalities of that great city of Glasgow where he lived and transacted business. The various personages, ministers of the church, municipal officers, mercantile bigwigs, whom he had occasion to introduce, were all alike denigrated, all served but as reflectors to cast back a flattering side-light on the house of Cauldstaneslap. The Provost, for whom Clem by exception entertained a measure of respect, he would liken to Hob. " He minds me o' the laird there," he would say. " He has some of Hob's grand, whunstane sense, and the same way with him of steiking his mouth when he's no' very pleased." And Hob, all unconscious, would draw down his upper lip and produce, as if for comparison, the formidable grimace referred to. The unsatisfactory incumbent of St. Enoch's Kirk was thus briefly dismissed : " If he had but twa fingers o' Gib's he would waken them up." And Gib, honest man ! would look down and secretly smile. Clem was a spy whom they had sent out into the world of men. He had come back with the good news that there was nobody to compare with the Four Black Brothers, no position that they would not adorn, no official that it would not be well they should replace, no interest of

F,

mankind, secular or spiritual, which would not immediately bloom under their supervision. The excuse of their folly is in two words : scarce the breadth of a hair divided them from the peasantry. The measure of their sense is this : that these symposia of rustic vanity were kept entirely within the family, like some secret ancestral practice. To the world their serious faces were never deformed by the suspicion of any simper of self-contentment. Yet it was known. " They hae a guid pride o' themsel's ! " was the word in the countryside.

Lastly, in a Border story, there should be added their " to-names." Hob was The Laird. " Roy ne puis, prince ne daigne " ; he was the laird of Cauldstaneslap— say fifty acres—*ipsissimus*. Clement was Mr. Elliott, as upon his door-plate, the earlier Dafty having been discarded as no longer applicable, and indeed only a reminder of misjudgment and the imbecility of the public ; and the youngest, in honour of his perpetual wanderings, was known by the sobriquet of Randy Dand.

It will be understood that not all this information was communicated by the aunt, who had too much of the family failing herself to appreciate it thoroughly in others. But as time went on, Archie began to observe an omission in the family chronicle.

" Is there not a girl too ? " he asked.

" Ay. Kirstie. She was named from me, or my grand-mother at least—it's the same thing," returned the aunt, and went on again about Dand, whom she secretly pre-ferred by reason of his gallantries.

" But what is your niece like ? " said Archie at the next opportunity.

" Her ? As black's your hat ! But I dinna suppose she would maybe be what you would ca' *ill-looked* a' thegither. Na, she's a kind of a handsome jaud—a kind o' gipsy," said the aunt, who had two sets of scales for men and women—or perhaps it would be more fair to say that she had three, and the third and the most loaded was for girls.

" How comes it that I never see her in church ? " said Archie.

" 'Deed, and I believe she's in Glesgie with Clem and his wife. A heap good she's like to get of it ! I dinna say for men folk, but where weemen folk are born, there let them bide. Glory to God, I was never far'er from here than Crossmichael.''

In the meantime it began to strike Archie as strange, that while she thus sang the praises of her kinsfolk, and manifestly relished their virtues and (I may say) their vices like a thing creditable to herself, there should appear not the least sign of cordiality between the house of Hermiston and that of Cauldstaneslap. Going to church of a Sunday, as the lady housekeeper stepped with her skirts kilted, three tucks of her white petticoat showing below, and her best India shawl upon her back (if the day were fine) in a pattern of radiant dyes, she would sometimes overtake her relatives preceding her more leisurely in the same direction. Gib of course was absent : by skriegh of day he had been gone to Crossmichael and his fellow heretics ; but the rest of the family would be seen marching in open order : Hob and Dand, stiff-necked, straight-backed six-footers, with severe dark faces, and their plaids about their shoulders ; the convoy of children scattering (in a state of high polish) on the wayside, and every now and again collected by the shrill summons of the mother ; and the mother herself, by a suggestive circumstance which might have afforded matter of thought to a more experienced observer than Archie, wrapped in a shawl nearly identical with Kirstie's but a thought more gaudy and conspicuously newer. At the sight, Kirstie grew more tall —Kirstie showed her classical profile, nose in air and nostril spread, the pure blood came in her cheek evenly in a delicate living pink.

" A braw day to ye, Mistress Elliott," said she, and hostility and gentility were nicely mingled in her tones. " A fine day, mem," the laird's wife would reply with a miraculous curtsey, spreading the while her plumage— setting off, in other words, and with arts unknown to the mere man, the pattern of her India shawl. Behind her, the whole Cauldstaneslap contingent marched in closer order, and with an indescribable air of being in the presence of the foe; and while Dandie saluted his aunt with a certain familiarity as of one who was well in court, Hob marched on in awful immobility. There appeared upon the face of this attitude in the family the consequences of some dreadful feud. Presumably the two women had been principals in the original encounter, and the laird had probably been drawn into the quarrel by the ears, too late to be included in the present skin-deep reconciliation.

"Kirstie," said Archie one day, "what is this you have against your family?"

"I dinna complean," said Kirstie, with a flush. "I say naething."

"I see you do not—not even good-day to your own nephew," said he.

"I hae naething to be ashamed of," said she. "I can say the Lord's Prayer with a good grace. If Hob was ill, or in preeson or poverty, I would see to him blithely. But for curtchying and complimenting and colloguing, thank ye kindly!"

Archie had a bit of a smile: he leaned back in his chair. "I think you and Mrs. Robert are not very good friends," says he slyly, "when you have your India shawls on?"

She looked upon him in silence, with a sparkling eye but an indecipherable expression; and that was all that Archie was ever destined to learn of the battle of the India shawls.

"Do none of them ever come here to see you?" he inquired.

"Mr. Archie," said she, "I hope that I ken my place better. It would be a queer thing, I think, if I was to clamjamfry up your faither's house—that I should say it!—wi' a dirty, black-a-vised clan, no ane o' them it was worth while to mar soap upon but just mysel'! Na, they're all damnifeed wi' the black Ellwalds. I have nae patience wi' black folk." Then, with a sudden consciousness of the case of Archie, "No' that it maitters for men sae muckle," she made haste to add, "but there's naebody can deny that it's unwomanly. Long hair is the ornament o' woman ony way; we've good warrandise for that—it's in the Bible—and wha can doubt that the Apostle had some gowden-haired lassie in his mind—Apostle and all, for what was he but just a man like yersel'?"

CHAPTER VI

A LEAF FROM CHRISTINA'S PSALM-BOOK

ARCHIE was sedulous at church. Sunday after Sunday he sat down and stood up with that small company, heard the voice of Mr. Torrance leaping like an ill-played clarionet from key to key, and had an opportunity to study his moth-eaten gown and the black thread mittens that he joined together in prayer, and lifted up with a reverent solemnity in the act of benediction. Hermiston pew was a little square box, dwarfish in proportion with the kirk itself, and enclosing a table not much bigger than a footstool. There sat Archie an apparent prince, the only undeniable gentleman and the only great heritor in the parish, taking his ease in the only pew, for no other in the kirk had doors. Thence he might command an undisturbed view of that congregation of solid plaided men, strapping wives and daughters, oppressed children, and uneasy sheep-dogs. It was strange how Archie missed the look of race ; except the dogs, with their refined foxy faces and inimitably curling tails, there was no one present with the least claim to gentility. The Cauldstaneslap party was scarcely an exception ; Dandie perhaps, as he amused himself making verses through the interminable burden of the service, stood out a little by the glow in his eye and a certain superior animation of face and alertness of body ; but even Dandie slouched like a rustic. The rest of the congregation, like so many sheep, oppressed him with a sense of hob-nailed routine, day following day—of physical labour in the open air, oatmeal porridge, peas bannock, the somnolent fire-side in the evening, and the night-long nasal slumbers in a box-bed. Yet he knew many of them to be shrewd and humorous, men of character, notable women, making a bustle in the world and radiating an influence from their low-browed doors. He knew besides they were like other men ; below the crust of custom, rapture found a way ; he had heard them beat the timbrel before Bacchus—had heard them shout and carouse over their whisky-toddy ; and not the most Dutch-bottomed and severe faces among them all, not even the solemn elders themselves, but were capable of singular gambols at the voice of love. Men drawing near to an end of life's adventurous journey—maids thrilling with fear and curiosity on the threshold of entrance—women who had borne and perhaps buried children, who could remember the clinging of the small dead hands and the patter of the little feet now silent—he marvelled that among all those faces there should be no face of expectation, none that was mobile, none into which the rhythm and poetry of life had entered. " O for a live face," he thought ; and at times he had a memory of Lady Flora ; and at times he would study the living gallery before him with despair, and would see himself go on to waste his days in that joyless, pastoral place, and death come to him, and his grave be dug under the rowans, and the Spirit of the Earth laugh out in a thunder-peal at the huge fiasco.

On this particular Sunday, there was no doubt but that the spring had come at last. It was warm, with a latent shiver in the air that made the warmth only the more welcome. The shallows of the stream glittered and tinkled among bunches of primrose. Vagrant scents of the earth arrested Archie by the way with moments of ethereal intoxication. The grey, Quakerish dale was still only awakened in places and patches from the sobriety of its wintry colouring ; and he wondered at its beauty ; an essential beauty of the old earth it seemed to him, not resident in particulars but breathing to him from the whole. He surprised himself by a sudden impulse to write poetry—he did so sometimes, loose, galloping octosyllabics in the vein of Scott—and when he had taken his place on a boulder, near some fairy falls and shaded by a whip of a tree that was already radiant with new leaves, it still more surprised him that he should find nothing to write. His heart perhaps beat in time to some vast indwelling rhythm of the universe. By the time he came to a corner of the valley and could see the kirk, he had so lingered by the way that the first psalm was finishing. The nasal psalmody, full of turns and trills and graceless graces, seemed the essential voice of the kirk itself upraised in thanksgiving. " Everything's alive," he said ; and again cries it aloud, " Thank God, everything's alive ! " He lingered yet a while in the kirk-yard. A tuft of primroses was blooming hard by the leg of an old, black table tombstone, and he stopped to contemplate the random apologue. They stood forth on the cold earth with a trenchancy of contrast ; and he was struck with a sense of incompleteness in the day, the season, and the beauty that surrounded him—the chill there was in the warmth, the gross black clods about the opening primroses, the damp earthy smell that was everywhere intermingled with the scents. The voice of the aged Torrance within rose in an ecstasy. And he wondered if Torrance also felt in his old bones the joyous influence of the spring morning ; Torrance, or the shadow of what once was Torrance, that must come so soon to lie outside here in the sun and rain with all his rheumatisms, while a new minister stood in his room and thundered from his own familiar pulpit ? The pity of it, and something of the chill of the grave, shook him for a moment as he made haste to enter.

He went up the aisle reverently and took his place in the pew with lowered eyes, for he feared he had already offended the kind old gentleman in the pulpit, and was sedulous to offend no further. He could not follow the prayer, not even the heads of it. Brightness of azure, clouds of fragrance, a tinkle of falling water and singing birds, rose like exhalations from some deeper, aboriginal memory, that was not his, but belonged to the flesh on his bones. His body remembered ; and it seemed to him that his body was in no way gross, but ethereal and perishable like a strain of music ; and he felt for it an exquisite tenderness as for a child, an innocent, full of beautiful instincts and destined to an early death. And he felt for old Torrance—of the many supplications, of the few days—a pity that was near to tears. The prayer ended. Right over him was a tablet in the wall, the only ornament in the roughly masoned chapel—for it was no more ; the tablet commemorated, I was about to say the virtues, but rather the existence of a former Rutherford of Hermiston ; and Archie, under that trophy of his long descent and local greatness, leaned back in the pew and contemplated vacancy with the shadow of a smile between playful and sad, that became him strangely. Dandie's sister, sitting by the side of Clem in her new Glasgow finery, chose that moment to observe the young laird. Aware of the stir of his entrance, the little formalist had kept her eyes fastened and her face prettily composed during the prayer. It was not hypocrisy, there was no one further from a hypocrite. The girl had been taught to behave : to look up, to look down, to look unconscious, to look seriously impressed in church, and in every conjuncture to look her best. That was the game of female life, and she played it frankly. Archie was the one person in church who was of interest, who was somebody new, reputed eccentric, known to be young, and a laird, and still unseen by Christina. Small wonder that, as she stood there in her attitude of pretty decency, her mind should run upon him ! If he spared a glance in her direction, he should know she was a well-behaved young lady who had been to Glasgow. In reason he must admire her clothes, and it was possible that he should think her pretty. At that her heart beat the least thing in the world ; and she proceeded, by way of a corrective, to call up and dismiss a series of fancied pictures of the young man who should now, by rights, be looking at her. She settled on the plainest of them, a pink short young man with a dish face and no figure, at whose admiration she could afford to smile ; but for all that, the consciousness of his gaze (which was really fixed on Torrance and his mittens) kept her in something of a flutter till the word Amen. Even then, she was far too well-bred to

gratify her curiosity with any impatience. She resumed
her seat languidly—this was a Glasgow touch—she .com-
posed her dress, rearranged her nosegay of primroses,
looked first in front, then behind upon the other side, and
at last allowed her eyes to move, without hurry, in the
direction of the Hermiston pew. For a moment, they were
riveted. Next she had plucked her gaze home again like
a tame bird who should have meditated flight. Possibilities crowded on her; she hung over the future and
grew dizzy ; the image of this young man, slim, graceful,
dark, with the inscrutable half-smile, attracted and re-
pelled her like a chasm. " I wonder, will I have met my
fate ? " she thought, and her heart swelled.

Torrance was got some way into his first exposition,
positing a deep layer of texts as he went along, laying the
foundations of his discourse, which was to deal with a nice
point in divinity, before Archie suffered his eyes to wander.
They fell first of all on Clem, looking insupportably pros-
perous and patronising Torrance with the favour of a
modified attention, as of one who was used to better things
in Glasgow. Though he had never before set eyes on
him, Archie had no difficulty in identifying him, and no
hesitation in pronouncing him vulgar, the worst of the
family. Clem was leaning lazily forward when Archie
first saw him. Presently he leaned nonchalantly back ;
and that deadly instrument, the maiden, was suddenly
unmasked in profile. Though not quite in the front of
the fashion (had anybody cared !), certain artful Glasgow
mantua-makers, and her own inherent taste, had arrayed
her to great advantage. Her accoutrement was, indeed, a
cause of heart-burning, and almost of scandal, in that
infinitesimal kirk company. Mrs. Hob had said her say
at Cauldstaneslap. " Daft-like ! " she had pronounced it.
" A jaiket that'll no' meet ! Whaur's the sense of a jaiket
that'll no' button upon ye, if it should come to be weet ?
What do ye ca' thir things ? Demmy brokens, d'ye say ?
They'll be brokens wi' a vengeance or ye can win back !
Weel, I have naething to do wi' it—it's no' good taste."
Clem, whose purse had thus metamorphosed his sister, and

who was not insensible to the advertisement, had come to
the rescue with a " Hoot, woman ! What do you ken of
good taste that has never been to the ceety ? " And Hob,
looking on the girl with pleased smiles, as she timidly displayed her finery in the midst of the dark kitchen, had
thus ended the dispute : " The cutty looks weel," he had
said, " and it's no' very like rain. Wear them the day,
hizzie ; but it's no' a thing to make a practice o'." In
the breasts of her rivals, coming to the kirk very conscious
of white underlinen, and their faces splendid with much
soap, the sight of the toilet had raised a storm of varying
emotion, from the mere unenvious admiration that was
expressed in the long-drawn " Eh ! " to the angrier feeling
that found vent in an emphatic " Set her up ! " Her frock
was of straw-coloured jaconet muslin, cut low at the bosom
and short at the ankle, so as to display her *demi-broquins*
of Regency violet, crossing with many straps upon a yellow
cobweb stocking. According to the pretty fashion in which
our grandmothers did not hesitate to appear, and our great-
aunts went forth armed for the pursuit and capture of our
great-uncles, the dress was drawn up so as to mould the
contour of both breasts, and in the nook between a cairngorm brooch maintained it. Here, too, surely in a very
enviable position, trembled the nosegay of primroses. She
wore on her shoulders—or rather, on her back and not
her shoulders, which it scarcely passed—a French coat of
sarsenet, tied in front with Margate braces, and of the
same colour with her violet shoes. About her face clustered
a disorder of dark ringlets, a little garland of yellow French
roses surmounted her brow, and the whole was crowned
by a village hat of chipped straw. Amongst all the rosy and
all the weathered faces that surrounded her in church, she
glowed like an open flower—girl and raiment, and the
cairngorm that caught the daylight and returned it in a
fiery flash, and the threads of bronze and gold that played
in her hair.

Archie was attracted by the bright thing like a child.
He looked at her again and yet again, and their looks
crossed. The lip was lifted from her little teeth. He saw

the red blood work vividly under her tawny skin. Her eye, which was great as a stag's, struck and held his gaze. He knew who she must be—Kirstie, she of the harsh diminutive, his housekeeper's niece, the sister of the rustic prophet, Gib—and he found in her the answer to his wishes.

Christina felt the shock of their encountering glances, and seemed to rise, clothed in smiles, into a region of the vague and bright. But the gratification was not more exquisite than it was brief. She looked away abruptly, and immediately began to blame herself for that abruptness. She knew what she should have done, too late—turned slowly with her nose in the air. And meantime his look was not removed, but continued to play upon her like a battery of cannon constantly aimed, and now seemed to isolate her alone with him, and now seemed to uplift her, as on a pillory, before the congregation. For Archie continued to drink her in with his eyes, even as a wayfarer comes to a well-head on a mountain, and stoops his face, and drinks with thirst unassuageable. In the cleft of her little breasts the fiery eye of the topaz and the pale florets of primrose fascinated him. He saw the breasts heave, and the flowers shake with the heaving, and marvelled what should so much discompose the girl. And Christina was conscious of his gaze—saw it, perhaps, with the dainty plaything of an ear that peeped among her ringlets ; she was conscious of changing colour, conscious of her unsteady breath. Like a creature tracked, run down, surrounded, she sought in a dozen ways to give herself a countenance. She used her handkerchief—it was a really fine one—then she desisted in a panic : " He would only think I was too warm." She took to reading in the metrical psalms, and then remembered it was sermon-time. Last she put a " sugar-bool " in her mouth, and the next moment repented of the step. It was such a homely-like thing ! Mr. Archie would never be eating sweeties in kirk ; and, with a palpable effort, she swallowed it whole, and her colour flamed high. At this signal of distress Archie awoke to a sense of his ill-behaviour. What had he been doing ? He had been exquisitely rude in church to the niece of his housekeeper ; he had stared like a lackey and a libertine at a beautiful and modest girl. It was possible, it was even likely, he would be presented to her after service in the kirk-yard, and then how was he to look ? And there was no excuse. He had marked the tokens of her shame, of her increasing indignation, and he was such a fool that he had not understood them. Shame bowed him down, and he looked resolutely at Mr. Torrance ; who little supposed, good, worthy man, as he continued to expound justification by faith, what was his true business : to play the part of derivative to a pair of children at the old game of falling in love.

Christina was greatly relieved at first. It seemed to her that she was clothed again. She looked back on what had passed. All would have been right if she had not blushed, a silly fool! There was nothing to blush at, if she *had* taken a sugar-bool. Mrs. MacTaggart, the elder's wife in St. Enoch's, took them often. And if he had looked at her, what was more natural than that a young gentleman should look at the best-dressed girl in church ? And at the same time, she knew far otherwise ; she knew there was nothing casual or ordinary in the look, and valued herself on its memory like a decoration. Well, it was a blessing he had found something else to look at ! And presently she began to have other thoughts. It was necessary, she fancied, that she should put herself right by a repetition of the incident, better managed. If the wish was father to the thought, she did not know or she would not recognise it. It was simply as a manœuvre of propriety, as something called for to lessen the significance of what had gone before, that she should a second time meet his eyes, and this time without blushing. And at the memory of the blush, she blushed again, and became one general blush burning from head to foot. Was ever anything so indelicate, so forward, done by a girl before ? And here she was, making an exhibition of herself before the congregation about nothing ! She stole a glance upon her neighbours, and behold ! they were steadily indifferent, and Clem had gone to sleep. And still the one idea was becoming more and more potent with her, that in common prudence she must look again before the service ended. Something of the same sort was going forward in the mind of Archie, as he struggled with the load of penitence. So it chanced that, in the flutter of the moment when the last psalm was given out, and Torrance was reading the verse, and the leaves of every psalm-book in church were rustling under busy fingers, two stealthy glances were sent out like antennæ among the pews and on the indifferent and absorbed occupants, and drew timidly nearer to the straight line between Archie and Christina. They met, they lingered together for the least fraction of time, and that was enough. A charge as of electricity passed through Christina, and behold ! the leaf of her psalm-book was torn across.

Archie was outside by the gate of the graveyard, conversing with Hob and the minister and shaking hands all round with the scattering congregation, when Clem and Christina were brought up to be presented. The laird took off his hat and bowed to her with grace and respect. Christina made her Glasgow curtsey to the laird, and went on again up the road for Hermiston and Cauldstaneslap, walking fast, breathing hurriedly with a heightened colour, and in this strange frame of mind, that when she was alone she seemed in high happiness, and when any one addressed her she resented it like a contradiction. A part of the way she had the company of some neighbour girls and a loutish young man ; never had they seemed so insipid, never had she made herself so disagreeable. But these struck aside to their various destinations or were outwalked and left behind ; and when she had driven off with sharp words the proffered convoy of some of her nephews and nieces, she was free to go on alone up Hermiston brae, walking on air, dwelling intoxicated among clouds of happiness. Near to the summit she heard steps behind her, a man's steps, light and very rapid. She knew the foot at once and walked the faster. "If it's me he's wanting he can run for it," she thought, smiling.

Archie overtook her like a man whose mind was made up.
" Miss Kirstie," he began.

" Miss Christina, if you please, Mr. Weir," she interrupted. " I canna bear the contraction."

" You forget it has a friendly sound for me. Your
aunt is an old friend of mine and a very good one. I
hope we shall see much of you at Hermiston ? "

" My aunt and my sister-in-law doesna agree very well.
Not that I have much ado with it. But still when I'm
stopping in the house, if I was to be visiting my aunt, it
would not look considerate-like."

" I am sorry," said Archie.

" I thank you kindly, Mr. Weir," she said. " I whiles
think myself it's a great peety."

" Ah, I am sure your voice would always be for peace ! "
he cried.

" I wouldna be too sure of that," she said. " I have
my days like other folk, I suppose."

" Do you know, in our old kirk, among our good old
grey dames, you made an effect like sunshine."

" Ah, but that would be my Glasgow clothes ! "

" I did not think I was so much under the influence
of pretty frocks."

She smiled with a half look at him. " There's more
than you ! " she said. " But you see I'm only Cinderella.
I'll have to put all these things by in my trunk ; next
Sunday I'll be as grey as the rest. They're Glasgow
clothes, you see, and it would never do to make a practice
of it. It would seem terrible conspicuous."

By that they were come to the place where their ways
severed. The old grey moors were all about them ; in
the midst a few sheep wandered ; and they could see on
the one hand the straggling caravan scaling the braes in
front of them for Cauldstaneslap, and on the other the
contingent from Hermiston bending off and beginning to
disappear by detachments into the policy gate. It was in
these circumstances that they turned to say farewell, and
deliberately exchanged a glance as they shook hands. All
passed as it should, genteelly ; and in Christina's mind,

as she mounted the first steep ascent for Cauldstaneslap, a gratifying sense of triumph prevailed over the recollection of minor lapses and mistakes. She had kilted her gown, as she did usually at that rugged pass ; but when she spied Archie still standing and gazing after her, the skirts came down again as if by enchantment. Here was a piece of nicety for that upland parish, where the matrons marched with their coats kilted in the rain, and the lasses walked barefoot to kirk through the dust of summer, and went bravely down by the burnside, and sat on stones to make a public toilet before entering ! It was perhaps an air wafted from Glasgow ; or perhaps it marked a stage of that dizziness of gratified vanity, in which the instinctive act passed unperceived. He was looking after ! She unloaded her bosom of a prodigious sigh that was all pleasure, and betook herself to run. When she had overtaken the stragglers of her family, she caught up the niece whom she had so recently repulsed, and kissed and slapped her, and drove her away again, and ran after her with pretty cries and laughter. Perhaps she thought the laird might still be looking ! But it chanced the little scene came under the view of eyes less favourable ; for she overtook Mrs. Hob marching with Clem and Dand.

" You're shürely fey,[1] lass ! " quoth Dandie.

" Think shame to yersel', miss ! " said the strident Mrs. Hob. " Is this the gait to guide yersel' on the way hame frae kirk ? You're shürely no' sponsible the day. And anyway I would mind my guid claes."

" Hoot ! " said Christina, and went on before them, head in air, treading the rough track with the tread of a wild doe.

She was in love with herself, her destiny, the air of the hills, the benediction of the sun. All the way home, she continued under the intoxication of these sky-scraping spirits. At table she could talk freely of young Hermiston ; gave her opinion of him offhand and with a loud voice, that he was a handsome young gentleman, real well-

[1] Unlike yourself, strange, as persons are observed to be in the hour of approaching death or calamity.

mannered and sensible-like, but it was a pity he looked
doleful. Only—the moment after—a memory of his eyes
in church embarrassed her. But for this inconsiderable
check, all through meal-time she had a good appetite, and
she kept them laughing at table, until Gib (who had
returned before them from Crossmichael and his separa-
tive worship) reproved the whole of them for their levity.

Singing " in to herself " as she went, her mind still in
the turmoil of a glad confusion, she rose and tripped upstairs to a little loft, lighted by four panes in the gable,
where she slept with one of her nieces. The niece, who
followed her, presuming on " Auntie's " high spirits, was
flounced out of the apartment with small ceremony, and
retired, smarting and half tearful, to bury her woes in
the byre among the hay. Still humming, Christina
divested herself of her finery, and put her treasures one
by one in her great green trunk. The last of these was the
psalm-book ; it was a fine piece, the gift of Mistress Clem,
in distinct old-faced type, on paper that had begun to grow
foxy in the warehouse—not by service—and she was used
to wrap it in a handkerchief every Sunday after its period
of service was over, and bury it end-wise at the head of
her trunk. As she now took it in hand the book fell open
where the leaf was torn, and she stood and gazed upon that
evidence of her bygone discomposure. There returned
again the vision of the two brown eyes staring at her,
intent and bright, out of that dark corner of the kirk. The
whole appearance and attitude, the smile, the suggested
gesture of young Hermiston came before her in a flash
at the sight of the torn page. " I was surely fey ! " she
said, echoing the words of Dandie, and at the suggested
doom her high spirits deserted her. She flung herself
prone upon the bed, and lay there, holding the psalm-
book in her hands for hours, for the more part in a mere
stupor of unconsenting pleasure and unreasoning fear.
The fear was superstitious ; there came up again and
again in her memory Dandie's ill-omened words, and a
hundred grisly and black tales out of the immediate
neighbourhood read her a commentary on their force.

G

The pleasure was never realised.   You might say the joints
of her body thought and remembered, and were gladdened,
but her essential self, in the immediate theatre of consciousness, talked feverishly of something else, like a
nervous person at a fire.   The image that she most com-
placently dwelt on was that of Miss Christina in her
character of the Fair Lass of Cauldstaneslap, carrying all
before her in the straw-coloured frock, the violet mantle,
and the yellow cobweb stockings.   Archie's image, on the
other hand, when it presented itself, was never welcomed
—far less welcomed with any ardour, and it was exposed
at times to merciless criticism.   In the long, vague dia-
logues she held in her mind, often with imaginary, often
with unrealised interlocutors, Archie, if he were referred
to at all, came in for savage handling.   He was described
as " looking like a stirk," " staring like a caulf," " a face
like a ghaist's."   " Do you call that manners ? " she said ;
or, " I soon put him in his place."   " ' Miss Christina, if
you please, Mr. Weir ! ' says I, and just flyped up my
skirt tails."   With gabble like this she would entertain
herself long whiles together, and then her eye would
perhaps fall on the torn leaf, and the eyes of Archie would
appear again from the darkness of the wall, and the voluble
words deserted her, and she would lie still and stupid, and
think upon nothing with devotion, and be sometimes raised
by a quiet sigh.   Had a doctor of medicine come into that
loft, he would have diagnosed a healthy, well-developed,
eminently vivacious lass lying on her face in a fit of the
sulks ; not one who had just contracted, or was just con-
tracting, a mortal sickness of the mind which should yet
carry her towards death and despair.   Had it been a doctor
of psychology, he might have been pardoned for divining
in the girl a passion of childish vanity, self-love *in excelsis*,
and no more.   It is to be understood that I have been
painting chaos and describing the inarticulate.   Every
lineament that appears is too precise, almost every word
used too strong.   Take a finger-post in the mountains on
a day of rolling mists ; I have but copied the names that
appear upon the pointers, the names of definite and famous

cities far distant, and now perhaps basking in sunshine ; but Christina remained all these hours, as it were, at the foot of the post itself, not moving, and enveloped in mutable and blinding wreaths of haze.

The day was growing late and the sunbeams long and level, when she sat suddenly up, and wrapped in its handkerchief and put by that psalm-book which had already played a part so decisive in the first chapter of her love-story. In the absence of the mesmerist's eye, we are told nowadays that the head of a bright nail may fill his place, if it be steadfastly regarded. So that torn page had riveted her attention on what might else have been but little, and perhaps soon forgotten ; while the ominous words of Dandie—heard, not heeded, and still remembered—had lent to her thoughts, or rather to her mood, a cast of solemnity, and that idea of Fate—a pagan Fate, uncontrolled by any Christian deity, obscure, lawless, and august—moving indissuadably in the affairs of Christian men. Thus even that phenomenon of love at first sight, which is so rare and seems so simple and violent, like a disruption of life's tissue, may be decomposed into a sequence of accidents happily concurring.

She put on a grey frock and a pink kerchief, looked at herself a moment with approval in the small square of glass that served her for a toilet mirror, and went softly downstairs through the sleeping house that resounded with the sound of afternoon snoring. Just outside the door Dandie was sitting with a book in his hand, not reading, only honouring the Sabbath by a sacred vacancy of mind. She came near him and stood still.

" I'm for off up the muirs, Dandie," she said.

There was something unusually soft in her tones that made him look up. She was pale, her eyes dark and bright ; no trace remained of the levity of the morning.

" Ay, lass ? Ye'll have yer ups and downs like me, I'm thinkin'," he observed.

" What for do ye say that ? " she asked.

" O, for naething," says Dand. " Only I think ye're mair like me than the lave of them. Ye've mair of the poetic temper, tho' Guid kens little enough of the poetic taalent. It's an ill gift at the best. Look at yoursel'. At denner you were all sunshine and flowers and laughter, and now you're like the star of evening on a lake."

She drank in this hackneyed compliment like wine, and it glowed in her veins.

" But I'm saying, Dand "—she came nearer him—" I'm for the muirs. I must have a braith of air. If Clem was to be speiring for me, try and quaiet him, will ye no' ? "

" What way ? " said Dandie. " I ken but the ae way, and that's leein'. I'll say ye had a sair heid, if ye like."

" But I havena," she objected.

" I daursay no," he returned. " I said I would say ye had ; and if ye like to nay-say me when ye come back, it'll no mateerially maitter, for my chara'ter's clean gane a'ready past reca'."

" O, Dand, are ye a leear ? " she asked, lingering.

" Folks say sae," replied the bard.

" Wha says sae ? " she pursued.

" Them that should ken the best," he responded. " The lassies, for ane."

" But, Dand, you would never lee to me ? " she asked.

" I'll leave that for your pairt of it, ye girzie," said he. " Ye'll lee to me fast eneuch, when ye hae gotten a jo. I'm tellin' ye and it's true ; when you have a jo, Miss Kirstie, it'll be for guid and ill. I ken : I was made that way mysel', but the deil was in my luck ! Here, gang awa wi' ye to your muirs, and let me be ; I'm in an hour of inspirauton, ye upsetting tawpie ! "

But she clung to her brother's neighbourhood, she knew not why.

" Will ye no gie's a kiss, Dand ? " she said. " I aye likit ye fine."

He kissed her and considered her a moment ; he found something strange in her. But he was a libertine through and through, nourished equal contempt and suspicion of all womankind, and paid his way among them habitually with idle compliments.

" Gae wa' wi' ye ! " said he. " Ye're a dentie baby, and be content wi' that ! "

That was Dandie's way ; a kiss and a comfit to Jenny— a bawbee and my blessing to Jill—and good-night to the whole clan of ye, my dears ! When anything approached the serious, it became a matter for men, he both thought and said. Women, when they did not absorb, were only children to be shoo'd away. Merely in his character of connoisseur, however, Dandie glanced carelessly after his sister as she crossed the meadow. " The brat's no' that bad ! " he thought with surprise, for though he had just been paying her compliments, he had not really looked at her. " Hey ! what's yon ? " For the grey dress was cut with short sleeves and skirts, and displayed her trim strong legs clad in pink stockings of the same shade as the kerchief she wore round her shoulders, and that shimmered as she went. This was not her way in undress ; he knew her ways and the ways of the whole sex in the country-side, no one better ; when they did not go barefoot, they wore stout " rig and furrow " woollen hose of an invisible blue mostly, when they were not black outright ; and Dandie, at sight of this daintiness, put two and two together. It was a silk handkerchief, then they would be silken hose ; they matched—then the whole outfit was a present of Clem's, a costly present, and not something to be worn through bog and briar, or on a late afternoon of Sunday. He whistled. " My denty May, either your heid's fair turned, or there's some on-goings ! " he observed, and dismissed the subject.

She went slowly at first, but ever straighter and faster for the Cauldstaneslap, a pass among the hills to which the farm owed its name. The Slap opened like a doorway between two rounded hillocks ; and through this ran the short cut to Hermiston. Immediately on the other side it went down through the Deil's Hags, a considerable marshy hollow of the hill tops, full of springs, and crouching junipers, and pools where the black peat-water slumbered. There was no view from here. A man might have sat upon the Praying Weaver's Stone a half-century, and seen none but the Cauldstaneslap children twice in the twenty-four hours on their way to the school and back again, an occasional shepherd, the irruption of a clan of sheep, or the birds who haunted about the springs, drinking and shrilly piping. So, when she had once passed the Slap, Kirstie was received into seclusion. She looked back a last time at the farm. It still lay deserted except for the figure of Dandie, who was now seen to be scribbling in his lap, the hour of expected inspiration having come to him at last. Thence she passed rapidly through the morass, and came to the farther end of it, where a sluggish burn discharges, and the path for Hermiston accompanies it on the beginning of its downward path. From this corner a wide view was opened to her of the whole stretch of braes upon the other side, still sallow and in places rusty with the winter, with the path marked boldly, here and there by the burnside a tuft of birches, and—three miles off as the crow flies—from its enclosures and young plantations, the windows of Hermiston glittering in the western sun.

Here she sat down and waited, and looked for a long time at these far-away bright panes of glass. It amused her to have so extended a view, she thought. It amused her to see the house of Hermiston—to see " folk " ; and there was an indistinguishable human unit, perhaps the gardener, visibly sauntering on the gravel paths.

By the time the sun was down and all the easterly braes lay plunged in clear shadow, she was aware of another figure coming up the path at a most unequal rate of approach, now half-running, now pausing and seeming to hesitate. She watched him at first with a total suspension of thought. She held her thought as a person holds his breathing. Then she consented to recognise him. " He'll no' be coming here, he canna be ; it's no' possible." And there began to grow upon her a subdued choking suspense. He *was* coming ; his hesitations had quite ceased, his step grew firm and swift ; no doubt remained ; and the question loomed up before her instant : what was she to do ? It was all very well to say that her brother was a laird himself; it was all very well to speak of casual intermarriages and to count cousinship, like Aunt Kirstie. The difference in their social station was trenchant; propriety, prudence, all that she had ever learned, all that she knew, bade her flee. But on the other hand the cup of life now offered to her was too enchanting. For one moment, she saw the question clearly, and definitely made her choice. She stood up and showed herself an instant in the gap relieved upon the sky line; and the next, fled trembling and sat down glowing with excitement on the Weaver's Stone. She shut her eyes, seeking, praying for composure. Her hand shook in her lap, and her mind was full of incongruous and futile speeches. What was there to make a work about? She could take care of herself, she supposed! There was no harm in seeing the laird. It was the best thing that could happen. She would mark a proper distance to him once and for all. Gradually the wheels of her nature ceased to go round so madly, and she sat in passive expectation, a quiet, solitary figure in the midst of the grey moss. I have said she was no hypocrite, but here I am at fault. She never admitted to herself that she had come up the hill to look for Archie. And perhaps after all she did not know, perhaps came as a stone falls. For the steps of love in the young, and especially in girls, are instinctive and unconscious.

In the meantime, Archie was drawing rapidly near, and he at least was consciously seeking her neighbourhood. The afternoon had turned to ashes in his mouth; the memory of the girl had kept him from reading and drawn him as with cords; and at last, as the cool of the evening began to come on, he had taken his hat and set forth, with a smothered ejaculation, by the moor path to Cauldstaneslap. He had no hope to find her; he took the off chance without expectation of result and to relieve his uneasiness. The greater was his surprise, as he surmounted the slope and came into the hollow of the Deil's Hags, to see there, like an answer to his wishes, the little womanly figure in the grey dress and the pink kerchief sitting little, and low, and lost, and acutely solitary, in these desolate surroundings and on the weather-beaten stone of the dead weaver. Those things that still smacked of winter were all rusty about her, and those things that already relished of the spring had put forth the tender and lively colours of the season. Even in the unchanging face of the death-stone changes were to be remarked; and in the channelled lettering, the moss began to renew itself in jewels of green. By an after-thought that was a stroke of art, she had turned up over her head the back of the kerchief; so that it now framed becomingly her vivacious and yet pensive face. Her feet were gathered under her on the one side, and she leaned on her bare arm, which showed out strong and round, tapered to a slim wrist, and shimmered in the fading light.

Young Hermiston was struck with a certain chill. He was reminded that he now dealt in serious matters of life and death. This was a grown woman he was approaching, endowed with her mysterious potencies and attractions, the treasury of the continued race, and he was neither better nor worse than the average of his sex and age. He had a certain delicacy which had preserved him hitherto unspotted, and which (had either of them guessed it) made him a more dangerous companion when his heart should be really stirred. His throat was dry as he came near; but the appealing sweetness of her smile stood between them like a guardian angel.

For she turned to him and smiled, though without rising. There was a shade in this cavalier greeting that neither of them perceived; neither he, who simply thought it gracious and charming as herself; nor yet she, who did not observe (quick as she was) the difference between rising to meet the laird and remaining seated to receive the expected admirer.

"Are ye stepping west, Hermiston?" said she, giving him his territorial name after the fashion of the country-side.

"I was," said he, a little hoarsely, "but I think I will be about the end of my stroll now. Are you like me,

Miss Christina? the house would not hold me. I came here seeking air."

He took his seat at the other end of the tombstone and studied her, wondering what was she. There was infinite import in the question alike for her and him.

"Ay," she said. "I couldna bear the roof either. It's a habit of mine to come up here about the gloaming when it's quaiet and caller."

"It was a habit of my mother's also," he said gravely. The recollection half startled him as he expressed it. He looked around. "I have scarce been here since. It's peaceful," he said, with a long breath.

"It's no' like Glasgow," she replied. "A weary place, yon Glasgow! But what a day have I had for my hame-coming, and what a bonny evening!"

"Indeed, it was a wonderful day," said Archie. "I think I will remember it years and years until I come to die. On days like this—I do not know if you feel as I do—but everything appears so brief, and fragile, and exquisite, that I am afraid to touch life. We are here for so short a time; and all the old people before us—Rutherfords of Hermiston, Elliotts of the Cauldstaneslap—that were here but a while since, riding about and keeping up a great noise in this quiet corner—making love too, and marrying—why, where are they now? It's deadly commonplace, but after all, the commonplaces are the great poetic truths."

He was sounding her, semi-consciously, to see if she could understand him; to learn if she were only an animal the colour of flowers, or had a soul in her to keep her sweet. She, on her part, her means well in hand, watched, womanlike, for any opportunity to shine, to abound in his humour, whatever that might be. The dramatic artist, that lies dormant or only half-awake in most human beings, had in her sprung to his feet in a divine fury, and chance had served her well. She looked upon him with a subdued twilight look that became the hour of the day and the train of thought; earnestness shone through her like stars in the purple west; and from the great but controlled upheaval of her whole nature there passed into her voice, and rang in her lightest words, a thrill of emotion.

"Have you mind of Dand's song?" she answered. "I think he'll have been trying to say what you have been thinking."

"No, I never heard it," he said. "Repeat it to me, can you?"

"It's nothing wanting the tune," said Kirstie.

"Then sing it me," said he.

"On the Lord's Day? That would never do, Mr. Weir!"

"I am afraid I am not so strict a keeper of the Sabbath, and there is no one in this place to hear us, unless the poor old ancient under the stone."

"No' that I'm thinking that really," she said. "By my way of thinking, it's just as serious as a psalm. Will I sooth it to ye, then?"

"If you please," said he, and, drawing near to her on the tombstone, prepared to listen.

She sat up as if to sing. "I'll only can sooth it to ye," she explained. "I woundna like to sing out loud on the Sabbath. I think the birds would carry news of it to Gilbert," and she smiled. "It's about the Elliotts," she continued, "and I think there's few bonnier bits in the book-poets, though Dand has never got printed yet."

And she began, in the low, clear tones of her half-voice, now sinking almost to a whisper, now rising to a particular note which was her best, and which Archie learned to wait for with growing emotion :—

"O they rade in the rain, in the days that are gane,
    In the rain and the wind and the lave,
  They shoutit in the ha' and they routit on the hill,
    But they're a' quaitit noo in the grave.
Auld, auld Elliotts, clay-cauld Elliotts, dour, bauld Elliotts of
    auld!"

All the time she sang she looked steadfastly before her, her knees straight, her hands upon her knee, her head cast back and up. The expression was admirable throughout, for had she not learned it from the lips and under the criticism of the author ? When it was done, she turned upon Archie a face softly bright, and eyes gently suffused and shining in the twilight, and his heart rose and went out to her with boundless pity and sympathy. His question was answered. She was a human being tuned to a sense of the tragedy of life ; there were pathos and music and a great heart in the girl.

He arose instinctively, she also, for she saw she had gained a point, and scored the impression deeper, and she had wit enough left to flee upon a victory. They were but commonplaces that remained to be exchanged, but the low, moved voices in which they passed made them sacred in the memory. In the falling greyness of the evening he watched her figure winding through the morass, saw it turn a last time and wave a hand, and then pass through the Slap ; and it seemed to him as if something went along with her out of the deepest of his heart. And something surely had come, and come to dwell there. He had retained from childhood a picture, now half-obliterated by the passage of time and the multitude of fresh impressions, of his mother telling him, with the fluttered earnestness of her voice, and often with dropping tears, the tale of the " Praying Weaver," on the very scene of his brief tragedy and long repose. And now there was a companion piece ; and he beheld, and he should behold for ever, Christina perched on the same tomb, in the grey colours of the evening, gracious, dainty, perfect as a flower, and she also singing—

> " Of old, unhappy far-off things,
>   And battles long ago,"

—of their common ancestors now dead, of their rude wars composed, their weapons buried with them, and of these strange changelings, their descendants, who lingered a little in their places, and would soon be gone also, and perhaps sung of by others at the gloaming hour. By one of the unconscious arts of tenderness the two women were enshrined together in his memory. Tears, in that hour of sensibility, came into his eyes indifferently at the thought of either, and the girl, from being something merely bright and shapely, was caught up into the zone of things serious as life and death and his dead mother. So that in all ways and on either side, Fate played his game artfully with this poor pair of children. The generations were prepared, the pangs were made ready, before the curtain rose on the dark drama.

In the same moment of time that she disappeared from Archie, there opened before Kirstie's eyes the cup-like hollow in which the farm lay. She saw, some five hundred feet below her, the house making itself bright with candles, and this was a broad hint to her to hurry. For they were only kindled on a Sabbath night with a view to that family worship which rounded in the incomparable tedium of the day and brought on the relaxation of supper. Already she knew that Robert must be within-sides at the head of the table, " waling the portions " ; for it was Robert in his quality of family priest and judge, not the gifted Gilbert, who officiated. She made good time accordingly down the steep ascent, and came up to the door panting as the three younger brothers, all roused at last from slumber, stood together in the cool and the dark of the evening with a fry of nephews and nieces about them, chatting and awaiting the expected signal. She stood back ; she had no mind to direct attention to her late arrival or to her labouring breath.

" Kirstie, ye have shaved it this time, my lass," said Clem. " Whaur were ye ? "

" O, just taking a dander by mysel'," said Kirstie.

And the talk continued on the subject of the American war, without further reference to the truant who stood by them in the covert of the dusk, thrilling with happiness and the sense of guilt.

The signal was given, and the brothers began to go in one after another, amid the jostle and throng of Hob's children.

Only Dandie, waiting till the last, caught Kirstie by the

arm. "When did ye begin to dander in pink hosen, Mistress Elliott?" he whispered slyly.

She looked down; she was one blush. "I maun have forgotten to change them," said she; and went in to prayers in her turn with a troubled mind, between anxiety as to whether Dand should have observed her yellow stockings at church, and should thus detect her in a palpable falsehood, and shame that she had already made good his prophecy. She remembered the words of it, how it was to be when she had gotten a jo, and that that would be for good and evil. "Will I have gotten my jo now?" she thought with a secret rapture.

And all through prayers, where it was her principal business to conceal the pink stockings from the eyes of the indifferent Mrs. Hob—and all through supper, as she made a feint of eating, and sat at the table radiant and constrained—and again when she had left them and come into her chamber, and was alone with her sleeping niece, and could at last lay aside the armour of society—the same words sounded within her, the same profound note of happiness, of a world all changed and renewed, of a day that had been passed in Paradise, and of a night that was to be heaven opened. All night she seemed to be conveyed smoothly upon a shallow stream of sleep and waking, and through the bowers of Beulah; all night she cherished to her heart that exquisite hope; and if, towards morning, she forgot it a while in a more profound unconsciousness, it was to catch again the rainbow thought with her first moment of awaking.

CHAPTER VII

ENTER MEPHISTOPHELES

TWO days later a gig from Crossmichael deposited Frank Innes at the doors of Hermiston. Once in a way, during the past winter, Archie, in some acute phase of boredom, had written him a letter. It had contained something in the nature of an invitation, or a reference to an invitation—precisely what, neither of them now remembered. When Innes had received it, there had been nothing further from his mind than to bury himself in the moors with Archie; but not even the most acute political heads are guided through the steps of life with unerring directness. That would require a gift of prophecy which has been denied to man. For instance, who could have imagined that, not a month after he had received the letter, and turned it into mockery, and put off answering it, and in the end lost it, misfortunes of a gloomy cast should begin to thicken over Frank's career? His case may be briefly stated. His father, a small Morayshire laird with a large family, became recalcitrant and cut off the supplies; he had fitted himself out with the beginnings of quite a good law library, which, upon some sudden losses on the turf, he had been obliged to sell before they were paid for; and his bookseller, hearing some rumour of the event, took out a warrant for his arrest. Innes had early word of it, and was able to take precautions. In this immediate welter of his affairs, with an unpleasant charge hanging over him, he had judged it the part of prudence to be off instantly, had written a fervid letter to his father at Inverauld, and put himself in the coach for Crossmichael. Any port in a storm! He was manfully turning his back on the Parliament House and its gay babble, on porter and oysters, the racecourse and the ring ; and manfully prepared, until these clouds should have blown by, to share a living grave with Archie Weir at Hermiston.

To do him justice, he was no less surprised to be going than Archie was to see him come ; and he carried off his wonder with an infinitely better grace.

" Well, here I am ! " said he, as he alighted. " Pylades has come to Orestes at last. By the way, did you get my answer ? No ? How very provoking ! Well, here I am to answer for myself, and that's better still."

" I am very glad to see you, of course," said Archie. " I make you heartily welcome, of course. But you surely have not come to stay, with the Courts still sitting ; is that not most unwise ? "

" Damn the Courts ! " says Frank. " What are the Courts to friendship and a little fishing ? "

And so it was agreed that he was to stay, with no term to the visit but the term which he had privily set to it himself—the day, namely, when his father should have come down with the dust, and he should be able to pacify the bookseller. On such vague conditions there began for these two young men (who were not even friends) a life of great familiarity and, as the days grew on, less and less intimacy. They were together at meal-times, together o' nights when the hour had come for whisky-toddy ; but it might have been noticed (had there been any one to pay heed) that they were rarely so much together by day. Archie had Hermiston to attend to, multifarious activities in the hills, in which he did not require, and had even refused, Frank's escort. He would be off sometimes in the morning and leave only a note on the breakfast-table to announce the fact ; and sometimes, with no notice at all, he would not return for dinner until the hour was long past. Innes groaned under these desertions ; it required all his philosophy to sit down to a solitary breakfast with composure, and all his unaffected good-nature to be able to greet Archie with friendliness on the more rare occasions when he came home late for dinner.

" I wonder what on earth he finds to do, Mrs. Elliott ? " said he one morning, after he had just read the hasty billet and sat down to table.

" I suppose it will be business, sir," replied the house-keeper dryly, measuring his distance off to him by an indicated curtsey.

" But I can't imagine what business ! " he reiterated.

" I suppose it will be *his* business," retorted the austere Kirstie.

He turned to her with that happy brightness that made the charm of his disposition, and broke into a peal of healthy and natural laughter.

" Well played, Mrs. Elliott ! " he cried, and the house-keeper's face relaxed into the shadow of an iron smile. " Well played indeed ! " said he. " But you must not be making a stranger of me like that. Why, Archie and I were at the High School together, and we've been to College together, and we were going to the Bar together, when—you know ! Dear me, dear me ! what a pity that was ! A life spoiled, a fine young fellow as good as buried here in the wilderness with rustics ; and all for what ? A frolic, silly, if you like, but no more. God, how good your scones are, Mrs. Elliott ! "

" They're no' mines, it was the lassie made them," said Kirstie ; " and, saving your presence, there's little sense in taking the Lord's name in vain about idle vivers that you fill your kyte wi'."

" I daresay you're perfectly right, ma'am," quoth the imperturbable Frank. " But, as I was saying, this is a pitiable business, this about poor Archie ; and you and I might do worse than put our heads together, like a couple of sensible people, and bring it to an end. Let me tell you, ma'am, that Archie is really quite a promising young man, and in my opinion he would do well at the Bar. As for his father, no one can deny his ability, and I don't fancy any one would care to deny that he has the deil's own temper——"

" If you'll excuse me, Mr. Innes, I think the lass is crying on me," said Kirstie, and flounced from the room.

"The damned, cross-grained old broomstick!" ejaculated Innes.

In the meantime, Kirstie had escaped into the kitchen, and before her vassal gave vent to her feelings.

"Here, ettercap! Ye'll have to wait on yon Innes! I canna haud myself in. 'Puir Erchie'! I'd 'puir Erchie' him, if I had my way! And Hermiston with the deil's ain temper! God, let him take Hermiston's scones out of his mouth first. There's no' a hair on ayther o' the Weirs that hasna mair spunk and dirdum to it than what he has in his hale dwaibly body! Settin' up his snash to me! Let him gang to the black toon where he's mebbe wantit—birling in a curricle—wi' pimatum on his heid—making a mess o' himsel' wi' nesty hizzies—a fair disgrace!" It was impossible to hear without admiration Kirstie's graduated disgust, as she brought forth, one after another, these somewhat baseless charges. Then she remembered her immediate purpose, and turned again on her fascinated auditor. "Do ye no' hear me, tawpie? Do ye no' hear what I'm tellin' ye? Will I have to shoo ye in to him? If I come to attend to ye, mistress!" And the maid fled the kitchen, which had become practically dangerous, to attend on Innes's wants in the front parlour.

Tantæne iræ? Has the reader perceived the reason? Since Frank's coming there were no more hours of gossip over the supper tray! All his blandishments were in vain; he had started handicapped on the race for Mrs. Elliott's favour.

But it was a strange thing how misfortune dogged him in his efforts to be genial. I must guard the reader against accepting Kirstie's epithets as evidence; she was more concerned for their vigour than for their accuracy. Dwaibly, for instance; nothing could be more calumnious. Frank was the very picture of good looks, good-humour, and manly youth. He had bright eyes with a sparkle and a dance to them, curly hair, a charming smile, brilliant teeth, an admirable carriage of the head, the look of a gentleman, the address of one accustomed to please at

H

first sight and to improve the impression. And with all these advantages, he failed with everyone about Hermiston; with the silent shepherd, with the obsequious grieve, with the groom who was also the ploughman, with the gardener and the gardener's sister—a pious, down-hearted woman with a shawl over her ears—he failed equally and flatly. They did not like him, and they showed it. The little maid, indeed, was an exception; she admired him devoutly, probably dreamed of him in her private hours; but she was accustomed to play the part of silent auditor to Kirstie's tirades and silent recipient of Kirstie's buffets, and she had learned not only to be a very capable girl of her years, but a very secret and prudent one besides. Frank was thus conscious that he had one ally and sympathiser in the midst of that general union of disfavour that surrounded, watched, and waited on him in the house of Hermiston; but he had little comfort or society from that alliance, and the demure little maid (twelve on her last birthday) preserved her own counsel, and tripped on his service, brisk, dumbly responsive, but inexorably un-conversational. For the others, they were beyond hope and beyond endurance. Never had a young Apollo been cast among such rustic barbarians. But perhaps the cause of his ill-success lay in one trait which was habitual and unconscious with him, yet diagnostic of the man. It was his practice to approach any one person at the expense of some one else. He offered you an alliance against the some one else; he flattered you by slighting him; you were drawn into a small intrigue against him before you knew how. Wonderful are the virtues of this process generally; but Frank's mistake was in the choice of the some one else. He was not politic in that; he listened to the voice of irritation. Archie had offended him at first by what he had felt to be rather a dry reception; had offended him since by his frequent absences. He was besides the one figure continually present in Frank's eye; and it was to his immediate dependants that Frank could offer the snare of his sympathy. Now the truth is that the Weirs, father and son, were surrounded by a posse of strenuous loyalists. Of my lord they were vastly proud. It was a distinction in itself to be one of the vassals of the "Hanging Judge," and his gross, formidable joviality was far from unpopular in the neighbourhood of his home. For Archie they had, one and all, a sensitive affection and respect which recoiled from a word of belittlement.

Nor was Frank more successful when he went farther afield. To the Four Black Brothers, for instance, he was antipathetic in the highest degree. Hob thought him too light, Gib too profane. Clem, who saw him but for a day or two before he went to Glasgow, wanted to know what the fule's business was, and whether he meant to stay here all session time! "Yon's a drone," he pronounced. As for Dand, it will be enough to describe their first meeting, when Frank had been whipping a river and the rustic celebrity chanced to come along the path.

"I'm told you are quite a poet," Frank had said.

"Wha tell 't ye that, mannie?" had been the unconciliating answer.

"O, everybody," says Frank.

"God! Here's fame!" said the sardonic poet, and he had passed on his way.

Come to think of it, we have here perhaps a truer explanation of Frank's failures. Had he met Mr. Sheriff Scott he could have turned a neater compliment, because Mr. Scott would have been a friend worth making. Dand, on the other hand, he did not value sixpence, and he showed it even while he tried to flatter. Condescension is an excellent thing, but it is strange how one-sided the pleasure of it is! He who goes fishing among the Scots peasantry with condescension for a bait will have an empty basket by evening.

In proof of this theory Frank made a great success of it at the Crossmichael Club, to which Archie took him immediately on his arrival; his own last appearance on that scene of gaiety. Frank was made welcome there at once, continued to go regularly, and had attended a meeting (as the members ever after loved to tell) on the evening before his death. Young Hay and young Pringle appeared again. There was another supper at Windielaws, another dinner at Driffel ; and it resulted in Frank being taken to the bosom of the county people as unreservedly as he had been repudiated by the country folk. He occupied Hermiston after the manner of an invader in a conquered capital. He was perpetually issuing from it, as from a base, to toddy parties, fishing parties, and dinner parties, to which Archie was not invited, or to which Archie would not go. It was now that the name of The Recluse became general for the young man. Some say that Innes invented it ; Innes, at least, spread it abroad.

"How's all with your Recluse to-day ? " people would ask.

"O, reclusing away ! " Innes would declare, with his bright air of saying something witty ; and immediately interrupt the general laughter which he had provoked much more by his air than his words, " Mind you, it's all very well laughing, but I'm not very well pleased. Poor Archie is a good fellow, an excellent fellow, a fellow I always liked. I think it small of him to take his little disgrace so hard and shut himself up. ' Grant that it is a ridiculous story, painfully ridiculous,' I keep telling him. ' Be a man ! Live it down, man ! ' But not he. Of course it's just solitude, and shame, and all that. But I confess I'm beginning to fear the result. It would be all the pities in the world if a really promising fellow like Weir was to end ill. I'm seriously tempted to write to Lord Hermiston, and put it plainly to him."

"I would if I were you," some of his auditors would say, shaking the head, sitting bewildered and confused at this new view of the matter, so deftly indicated by a single word. " A capital idea ! " they would add, and wonder at the *aplomb* and position of this young man, who talked as a matter of course of writing to Hermiston and correcting him upon his private affairs.

And Frank would proceed, sweetly confidential : " I'll give you an idea, now. He's actually sore about the way that I'm received and he's left out in the county—actually jealous and sore. I've rallied him and I've reasoned with him, told him that every one was most kindly inclined towards him, told him even that *I* was received merely because I was his guest. But it's no use. He will neither accept the invitations he gets, nor stop brooding about the ones where he's left out. What I'm afraid of is that the wound's ulcerating. He had always one of those dark, secret, angry natures—a little underhand and plenty of bile—you know the sort. He must have inherited it from the Weirs, whom I suspect to have been a worthy family of weavers somewhere ; what's the cant phrase !—sedentary occupation. It's precisely the kind of character to go wrong in a false position like what his father's made for him, or he's making for himself, whichever you like to call it. And for my part, I think it a disgrace," Frank would say generously.

Presently the sorrow and anxiety of this disinterested friend took shape. He began in private, in conversations of two, to talk vaguely of bad habits and low habits. " I must say I'm afraid he's going wrong altogether," he would say. " I'll tell you plainly, and between ourselves, I scarcely like to stay there any longer ; only, man, I'm positively afraid to leave him alone. You'll see, I shall be blamed for it later on. I'm staying at a great sacrifice. I'm hindering my chances at the Bar, and I can't blind my eyes to it. And what I'm afraid of is that I'm going to get kicked for it all round before all's done. You see, nobody believes in friendship nowadays."

" Well, Innes," his interlocutor would reply, " it's very good of you, I must say that. If there's any blame going you'll always be sure of *my* good word, for one thing."

" Well," Frank would continue, " candidly, I don't say it's pleasant. He has a very rough way with him ; his father's son, you know. I don't say he's rude—of course, I couldn't be expected to stand that—but he steers very near the wind. No, it's not pleasant ; but I tell ye, man, in conscience I don't think it would be fair to leave him.

Mind you, I don't say there's anything actually wrong. What I say is that I don't like the looks of it, man ! " and he would press the arm of his momentary confidant.

In the early stages I am persuaded there was no malice. He talked but for the pleasure of airing himself. He was essentially glib, as becomes the young advocate, and essentially careless of the truth, which is the mark of the young ass ; and so he talked at random. There was no particular bias, but that one which is indigenous and universal, to flatter himself and to please and interest the present friend. And by thus milling air out of his mouth, he had presently built up a presentation of Archie which was known and talked of in all corners of the county. Wherever there was a residential house and a walled garden, wherever there was a dwarfish castle and a park, wherever a quadruple cottage by the ruins of a peel-tower showed an old family going down, and wherever a handsome villa with a carriage approach and a shrubbery marked the coming up of a new one—probably on the wheels of machinery—Archie began to be regarded in the light of a dark, perhaps a vicious mystery, and the future developments of his career to be looked for with uneasiness and confidential whispering. He had done something disgraceful, my dear. What, was not precisely known, and that good kind young man, Mr. Innes, did his best to make light of it. But there it was. And Mr. Innes was very anxious about him now ; he was really uneasy, my dear ; he was positively wrecking his own prospects because he dared not leave him alone. How wholly we all lie at the mercy of a single prater, not needfully with any malign purpose ! And if a man but talks of himself in the right spirit, refers to his virtuous actions by the way, and never applies to them the name of virtue, how easily his evidence is accepted in the court of public opinion !

All this while, however, there was a more poisonous ferment at work between the two lads, which came late indeed to the surface, but had modified and magnified their dissensions from the first. To an idle, shallow, easy-going customer like Frank, the smell of a mystery was attractive. It gave his mind something to play with, like a new toy to a child; and it took him on the weak side, for like many young men coming to the Bar, and before they have been tried and found wanting, he flattered himself he was a fellow of unusual quickness and penetration. They knew nothing of Sherlock Holmes in these days, but there was a good deal said of Talleyrand. And if you could have caught Frank off his guard, he would have confessed with a smirk, that, if he resembled any one, it was the Marquis de Talleyrand-Périgord. It was on the occasion of Archie's first absence that this interest took root. It was vastly deepened when Kirstie resented his curiosity at breakfast, and that same afternoon there occurred another scene which clinched the business. He was fishing Swingleburn, Archie accompanying him, when the latter looked at his watch.

" Well, good-bye," said he. " I have something to do. See you at dinner."

" Don't be in such a hurry," cries Frank. " Hold on till I get my rod up. I'll go with you; I'm sick of flogging this ditch."

And he began to reel up his line.

Archie stood speechless. He took a long while to recover his wits under this direct attack; but by the time he was ready with his answer, and the angle was almost packed up, he had become completely Weir, and the hanging face gloomed on his young shoulders. He spoke with a laboured composure, a laboured kindness even; but a child could see that his mind was made up.

" I beg your pardon, Innes; I don't want to be disagreeable, but let us understand one another from the beginning. When I want your company, I'll let you know."

" Oh!" cries Frank, " you don't want my company, don't you?"

" Apparently not just now," replied Archie. " I even indicated to you when I did, if you'll remember—and that was at dinner. If we two fellows are to live together pleasantly—and I see no reason why we should not—it can only be by respecting each other's privacy. If we begin intruding——"

"Oh, come ! I'll take this at no man's hands. Is this the way you treat a guest and an old friend ? " cried Innes.

"Just go home and think over what I said by yourself," continued Archie, "whether it's reasonable, or whether it's really offensive or not ; and let's meet at dinner as though nothing had happened. I'll put it this way, if you like—that I know my own character, that I'm looking forward (with great pleasure, I assure you) to a long visit from you, and that I'm taking precautions at the first. I see the thing that we—that I, if you like—might fall out upon, and I step in and *obsto principiis*. I wager you five pounds you'll end by seeing that I mean friendliness, and I assure you, Francie, I do," he added, relenting.

Bursting with anger, but incapable of speech, Innes shouldered his rod, made a gesture of farewell, and strode off down the burnside. Archie watched him go without moving. He was sorry, but quite unashamed. He hated to be inhospitable, but in one thing he was his father's son. He had a strong sense that his house was his own and no man else's ; and to lie at a guest's mercy was what he refused. He hated to seem harsh. But that was Frank's look-out. If Frank had been commonly discreet, he would have been decently courteous. And there was another consideration. The secret he was protecting was not his own merely ; it was hers ; it belonged to that inexpressible she who was fast taking possession of his soul, and whom he would soon have defended at the cost of burning cities. By the time he had watched Frank as far as the Swingleburnfoot, appearing and disappearing in the tarnished heather, still stalking at a fierce gait but already dwindled in the distance into less than the smallness of Lilliput, he could afford to smile at the occurrence. Either Frank would go, and that would be a relief—or he would continue to stay, and his host must continue to endure him. And Archie was now free—by devious paths, behind hillocks and in the hollow of burns—to make for the trysting-place where Kirstie, cried about by the curlew and the plover, waited and burned for his coming by the Covenanter's stone.

Innes went off down-hill in a passion of resentment, easy to be understood, but which yielded progressively to the needs of his situation. He cursed Archie for a cold-hearted, unfriendly, rude dog; and himself still more passionately for a fool in having come to Hermiston when he might have sought refuge in almost any other house in Scotland, but the step once taken was practically irretrievable. He had no more ready money to go any-where else; he would have to borrow from Archie the next club-night; and ill as he thought of his hoot's manners, he was sure of his practical generosity. Frank's resem-blance to Talleyrand strikes me as imaginary; but at least not Talleyrand himself could have more obediently taken his lesson from the facts. He met Archie at dinner without resentment, almost with cordiality. You must take your friends as you find them, he would have said. Archie couldn't help being his father's son, or his grand-father's, the hypothetical weaver's, grandson. The son of a hunks, he was still a hunks at heart, incapable of true generosity and consideration; but he had other qualities with which Frank could divert himself in the meanwhile, and to enjoy which it was necessary that Frank should keep his temper.

So excellently was it controlled that he awoke next morning with his head full of a different, though a cog-nate subject. What was Archie's little game? Why did he shun Frank's company? What was he keeping secret? Was he keeping tryst with somebody, and was it a woman? It would be a good joke and a fair revenge to discover. To that task he set himself with a great deal of patience, which might have surprised his friends, for he had been always credited not with patience so much as brilliancy; and little by little, from one point to another, he at last succeeding in piecing out the situation. First he remarked that, although Archie set out in all the directions of the compass, he always came home again from some point between the south and west. From the study of a map, and in consideration of the great expanse of untenanted moorland running in that direction towards the sources of the Clyde, he laid his finger on Cauldstaneslap and two other neighbouring farms, Kingsmuirs and Polintarf. But it was difficult to advance farther. With his rod for a pretext, he vainly visited each of them in turn ; nothing was to be seen suspicious about this trinity of moorland settlements. He would have tried to follow Archie, had it been the least possible, but the nature of the land precluded the idea. He did the next best, ensconced himself in a quiet corner, and pursued his movements with a telescope. It was equally in vain, and he soon wearied of his futile vigilance, left the telescope at home, and had almost given the matter up in despair, when, on the twenty-seventh day of his visit, he was suddenly confronted with the person whom he sought. The first Sunday Kirstie had managed to stay away from kirk on some pretext of indisposition, which was more truly modesty ; the pleasure of beholding Archie seeming too sacred, too vivid for that public place. On the two following, Frank had himself been absent on some of his excursions among the neighbouring families. It was not until the fourth, accordingly, that Frank had occasion to set eyes on the enchantress. With the first look, all hesitation was over. She came with the Cauldstaneslap party ; then she lived at Cauldstaneslap. Here was Archie's secret, here was the woman, and more than that—though I have need here of every manageable attenuation of language—with the first look, he had already entered himself as rival. It was a good deal in pique, it was a little in revenge, it was much in genuine admiration : the devil may decide the proportions ; I cannot, and it is very likely that Frank could not.

" Mighty attractive milkmaid," he observed, on the way home.

" Who ? " said Archie.

" O, the girl you're looking at—aren't you ? Forward there on the road. She came attended by the rustic bard ; presumably, therefore, belongs to his exalted family. The single objection ! for the Four Black Brothers are awkward customers. If anything were to go wrong, Gib would gibber, and Clem would prove inclement ; and Dand fly in danders, and Hob blow up in gobbets. It would be a Helliott of a business ! "

" Very humorous, I am sure," said Archie.

" Well, I am trying to be so," said Frank. " It's none too easy in this place, and with your solemn society, my dear fellow. But confess that the milkmaid has found favour in your eyes or resign all claim to be a man of taste."

" It is no matter," returned Archie.

But the other continued to look at him, steadily and quizzically, and his colour slowly rose and deepened under the glance, until not impudence itself could have denied that he was blushing. And at this Archie lost some of his control. He changed his stick from one hand to the other, and—" O, for God's sake, don't be an ass ! " he cried.

" Ass ? That's the retort delicate without doubt," says Frank. " Beware of the homespun brothers, dear. If they come into the dance, you'll see who's an ass. Think now, if they only applied (say) a quarter as much talent as I have applied to the question of what Mr. Archie does with his evening hours, and why he is so unaffectedly nasty when the subject's touched on——"

" You are touching on it now," interrupted Archie, with a wince.

" Thank you. That was all I wanted, an articulate confession," said Frank.

" I beg to remind you——" began Archie.

But he was interrupted in turn. " My dear fellow, don't. It's quite needless. The subject's dead and buried."

And Frank began to talk hastily on other matters, an art in which he was an adept, for it was his gift to be fluent on anything or nothing. But although Archie had the grace or the timidity to suffer him to rattle on, he was by no means done with the subject. When he came home to dinner, he was greeted with a sly demand, how things were looking " Cauldstaneslap ways." Frank took his first glass of port out after dinner to the toast of Kirstie, and later in the evening he returned to the charge again.

"I say, Weir, you'll excuse me for returning again to this affair. I've been thinking it over, and I wish to beg you very seriously to be more careful. It's not a safe business. Not safe, my boy," said he.

"What ? " said Archie.

"Well, it's your own fault if I must put a name on the thing ; but really, as a friend, I cannot stand by and see you rushing head down into these dangers. My dear boy," said he, holding up a warning cigar, " consider what is to be the end of it ? "

"The end of what ? "—Archie, helpless with irritation, persisted in this dangerous and ungracious guard.

"Well, the end of the milkmaid ; or, to speak more by the card, the end of Miss Christina Elliott of the Cauldstaneslap ? "

"I assure you," Archie broke out, " this is all a figment of your imagination. There is nothing to be said against that young lady ; you have no right to introduce her name into the conversation."

"I'll make a note of it," said Frank. " She shall henceforth be nameless, nameless, nameless, Gregarach ! I make a note besides of your valuable testimony to her character. I only want to look at this thing as a man of the world. Admitted she's an angel—but, my good fellow, is she a lady ? "

This was torture to Archie. "I beg your pardon," he said, struggling to be composed, " but because you have wormed yourself into my confidence——"

"Oh, come ! " cried Frank. " Your confidence ? It was rosy but unconsenting. Your confidence, indeed !

Now, look ! This is what I must say, Weir, for it concerns your safety and good character, and therefore my honour as your friend. You say I wormed myself into your confidence. Wormed is good. But what have I done ? I have put two and two together, just as the parish will be doing to-morrow, and the whole of Tweeddale in two weeks, and the Black Brothers—well, I won't put a date on that ; it will be a dark and stormy morning. Your secret, in other words, is poor Poll's. And I want to ask of you as a friend whether you like the prospect ? There are two horns to your dilemma, and I must say for myself I should look mighty ruefully on either. Do you see yourself explaining to the Four Black Brothers ? or do you see yourself presenting the milkmaid to papa as the future lady of Hermiston ? Do you ? I tell you plainly, I don't."

Archie rose. "I will hear no more of this," he said in a trembling voice.

But Frank again held up his cigar. "Tell me one thing first. Tell me if this is not a friend's part that I am playing ? "

"I believe you think it so," replied Archie. "I can go as far as that. I can do so much justice to your motives. But I will hear no more of it. I am going to bed."

"That's right, Weir," said Frank, heartily. "Go to bed and think over it ; and I say, man, don't forget your prayers ! I don't often do the moral—don't go in for that sort of thing—but when I do there's one thing sure, that I mean it."

So Archie marched off to bed, and Frank sat alone by the table for another hour or so, smiling to himself richly. There was nothing vindictive in his nature ; but, if revenge came in his way, it might as well be good, and the thought of Archie's pillow reflections that night was indescribably sweet to him. He felt a pleasant sense of power. He looked down on Archie as on a very little boy whose strings he pulled—as on a horse whom he had backed and bridled by sheer power of intelligence, and whom he might

ride to glory or the grave at pleasure. Which was it to be?
He lingered long, relishing the details of schemes that he
was too idle to pursue. Poor cork upon a torrent, he
tasted that night the sweets of omnipotence, and brooded
like a deity over the strands of that intrigue which was
to shatter him before the summer waned.

CHAPTER VIII

A NOCTURNAL VISIT

KIRSTIE had many causes of distress. More and more as we grow old—and yet more and more as we grow old and are women, frozen by the fear of age—we come to rely on the voice as the single outlet of the soul. Only thus, in the curtailment of our means, can we relieve the straitened cry of the passion within us ; only thus, in the bitter and sensitive shyness of advancing years, can we maintain relations with those vivacious figures of the young that still show before us and tend daily to become no more than the moving wallpaper of life. Talk is the last link, the last relation. But with the end of the conversation, when the voice stops and the bright face of the listener is turned away, solitude falls again on the bruised heart. Kirstie had lost her " cannie hour at e'en " ; she could no more wander with Archie, a ghost, if you will, but a happy ghost, in fields Elysian. And to her it was as if the whole world had fallen silent ; to him, but an unremarkable change of amusements. And she raged to know it. The effervescency of her passionate and irritable nature rose within her at times to bursting point.

This is the price paid by age for unseasonable ardours of feeling. It must have been so for Kirstie at any time when the occasion chanced ; but it so fell out that she was deprived of this delight in the hour when she had most need of it, when she had most to say, most to ask, and when she trembled to recognise her sovereignty not merely in abeyance but annulled. For, with the clairvoyance of a genuine love, she had pierced the mystery that had so long embarrassed Frank. She was conscious, even before it was carried out, even on that Sunday night when it began, of an invasion of her rights ; and a voice told her the invader's name. Since then, by arts, by accident, by small things observed, and by the general drift of Archie's humour, she had passed beyond all possibility of doubt. With a sense of justice that Lord Hermiston might have envied, she had that day in church considered and admitted the attractions of the younger Kirstie ; and with the profound humanity and sentimentality of her nature, she had recognised the coming of fate. Not thus would she have chosen. She had seen, in imagination, Archie wedded to some tall, powerful, and rosy heroine of the golden locks, made in her own image, for whom she would have strewed the bride-bed with delight ; and now she could have wept to see the ambition falsified. But the gods had pronounced, and her doom was otherwise.

She lay tossing in bed that night, besieged with feverish thoughts. There were dangerous matters pending, a battle was toward, over the fate of which she hung in jealousy, sympathy, fear, and alternate loyalty and disloyalty to either side. Now she was reincarnated in her niece, and now in Archie. Now she saw, through the girl's eyes, the youth on his knees to her, heard his persuasive instances with a deadly weakness, and received his over-mastering caresses. Anon, with a revulsion, her temper raged to see such utmost favours of fortune, and love squandered on a brat of a girl, one of her own house, using her own name—a deadly ingredient—and that " didna ken her ain mind an' was as black's your hat." Now she trembled lest her deity should plead in vain, loving the idea of success for him like a triumph of nature ; anon, with returning loyalty to her own family and sex, she trembled for Kirstie and the credit of the Elliotts. And again she had a vision of herself, the day over for her old-world tales and local gossip, bidding farewell to her last link with life and brightness and love ; and behind and beyond, she saw but the blank butt-end where she must crawl to die. Had she then come to the lees ? she, so great, so beautiful, with a heart as fresh as a girl's and strong as womanhood? It could not be, and yet it was so; and for a moment her bed was horrible to her as the sides of the grave. And she looked forward over a waste of hours, and saw herself go on to rage, and tremble, and be softened, and rage again, until the day came and the labours of the day must be renewed.

Suddenly she heard feet on the stairs—his feet, and soon after the sound of a window-sash flung open. She sat up with her heart beating. He had gone to his room alone, and he had not gone to bed. She might again have one of her night cracks; and at the entrancing prospect, a change came over her mind; with the approach of this hope of pleasure, all the baser metal became immediately obliterated from her thoughts. She rose, all woman, and all the best of woman, tender, pitiful, hating the wrong, loyal to her own sex—and all the weakest of that dear miscellany, nourishing, cherishing next her soft heart, voicelessly flattering, hopes that she would have died sooner than have acknowledged. She tore off her night-cap, and her hair fell about her shoulders in profusion. Undying coquetry awoke. By the faint light of her nocturnal rush, she stood before the looking-glass, carried her shapely arms above her head, and gathered up the treasures of her tresses. She was never backward to admire herself; that kind of modesty was a stranger to her nature; and she paused, struck with a pleased wonder at the sight. " Ye daft auld wife ! " she said, answering a thought that was not ; and she blushed with the innocent consciousness of a child. Hastily she did up the massive and shining coils, hastily donned a wrapper, and with the rush-light in her hand, stole into the hall. Below stairs she heard the clock ticking the deliberate seconds, and Frank jingling with the decanters in the dining-room. Aversion rose in her, bitter and momentary. " Nesty, tippling puggy ! " she thought ; and the next moment she had knocked guardedly at Archie's door and was bidden enter.

Archie had been looking out into the ancient blackness,

I

pierced here and there with a rayless star; taking the sweet air of the moors and the night into his bosom deeply; seeking, perhaps finding, peace after the manner of the unhappy. He turned round as she came in, and showed her a pale face against the window-frame.

" Is that you, Kirstie ? " he asked. " Come in ! "

" It's unco' late, my dear," said Kirstie, affecting unwillingness.

" No, no," he answered, " not at all. Come in, if you want a crack. I am not sleepy, God knows ! "

She advanced, took a chair by the toilet-table and the candle, and set the rush-light at her foot. Something— it might be in the comparative disorder of her dress, it might be the emotion that now welled in her bosom— had touched her with a wand of transformation, and she seemed young with the youth of goddesses.

" Mr. Erchie," she began, " what's this that's come to ye ? "

" I am not aware of anything that has come," said Archie, and blushed and repented bitterly that he had let her in.

" Oh, my dear, that'll no dae ! " said Kirstie. " It's ill to blind the eyes of love. Oh, Mr. Erchie, tak' a thocht ere it's ower late. Ye shouldna be impatient o' the braws o' life, they'll a' come in their saison, like the sun and the rain. Ye're young yet; ye've mony cantie years afore ye. See and dinna wreck yersel' at the outset like sae mony ithers ! Hae patience—they telled me aye that was the overcome o' life—hae patience, there's a braw day coming yet. Gude kens it never cam' to me; and here I am wi' nayther man nor bairn to ca' my ain, wearyin' a' folks wi' my ill tongue, and you just the first, Mr. Erchie ! "

" I have a difficulty in knowing what you mean," said Archie.

" Weel, and I'll tell ye," she said. " It's just this, that I'm feared. I'm feared for ye, my dear. Remember, your faither is a hard man, reapin' where he hasna sowed and gaitherin' where he hasna strawed. It's easy speakin', but mind ! Ye'll have to look in the gurly face o'm, where it's ill to look, and vain to look for mercy. Ye mind me o' a bonny ship pitten oot into the black and gowsty seas—ye're a' safe still, sittin' quait and crackin' wi' Kirstie in your lown chalmer ; but whaur will ye be the morn, and in whatten horror o' the fearsome tempest, cryin' on the hills to cover ye ? "

"Why, Kirstie, you're very enigmatical to-night—and very eloquent," Archie put in.

"And, my dear Mr. Erchie," she continued, with a change of voice, " ye mauna think that I canna sympathise wi' ye. Ye mauna think that I havena been young mysel'. Lang syne, when I was a bit lassie, no' twenty yet——" She paused and sighed. " Clean and caller, wi' a fit like the hinney bee," she continued, " I was aye big and buirdly, ye maun understand ; a bonny figure o' a woman, though I say it that suldna—built to rear bairns —braw bairns they suld hae been, and grand I would hae likit it ! But I was young, dear, wi' the bonny glint o' youth in my e'en, and little I dreamed I'd ever be tellin' ye this, an auld, lanely, rudas wife ! Weel, Mr. Erchie, there was a lad cam' courtin' me, as was but naetural. Mony had come before, and I would nane o' them. But this yin had a tongue to wile the birds frae the lift and the bees frae the foxglove bells. Deary me, but it's lang syne. Folk have dee'd sinsyne and been buried, and are forgotten, and bairns been born and got merrit and got bairns o' their ain. Sinsyne woods have been plantit, and have grawn up and are bonny trees, and the joes sit in their shadow, and sinsyne auld estates have changed hands, and there have been wars and rumours of wars on the face of the earth. And here I'm still—like an auld droopit craw—lookin' on and craikin'. But, Mr. Erchie, do ye no' think that I have mind o' it a' still ? I was dwallin' then in my faither's house ; and it's a curious thing that we were whiles trysted in the Deil's Hags. And do ye no' think that I have mind of the bonny simmer days, the lang miles o' the bluid-red heather, the cryin' o' the whaups, and the lad and the lassie that was trysted ?

Do ye no' think that I mind how the hilly sweetness ran about my hairt ? Ay, Mr. Erchie, I ken the way o' it— fine do I ken the way—how the grace o' God takes them like Paul of Tarsus, when they think it least, and drives the pair o' them into a land which is like a dream, and the world and the folks in't are nae mair than clouds to the puir lassie, and Heeven nae mair than windlestraes, if she can but pleesure him ! Until Tam dee'd—that was my story," she broke off to say, " he dee'd, and I wasna at the buryin'. But while he was here, I could take care o' mysel'. And can yon puir lassie ? "

Kirstie, her eyes shining with unshed tears, stretched out her hand towards him appealingly ; the bright and the dull gold of her hair flashed and smouldered in the coils behind her comely head, like the rays of an eternal youth ; the pure colour had risen in her face ; and Archie was abashed alike by her beauty and her story. He came towards her slowly from the window, took up her hand in his and kissed it.

" Kirstie," he said hoarsely, " you have misjudged me sorely. I have always thought of her, I wouldna harm her for the universe, my woman ! "

" Eh, lad, and that's easy sayin'," cried Kirstie, " but it's nae sae easy doin' ! Man, do ye no' comprehend that it's God wull we should be blendit and glamoured, and have nae command over our ain members at a time like that ? My bairn," she cried, still holding his hand, " think o' the puir lass ! have pity upon her, Erchie ! and O, be wise for twa ! Think o' the risk she rins ! I have seen ye, and what's to prevent ithers ? I saw ye once in the Hags, in my ain howf, and I was wae to see ye there —in pairt for the omen, for I think there's a weird on the place—and in pairt for puir nakit envy and bitterness o' hairt. It's strange ye should forgather there tae ! God ! but yon puir, thrawn, auld Covenanter's seen a heap o' human natur since he lookit his last on the musket-barrels, if he never saw nane afore," she added, with a kind of wonder in her eyes.

"I swear by my honour I have done her no wrong," said Archie. "I swear by my honour and the redemption of my soul that there shall none be done her. I have heard of this before. I have been foolish, Kirstie, not unkind, and, above all, not base."

"There's my bairn!" said Kirstie, rising. "I'll can trust ye noo, I'll can gang to my bed wi' an easy hairt." And then she saw in a flash how barren had been her triumph. Archie had promised to spare the girl, and he would keep it; but who had promised to spare Archie? What was to be the end of it? Over a maze of difficulties she glanced, and saw, at the end of every passage, the flinty countenance of Hermiston. And a kind of horror fell upon her at what she had done. She wore a tragic mask. "Erchie, the Lord peety you, dear, and peety me! I have buildit on this foundation,"—laying her hand heavily on his shoulder—"and buildit hie, and pit my hairt in the buildin' of it. If the hale hypothec were to fa', I think, laddie, I would dee! Excuse a daft wife that loves ye, and that kenned your mither. And for His name's sake keep yersel' frae inordinate desires; haud your hairt in baith your hands, carry it canny and laigh; dinna send it up like a bairn's kite into the collieshangie o' the wunds! Mind, Maister Erchie dear, that this life's a disappointment, and a mouthfu' o' mools is the appointed end."

"Ay, but Kirstie, my woman, you're asking me ower much at last," said Archie, profoundly moved, and lapsing into the broad Scots. "Ye're asking what nae man can grant ye, what only the Lord of heaven can grant ye if He see fit. Ay! And can even He? I can promise ye what I shall do, and you can depend on that. But how I shall feel—my woman, that is long past thinking of!"

They were both standing by now opposite each other. The face of Archie wore the wretched semblance of a smile; hers was convulsed for a moment.

"Promise me ae thing," she cried, in a sharp voice.

"Promise me ye'll never do naething without telling me."

"No, Kirstie, I canna promise ye that," he replied. "I have promised enough, God kens!"

"May the blessing of God lift and rest upon ye, dear!" she said.

"God bless ye, my old friend," said he.

CHAPTER IX

AT THE WEAVER'S STONE

IT was late in the afternoon when Archie drew near by the hill path to the Praying Weaver's Stone. The Hags were in shadow. But still, through the gate of the Slap, the sun shot a last arrow, which sped far and straight across the surface of the moss, here and there touching and shining on a tussock, and lighted at length on the gravestone and the small figure awaiting him there. The emptiness and solitude of the great moors seemed to be concentred there, and Kirstie pointed out by that finger of sunshine for the only inhabitant. His first sight of her was thus excruciatingly sad, like a glimpse of a world from which all light, comfort, and society were on the point of vanishing. And the next moment, when she had turned her face to him and the quick smile had enlightened it, the whole face of nature smiled upon him in her smile of welcome. Archie's slow pace was quickened ; his legs hasted to her though his heart was hanging back. The girl, upon her side, drew herself together slowly and stood up, expectant ; she was all languor, her face was gone white ; her arms ached for him, her soul was on tip-toes. But he deceived her, pausing a few steps away, not less white than herself, and holding up his hand with a gesture of denial.

" No, Christina, not to-day," he said. " To-day I have to talk to you seriously. Sit ye down, please, there where you were. Please ! " he repeated.

The revulsion of feeling in Christina's heart was violent. To have longed and waited these weary hours for him, re-hearsing her endearments—to have seen him at last come —to have been ready there, breathless, wholly passive, his to do what he would with—and suddenly to have found herself confronted with a grey-faced, harsh school-master—it was too rude a shock. She could have wept, but pride withheld her. She sat down on the stone, from which she had arisen, part with the instinct of obedience, part as though she had been thrust there. What was this? Why was she rejected? Had she ceased to please? She stood here offering her wares, and he would none of them! And yet they were all his! His to take and keep; not his to refuse, though! In her quick petulant nature, a moment ago on fire with hope, thwarted love and wounded vanity wrought. The schoolmaster that there is in all men, to the despair of all girls and most women, was now completely in possession of Archie. He had passed a night of sermons; a day of reflection; he had come wound up to do his duty; and the set mouth, which in him only betrayed the effort of his will, to her seemed the expression of an averted heart. It was the same with his constrained voice and embarrassed utterance; and if so—if it was all over—the pang of the thought took away from her the power of thinking.

He stood before her some way off. "Kirstie, there's been too much of this. We've seen too much of each other." She looked up quickly and her eyes contracted. "There's no good ever comes of these secret meetings. They're not frank, not honest truly, and I ought to have seen it. People have begun to talk; and it's not right of me. Do you see?"

"I see somebody will have been talking to ye," she said sullenly.

"They have, more than one of them," replied Archie.

"And whae were they?" she cried. "And what kind o' love do ye ca' that, that's ready to gang round like a whirligig at folk talking? Do ye think they havena talked to me?"

"Have they indeed?" said Archie, with a quick breath. "That is what I feared. Who were they? Who has dared——"

Archie was on the point of losing his temper.

As a matter of fact, not any one had talked to Christina on the matter ; and she strenuously repeated her own first question in a panic of self-defence.

" Ah, well ! what does it matter ? " he said. " They were good folk that wished well to us, and the great affair is that there are people talking. My dear girl, we have to be wise. We must not wreck our lives at the outset. They may be long and happy yet, and we must see to it, Kirstie, like God's rational creatures and not like fool children. There is one thing we must see to before all. You're worth waiting for, Kirstie ! worth waiting for a generation ; it would be enough reward."—And here he remembered the schoolmaster again, and very unwisely took to following wisdom. " The first thing that we must see to, is that there shall be no scandal about, for my father's sake. That would ruin all ; do ye no' see that ? "

Kirstie was a little pleased, there had been some show of warmth of sentiment in what Archie had said last. But the dull irritation still persisted in her bosom ; with the aboriginal instinct, having suffered herself, she wished to make Archie suffer.

And besides, there had come out the word she had always feared to hear from his lips, the name of his father. It is not to be supposed that, during so many days with a love avowed between them, some reference had not been made to their conjoint future. It had in fact been often touched upon, and from the first had been the sore point. Kirstie had wilfully closed the eye of thought ; she would not argue even with herself ; gallant, desperate little heart, she had accepted the command of that supreme attraction like the call of fate and marched blindfold on her doom. But Archie, with his masculine sense of responsibility, must reason ; he must dwell on some future good, when the present good was all in all to Kirstie ; he must talk— and talk lamely, as necessity drove him—of what was to be. Again and again he had touched on marriage ; again and again been driven back into indistinctness by a memory of Lord Hermiston. And Kirstie had been swift to under-

stand and quick to choke down and smother the understanding ; swift to leap up in flame at a mention of that
hope, which spoke volumes to her vanity and her love,
that she might one day be Mrs. Weir of Hermiston ; swift,
also, to recognise in his stumbling or throttled utterance
the death-knell of these expectations, and constant, poor
girl ! in her large-minded madness, to go on and to reck
nothing of the future. But these unfinished references,
these blinks in which his heart spoke, and his memory and
reason rose up to silence it before the words were well
uttered, gave her unqualifiable agony. She was raised up
and dashed down again bleeding. The recurrence of the
subject forced her, for however short a time, to open her
eyes on what she did not wish to see ; and it had invariably
ended in another disappointment. So now again, at the
mere wind of its coming, at the mere mention of his
father's name—who might seem indeed to have accompanied them in their whole moorland courtship, an awful
figure in a wig with an ironical and bitter smile, present
to guilty consciousness—she fled from it head down.

" Ye havena told me yet," she said, " who was it spoke ? "

" Your aunt for one," said Archie.

" Auntie Kirstie ? " she cried. " And what do I care
for my Auntie Kirstie ? "

" She cares a great deal for her niece," replied Archie,
in kind reproof.

" Troth, and it's the first I've heard of it," retorted the
girl.

" The question here is not who it is, but what they say,
what they have noticed," pursued the lucid schoolmaster.
" That is what we have to think of in self-defence ! "

" Auntie Kirstie, indeed ! A bitter, thrawn auld maid
that's fomented trouble in the country before I was born,
and will be doing it still, I daur say, when I'm deid ! It's
in her nature ; it's as natural for her as it's for a sheep
to eat."

" Pardon me, Kirstie, she was not the only one," interposed Archie. " I had two warnings, two sermons, last
night, both most kind and considerate. Had you been

there, I promise you you would have grat, my dear !
And they opened my eyes. I saw we were going a wrong
way."

" Who was the other one ? " Kirstie demanded.

By this time Archie was in the condition of a hunted
beast. He had come, braced and resolute ; he was to
trace out a line of conduct for the pair of them in a few
cold, convincing sentences ; he had now been there some
time, and he was still staggering round the outworks and
undergoing what he felt to be a savage cross-examination.

" Mr. Frank ! " she cried. " What nex', I would like
to ken ? "

" He spoke most kindly and truly."

" What like did he say ? "

" I am not going to tell you ; you have nothing to do
with that," cried Archie, startled to find he had admitted
so much.

" Oh, I have naething to do with it ! " she repeated,
springing to her feet. " A'body at Hermiston's free to
pass their opinions upon me, but I have naething to do
wi' it ! Was this at prayers like ? Did ye ca' the grieve
into the consultation ? Little wonder if a'body's talking,
when you make a'body ye're confidants ! But as you say,
Mr. Weir,—most kindly, most considerately, most truly,
I'm sure,—I have naething to do with it. And I think
I'll better be going. I'll be wishing you good-evening,
Mr. Weir." And she made him a stately curtsey, shaking
as she did so from head to foot, with the barren ecstasy
of temper.

Poor Archie stood dumbfounded. She had moved some
steps away from him before he recovered the gift of
articulate speech.

" Kirstie ! " he cried. " Oh, Kirstie woman ! "

There was in his voice a ring of appeal, a clang of mere
astonishment that showed the schoolmaster was vanquished.

She turned round on him. " What do ye Kirstie me
for ? " she retorted. " What have ye to do wi' me ? Gang
to your ain freends and deave them ! "

He could only repeat the appealing " Kirstie ! "

" Kirstie, indeed ! " cried the girl, her eyes blazing in her white face. " My name is Miss Christina Elliott, I would have ye to ken, and I daur ye to ca' me out of it. If I canna get love, I'll have respect, Mr. Weir. I'm come of decent people, and I'll have respect. What have I done that ye should lightly me ? What have I done ? What have I done ? Oh, what have I done ? " and her voice rose upon the third repetition. " I thocht—I thocht—I thocht I was sae happy ! " and the first sob broke from her like the paroxysm of some mortal sickness.

Archie ran to her. He took the poor child in his arms, and she nestled to his breast as to a mother's, and clasped him in hands that were strong like vices. He felt her whole body shaken by the throes of distress, and had pity upon her beyond speech. Pity, and at the same time a bewildered fear of this explosive engine in his arms, whose works he did not understand, and yet had been tampering with. There arose from before him the curtains of boyhood, and he saw for the first time the ambiguous face of woman as she is. In vain he looked back over the interview ; he saw not where he had offended. It seemed unprovoked, a wilful convulsion of brute nature. . . .

EDITORIAL NOTE

By Sir Sidney Colvin

WITH the words last printed, "a wilful convulsion of brute nature," the romance of *Weir of Hermiston* breaks off. They were dictated, I believe, on the very morning of the writer's sudden seizure and death. *Weir of Hermiston* thus remains in the work of Stevenson what *Edwin Drood* is in the work of Dickens, or *Denis Duval* in that of Thackeray : or rather it remains relatively more, for if each of those fragments holds an honourable place among its author's writings, among Stevenson's the fragment of *Weir* holds, at least to my mind, certainly the highest.

Readers may be divided in opinion on the question whether they would or they would not wish to hear more of the intended course of the story and destinies of the characters. To some, silence may seem best, and that the mind should be left to its own conjectures as to the sequel, with the help of such indications as the text affords. I confess that this is the view which has my sympathy. But since others, and those almost certainly a majority, are anxious to be told all they can, and since editors and publishers join in the request, I can scarce do otherwise than comply. The intended argument, then, so far as it was known at the time of the writer's death to his step-daughter and devoted amanuensis, Mrs. Strong, was nearly as follows :—

Archie persists in his good resolution of avoiding further conduct compromising to young Kirstie's good name. Taking advantage of the situation thus created, and of the girl's unhappiness and wounded vanity, Frank Innes pursues his purpose of seduction ; and Kirstie, though still caring for Archie in her heart, allows herself to become Frank's victim. Old Kirstie is the first to perceive something amiss with her, and believing Archie to be the culprit, accuses him, thus making him aware for the first time that mischief has happened. He does not at once deny the charge, but seeks out and questions young Kirstie, who confesses the truth to him ; and he, still loving her, promises to protect and defend her in her trouble. He then has an interview with Frank Innes on the moor, which ends in a quarrel and in Archie killing Frank beside the Weaver's Stone. Meanwhile the Four Black Brothers, having become aware of their sister's betrayal, are bent on vengeance against Archie as her supposed seducer. They are about to close in upon him with this purpose, when he is arrested by the officers of the law for the murder of Frank. He is tried before his own father, the Lord Justice-Clerk, found guilty, and condemned to death. Meanwhile the elder Kirstie, having discovered from the girl how matters really stand, informs her nephews of the truth : and they, in a great revulsion of feeling in Archie's favour, determine on an action after the ancient manner of their house. They gather a following, and after a great fight break the prison where Archie lies confined, and rescue him. He and young Kirstie thereafter escape to America. But the ordeal of taking part in the trial of his own son has been too much for the Lord Justice-Clerk, who dies of the shock. " I do not know," adds the amanuensis, " what becomes of old Kirstie, but that character grew and strengthened so in the writing that I am sure he had some dramatic destiny for her."

The plan of every imaginative work is subject, of course, to change under the artist's hand as he carries it out ; and not merely the character of the elder Kirstie, but other elements of the design no less, might well have deviated from the lines originally traced. It seems certain, however, that the next stage in the relations of Archie and the younger Kirstie would have been as above foreshadowed ; this conception of the lover's unconventional chivalry and unshaken devotion to his mistress after her fault is very characteristic of the author's mind. The vengeance to be taken on the seducer beside the Weaver's Stone is prepared for in the first words of the Introduction : while the situation and fate of the judge, confronting like a Brutus, but unable to survive, the duty of sending his own son to the gallows, seems clearly to have been destined to furnish the climax and essential tragedy of the tale. How this circumstance was to have been brought about within the limits of legal usage and social possibility, seems hard to conjecture ; but it was a point to which the author had evidently given careful consideration. Mrs. Strong says simply that the Lord Justice-Clerk, like an old Roman, condemns his son to death ; but I am assured on the best legal authority of Scotland that no judge, however powerful either by character or office, could have insisted on presiding at the trial of a near kinsman of his own. The Lord Justice-Clerk was head of the criminal justiciary of the country ; he might have insisted on his right of being present on the bench when his son was tried ; but he would never have been allowed to preside or to pass sentence. Now in a letter of Stevenson's to Mr. Baxter, of October, 1892, I find him asking for materials in terms which seem to indicate that he knew this quite well :—" I wish Pitcairn's ' Criminal Trials,' *quam primum.* Also an absolutely correct text of the Scots judiciary oath. Also, in case Pitcairn does not come down late enough, I wish as full a report as possible of a Scots murder trial between 1790–1820. Understand, *the fullest possible.* Is there any book which would guide me to the following facts ? The Justice-Clerk tries some people capitally on circuit. Certain evidence cropping up, the charge is transferred to the Justice-Clerk's own son. Of course in the next trial the Justice-Clerk is excluded, and the case is called before the Lord Justice-General. Where would this trial have to be ? I fear in Edinburgh, which would not suit my view. Could it be again at the circuit town ? " The point was referred to a quondam fellow-member with Stevenson of the Edinburgh Speculative Society, Mr. Graham Murray, the present Solicitor-General for Scotland, whose reply was to the effect that there would be no difficulty in making the new trial take place at the circuit town : that it would have to be held there in spring or autumn, before two Lords of Justiciary ; and that the Lord Justice-General would have nothing to do with it, this title being at the date in question only a nominal one held by a layman (which is no longer the case). On this Stevenson writes, " Graham Murray's note *re* the venue was highly satisfactory, and did me all the good in the world." The terms of his inquiry seem to imply that he intended other persons, before Archie, to have fallen first under suspicion of the murder ; and also—doubtless in order to make the rescue by the Black Brothers possible—that he wanted Archie to be imprisoned not in Edinburgh but in the circuit town. But they do not show how he meant to get over the main difficulty, which at the same time he fully recognises. Can it have been that Lord Hermiston's part was to have been limited to presiding at the *first* trial, where the evidence incriminating Archie was unexpectedly brought forward, and to directing that the law should take its course ?

Whether the final escape and union of Archie and Christina would have proved equally essential to the plot may perhaps to some readers seem questionable. They may rather feel that a tragic destiny is foreshadowed from the beginning for all concerned, and is inherent in the very conditions of the tale. But on this point, and other matters of general criticism connected with it, I find an interesting discussion by the author himself in his correspondence. Writing to Mr. J. M. Barrie, under date November 1, 1892, and criticising that author's famous story of *The Little Minister*, Stevenson says :—

" Your descriptions of your dealings with Lord Rintoul are frightfully unconscientious. . . . *The Little Minister* ought to have ended badly ; we all know it *did*, and we are infinitely grateful to you for the grace and good feeling with which you have lied about it. If you had told the truth, I for one could never have forgiven you. As you had conceived and written the earlier parts, the truth about the end, though indisputably true to fact, would have been a lie, or what is worse, a discord, in art. If you are going to make a book end badly, it must end badly from the beginning. Now, your book began to end well. You let yourself fall in love with, and fondle, and smile at your puppets. Once you had done that, your honour was committed—at the cost of truth to life you were bound to save them. It is the blot on *Richard Feverel*, for instance, that it begins to end well ; and then tricks you and ends ill. But in this case, there is worse behind, for the ill ending does not inherently issue from the plot—the story had, in fact, ended well after the great last interview between Richard and Lucy—and the blind, illogical bullet which smashes all has no more to do between the boards than a fly has to do with a room into whose open window it comes buzzing. It might have so happened ; it needed not ; and unless needs must, we have no right to pain our readers. I have had a heavy case of conscience of the same kind about my Braxfield story. Braxfield—only his name is Hermiston—has a son who is condemned to death ; plainly there is a fine tempting fitness about this —and I meant he was to hang. But on considering my minor characters, I saw there were five people who would —in a sense, who must—break prison and attempt his rescue. They are capable hardy folks too, who might very well succeed. Why should they not then ? Why should not young Hermiston escape clear out of the country ? and be happy, if he could, with his—but soft ! I will not betray my secret nor my heroine. . . ."

To pass, now, from the question how the story would have ended to the question how it originated and grew in the writer's mind. The character of the hero, Weir of Hermiston, is avowedly suggested by the historical personality of Robert Macqueen, Lord Braxfield. This famous judge has been for generations the subject of a hundred Edinburgh tales and anecdotes. Readers of Stevenson's essay on the Raeburn exhibition, in *Virginibus Puerisque*, will remember how he is fascinated by

J

Raeburn's portrait of Braxfield, even as Lockhart had been fascinated by a different portrait of the same worthy sixty years before (see *Peter's Letters to his Kinsfolk*) ; nor did his interest in the character diminish in later life.

Again, the case of a judge involved by the exigencies of his office in a strong conflict between public duty and private interest or affection, was one which had always attracted and exercised Stevenson's imagination. In the days when he and Mr. Henley were collaborating with a view to the stage, Mr. Henley once proposed a plot founded on the story of Mr. Justice Harbottle in Sheridan Le Fanu's *In a Glass Darkly*, in which the wicked judge goes headlong *per fas et nefas* to his object of getting the husband of his mistress hanged. Some time later Stevenson and his wife together wrote a play called *The Hanging Judge*. In this, the title character is tempted for the first time in his life to tamper with the course of justice, in order to shield his wife from persecution by a former husband who re-appears after being supposed dead. Bulwer's novel of *Paul Clifford*, with its final situation of the worldly-minded judge, Sir William Brandon, learning that the highwayman whom he is in the act of sentencing is his own son, and dying of the knowledge, was also well known to Stevenson, and no doubt counted for something in the suggestion of the present story.

Once more, the difficulties often attending the relation of father and son in actual life had pressed heavily on Stevenson's mind and conscience from the days of his youth, when in obeying the law of his own nature he had been constrained to disappoint, distress, and for a time to be much misunderstood by, a father whom he justly loved and admired with all his heart. Difficulties of this kind he had already handled in a lighter vein once or twice in fiction—as for instance in the *Story of a Lie* and in *The Wrecker*—before he grappled with them in the acute and tragic phase in which they occur in the present story.

These three elements, then, the interest of the historical personality of Lord Braxfield, the problems and emotions arising from a violent conflict between duty and nature in a judge, and the difficulties due to incompatibility and misunderstanding between father and son, lie at the foundations of the present story. To touch on minor matters, it is perhaps worth notice, as Mr. Henley reminds me, that the name of Weir had from of old a special significance for Stevenson's imagination, from the traditional fame in Edinburgh of Major Weir, burned as a warlock, together with his sister, under circumstances of peculiar atrocity. Another name, that of the episodical personage of Mr. Torrance the minister, is borrowed direct from life, as indeed are the whole figure and its surroundings—kirkyard, kirk, and manse—down even to the black thread mittens : witness the following passage from a letter of the early seventies :—" I've been to church and am not depressed—a great step. It was at that beautiful church [of Glencorse in the Pentlands, three miles from his father's country house at Swanston]. It is a little cruciform place, with a steep slate roof. The small kirkyard is full of old gravestones ; one of a Frenchman from Dunkerque, I suppose he died prisoner in the military prison hard by. And one, the most pathetic memorial I ever saw : a poor school-slate, in a wooden frame, with the inscription cut into it evidently by the father's own hand. In church, old Mr. Torrance preached, over eighty and a relic of times forgotten, with his black thread gloves and mild old face." A side hint for a particular trait in the character of Mrs. Weir we can trace in some family traditions concerning the writer's own grandmother, who is reported to have valued piety much more than efficiency in her domestic servants. The other women characters seem, so far as his friends know, to have been pure creation, and especially that new and admirable incarnation of the eternal feminine in the elder Kirstie. The little that he says about her himself is in a letter written a few days before his death to Mr. Gosse. The allusions are to the various moods and attitudes of people in regard to middle age, and are suggested by Mr. Gosse's volume of poems, *In Russet and Silver*. " It seems rather funny," he writes,

" that this matter should come up just now, as I am at present engaged in treating a severe case of middle age in one of my stories, *The Justice-Clerk*. The case is that of a woman, and I think I am doing her justice. You will be interested, I believe, to see the difference in our treatments. *Secreta Vitae* [the title of one of Mr. Gosse's poems] comes nearer to the case of my poor Kirstie." From the wonderful midnight scene between her and Archie, we may judge what we have lost in those later scenes where she was to have taxed him with the fault that was not his—to have presently learned his innocence from the lips of his supposed victim—to have then vindicated him to her kinsmen and fired them to the action of his rescue. The scene of the prison-breaking here planned by Stevenson would have gained interest (as will already have occurred to readers) from comparison with the two famous precedents in Scott, the Porteous mob and the breaking of Portanferry Jail.

The best account of Stevenson's methods of imaginative work is in the following sentences from a letter of his own to Mr. W. Craibe Angus of Glasgow :—" I am still a ' slow study,' and sit for a long while silent on my eggs. Unconscious thought, there is the only method : macerate your subject, let it boil slow, then take the lid off and look in—and there your stuff is—good or bad." The several elements above noted having been left to work for many years in his mind, it was in the autumn of 1892 that he was moved to " take the lid off and look in,"—under the influence, it would seem, of a special and overmastering wave of that feeling for the romance of Scottish scenery and character which was at all times so strong in him, and which his exile did so much to intensify. I quote again from his letter to Mr. Barrie on November 1st in that year :—" It is a singular thing that I should live here in the South Seas under conditions so new and so striking, and yet my imagination so continually inhabit the cold old huddle of grey hills from which we come. I have finished *David Balfour*, I have another book on the stocks, *The Young Chevalier*, which is to be part in France and part in Scotland and to deal with Prince Charlie about the year 1749 ; and now what have I done but begun a third, which is to be all moorland together, and is to have for a centre-piece a figure that I think you will appreciate—that of the immortal Braxfield. Braxfield himself is my grand premier—or since you are so much involved in the British drama, let me say my heavy lead."

Writing to me at the same date he makes the same announcement more briefly, with a list of the characters and an indication of the scene and date of the story. To Mr. Baxter he writes a month later, " I have a novel on the stocks to be called *The Justice-Clerk*. It is pretty Scotch ; the grand premier is taken from Braxfield (O, by the by, send me Cockburn's *Memorials*), and some of the story is, well, queer. The heroine is seduced by one man, and finally disappears with the other man who shot him. . . . Mind you, I expect *The Justice-Clerk* to be my master-piece. My Braxfield is already a thing of beauty and a joy for ever, and so far as he has gone far my best character." From the last extract it appears that he had already at this date drafted some of the earlier chapters of the book. He also about the same time composed the dedication to his wife, who found it pinned to her bed-curtains one morning on awaking. It was always his habit to keep several books in progress at the same time, turning from one to another as the fancy took him, and finding rest in the change of labour ; and for many months after the date of this letter, first illness,—then a voyage to Auckland, —then work on the *Ebb-Tide*, on a new tale called *St. Ives*, which was begun during an attack of influenza, and on his projected book of family history,—prevented his making any continuous progress with *Weir*. In August, 1893, he says he has been recasting the beginning. A year later, still only the first four or five chapters had been drafted. Then, in the last weeks of his life, he attacked the task again, in a sudden heat of inspiration, and worked at it ardently and without interruption until the end came. No wonder if during these weeks he was sometimes aware of a tension of the spirit difficult to sustain. " How can I keep this pitch ? " he is reported to have said after finishing one of the chapters. To keep the pitch proved indeed beyond his strength ; and that frail organism, taxed so long and so unsparingly in obedience to his indomitable will, at last betrayed him in mid effort.

There remains one more point to be mentioned, as to the speech and manners of the Hanging Judge himself. That these are not a whit exaggerated, in comparison with what is recorded of his historic prototype, Lord Braxfield, is certain. The *locus classicus* in regard to this personage is in Lord Cockburn's *Memorials of his Time*. " Strong built and dark, with rough eyebrows, powerful eyes, threatening lips, and a low growling voice, he was like a formidable blacksmith. His accent and dialect were exaggerated Scotch ; his language, like his thoughts, short, strong, and conclusive. Illiterate and without any taste for any refined enjoyment, strength of understanding, which gave him power without cultivation, only encouraged him to a more contemptuous disdain of all natures less coarse than his own. It may be doubted if he was ever so much in his element as when tauntingly repelling the last despairing claim of a wretched culprit, and sending him to Botany Bay or the gallows with an insulting jest. Yet this was not from cruelty, for which he was too strong and too jovial, but from cherished coarseness." Readers, nevertheless, who are at all acquainted with the social history of Scotland will hardly have failed to make the observation that Braxfield's is an extreme case of eighteenth-century manners, as he himself was an eighteenth-century personage (he died in 1799 in his seventy-eighth year) ; and that for the date in which the story is cast (1814) such manners are somewhat of an anachronism. During the generation contemporary with the French Revolution and the Napoleonic wars,—or to put it another way, the generation that elapsed between the days when Scott roamed the country as a High School and University student and those when he settled in the fulness of fame and prosperity at Abbotsford,—or again (the allusions will appeal to readers of the admirable Galt) during the intervals between the first and the last pro-vostry of Bailie Pawkie in the borough of Gudetown, or between the earlier and the final ministrations of Mr. Balwhidder in the parish of Dalmailing,—during this period a great softening had taken place in Scottish manners generally, and in those of the Bar and Bench not least. "Since the death of Lord Justice-Clerk Macqueen of Braxfield," says Lockhart, writing about 1817, "the whole exterior of judicial deportment has been quite altered." A similar criticism may probably hold good on the pic-ture of border life contained in the chapter concerning the Four Black Brothers of Cauldstaneslap, namely, that it rather suggests the ways of an earlier generation ; nor have I any clew to the reasons which led Stevenson to choose this particular date, in the year preceding Waterloo, for a story which, in regard to some of its features at least, might seem more naturally placed some twenty-five or thirty years before.

If the reader seeks, further, to know whether the scenery of Hermiston can be identified with any one special place familiar to the writer's early experience, the answer, I think, must be in the negative. Rather it is distilled from a number of different haunts and associations among the moorlands of southern Scotland. In the dedication and in a letter to me he indicates the Lammermuirs as the scene of his tragedy, and Mrs. Stevenson (his mother) told me that she thought he was inspired by recollections of a visit paid in boyhood to an uncle living at a remote farmhouse in that district called Overshiels, in the parish of Stow. But although he may have thought of the Lammermuirs in the first instance, we have already found him drawing his description of the kirk and manse from another haunt of his youth, namely, Glencorse in the Pentlands. And passages in chapters v. and viii. point explicitly to a third district, that is, the country bordering upon Upper Tweeddale, with the country stretching thence to the headwaters of the Clyde. With this country also holiday rides and excursions from Peebles had made him familiar as a boy : and this seems certainly the most natural scene of the story, if only from its proximity to the proper home of the Elliotts, which of course is in the heart of the Border, especially Teviotdale and Ettrick. Some of the geographical names mentioned are clearly not meant to furnish literal indications. The Spango, for instance, is a water running, I believe, not into the Tweed but into the Nith, and Crossmichael as the name of a town is borrowed from Galloway; but it may be taken to all intents and purposes as standing for Peebles, where I am told by Sir George Douglas there existed in the early years of the century a well-known club of the same character as that described in the story. Lastly, the name of Hermiston itself is taken from a farm on the Water of Ale, between Ettrick and Teviotdale, and close to the proper country of the Elliotts.

But it is with the general and essential that the artist deals, and questions of strict historical perspective or local definition are beside the mark in considering his work. Nor will any reader expect, or be grateful for, comment in this place on matters which are more properly to the point—on the seizing and penetrating power of the author's ripened art as exhibited in the foregoing pages, the wide range of character and emotion over which he sweeps with so assured a hand, his vital poetry of vision and magic of presentment. Surely no son of Scotland has died leaving with his last breath a worthier tribute to the land he loved.

SIDNEY COLVIN.

GLOSSARY

ae, *one.*

antinomian, *one of a sect which holds that under the Gospel dispensation the moral law is not obligatory.*

Auld Hornie, *the Devil.*

ballant, *ballad.*

bauchles, *brogues, old shoes.*

bauld, *bold.*

bees in their bonnet, *eccentricities.*

birling, *whirling.*

black-a-vised, *dark - complexioned.*

bonnet-laird, *small landed proprietor, yeoman.*

bool, *ball,* technically, *marble;* here, *sugar-plum.*

brae, *rising ground.*

brig, *bridge.*

buff, play buff on, *to make a fool of, to deceive.*

burn, *stream.*

butt end, *end of a cottage.*

byre, *cow-house.*

ca', *drive.*

caller, *fresh.*

canna, *cannot.*

canny, *careful, shrewd.*

cantie, *cheerful.*

carline, *an old woman.*

chalmer, *chamber.*

claes, *clothes.*

clamjamfry, *crowd.*

clavers, *idle talk.*

cock-laird, *a yeoman.*

collieshangie, *turmoil.*

crack, *to converse.*

cuddy, *donkey.*

cuist, *cast.*

cutty, *jade ;* also used playfully = *brat.*

daft, *mad, frolicsome.*

dander, *to saunter.*

danders, *cinders.*

daurna, *dare not.*

deave, *to deafen.*

demmy brokens, *demi-broquins.*

denty, *dainty.*

dirdum, *vigour.*

disjaskit, *worn-out, disreputable-looking.*

doer, *law agent.*

dour, *hard.*

drumlie, *dark.*

dule-tree, *the tree of lamentation, the hanging tree;* dule *is also Scots for boundary, and it may mean the boundary tree, the tree on which the baron hung interlopers.*

dunting, *knocking.*

dwaibly, *infirm, rickety.*

earrand, *errand.*

ettercap, *vixen.*

fechting, *fighting.*

feck, *quantity, portion.*

feckless, *feeble, powerless.*

fell, *strong and fiery.*

fey, *unlike yourself, strange, as persons are observed to be in the hour of approaching death or disaster.*

fit, *foot.*

flit, *to depart.*

flyped, *turned up, turned inside out.*

forbye, *in addition to.*

forgather, *to fall in with.*

fower, *four.*

fule, *fool.*

füshionless, *pithless, weak.*

fyle, *to soil, to defile.*

fylement, *obloquy, defilement.*

gaed, *went.*

gang, *to go.*

gey an', *very.*

gigot, *leg of mutton.*

girzie, *lit., diminutive of Grizel; here, a playful nickname.*

glaur, *mud.*

glint, *glance, sparkle.*

gloaming, *twilight.*

glower, *to scowl.*

gobbets, *small lumps.*

gowden, *golden.*

gowsty, *gusty.*

grat, *wept.*

grieve, *land-steward.*

guddle, *to catch fish with the hands by groping under the stones or banks.*

guid, *good.*

gumption, *common-sense, judgment.*

gurley, *stormy, surly.*

gyte, *beside itself.*

haddit, *held.*

hae, *have, take.*

hale, *whole.*

heels-ower-hurdie, *heels over head.*

hinney, *honey.*

hirstle, *to bustle.*

hizzie, *wench.*

howe, *hollow.*

howf, *haunt.*

hunkered, *crouched.*

hypothec, *lit., a term in Scots law meaning the security given by a tenant to a landlord, as furniture, produce, etc.; by metonymy and colloquially, "the whole structure," "the whole affair."*

idleset, *idleness.*

infeftment, *a term in Scots law originally synonymous with investiture.*

jaud, *jade.*

jeely-piece, *a slice of bread and jelly.*

jennipers, *juniper.*

jo, *sweetheart.*

justifeed, *executed, made the victim of justice.*

jyle, *jail.*

kebbuck, *cheese.*

ken, *to know.*

kenspeckle, *conspicuous.*

kilted, *tucked up.*

kyte, *belly.*

laigh, *low.*

laird, *landed proprietor.*

lane, *alone.*

lave, *rest, remainder.*

linking, *tripping.*

lown, *lonely, still.*

lynn, *cataract.*

Lyon King of Arms, *the chief of the Court of Heraldry in Scotland.*

macers, *officers of the supreme court [cf. Guy Mannering, last chapter].*

maun, *must.*

menseful, *of good manners.*

mirk, *dark.*

misbegowk, *deception, disappointment.*

mools, *mould, earth.*

muckle, *much, great, big.*
my lane, *by myself.*

nowt, *black cattle.*

palmering, *walking infirmly.*
panel, in Scots law, *the accused person in a criminal action, the prisoner.*
peel, *a fortified watch-tower.*
plew-stilts, *plough-handles.*
policy, *ornamental grounds of a country mansion.*
puddock, *frog.*

quean, *wench.*

rair, *to roar.*
riffraff, *rabble.*
risping, *grating.*
rowt, *to roar, to rant.*
rowth, *abundance.*
rudas, *haggard (old woman).*
runt, *an old cow past breeding; opprobriously, an old woman.*

sab, *sob.*
sanguishes, *sandwiches.*
sasine, in Scots law, *the act of giving legal possession of feudal property,* or, colloquially, *the deed by which that possession is proved.*
sclamber, *to scramble.*
sculduddery, *impropriety, grossness.*
session, *the Court of Session, the supreme court of Scotland.*
shauchling, *shuffling.*
shoo, *to chase gently.*
siller, *money.*
sinsyne, *since then.*
skailing, *dispersing.*
skelp, *slap.*
skirling, *screaming.*
skreigh-o'-day, *daybreak.*

snash, *abuse.*
sneisty, *supercilious.*
sooth, *to hum.*
sough, *sound, murmur.*
Spec., *The Speculative Society,* a debating society connected with Edinburgh University.
speir, *to ask.*
speldering, *sprawling.*
splairge, *to splash.*
spunk, *spirit, fire.*
steik, *to shut.*
stirk, *a young bullock.*
stockfish, *hard, savourless.*
sugar-bool, *sugar-plum.*
syne, *since.*

tawpie, *a slow, foolish slut.*
telling you, *a good thing for you.*
thir, *these.*
thrawn, *cross-grained.*
toon, *town.*
two-names, *local sobriquets in addition to patronymic.*
tyke, *dog.*

unchancy, *unlucky.*
unco, *strange, extraordinary, very.*
upsitten, *impertinent.*

vivers, *victuals.*

wae, *sad, unhappy.*
waling, *choosing.*
warrandise, *warranty.*
waur, *worse.*
weird, *destiny.*
whammle, *to upset.*
whaup, *curlew.*
windlestrae, *crested dog's-tail grass.*
wund, *wind.*

yin, *one.*

HEATHERCAT
A FRAGMENT

HEATHERCAT

PART I

THE KILLING-TIME

CHAPTER I

TRAQUAIRS OF MONTROYMONT

THE period of this tale is in the heat of the *killing-time*; the scene laid for the most part in solitary hills and morasses, haunted only by the so-called Mountain Wanderers, the dragoons that came in chase of them, the women that wept on their dead bodies, and the wild birds of the moorland that have cried there since the beginning. It is a land of many rain-clouds; a land of much mute history, written there in prehistoric symbols. Strange green raths are to be seen commonly in the country, above all by the kirkyards; barrows of the dead, standing stones; beside these, the faint, durable footprints and handmarks of the Roman; and an antiquity older perhaps than any, and still living and active—a complete Celtic nomenclature and a scarce-mingled Celtic population. These rugged and grey hills were once included in the boundaries of the Caledonian Forest. Merlin sat here below his apple-tree and lamented Gwendolen; here spoke with Kentigern; here fell into his enchanted trance. And the legend of his slumber seems to body forth the story of that Celtic race, deprived for so many centuries of their authentic speech, surviving with their ancestral inheritance of melancholy perversity and patient, unfortunate courage.

The Traquairs of Montroymont (*Mons Romanus*, as the erudite expound it) had long held their seat about the head waters of the Dule and in the back parts of the moorland parish of Balweary. For two hundred years they had enjoyed in these upland quarters a certain decency (almost to be named distinction) of repute; and the annals of their house, or what is remembered of them, were obscure and bloody. Ninian Traquair was "cruallie slochtered" by the Crozers at the kirk-door of Balweary, anno 1482. Francis killed Simon Ruthven of Drumshoreland, anno 1540; bought letters of slayers at the widow and heir, and, by a barbarous form of compounding, married (without tocher) Simon's daughter Grizzel, which is the way the Traquairs and Ruthvens came first to an intermarriage. About the last Traquair and Ruthven marriage, it is the business of this book, among many other things, to tell.

The Traquairs were always strong for the Covenant; for the King also, but the Covenant first; and it began to be ill days for Montroymont when the Bishops came in and the dragoons at the heels of them. Ninian (then laird) was an anxious husband of himself and the property, as the times required, and it may be said of him that he lost both. He was heavily suspected of the Pentland Hills rebellion. When it came the length of Bothwell Brig, he stood his trial before the Secret Council, and was convicted of talking to some insurgents by the wayside, the subject of the conversation not very clearly appearing, and of the reset and maintenance of one Gale, a gardener-man, who was seen before Bothwell with a musket, and afterwards, for a continuance of months, delved the garden at Montroymont. Matters went very ill with Ninian at the Council; some of the lords were clear for treason; and even the boot was talked of. But he was spared that torture; and at last, having pretty good friendship among great men, he came off with a fine of seven thousand marks, that caused the estate to groan. In this case, as in so many others, it was the wife that made the trouble. She was a great keeper of conventicles; would ride ten miles to one, and when she was fined, rejoiced greatly to suffer for the Kirk; but it was rather her husband that suffered. She had their only son, Francis, baptised privately by the hands of Mr. Kidd; there was that much the more to pay for! She could neither be driven nor wiled into the parish kirk; as for taking the sacrament at the hands of any Episcopalian curate, and tenfold more at those of Curate Haddo, there was nothing further from her purposes; and Montroymont had to put his hand in his pocket month by month and year by year. Once, indeed, the little lady was cast in prison, and the laird, worthy, heavy, uninterested man, had to ride up and take her place; from which he was not discharged under nine months and a sharp fine. It scarce seemed she had any gratitude to him; she came out of jail herself, and plunged immediately deeper in conventicles, resetting recusants, and all her old, expensive folly, only with greater vigour and openness, because Montroymont was safe in the Tolbooth and she had no witness to consider. When he was liberated and came back, with his fingers singed, in December, 1680, and late in the black night, my lady was from home. He came into the house at his alighting, with a riding-rod yet in his hand; and, on the servant-maid telling him, caught her by the scruff of the neck, beat her violently, flung her down in the passageway, and went upstairs to his bed fasting and without a light. It was three in the morning when my lady returned from that conventicle, and, hearing of the assault (because the maid had sat up for her, weeping), went to their common chamber with a lantern in hand and stamping with her shoes so as to wake the dead; it was supposed, by those that heard her, from a design to have it out with the goodman at once. The house-servants gathered on the stair, because it was a main interest with them to know which of these two was the better horse; and for the space of two hours they were heard to go at the matter, hammer and tongs. Montroymont alleged he was at the end of his possibilities; it was no longer within his power to pay the annual rents; she had served him basely by keeping conventicles while he lay in prison for her sake; his friends

K

were weary, and there was nothing else before him but
the entire loss of the family lands, and to begin life again
by the wayside as a common beggar. She took him up
very sharp and high : called upon him, if he were a Christian ? and which he most considered, the loss of a few
dirty, miry glebes, or of his soul ? Presently he was heard
to weep, and my lady's voice to go on continually like a
running burn, only the words indistinguishable ; whereupon it was supposed a victory for her ladyship, and the
domestics took themselves to bed. The next day Traquair
appeared like a man who had gone under the harrows ;
and his lady wife thenceforward continued in her old
course without the least deflection.

Thenceforward Ninian went on his way without complaint, and suffered his wife to go on hers without remon-
strance. He still minded his estate, of which, it might
be said, he took daily a fresh farewell, and counted it
already lost ; looking ruefully on the acres and the graves
of his fathers, on the moorlands where the wild-fowl con-
sorted, the low, gurgling pool of the trout, and the high,
windy place of the calling curlews—things that were yet
his for the day and would be another's to-morrow ; coming
back again, and sitting ciphering till the dusk at his approaching ruin, which no device of arithmetic could post-
pone beyond a year or two. He was essentially the simple
ancient man, the farmer and landholder ; he would have
been content to watch the seasons come and go, and his
cattle increase, until the limit of age ; he would have been
content at any time to die, if he could have left the estates
undiminished to an heir male of his ancestors, that duty
standing first in his instinctive calendar. And now he
saw everywhere the image of the new proprietor come to
meet him, and go sowing and reaping, or fowling for his
pleasure on the red moors, or eating the very gooseberries
in the Place garden ; and saw always, on the other hand,
the figure of Francis go forth, a beggar, into the broad
world.

It was in vain the poor gentleman sought to moderate ;
took every test and took advantage of every indulgence ;

went and drank with the dragoons in Balweary; attended
the communion and came regularly to the church to Curate
Haddo, with his son beside him. The mad, raging,
Presbyterian zealot of a wife at home made all of no avail;
and indeed the house must have fallen years before if it
had not been for the secret indulgence of the curate, who
had a great sympathy with the laird, and winked hard at
the doings in Montroymont. This curate was a man very
ill reputed in the countryside, and indeed in all Scotland.
" Infamous Haddo " is Shield's expression. But Patrick
Walker is more copious. " Curate Hall Haddo," says he,
sub voce Peden, " or *Hell* Haddo as he was more justly
to be called, a pokeful of old condemned errors and the
filthy vile lusts of the flesh, a published whoremonger, a
common gross drunkard, continually and godlessly scrap-
ing and skirling on a fiddle, continually breathing flames
against the remnant of Israel. But the Lord put an end
to his piping, and all these offences were composed into
one bloody grave." No doubt this was written to excuse
his slaughter; and I have never heard it claimed for
Walker that he was either a just witness or an indulgent
judge. At least, in a merely human character, Haddo
comes off not wholly amiss in the matter of these Traquairs: not that he showed any graces of the Christian,
but had a sort of Pagan decency, which might almost
tempt one to be concerned about his sudden, violent, and
unprepared fate.

CHAPTER II

FRANCIE

FRANCIE was eleven years old, shy, secret, and rather childish of his age, though not backward in schooling, which had been pushed on far by a private governor, one M'Brair, a forfeited minister harboured in that capacity at Montroymont. The boy, already much employed in secret by his mother, was the most apt hand conceivable to run upon a message, to carry food to lurking fugitives, or to stand sentry on the sky-line above a conventicle. It seemed no place on the moorlands was so naked but what he would find cover there; and as he knew every hag, boulder, and heatherbush in a circuit of seven miles about Montroymont, there was scarce any spot but what he could leave or approach it unseen. This dexterity had won him a reputation in that part of the country; and among the many children employed in these dangerous affairs, he passed under the by-name of Heathercat.

How much his father knew of this employment might be doubted. He took much forethought for the boy's future, seeing he was like to be left so poorly, and would sometimes assist at his lessons, sighing heavily, yawning deep, and now and again patting Francie on the shoulder if he seemed to be doing ill, by way of a private, kind encouragement. But a great part of the day was passed in aimless wanderings with his eyes sealed, or in his cabinet sitting bemused over the particulars of the coming bankruptcy; and the boy would be absent a dozen times for once that his father would observe it.

On the 2nd of July, 1682, the boy had an errand from his mother, which must be kept private from all, the father

included in the first of them. Crossing the braes, he hears
the clatter of a horse's shoes, and claps down incontinent
in a hag by the wayside. And presently he spied his father
come riding from one direction, and Curate Haddo walking from another; and Montroymont leaning down from
the saddle, and Haddo getting on his toes (for he was a
little, ruddy, bald-pated man, more like a dwarf), they
greeted kindly, and came to a halt within two fathoms
of the child.

"Montroymont," the curate said, "the de'il 's in 't
but I'll have to denunciate your leddy again."

"De'il 's in 't indeed!" says the laird.

"Man! can ye no induce her to come to the kirk?"
pursues Haddo; "or to a communion at the least of it.
For the conventicles, let be! and the same for yon solemn
fule, M'Brair: I can blink at them. But she's got to
come to the kirk, Montroymont."

"Dinna speak of it," says the laird. "I can do nothing
with her."

"Couldn't ye try the stick to her? It works wonders
whiles," suggested Haddo. "No? I'm wae to hear it.
And I suppose ye ken where you're going?"

"Fine!" said Montroymont. "Fine do I ken where:
Bankrup'cy and the Bass Rock!"

"Praise to my bones that I never married!" cried the
curate. "Well, it's a grievous thing to me to see an
auld house dung down that was here before Flodden
Field. But naebody can say it was with my wish."

"No more they can, Haddo!" says the laird. "A
good friend ye've been to me, first and last. I can give
you that character with a clear conscience."

Whereupon they separated, and Montroymont rode
briskly down into the Dule Valley. But of the curate
Francie was not to be quit so easily. He went on with
his little, brisk steps to the corner of a dyke, and stopped
and whistled and waved upon a lassie that was herding
cattle there. This Janet M'Clour was a big lass, being
taller than the curate; and what made her look the more
so, she was kilted very high. It seemed for a while she

would not come, and Francie heard her calling Haddo a "daft auld fule," and saw her running and dodging him among the whins and hags till he was fairly blown. But at the last he gets a bottle from his plaid-neuk and holds it up to her; whereupon she came at once into a composition, and the pair sat, drinking of the bottle, and daffing and laughing together, on a mound of heather. The boy had scarce heard of these vanities, or he might have been minded of a nymph and satyr, if anybody could have taken long-leggit Janet for a nymph. But they seemed to be huge friends, he thought; and was the more surprised, when the curate had taken his leave, to see the lassie fling stones after him with screeches of laughter, and Haddo turn about and caper, and shake his staff at her, and laugh louder than herself. A wonderful merry pair, they seemed; and when Francie crawled out of the hag, he had a great deal to consider in his mind. It was possible they were all fallen in error about Mr. Haddo, he reflected,—having seen him so tender with Montroymont, and so kind and playful with the lass Janet; and he had a temptation to go out of his road and question her herself upon the matter. But he had a strong spirit of duty on him; and plodded on instead over the braes till he came near the House of Cairngorm. There, in a hollow place by the burn-side that was shaded by some birks, he was aware of a barefoot boy, perhaps a matter of three years older than himself. The two approached with the precautions of a pair of strange dogs, looking at each other queerly.

"It's ill weather on the hills," said the stranger, giving the watchword.

"For a season," said Francie, "but the Lord will appear."

"Richt," said the barefoot boy. "Wha're ye frae?"

"The Leddy Montroymont," says Francie.

"Ha'e then!" says the stranger, and handed him a folded paper, and they stood and looked at each other again. "It's unco' het," said the boy.

"Dooms het," says Francie.

" What do they ca' ye ? " says the other.

" Francie," says he. " I'm young Montroymont. They ca' me Heathercat."

" I'm Jock Crozer," said the boy. And there was another pause, while each rolled a stone under his foot.

" Cast your jaiket and I'll fecht ye for a bawbee," cried the elder boy, with sudden violence, and dramatically throwing back his jacket.

" Na, I have nae time the now," said Francie, with a sharp thrill of alarm, because Crozer was much the heavier boy.

" Ye're feared. Heathercat indeed ! " said Crozer, for among this infantile army of spies and messengers the fame of Crozer had gone forth and was resented by his rivals. And with that they separated.

On his way home Francie was a good deal occupied with the recollection of this untoward incident. The challenge had been fairly offered and basely refused : the tale would be carried all over the country, and the lustre of the name of Heathercat be dimmed. But the scene between Curate Haddo and Janet M'Clour had also given him much to think of ; and he was still puzzling over the case of the curate, and why such ill words were said of him, and why, if he were so merry-spirited, he should yet preach so dry, when, coming over a knowe, whom should he see but Janet, sitting with her back to him, minding her cattle ! He was always a great child for secret, stealthy ways, having been employed by his mother on errands when the same was necessary ; and he came behind the lass without her hearing.

" Jennet," says he.

" Keep me ! " cries Janet, springing up. " O, it's you, Maister Francie ! Save us, what a fricht ye gied me ! "

" Ay, it's me," said Francie. " I've been thinking, Jennet ; I saw you and the curate a while back——"

" Brat ! " cried Janet, and coloured up crimson ; and the one moment made as if she would have stricken him with a ragged stick she had to chase her bestial with, and the next was begging and praying that he would mention it to none. It was "naebody's business, whatever," she said ; " it would just start a clash in the country " ; and there would be nothing left for her but to drown herself in Dule Water.

" Why ? " says Francie.

The girl looked at him and grew scarlet again.

" And it isna that, anyway," continued Francie. " It was just that he seemed so good to ye—like our Father in Heaven, I thought ; and I thought that mebbe, perhaps, we had all been wrong about him from the first. But I'll have to tell Mr. M'Brair, I'm under a kind of a bargain to him to tell him all."

" Tell it to the divil if ye like for me ! " cried the lass. " I've naething to be ashamed of. Tell M'Brair to mind his ain affairs," she cried again ; " they'll be hot eneuch for him, if Haddie likes ! " And so strode off, shoving her beasts before her, and ever and again looking back and crying angry words to the boy, where he stood mystified.

By the time he had got home his mind was made up that he would say nothing to his mother. My Lady Montroymont was in the keeping-room, reading a godly book ; she was a wonderful frail little wife to make so much noise in the world and be able to steer about that patient sheep her husband ; her eyes were like sloes, the fingers of her hands were like tobacco-pipe shanks, her mouth shut tight like a trap ; and even when she was the most serious, and still more when she was angry, there hung about her face the terrifying semblance of a smile.

" Have ye gotten the billet, Francie ? " said she ; and when he had handed it over, and she had read and burned it, " Did you see anybody ? " she asked.

" I saw the laird," said Francie.

" He didna see you, though ? " asked his mother.

" De'il a fear," from Francie.

" Francie ! " she cried. " What's that I hear ? an aith ? The Lord forgive me, have I broughten forth a brand for the burning, a fagot for hell-fire ? "

"I'm very sorry, ma'am," said Francie. "I humbly beg the Lord's pardon, and yours, for my wickedness."

"H'm," grunted the lady. "Did ye see nobody else?"

"No, ma'am," said Francie, with the face of an angel, "except Jock Crozer, that gied me the billet."

"Jock Crozer!" cried the lady. "I'll Crozer them! Crozers indeed! What next? Are we to repose the lives of a suffering remnant in Crozers? The whole clan of them wants hanging, and if I had my way of it, they wouldna want it long. Are you aware, sir, that these Crozers killed your forebear at the kirk-door?"

"You see, he was bigger 'n me," said Francie.

"Jock Crozer," continued the lady. "That'll be Clement's son, the biggest thief and reiver in the countryside. To trust a note to him! But I'll give the benefit of my opinions to Lady Whitecross when we two forgather. Let her look to herself! I have no patience with half-hearted carlines, that complies on the Lord's day morning with the kirk, and comes taigling the same night to the conventicle. The one or the other! is what I say: Hell or Heaven—Haddie's abominations or the pure word of God dreeping from the lips of Mr. Arnot.

"'Like honey from the honeycomb
That dreepeth, sweeter far.'"

My lady was now fairly launched, and that upon two congenial subjects: the deficiencies of the Lady Whitecross, and the turpitudes of the whole Crozer race—which, indeed, had never been conspicuous for respectability. She pursued the pair of them for twenty minutes on the clock with wonderful animation and detail, something of the pulpit manner, and the spirit of one possessed. "O hellish compliance!" she exclaimed. "I would not suffer a complier to break bread with Christian folk. Of all the sins of this day there is not one so God-defying, so Christ-humiliating, as damnable compliance"; the boy standing before her meanwhile, and brokenly pursuing other thoughts, mainly of Haddo and Janet, and Jock

Crozer stripping off his jacket. And yet, with all his distraction, it might be argued that he heard too much; his father and himself being "compliers"—that is to say, attending the church of the parish as the law required.

Presently, the lady's passion beginning to decline or her flux of ill words to be exhausted, she dismissed her audience. Francie bowed low, left the room, closed the door behind him; and then turned him about in the passageway, and with a low voice, but a prodigious deal of sentiment, repeated the name of the evil one twenty times over, to the end of which, for the greater efficacy, he tacked on "damnable" and "hellish." *Fas est ab hoste doceri*—disrespect is made more pungent by quotation; and there is no doubt but he felt relieved, and went upstairs into his tutor's chamber with a quiet mind. M'Brair sat by the cheek of the peat-fire and shivered, for he had a quartan ague and this was his day. The great nightcap and plaid, the dark unshaven cheeks of the man, and the white, thin hands that held the plaid about his chittering body, made a sorrowful picture. But Francie knew and loved him; came straight in, nestled close to the refugee, and told his story. M'Brair had been at the College with Haddo; the Presbytery had licensed both on the same day; and at this tale, told with so much innocency by the boy, the heart of the tutor was commoved.

"Woe upon him! Woe upon that man!" he cried. "O the unfaithful shepherd! O the hireling and apostate minister! Make my matters hot for me? quo' she! the shameless limmer! And true it is that he could repose me in that nasty, stinking hole, the Canongate Tolbooth, from which your mother drew me out—the Lord reward her for it!—or to that cold, unbieldy, marine place of the Bass Rock, which, with my delicate kist, would be fair ruin to me. But I will be valiant in my Master's service. I have a duty here: a duty to my God, to myself, and to Haddo: in His strength, I will perform it."

Then he straightly discharged Francie to repeat the tale, and bade him in the future to avert his very eyes from the doings of the curate. "You must go to his

place of idolatry; look upon him there!" says he, "but
nowhere else. Avert your eyes, close your ears, pass him
by like a three days' corp'. He is like that damnable
monster Basiliscus, which defiles—yea, poisons!—by the
sight." All which was hardly claratory to the boy's mind.

Presently Montroymont came home, and called up the
stairs to Francie. Traquair was a good shot and swords-
man; and it was his pleasure to walk with his son over
the braes of the moorfowl, or to teach him arms in the
back court, when they made a mighty comely pair, the
child being so lean and light and active, and the laird
himself a man of a manly, pretty stature, his hair (the
periwig being laid aside) showing already white with many
anxieties, and his face of an even, flaccid red. But this
day Francie's heart was not in the fencing.

"Sir," says he, suddenly lowering his point, "will ye
tell me a thing if I was to ask it?"

"Ask away," says the father.

"Well, it's this," said Francie: "Why do you and me
comply if it's so wicked?"

"Ay, ye have the cant of it, too!" cries Montroymont.
"But I'll tell ye for all that. It's to try and see if we can
keep the rigging on this house, Francie. If she had her
way, we would be beggar-folk and hold our hands out
by the wayside. When ye hear her—when ye hear folk,"
he corrected himself briskly, "call me a coward, and one
that betrayed the Lord, and I kenna what else, just mind
it was to keep a bed to ye to sleep in and a bite for ye to
eat.—On guard!" he cried, and the lesson proceeded
again till they were called to supper.

"There's another thing yet," said Francie, stopping
his father. "There's another thing that I am not sure
I am very caring for. She—she sends me errands."

"Obey her, then, as is your bounden duty," said
Traquair.

"Ay, but wait till I tell ye," says the boy. "If I was
to see you I was to hide."

Montroymont sighed. "Well, and that's good of her,
too," said he. "The less that I ken of thir doings the

better for me ; and the best thing you can do is just to obey her, and see and be a good son to her, the same as ye are to me, Francie."

At the tenderness of this expression the heart of Francie swelled within his bosom, and his remorse was poured out. "Faither!" he cried, "I said 'de'il' to-day; many's the time I said it, and '*damnable*' too, and '*hellitsh*.' I ken they're all right; they're beeblical. But I didna say them beeblically; I said them for sweir-words—that's the truth of it."

"Hout, ye silly bairn!" said the father; "dinna do it nae mair, and come in by to your supper." And he took the boy, and drew him close to him a moment, as they went through the door, with something very fond and secret, like a caress between a pair of lovers.

The next day M'Brair was abroad in the afternoon, and had a long advising with Janet on the braes where she herded cattle. What passed was never wholly known ; but the lass wept bitterly, and fell on her knees to him among the whins. The same night, as soon as it was dark, he took the road again for Balweary. In the Kirkton, where the dragoons quartered, he saw many lights, and heard the noise of a ranting song and people laughing grossly, which was highly offensive to his mind. He gave it the wider berth, keeping among the fields ; and came down at last by the water-side, where the manse stands solitary between the river and the road. He tapped at the back door, and the old woman called upon him to come in, and guided him through the house to the study, as they still called it, though there was little enough study there in Haddo's days, and more song-books than theology.

"Here's yin to speak wi' ye, Mr. Haddie!" cries the old wife.

And M'Brair, opening the door and entering, found the little, round, red man seated in one chair and his feet upon another. A clear fire and a tallow dip lighted him barely. He was taking tobacco in a pipe, and smiling to himself ; and a brandy-bottle and glass, and his fiddle and bow, were beside him on the table.

"Hech, Patey M'Brair, is this you?" said he, a trifle tipsily. "Step in by, man, and have a drop brandy: for the stomach's sake! Even the de'il can quote Scripture—eh, Patey?"

"I will neither eat nor drink with you," replied M'Brair. "I am come upon my Master's errand: woe be upon me if I should anyways mince the same. Hall Haddo, I summon you to quit this kirk which you encumber."

"Muckle obleeged!" says Haddo, winking.

"You and me have been to kirk and market together," pursued M'Brair: "we have had blessed seasons in the kirk, we have sat in the same teaching-rooms and read in the same book; and I know you still retain for me some carnal kindness. It would be my shame if I denied it; I live here at your mercy and by your favour, and glory to acknowledge it. You have pity on my wretched body, which is but grass, and must soon be trodden under; but O, Haddo! how much greater is the yearning with which I yearn after and pity your immortal soul! Come now, let us reason together! I drop all points of controversy, weighty though these be; I take your defaced and damnified kirk on your own terms; and I ask you, Are you a worthy minister? The communion season approaches; how can you pronounce thir solemn words, 'The elders will now bring forrit the elements,' and not quail? A parishioner may be summoned to-night; you may have to rise from your miserable orgies; and I ask you, Haddo, what does your conscience tell you? Are you fit? Are you fit to smooth the pillow of a parting Christian? And if the summons should be for yourself, how then?"

Haddo was startled out of all composure and the better part of his temper. "What's this of it?" he cried. "I'm no waur than my neebours. I never set up to be speeritual; I never did. I'm a plain, canty creature; godliness is cheerfulness, says I; give me my fiddle and a dram, and I wouldna hairm a flee."

"And I repeat my question," said M'Brair: "Are you fit—fit for this great charge? fit to carry and save souls?"

" Fit ? Blethers ! As fit's yoursel'," cried Haddo.

" Are you so great a self-deceiver ? " said M'Brair.
" Wretched man, trampler upon God's covenants, crucifier
of your Lord afresh ! I will ding you to the earth with
one word : How about the young woman, Janet
M'Clour ? "

" Well, what about her ? what do I ken ? " cries Haddo.
" M'Brair, ye daft auld wife, I tell ye as true's truth, I
never meddled her. It was just daffing, I tell ye : daffing,
and nae mair : a piece of fun, like ! I'm no' denying but
what I'm fond of fun, sma' blame to me ! But for ony-
thing sarious—hout, man, it might come to a deposeetion !
I'll sweir it to ye. Where's a Bible, till you hear me
sweir ? "

" There is nae Bible in your study," said M'Brair
severely.

And Haddo, after a few distracted turns, was constrained to accept the fact.

" Weel, and suppose there isna ? " he cried, stamping.
" What mair can ye say of us, but just that I'm fond of
my joke, and so's she ? I declare to God, by what I ken,
she might be the Virgin Mary—if she would just keep
clear of the dragoons. But me ! na, de'il haet o' me ! "

" She is penitent at least," said M'Brair.

" Do you mean to actually up and tell me to my face
that she accused me ? " cried the curate.

" I canna just say that," replied M'Brair. " But I
rebuked her in the name of God, and she repented before
me on her bended knees."

" Weel, I daursay she's been ower far wi' the dragoons,"
said Haddo. " I never denied that. I ken naething by
it."

" Man, you but show your nakedness the more plainly,"
said M'Brair. " Poor, blind, besotted creature—and I see
you stoitering on the brink of dissolution : your light out,
and your hours numbered. Awake, man ! " he shouted
with a formidable voice, " awake, or it be ower late."

" Be damned if I stand this ! " exclaimed Haddo, cast-
ing his tobacco-pipe violently on the table, where it was

smashed in pieces. "Out of my house with ye, or I'll call for the dragoons."

"The speerit of the Lord is upon me," said M'Brair, with solemn ecstasy. "I sist you to compear before the Great White Throne, and I warn you the summons shall be bloody and sudden."

And at this, with more agility than could have been expected, he got clear of the room and slammed the door behind him in the face of the pursuing curate. The next Lord's day the curate was ill, and the kirk closed, but, for all his ill words, Mr. M'Brair abode unmolested in the house of Montroymont.

CHAPTER III

THE HILL-END OF DRUMLOWE

THIS was a bit of a steep broken hill that overlooked upon the west a moorish valley, full of ink-black pools. These presently drained into a burn that made off, with little noise and no celerity of pace, about the corner of the hill. On the far side the ground swelled into a bare heath, black with junipers, and spotted with the presence of the standing stones for which the place was famous. They were many in that part, shapeless, white with lichen—you would have said with age; and had made their abode there for untold centuries, since first the heathens shouted for their installation. The ancients had hallowed them to some ill religion, and their neighbourhood had long been avoided by the prudent before the fall of day; but of late, on the upspringing of new requirements, these lonely stones on the moor had again become a place of assembly. A watchful picket on the Hill-end commanded all the northern and eastern approaches; and such was the disposition of the ground, that by certain cunningly posted sentries the west also could be made secure against surprise: there was no place in the country where a conventicle could meet with more quiet of mind or a more certain retreat open, in the case of interference from the dragoons. The minister spoke from a knowe close to the edge of the Ring, and poured out the words God gave him on the very threshold of the devils of yore. When they pitched a tent (which was often in wet weather, upon a communion occasion) it was rigged over the huge isolated pillar that had the name of Anes-Errand, none knew why. And the congregation sat partly clustered on the slope below, and partly among the idolatrous monoliths and on the turfy soil of the Ring itself. In truth the situation was well qualified to give a zest to Christian doctrines, had there been any wanted. But these congregations assembled under conditions at once so formidable and romantic as made a zealot of the most cold. They were the last of the faithful; God, who had averted His face from all other countries of the world, still leaned from Heaven to observe, with swelling sympathy, the doings of His moorland remnant; Christ was by them with His eternal wounds, with dropping tears; the Holy Ghost (never perfectly realised nor firmly adopted by Protestant imaginations) was dimly supposed to be in the heart of each and on the lips of the minister. And over against them was the army of the hierarchies, from the men Charles and James Stuart, on to King Lewie and the Emperor; and the scarlet Pope, and the muckle black devil himself, peering out the red mouth of hell in an ecstasy of hate and hope. " One pull more ! " he seemed to cry; "one pull more, and it's done. There's only Clydesdale and the Stewartry, and the three Bailieries of Ayr, left for God." And with such an august assistance of powers and principalities looking on at the last conflict of good and evil, it was scarce possible to spare a thought to those old, infirm, debile *ab agendo* devils whose holy place they were now violating.

There might have been three hundred to four hundred present. At least there were three hundred horses tethered for the most part in the Ring; though some of the hearers on the outskirts of the crowd stood with their bridles in their hand, ready to mount at the first signal. The circle of faces was strangely characteristic; long, serious, strongly marked, the tackle standing out in the lean brown cheeks, the mouth set and the eyes shining with a fierce enthusiasm; the shepherd, the labouring man, and the rarer laird, stood there in their broad blue bonnets or laced hats, and presenting an essential identity of type. From time to time a long-drawn groan of adhesion rose in this audience, and was propagated like a wave to the outskirts, and died away among the keepers of

L

the horses. It had a name; it was called "a holy groan."

A squall came up; a great volley of flying mist went out before it and whelmed the scene; the wind stormed with a sudden fierceness that carried away the minister's voice and twitched his tails and made him stagger, and turned the congregation for a moment into a mere pother of blowing plaid-ends and prancing horses; and the rain followed and was dashed straight into their faces. Men and women panted aloud in the shock of that violent shower-bath; the teeth were bared along all the line in an involuntary grimace; plaids, mantles, and riding-coats were proved vain, and the worshippers felt the water stream on their naked flesh. The minister, reinforcing his great and shrill voice, continued to contend against and triumph over the rising of the squall and the dashing of the rain.

"In that day ye may go thirty mile and not hear a crawing cock," he said; "and fifty mile and not get a light to your pipe; and an hundred mile and not see a smoking house. For there'll be naething in all Scotland but deid men's banes and blackness, and the living anger of the Lord. O, where to find a bield—O sirs, where to find a bield from the wind of the Lord's anger? Do ye call *this* a wind? Bethankit! Sirs, this is but a temporary dispensation; this is but a puff of wind, this is but a spit of rain and by with it. Already there's a blue bow in the west, and the sun will take the crown of the causeway again, and your things'll be dried upon ye, and your flesh will be warm upon your bones. But O, sirs, sirs! for the day of the Lord's anger!"

His rhetoric was set forth with an ear-piercing elocution, and a voice that sometimes crashed like cannon. Such as it was, it was the gift of all hill-preachers, to a singular degree of likeness or identity. Their images scarce ranged beyond the red horizon of the moor and the rainy hill-top, the shepherd and his sheep, a fowling-piece, a spade, a pipe, a dunghill, a crowing cock, the shining and the withdrawal of the sun. An occasional pathos of simple humanity, and frequent patches of big biblical words, relieved the homely tissue. It was a poetry apart; bleak, austere, but genuine, and redolent of the soil.

A little before the coming of the squall there was a different scene enacting at the outposts. For the most part the sentinels were faithful to their important duty; the Hill-end of Drumlowe was known to be a safe meeting-place; and the out-pickets on this particular day had been somewhat lax from the beginning, and grew laxer during the inordinate length of the discourse. Francie lay there in his appointed hiding-hole, looking abroad between two whin-bushes. His view was across the course of the burn, then over a piece of plain moorland, to a gap between two hills; nothing moved but grouse, and some cattle who slowly traversed his field of view, heading north-ward: he heard the psalms, and sang words of his own to the savage and melancholy music; for he had his own design in hand, and terror and cowardice prevailed in his bosom alternately, like the hot and the cold fit of an ague. Courage was uppermost during the singing, which he accompanied through all its length with this impromptu strain:

> "And I will ding Jock Crozer down
> No later than the day."

Presently the voice of the preacher came to him in wafts, at the wind's will, as by the opening and shutting of a door; wild spasms of screaming, as of some undiscerned gigantic hill-bird stirred with inordinate passion, succeeded to intervals of silence; and Francie heard them with a critical ear. "Ay," he thought at last, "he'll do; he has the bit in his mou' fairly."

He had observed that his friend, or rather his enemy, Jock Crozer, had been established at a very critical part of the line of outposts; namely, where the burn issues by an abrupt gorge from the semicircle of high moors. If anything was calculated to nerve him to battle it was this. The post was important; next to the Hill-end itself, it might be called the key to the position; and it was where the cover was bad, and in which it was most natural to place a child. It should have been Heathercat's; why had it been given to Crozer? An exquisite fear of what should be the answer passed through his marrow every time he faced the question. Was it possible that Crozer could have boasted? that there were rumours abroad to his—Heathercat's—discredit? that his honour was publicly sullied? All the world went dark about him at the thought; he sank without a struggle into the midnight pool of despair; and every time he so sank, he brought back with him—not drowned heroism indeed, but half-drowned courage by the locks. His heart beat very slowly as he deserted his station, and began to crawl towards that of Crozer. Something pulled him back, and it was not the sense of duty, but a remembrance of Crozer's build and hateful readiness of fist. Duty, as he conceived it, pointed him forward on the rueful path that he was travelling. Duty bade him redeem his name if he were able, at the risk of broken bones; and his bones and every tooth in his head ached by anticipation. An awful subsidiary fear whispered him that if he were hurt, he should disgrace himself by weeping. He consoled himself, boy-like, with the consideration that he was not yet committed; he could easily steal over unseen to Crozer's post, and he had a continuous private idea that he would very probably steal back again. His course took him so near the minister that he could hear some of his words: " What news, minister, of Claver'se? He's going round like a roaring, rampaging lion . . ."

EDITORIAL NOTE

By Sir Sidney Colvin

THE story, which opens with these scenes of covenanting life and character in Scotland, was intended to
shift presently across the Atlantic, first to the Carolina
plantations, and next to the ill-fated Scotch settlement
in Darien. Practically all that we know of it is contained
in one or two passages of letters from the author to Mr.
Charles Baxter and Mr. S. R. Crockett. To Mr. Baxter
he writes as follows :

"6 Decr., 1893.

" ' Oct. 25, 1685, at Privy Council, George Murray,
Lieutenant of the King's Guard, and others, did, on the
21 of September last, obtain a clandestine order of Privy
Council to apprehend the person of Janet Pringle, daughter
to the late Clifton, and she having retired out of the way
upon information, he got an order against Andrew Pringle,
her uncle, to produce her. . . . But she having married
Andrew Pringle, her uncle's son (to disappoint all their
designs of selling her), a boy of 13 years old '—but my boy
is 14, so I extract no farther (*Fountainhall*, i. 320). May 6,
1685, Wappus Pringle of Clifton was still alive after all,[1]
and in prison for debt, and transacts with Lieutenant
Murray, giving security for 7000 marks (i. 320).

" My dear Charles, the above is my story, and I wonder
if any light can be thrown on it. I prefer the girl's father
dead ; and the question is how in that case could Lieutenant George Murray get his order to apprehend and
his power to sell her in marriage ? Or . . . might Lieutenant G. be her tutor, and the fugitive to the Pringles,

---

[1] No; it seems to have been *her* brother who had succeeded.

and on the discovery of her whereabouts hastily married ? A good legal note on these points is very ardently desired by me ; it will be the corner-stone of my novel.

" This is for—I am quite wrong to tell you, for you will tell others and nothing will teach you that all my schemes are in the air, and vanish and re-appear again like shapes in the clouds—it is for *Heathercat :* whereof the first volume will be called *The Killing-Time ;* and I believe I have authorities ample for that. But the second volume is to be called, I believe, *Darien,* and for that I want, I fear, a good deal of truck.

> Darien papers,
> Carstairs papers,
> Marchmont papers,
> Jerviswood correspondence—

I hope may do me ; some sort of general history of the Darien affair (if there is a decent one, which I misdoubt) it would also be well to have ; the one with most details, if possible. It is singular how obscure to me this decade of Scots History remains, 1690-1700 : a deuce of a want of light and grouping to it. However, I believe I shall be mostly out of Scotland in my tale ; first in Carolina and next in Darien."

The place of Andrew Pringle, in the historical extract above quoted, was evidently to be taken in Stevenson's story by Ninian Traquair of Montroymont. In a rough draft of chapter headings, chap. vi. bears the title, " The Ward Comes Home "; another chapter shows that her name was to have been Jean Ruthven ; plainly Francie Traquair was to be the boy-husband to whom this Jean was to be united in order to frustrate the designs of those who hoped to control her person and traffic in her marriage.

The references in the author's letters to Mr. Crockett date from June 30, 1893, and afterwards. His correspondent was about this time engaged in preparing a covenanting romance of his own—*The Men of the Moss-Hags.* On the first-named date Stevenson writes : " It may interest you to know that *Weir of Hermiston,* or *The*

Hanging Judge, or whatever the mischief the thing is to be called, centres about the grave of the Praying Weaver of Balweary. And when *Heathercat* is written, if it ever is, O, then there will be another chance for the Societies " (i.e., the United Societies, generally known in history as the Cameronians). A little later Stevenson received from the same correspondent, at his own request, materials for his work in the shape of extracts collected from the Earlston papers by the Rev. John Anderson, Assistant Curator of the Historical Department, Register House, Edinburgh ; the minutes of the Societies, edited by the Rev. John Howie of Lochgoin, entitled " Faithful Contendings," etc., etc. Later, he sends a humorous sketch of a trespassing board and gallows, with R. L. S. in the act of hanging S. R. C., and on the board the words : " Notice—The Cameronians are the proppaty of me, R. L. S.—trespassers and Raiders will be hung." In the letter accompanying this, he says : " I have made many notes for *Heathercat*, but do not get much forrader. For one thing, I am not inside these people yet. Wait three years and *I'll race you*. For another thing, I am not a keen partisan, and to write a good book you must be. The Society men were brave, dour-headed, strong-hearted men fighting a hard battle and fighting it hardly. That is about all the use I have for them." Finally, in a letter written shortly before his death, he mentions having laid the story on the shelf, whether permanently or only for a while he does not know.

SIDNEY COLVIN.

THE YOUNG CHEVALIER
A FRAGMENT

THE YOUNG CHEVALIER

PROLOGUE

THE WINE-SELLER'S WIFE

THERE was a wine-seller's shop, as you went down
to the river in the city of the Anti-popes. There
a man was served with good wine of the country and
plain country fare ; and the place being clean and quiet,
with a prospect on the river, certain gentlemen who dwelt
in that city in attendance on a great personage made it a
practice (when they had any silver in their purses) to
come and eat there and be private.

They called the wine-seller Paradou. He was built
more like a bullock than a man, huge in bone and brawn,
high in colour, and with a hand like a baby for size. Marie-
Madeleine was the name of his wife ; she was of Mar-
seilles, a city of entrancing women, nor was any fairer
than herself. She was tall, being almost of a height with
Paradou ; full-girdled, point-device in every form, with an
exquisite delicacy in the face ; her nose and nostrils a
delight to look at from the fineness of the sculpture, her
eyes inclined a hair's-breadth inward, her colour between
dark and fair, and laid on even like a flower's. A faint
rose dwelt in it, as though she had been found unawares
bathing, and had blushed from head to foot. She was of
a grave countenance, rarely smiling ; yet it seemed to be
written upon every part of her that she rejoiced in life.
Her husband loved the heels of her feet and the knuckles
of her fingers ; he loved her like a glutton and a brute ; his
love hung about her like an atmosphere ; one that came

by chance into the wine-shop was aware of that passion ;
and it might be said that by the strength of it the woman
had been drugged or spell-bound. She knew not if she
loved or loathed him ; he was always in her eyes like something monstrous—monstrous in his love, monstrous in his
person, horrific but imposing in his violence ; and her
sentiment swung back and forward from desire to sickness. But the mean, where it dwelt chiefly, was an
apathetic fascination, partly of horror ; as of Europa in
mid-ocean with her bull.

On the 10th November, 1749, there sat two of the
foreign gentlemen in the wine-seller's shop. They were
both handsome men of a good presence, richly dressed.
The first was swarthy and long and lean, with an alert,
black look, and a mole upon his cheek. The other was
more fair. He seemed very easy and sedate, and a little
melancholy for so young a man, but his smile was charming. In his grey eyes there was much abstraction, as of
one recalling fondly that which was past and lost. Yet
there was strength and swiftness in his limbs ; and his
mouth set straight across his face, the under lip a thought
upon side, like that of a man accustomed to resolve.
These two talked together in a rude outlandish speech
that no frequenter of that wine-shop understood. The
swarthy man answered to the name of *Ballantrae ;* he of
the dreamy eyes was sometimes called *Balmile*, and sometimes *my Lord*, or *my Lord Gladsmuir ;* but when the
title was given him, he seemed to put it by as if in jesting,
not without bitterness.

The mistral blew in the city. The first day of that
wind, they say in the countries where its voice is heard,
it blows away all the dust, the second all the stones, and
the third it blows back others from the mountains. It was
now come to the third day ; outside the pebbles flew like
hail, and the face of the river was puckered, and the very
building-stones in the walls of houses seemed to be
curdled, with the savage cold and fury of that continuous
blast. It could be heard to hoot in all the chimneys of
the city ; it swept about the wine-shop, filling the room

with eddies; the chill and gritty touch of it passed between the nearest clothes and the bare flesh; and the two gentlemen at the far table kept their mantles loose about their shoulders. The roughness of these outer hulls, for they were plain travellers' cloaks that had seen service, set the greater mark of richness on what showed below of their laced clothes; for the one was in scarlet and the other in violet and white, like men come from a scene of ceremony; as indeed they were.

It chanced that these fine clothes were not without their influence on the scene which followed, and which makes the prologue of our tale. For a long time Balmile was in the habit to come to the wine-shop and eat a meal or drink a measure of wine; sometimes with a comrade; more often alone, when he would sit and dream and drum upon the table, and the thoughts would show in the man's face in little glooms and lightenings, like the sun and the clouds upon a water. For a long time Marie-Madeleine had observed him apart. His sadness, the beauty of his smile when by any chance he remembered her existence and addressed her, the changes of his mind signalled forth by an abstruse play of feature, the mere fact that he was foreign and a thing detached from the local and the accustomed, insensibly attracted and affected her. Kindness was ready in her mind; it but lacked the touch of an occasion to effervesce and crystallise. Now, Balmile had come hitherto in a very poor plain habit; and this day of the mistral, when his mantle was just open, and she saw beneath it the glancing of the violet and the velvet and the silver, and the clustering fineness of the lace, it seemed to set the man in a new light, with which he shone resplendent to her fancy.

The high inhuman note of the wind, the violence and continuity of its outpouring, and the fierce touch of it upon man's whole periphery, accelerated the functions of the mind. It set thoughts whirling, as it whirled the trees of the forest; it stirred them up in flights, as it stirred up the dust in chambers. As brief as sparks, the fancies glittered and succeeded each other in the mind of Marie-

Madeleine ; and the grave man with the smile, and the bright clothes under the plain mantle, haunted her with incongruous explanations. She considered him, the unknown, the speaker of an unknown tongue, the hero (as she placed him) of an unknown romance, the dweller upon unknown memories. She recalled him sitting there alone, so immersed, so stupefied ; yet she was sure he was not stupid. She recalled one day when he had remained a long time motionless, with parted lips, like one in the act of starting up, his eyes fixed on vacancy. Any one else must have looked foolish ; but not he. She tried to conceive what manner of memory had thus entranced him ; she forged for him a past ; she showed him to herself in every light of heroism and greatness and misfortune ; she brooded with petulant intensity on all she knew and guessed of him. Yet, though she was already gone so deep, she was still unashamed, still unalarmed ; her thoughts were still disinterested ; she had still to reach the stage at which —beside the image of that other whom we love to contemplate and to adorn—we place the image of ourself and behold them together with delight.

She stood within the counter, her hands clasped behind her back, her shoulders pressed against the wall, her feet braced out. Her face was bright with the wind and her own thoughts ; as a fire in a similar day of tempest glows and brightens on a hearth, so she seemed to glow, standing there, and to breathe out energy. It was the first time Ballantrae had visited that wine-seller's, the first time he had seen the wife ; and his eyes were true to her.

"I perceive your reason for carrying me to this very draughty tavern," he said at last.

"I believe it is propinquity," returned Balmile.

"You play dark," said Ballantrae, "but have a care ! Be more frank with me, or I will cut you out. I go through no form of qualifying my threat, which would be commonplace and not conscientious. There is only one point in these campaigns : that is the degree of admiration offered by the man ; and to our hostess I am in a posture to make victorious love."

"If you think you have the time, or the game worth the candle," replied the other, with a shrug.

"One would suppose you were never at the pains to observe her," said Ballantrae.

"I am not very observant," said Balmile. "She seems comely."

"You very dear and dull dog!" cried Ballantrae; "chastity is the most besotting of the virtues. Why, she has a look in her face beyond singing! I believe, if you were to push me hard, I might trace it home to a trifle of a squint. What matters? The height of beauty is in the touch that's wrong, that's the modulation in a tune. 'Tis the devil we all love; I owe many a conquest to my mole"—he touched it as he spoke with a smile, and his eyes glittered; "we are all hunchbacks, and beauty is only that kind of deformity that I happen to admire. But come! Because you are chaste, for which I am sure I pay you my respects, that is no reason why you should be blind. Look at her, look at the delicious nose of her, look at her cheek, look at her ear, look at her hand and wrist—look at the whole baggage from heels to crown, and tell me if she wouldn't melt on a man's tongue."

As Ballantrae spoke, half jesting, half enthusiastic, Balmile was constrained to do as he was bidden. He looked at the woman, admired her excellences, and was at the same time ashamed for himself and his companion. So it befell that when Marie-Madeleine raised her eyes, she met those of the subject of her contemplations fixed directly on herself with a look that is unmistakable, the look of a person measuring and valuing another,—and, to clench the false impression, that his glance was instantly and guiltily withdrawn. The blood beat back upon her heart and leaped again; her obscure thoughts flashed clear before her; she flew in fancy straight to his arms like a wanton, and fled again on the instant like a nymph. And at that moment there chanced an interruption, which not only spared her embarrassment, but set the last consecration on her now articulate love.

Into the wine-shop there came a French gentleman,

arrayed in the last refinement of the fashion, though a
little tumbled by his passage in the wind. It was to be
judged he had come from the same formal gathering at
which the others had preceded him ; and perhaps that he
had gone there in the hope to meet with them, for he came
up to Ballantrae with unceremonious eagerness.

"At last, here you are !" he cried in French. " I
thought I was to miss you altogether."

The Scotsmen rose, and Ballantrae, after the first
greetings, laid his hand on his companion's shoulder.

" My Lord," said he, " allow me to present to you one
of my best friends and one of our best soldiers, the Lord
Viscount Gladsmuir."

The two bowed with the elaborate elegance of the
period.

" *Monseigneur,*" said Balmile, " *je n'ai pas la prétention
de m'affubler d'un titre que la mauvaise fortune de mon roi
ne me permet pas de porter comme il sied. Je m'appelle,
pour vous servir, Blair de Balmile tout court.*" (" My
Lord, I have not the effrontery to cumber myself with a
title which the ill fortunes of my king will not suffer me
to bear the way it should be. I call myself, at your
service, plain Blair of Balmile.")

" *Monsieur le Vicomte ou Monsieur Blèr' de Balmaîl,*"
replied the new-comer, " *le nom n'y fait rien, et l'on con-
naît vos beaux faits.*" (" The name matters nothing ;
your gallant actions are known.")

A few more ceremonies, and these three, sitting down
together to the table, called for wine. It was the happiness of Marie-Madeleine to wait unobserved upon the
prince of her desires. She poured the wine, he drank of
it ; and that link between them seemed to her, for the
moment, close as a caress. Though they lowered their
tones, she surprised great names passing in their conversation, names of kings, the names of de Gesvre and
Belle-Isle ; and the man who dealt in these high matters,
and she who was now coupled with him in her own
thoughts, seemed to swim in mid-air in a transfiguration.
Love is a crude core, but it has singular and far-reaching

fringes ; in that passionate attraction for the stranger that now swayed and mastered her, his harsh incomprehensible language and these names of grandees in his talk, were each an element.

The Frenchman stayed not long, but it was plain he left behind him matter of much interest to his companions ; they spoke together earnestly, their heads down, the woman of the wine-shop totally forgotten ; and they were still so occupied when Paradou returned.

This man's love was unsleeping. The even bluster of the mistral, with which he had been combating some hours, had not suspended, though it had embittered, that predominant passion. His first look was for his wife, a look of hope and suspicion, menace and humility and love, that made the over-blooming brute appear for the moment almost beautiful. She returned his glance, at first as though she knew him not, then with a swiftly waxing coldness of intent ; and at last, without changing their direction, she had closed her eyes.

There passed across her mind during that period much that Paradou could not have understood had it been told to him in words : chiefly the sense of an enlightening contrast betwixt the man who talked of kings and the man who kept a wine-shop, betwixt the love she yearned for and that to which she had been long exposed like a victim bound upon the altar. There swelled upon her, swifter than the Rhone, a tide of abhorrence and disgust. She had succumbed to the monster, humbling herself below animals ; and now she loved a hero, aspiring to the semi-divine. It was in the pang of that humiliating thought that she had closed her eyes.

Paradou—quick, as beasts are quick, to translate silence —felt the insult through his blood ; his inarticulate soul bellowed within him for revenge. He glanced about the shop. He saw the two indifferent gentlemen deep in talk, and passed them over : his fancy flying not so high. There was but one other present, a country lout who stood swallowing his wine, equally unobserved by all and unobserving ; to him he dealt a glance of murderous

M

suspicion and turned direct upon his wife. The wine-shop had lain hitherto, a space of shelter, the scene of a few ceremonial passages and some whispered conversation, in the howling river of the wind ; the clock had not yet ticked a score of times since Paradou's appearance ; and now, as he suddenly gave tongue, it seemed as though the mistral had entered at his heels.

"What ails you, woman ? " he cried, smiting on the counter.

"Nothing ails me," she replied. It was strange ; but she spoke and stood at that moment like a lady of degree, drawn upward by her aspirations.

"You speak to me, by God, as though you scorned me ! " cried the husband.

The man's passion was always formidable ; she had often looked on upon its violence with a thrill—it had been one ingredient in her fascination ; and she was now surprised to behold him, as from afar off, gesticulating but impotent. His fury might be dangerous like a torrent or a gust of wind, but it was inhuman ; it might be feared or braved, it should never be respected. And with that there came in her a sudden glow of courage and that readiness to die which attends so closely upon all strong passions.

"I do scorn you," she said.

"What is that ? " he cried.

"I scorn you," she repeated, smiling.

"You love another man ! " said he.

"With all my soul," was her reply.

The wine-seller roared aloud so that the house rang and shook with it.

"Is this the—— ? " he cried, using a foul word, common in the South ; and he seized the young countryman and dashed him to the ground. There he lay for the least interval of time insensible ; then fled from the house, the most terrified person in the county. The heavy measure had escaped from his hands, splashing the wine high upon the wall. Paradou caught it. "And you ? " he roared to his wife, giving her the same name in the feminine, and he aimed at her the deadly missile. She expected it, motionless, with radiant eyes.

But before it sped, Paradou was met by another adversary, and the unconscious rivals stood confronted. It was hard to say at that moment which appeared the more formidable. In Paradou, the whole muddy and truculent depths of the half-man were stirred to frenzy; the lust of destruction raged in him; there was not a feature in his face but it talked murder. Balmile had dropped his cloak; he shone out at once in his finery, and stood to his full stature; girt in mind and body; all his resources, all his temper, perfectly in command; in his face the light of battle. Neither spoke; there was no blow nor threat of one; it was war reduced to its last element, the spiritual; and the huge wine-seller slowly lowered his weapon. Balmile was a noble, he a commoner; Balmile exulted in an honourable cause. Paradou already perhaps began to be ashamed of his violence. Of a sudden, at least, the tortured brute turned and fled from the shop, in the footsteps of his former victim, to whose continued flight his reappearance added wings.

So soon as Balmile appeared between her husband and herself, Marie-Madeleine transferred to him her eyes. It might be her last moment, and she fed upon that face; reading there inimitable courage and illimitable valour to protect. And when the momentary peril was gone by, and the champion turned a little awkwardly towards her whom he had rescued, it was to meet, and quail before, a gaze of admiration more distinct than words. He bowed, he stammered, his words failed him; he who had crossed the floor a moment ago, like a young god, to smite, returned like one discomfited: got somehow to his place by the table, muffled himself again in his discarded cloak, and for a last touch of the ridiculous, seeking for anything to restore his countenance, drank of the wine before him, deep as a porter after a heavy lift. It was little wonder if Ballantrae, reading the scene with malevolent eyes, laughed out loud and brief, and drank with raised glass, "To the champion of the Fair."

Marie-Madeleine stood in her old place within the counter ; she disdained the mocking laughter ; it fell on her ears, but it did not reach her spirit. For her, the world of living persons was all resumed again into one pair, as in the days of Eden ; there was but the one end in life, the one hope before her, the one thing needful, the one thing possible,—to be his.

CHAPTER I

THE PRINCE

THAT same night there was in the city of Avignon a young man in distress of mind. Now he sat, now walked in a high apartment, full of draughts and shadows. A single candle made the darkness visible; and the light scarce sufficed to show upon the wall, where they had been recently and rudely nailed, a few miniatures and a copper medal of the young man's head. The same was being sold that year in London to admiring thousands. The original was fair; he had beautiful brown eyes, a beautiful bright open face; a little feminine, a little hard, a little weak; still full of the light of youth, but already beginning to be vulgarised; a sordid bloom come upon it, the lines coarsened with a touch of puffiness. He was dressed, as for a gala, in peach-colour and silver; his breast sparkled with stars and was bright with ribbons; for he had held a levee in the afternoon and received a distinguished personage incognito. Now he sat with a bowed head, now walked precipitately to and fro, now went and gazed from the uncurtained window, where the wind was still blowing, and the lights winked in the darkness.

The bells of Avignon rose into song as he was gazing; and the high notes and the deep tossed and drowned, boomed suddenly near or were suddenly swallowed up, in the current of the mistral. Tears sprang in the pale blue eyes; the expression of his face was changed to that of a more active misery; it seemed as if the voices of the bells reached and touched and pained him, in a waste of vacancy where even pain was welcome. Outside in the night they continued to sound on, swelling and fainting;

and the listener heard in his memory, as it were, their harmonies, joy-bells clashing in a northern city, and the acclamations of a multitude, the cries of battle, the gross voices of cannon, the stridor of an animated life. And then all died away, and he stood face to face with himself in the waste of vacancy, and a horror came upon his mind, and a faintness on his brain, such as seizes men upon the brink of cliffs.

On the table, by the side of the candle, stood a tray of glasses, a bottle, and a silver bell. He went thither swiftly, then his hand lowered first above the bell, then settled on the bottle. Slowly he filled a glass, slowly drank it out ; and, as a tide of animal warmth recomforted the recesses of his nature, stood there smiling at himself. He remembered he was young ; the funeral curtains rose, and he saw his life shine and broaden and flow out majestically, like a river sunward. The smile still on his lips, he lit a second candle, and a third ; a fire stood ready built in a chimney, he lit that also ; and the fir-cones and the gnarled olive billets were swift to break in flame and to crackle on the hearth, and the room brightened and enlarged about him like his hopes. To and fro, to and fro, he went, his hands lightly clasped, his breath deeply and pleasurably taken. Victory walked with him ; he marched to crowns and empires among shouting followers ; glory was his dress. And presently again the shadows closed upon the solitary. Under the gilt of flame and candle-light, the stone walls of the apartment showed down bare and cold ; behind the depicted triumph loomed up the actual failure : defeat, the long distress of the flight, exile, despair, broken followers, mourning faces, empty pockets, friends estranged. The memory of his father rose in his mind : he, too, estranged and defied ; despair sharpened into wrath. There was one who had led armies in the field, who had staked his life upon the family enterprise, a man of action and experience, of the open air, the camp, the court, the council-room ; and he was to accept direction from an old, pompous gentleman in a home in Italy, and buzzed about by priests ? A pretty king, if he had not a martial son to lean upon ! A king at all ?

"There was a weaver (of all people) joined me at St. Ninians ; he was more of a man than my papa ! " he thought. "I saw him lie doubled in his blood and a grenadier below him—and he died for my papa ! All died for him, or risked the dying, and I lay for him all those months in the rain and skulked in heather like a fox ; and now he writes me his advice ! calls me Carluccio—me, the man of the house, the only king in that king's race ! " He ground his teeth. "The only king in Europe ! Who else ? Who has done and suffered except me ? who has lain and run and hidden with his faithful subjects, like a second Bruce ? Not my accursed cousin, Louis of France, at least, the lewd effeminate traitor ! " And filling the glass to the brim, he drank a king's damnation. Ah, if he had the power of Louis, what a king were here !

The minutes followed each other into the past, and still he persevered in this debilitating cycle of emotions, still fed the fire of his excitement with driblets of Rhine wine ; a boy at odds with life, a boy with a spark of the heroic, which he was now burning out and drowning down in futile reverie and solitary excess.

From two rooms beyond, the sudden sound of a raised voice attracted him.

"By . . .

EDITORIAL NOTE

By Sir Sidney Colvin

THE first suggestion for the story of which the above is the opening was received by the author from Mr. Andrew Lang. It is mentioned in *Vailima Letters* under date January 3, 1892. Writing of the subject again on March 25 of the same year, Mr. Stevenson speculates on the title to be chosen and the turn the plot is to take; and later again, towards the end of May, announces that he has written the first " prologuial episode," that namely, which the reader has now before him. " There are only four characters," he observes : " Francis Blair of Balmile (Jacobite Lord Gladsmuir), my hero; the Master of Ballantrae ; Paradou, a wine-seller of Avignon ; Marie-Madeleine, his wife. These last two I am now done with, and I think they are successful, and I hope I have Balmile on his feet ; and the style seems to be found. It is a little charged and violent ; sins on the side of violence ; but I think will carry the tale. I think it is a good idea so to introduce my hero, being made love to by an episodic woman." If the reader will turn to the passage, he will find more about the intended developments of the story, which was to hinge on the rescue by the Prince of a young lady from a fire at an inn, and to bring back upon the scene not only the Master of Ballantrae, but one of the author's and his readers' favourite characters, Alan Breck. Mr. Lang has been good enough to furnish the following interesting notes as to its origin :

" The novel of *The Young Chevalier*," writes Mr. Lang, " of which only the fragment here given exists, was based on a suggestion of my own. But it is plain that Mr.

Stevenson's purpose differed widely from my crude idea. In reading the curious *Tales of the Century* (1847), by 'John Sobieski Holberg Stuart and Charles Edward Stuart,' I had been struck by a long essay on Prince Charles's mysterious incognito. Expelled from France after the treaty of Aix-la-Chapelle, His Royal Highness, in December, 1748, sought refuge in the papal city of Avignon, whence, annoyed by English remonstrances with the Vatican, he vanished in the last days of February, 1749. The Jacobite account of his secret adventures is given in a little romance, purporting to be a 'Letter from Henry Goring,' his equerry, brother of Sir Charles Goring. I had a transcript made from this rather scarce old pamphlet, and sent it to Mr. Stevenson, in Samoa. According to the pamphlet (which is perfectly untrustworthy) a mysterious stranger, probably meant for the Earl Marischal, came to Avignon. There came, too, an equally mysterious Scottish exile. Charles eloped in company with Henry Goring (which is true), joined the stranger, travelled to a place near Lyons, and thence to Strasbourg, which is probable. Here he rescued from a fire a lovely girl, travelling alone, and disdained to profit by her sudden passion for 'le Comte d'Espoir,' his travelling-name. Moving into Germany, he was attacked by assassins, headed by the second mysterious stranger, a Scottish spy; he performs prodigies of valour. He then visits foreign courts, Berlin being indicated, and wins the heart of a lady, probably the Princess Radziwill, whom he is to marry when his prospects improve. All or much of this is false. Charles really visited Paris, by way of Dijon, and Mme. de Talmont; thence he went to Venice. But the stories about Berlin and the Polish marriage were current at the time among bewildered diplomatists.[1]

"My idea was to make the narrator a young Scottish Jacobite at Avignon. He was to be sent by Charles to seek an actual hidden treasure—the fatal gold of the hoard buried at Loch Arkaig a few days after Culloden.

[1] The real facts, as far as known, are given in *Pickle the Spy*.—[A. L.]

He was to be a lover of Miss Clementina Walkinshaw, who later played the part of Beatrix Esmond to the Prince.

" Mr. Stevenson liked something in the notion, to which he refers in his *Vailima Letters.* He told me that Alan Breck and the Master of Ballantrae were to appear in the tale. I sent him such books about Avignon as I could collect, and he also made inquiries about Mandrin, the famous French brigand. Shortly before his death, I sent him transcripts of the unpublished letters of his old friend, James More Macgregor, and of Pickle the Spy, from the Pelham MSS. in the British Museum. But these, I think, arrived too late for his perusal. In Pickle he would have found some one not very unlike his Ballantrae. The fragment, as it stands, looks as if the Scottish assassin and the other mysterious stranger were not to appear, or not so early as one had supposed. The beautiful woman of the inn and her surly husband (Mandrin ?) were inventions of his own. Other projects superseded his interest in this tale, and deprived us of a fresh view of Alan Breck. His dates, as indicated in the fragment, are not exact ; and there is no reason to believe that Charles's house at Avignon (that of the de Rochefort family) was dismantled and comfortless, as here represented.

" Mr. Stevenson made, as was his habit, a list of chapter headings, which I unluckily did not keep. One, I remember, was ' Ballantrae to the Rescue,' of whom or of what did not appear. It is impossible to guess how the story would have finally shaped itself in his fancy. One naturally regrets what we have lost, however great the compensation in the works which took the place of the sketch. Our Prince Charles of romance must remain the Prince of *Waverley* and the King of *Redgauntlet.* No other hand now can paint him in the adventurous and mysterious years of 1749-59. Often, since Mr. Stevenson's death, in reading Jacobite MSS. unknown to me or to any one when the story was planned, I have thought, ' He could have done something with this,' or ' This would have interested him.' *Eheu !* "

SIDNEY COLVIN.

THE GREAT NORTH ROAD

THE GREAT NORTH ROAD

CHAPTER I

NANCE AT THE "GREEN DRAGON"

NANCE HOLDAWAY was on her knees before the fire, blowing the green wood that voluminously smoked upon the dogs, and only now and then shot forth a smothered flame; her knees already ached and her eyes smarted, for she had been some while at this ungrateful task, but her mind was gone far away to meet the coming stranger. Now she met him in the wood, now at the castle gate, now in the kitchen by candle-light; each fresh presentment eclipsed the one before; a form so elegant, manners so sedate, a countenance so brave and comely, a voice so winning and resolute—sure such a man was never seen! The thick-coming fancies poured and brightened in her head like the smoke and flames upon the hearth.

Presently the heavy foot of her Uncle Jonathan was heard upon the stair, and as he entered the room she bent the closer to her work. He glanced at the green fagots with a sneer, and looked askance at the bed and the white sheets, at the strip of carpet laid, like an island, on the great expanse of the stone floor, and at the broken glazing of the casement clumsily repaired with paper.

"Leave that fire a-be," he cried. "What, have I toiled all my life to turn innkeeper at the hind end? Leave it a-be, I say."

"La, uncle, it doesn't burn a bit; it only smokes," said Nance, looking up from her position.

" You are come of decent people on both sides," returned the old man. " Who are you to blow the coals for any Robin-run-agate ? Get up, get on your hood, make yourself useful, and be off to the ' Green Dragon.' "

" I thought you was to go yourself," Nance faltered.

" So did I," quoth Jonathan ; " but it appears I was mistook."

The very excess of her eagerness alarmed her, and she began to hang back. " I think I would rather not, dear uncle," she said. " Night is at hand, and I think, dear, I would rather not."

" Now you look here," replied Jonathan ; " I have my lord's orders, have I not ? Little he gives me, but it's all my livelihood. And do you fancy, if I disobey my lord, I'm likely to turn round for a lass like you ? No ; I've that hell-fire of pain in my old knee, I wouldn't walk a mile, not for King George upon his bended knees." And he walked to the window and looked down the steep scarp to where the river foamed in the bottom of the dell.

Nance stayed for no more bidding. In her own room, by the glimmer of the twilight, she washed her hands and pulled on her Sunday mittens ; adjusted her black hood, and tied a dozen times its cherry ribbons ; and in less than ten minutes, with a fluttering heart and excellently bright eyes, she passed forth under the arch and over the bridge, into the thickening shadows of the groves. A well-marked wheel-track conducted her. The wood, which upon both sides of the river dell was a mere scrambling thicket of hazel, hawthorn, and holly, boasted on the level of more considerable timber. Beeches came to a good growth, with here and there an oak ; and the track now passed under a high arcade of branches, and now ran under the open sky in glades. As the girl proceeded these glades became more frequent, the trees began again to decline in size, and the wood to degenerate into furzy coverts. Last of all there was a fringe of elders ; and beyond that the track came forth upon an open, rolling moorland, dotted with wind-bowed and scanty bushes, and all golden-brown with the winter, like a grouse. Right over against the girl the last red embers of the sunset burned under horizontal clouds; the night fell clear and still and frosty, and the track in low and marshy passages began to crackle underfoot with ice.

Some half a mile beyond the borders of the wood the lights of the "Green Dragon" hove in sight, and running close beside them, very faint in the dying dusk, the pale ribbon of the Great North Road. It was the back of the post-house that was presented to Nance Holdaway; and as she continued to draw near and the night to fall more completely, she became aware of an unusual brightness and bustle.

A post-chaise stood in the yard, its lamps already lighted: light shone hospitably in the windows and from the open door; moving lights and shadows testified to the activity of servants bearing lanterns. The clank of pails, the stamping of hoofs on the firm causeway, the jingle of harness, and, last of all, the energetic hissing of a groom, began to fall upon her ear. By the stir you would have thought the mail was at the door, but it was still too early in the night. The down mail was not due at the "Green Dragon" for hard upon an hour; the up mail from Scotland not before two in the black morning.

Nance entered the yard somewhat dazzled. Sam, the tall hostler, was polishing the curb-chain with sand; the lantern at his feet letting up spouts of candle-light through the holes with which its conical roof was peppered.

"Hey, miss," said he, jocularly, "you won't look at me any more, now you have gentry at the castle."

Her cheeks burned with anger.

"That's my lord's chay," the man continued, nodding at the chaise; "Lord Windermoor's. Came all in a fluster—dinner, bowl of punch, and put the horses to. For all the world like a runaway match, my dear—bar the bride. He brought Mr. Archer in the chay with him."

"Is that Holdaway?" cried the landlord from the lighted entry, where he stood shading his eyes.

"Only me, sir," answered Nance.

" O, you, Miss Nance," he said. " Well, come in quick, my pretty. My lord is waiting for your uncle."

And he ushered Nance into a room cased with yellow wainscot and lighted by tall candles, where two gentlemen sat at a table finishing a bowl of punch. One of these was stout, elderly, and irascible, with a face like a full moon, well dyed with liquor, thick tremulous lips, a short purple hand, in which he brandished a long pipe, and an abrupt and gobbling utterance. This was my Lord Windermoor. In his companion Nance beheld a younger man, tall, quiet, grave, demurely dressed, and wearing his own hair. Her glance but lighted on him, and she flushed, for in that second she made sure that she had twice betrayed herself—betrayed by the involuntary flash of her black eyes her secret impatience to behold this new companion, and, what was far worse, betrayed her disappointment in the realisation of her dreams. He, meanwhile, as if unconscious, continued to regard her with unmoved decorum.

" O, a man of wood," thought Nance.

" What—what ? " said his lordship. " Who is this ? "

" If you please, my lord, I am Holdaway's niece," replied Nance, with a curtsey.

" Should have been here himself," observed his lordship. " Well, you tell Holdaway that I'm aground ; not a stiver—not a stiver. I'm running for the beagles— going abroad, tell Holdaway. And he need look for no more wages : glad of 'em myself, if I could get 'em. He can live in the castle if he likes, or go to the devil. O, and here is Mr. Archer ; and I recommend him to take him in—a friend of mine—and Mr. Archer will pay, as I wrote. And I regard that in the light of a precious good thing for Holdaway, let me tell you, and a set-off against the wages."

" But O, my lord ! " cried Nance, " we live upon the wages, and what are we to do without ? "

" What am I to do ?—what am I to do ? " replied Lord Windermoor, with some exasperation. " I have no wages. And there is Mr. Archer. And if Holdaway

doesn't like it, he can go to the devil, and you with him !
—and you with him ! "

" And yet, my lord," said Mr. Archer, " these good
people will have as keen a sense of loss as you or I ; keener,
perhaps, since they have done nothing to deserve it."

" Deserve it ? " cried the peer. " What ? What ? If
a rascally highwayman comes up to me with a confounded
pistol, do you say that I've deserved it ? How often am
I to tell you, sir, that I was cheated—that I was cheated ? "

" You are happy in the belief," returned Mr. Archer,
gravely.

" Archer, you would be the death of me ! " exclaimed
his lordship. " You know you're drunk ; you know it,
sir ; and yet you can't get up a spark of animation."

" I have drunk fair, my lord," replied the younger
man ; " but I own I am conscious of no exhilaration."

" If you had as black a look-out as me, sir," cried the
peer, " you would be very glad of a little innocent exhilaration, let me tell you. I am glad of it—glad of it, and
I only wish I was drunker. For let me tell you it's a cruel
hard thing upon a man of my time of life and my position,
to be brought down to beggary because the world is full
of thieves and rascals—thieves and rascals. What ? For
all I know, you may be a thief and a rascal yourself ; and
I would fight you for a pinch of snuff—a pinch of snuff,"
exclaimed his lordship.

Here Mr. Archer turned to Nance Holdaway with a
pleasant smile, so full of sweetness, kindness, and composure that, at one bound, her dreams returned to her.

" My good Miss Holdaway," said he, " if you are willing
to show me the road, I am eager to be gone. As for his
lordship and myself, compose yourself ; there is no fear ;
this is his lordship's way."

" What ? What ? " cried his lordship. " My way ?
Ish no such a thing, my way."

" Come, my lord," cried Archer ; " you and I very
thoroughly understand each other ; and let me suggest, it
is time that both of us were gone. The mail will soon be
due. Here, then, my lord, I take my leave of you, with

N

the most earnest assurance of my gratitude for the past, and a sincere offer of any services I may be able to render in the future."

"Archer," exclaimed Lord Windermoor, "I love you like a son. Le' 's have another bowl."

"My lord, for both our sakes, you will excuse me," replied Mr. Archer. "We both require caution; we must both, for some while at least, avoid the chance of a pursuit."

"Archer," quoth his lordship, "this is a rank ingratishood. What? I'm to go firing away in the dark in the cold po'-chaise, and not so much as a game of écarté possible, unless I stop and play with the postillion—the postillion; and the whole country swarming with thieves and rascals and highwaymen."

"I beg your lordship's pardon," put in the landlord, who now appeared in the doorway to announce the chaise, 'but this part of the North Road is known for safety. There has not been a robbery, to call a robbery, this five years' time. Farther south, of course, it's nearer London, and another story," he added.

"Well, then, if that's so," concluded my lord, "le' 's have t' other bowl and a pack of cards."

"My lord, you forget," said Archer, "I might still gain, but it is hardly possible for me to lose."

"Think I'm a sharper?" inquired the peer. "Gen'leman's parole's all I ask."

But Mr. Archer was proof against these blandishments, and said farewell gravely enough to Lord Windermoor, shaking his hand and at the same time bowing very low. "You will never know," said he, "the service you have done me." And with that, and before my lord had finally taken up his meaning, he had slipped about the table, touched Nance lightly but imperiously on the arm, and left the room. In face of the outbreak of his lordship's lamentations, she made haste to follow the truant.

CHAPTER II

IN WHICH MR. ARCHER IS INSTALLED

THE chaise had been driven around to the front door ;
the courtyard lay all deserted, and only lit by a lantern
set upon a window-sill. Through this Nance rapidly
led the way, and began to ascend the swellings of the moor
with a heart that somewhat fluttered in her bosom. She
was not afraid, but in the course of these last passages
with Lord Windermoor Mr. Archer had ascended to that
pedestal on which her fancy waited to install him. The
reality, she felt, excelled her dreams, and this cold night
walk was the first romantic incident in her experience.

It was the rule in those days to see gentlemen unsteady
after dinner, yet Nance was both surprised and amused
when her companion, who had spoken so soberly, began
to stumble and waver by her side with the most airy
divagations. Sometimes he would get so close to her that
she must edge away ; and at others lurch clear out of the
track and plough among deep heather. His courtesy and
gravity meanwhile remained unaltered. He asked her how
far they had to go ; whether the way lay all upon the moorland, and when he learned they had to pass a wood expressed his pleasure. " For," said he, " I am passionately
fond of trees. Trees and fair lawns, if you consider of
it rightly, are the ornaments of nature, as palaces and fine
approaches——" And here he stumbled into a patch of
slough and nearly fell. The girl had hard work not to
laugh, but at heart she was lost in admiration for one who
talked so elegantly.

They had got to about a quarter of a mile from the
" Green Dragon," and were near the summit of the rise,
when a sudden rush of wheels arrested them. Turning

and looking back, they saw the post-house, now much declined in brightness ; and speeding away northward the two tremulous bright dots of my Lord Windermoor's chaise-lamps. Mr. Archer followed these yellow and unsteady stars until they dwindled into points and disappeared.

"There goes my only friend," he said. "Death has cut off those that loved me, and change of fortune estranged my flatterers ; and but for you, poor bankrupt, my life is as lonely as this moor."

The tone of his voice affected both of them. They stood there on the side of the moor, and became thrillingly conscious of the void waste of the night, without a feature for the eye, and except for the fainting whisper of the carriage-wheels without a murmur for the ear. And instantly, like a mockery, there broke out, very far away, but clear and jolly, the note of the mail-guard's horn. "Over the hills," was his air. It rose to the two watchers on the moor with the most cheerful sentiment of human company and travel, and at the same time in and around the "Green Dragon" it woke up a great bustle of lights running to and fro and clattering hoofs. Presently after, out of the darkness to southward, the mail drew near with a growing rumble. Its lamps were very large and bright, and threw their radiance forward in overlapping cones ; the four cantering horses swarmed and steamed ; the body of the coach followed like a great shadow ; and this lit picture slid with a sort of ineffectual swiftness over the black field of night, and was eclipsed by the buildings of the "Green Dragon."

Mr. Archer turned abruptly and resumed his former walk ; only that he was now more steady, kept better alongside his young conductor, and had fallen into a silence broken by sighs. Nance waxed very pitiful over his fate, contrasting an imaginary past of courts and great society, and perhaps the King himself, with the tumbledown ruin in a wood to which she was now conducting him.

"You must try, sir, to keep your spirits up," said she.

" To be sure, this is a great change for one like you ; but who knows the future ? "

Mr. Archer turned towards her in the darkness, and she could clearly perceive that he smiled upon her very kindly. " There spoke a sweet nature," said he, " and I must thank you for these words. But I would not have you fancy that I regret the past for any happiness found in it, or that I fear the simplicity and hardship of the country. I am a man that has been much tossed about in life ; now up, now down ; and do you think that I shall not be able to support what you support—you who are kind, and therefore know how to feel pain ; who are beautiful, and therefore hope ; who are young, and there-fore (or am I the more mistaken ?) discontented ? "

" Nay, sir, not that, at least," said Nance ; " not dis-contented. If I were to be discontented how should I look those that have real sorrows in the face ? I have faults enough, but not that fault ; and I have my merits too, for I have a good opinion of myself. But for beauty, I am not so simple but that I can tell a banter from a compliment."

" Nay, nay," said Mr. Archer, " I had half forgotten ; grief is selfish, and I was thinking of myself and not of you, or I had never blurted out so bold a piece of praise. 'Tis the best proof of my sincerity. But come, now, I would lay a wager you are no coward ? "

" Indeed, sir, I am not more afraid than another," said Nance. " None of my blood are given to fear."

" And you are honest ? " he returned.

" I will answer for that," said she.

" Well, then, to be brave, to be honest, to be kind, and to be contented, since you say you are so—is not that to fill up a great part of virtue ? "

" I fear you are but a flatterer," said Nance, but she did not say it clearly, for what with bewilderment and satisfaction, her heart was quite oppressed.

There could be no harm, certainly, in these grave com-pliments ; but yet they charmed and frightened her, and to find favour, for reasons however obscure, in the eyes of this elegant, serious, and most unfortunate young gentleman, was a giddy elevation, was almost an apotheosis, for a country maid.

But she was to be no more exercised; for Mr. Archer, disclaiming any thought of flattery, turned off to other subjects, and held her all through the wood in conversation, addressing her with an air of perfect sincerity, and listening to her answers with every mark of interest. Had open flattery continued, Nance would have soon found refuge in good sense; but the more subtle lure she could not suspect, much less avoid. It was the first time she had ever taken part in a conversation illuminated by any ideas. All was then true that she had heard and dreamed of gentlemen; they were a race apart, like deities knowing good and evil. And then there burst upon her soul a divine thought, hope's glorious sunrise: since she could understand, since it seemed that she too, even she, could interest this sorrowful Apollo, might she not learn? Or was she not learning? Would not her soul awake and put forth wings? Was she not, in fact, an enchanted princess, waiting but a touch to become royal? She saw herself transformed, radiantly attired, but in the most exquisite taste; her face grown longer and more refined; her tint etherealised; and she heard herself with delighted wonder talking like a book.

Meanwhile they had arrived at where the track comes out above the river dell, and saw in front of them the castle, faintly shadowed on the night, covering with its broken battlements a bold projection of the bank, and showing at the extreme end, where were the habitable tower and wing, some crevices of candle-light. Hence she called loudly upon her uncle, and he was seen to issue, lantern in hand, from the tower door, and, where the ruins did not intervene, to pick his way over the swarded courtyard, avoiding treacherous cellars and winding among blocks of fallen masonry. The arch of the great gate was still entire, flanked by two tottering bastions, and it was here that Jonathan met them, standing at the edge of the bridge, bent somewhat forward, and blinking at them through the glow of his own lantern. Mr. Archer greeted him with civility ; but the old man was in no humour of compliance. He guided the new-comer across the court-yard, looking sharply and quickly in his face, and grumbling all the time about the cold, and the discomfort and dilapida-tion of the castle.

He was sure he hoped that Mr. Archer would like it ; but in truth he could not think what brought him there. Doubtless he had a good reason—this with a look of cunning scrutiny—but, indeed, the place was quite unfit for any person of repute ; he himself was eaten up with the rheumatics. It was the most rheumaticky place in England, and, some fine day, the whole habitable part (to call it habitable) would fetch away bodily and go down the slope into the river. He had seen the cracks widen-ing ; there was a plaguy issue in the bank below ; he thought a spring was mining it ; it might be to-morrow, it might be next day ; but they were all sure of a come-down sooner or later. " And that is a poor death," said he, " for any one, let alone a gentleman, to have a whole old ruin dumped upon his belly. Have a care to your left there : these cellar vaults have all broke down, and the grass and the hemlock hide 'em. Well, sir, here is welcome to you, such as it is, and wishing you well away."

And with that Jonathan ushered his guest through the tower door, and down three steps on the left hand into the kitchen or common room of the castle. It was a huge, low room, as large as a meadow, occupying the whole width of the habitable wing, with six barred windows looking on the court, and two into the river valley. A dresser, a table, and a few chairs stood dotted here and there upon the uneven flags. Under the great chimney a good fire burned in an iron fire-basket ; a high old settle, rudely carved with figures and Gothic lettering, flanked it on either side ; there were a hinge table and a stone bench in the chimney corner, and above the arch hung guns, axes, lanterns, and great sheaves of rusty keys.

Jonathan looked about him, holding up the lantern, and shrugged his shoulders with a pitying grimace. " Here it is," he said. " See the damp on the floor, look at the moss ; where there's moss you may be sure that it's rheumaticky. Try and get near that fire for to warm yourself ; it'll blow the coat off your back. And with a young gentleman with a face like yours, as pale as a tallow candle, I'd be afeard of a churchyard cough and a galloping decline," said Jonathan, naming the maladies with gloomy gusto, " or the cold might strike and turn your blood," he added.

Mr. Archer fairly laughed. " My good Mr. Holdaway," said he, " I was born with that same tallow-candle face, and the only fear that you inspire me with is the fear that I intrude unwelcomely upon your private hours. But I think I can promise you that I am very little troublesome, and I am inclined to hope that the terms which I can offer may still pay you the derangement."

" Yes, the terms," said Jonathan, " I was thinking of that. As you say, they are very small," and he shook his head.

" Unhappily, I can afford no more," said Mr. Archer. " But this we have arranged already," he added with a certain stiffness ; " and as I am aware that Miss Holdaway has matter to communicate, I will, if you permit, retire at once. To-night I must bivouac ; to-morrow my trunk is to follow from the ' Dragon.' So, if you will show me to my room I shall wish you a good slumber and a better awakening."

Jonathan silently gave the lantern to Nance, and she, turning and curtseying in the doorway, proceeded to conduct their guest up the broad winding staircase of the tower. He followed with a very brooding face.

" Alas ! " cried Nance, as she entered the room, " your fire is black out," and setting down the lantern, she clapped upon her knees before the chimney and began to rearrange the charred and still smouldering remains. Mr. Archer looked about the gaunt apartment with a sort of shudder. The great height, the bare stone, the shattered windows, the aspect of the uncurtained bed, with one of its four fluted columns broken short, all struck a chill upon his fancy. From this dismal survey his eyes turned to Nance crouching before the fire, the candle in one hand and artfully puffing at the embers; the flames as they broke forth played upon the soft outline of her cheek—she was alive and young, coloured with the bright hues of life, and a woman. He looked upon her, softening; and then sat down and continued to admire the picture.

"There, sir," said she, getting upon her feet, "your fire is doing bravely now. Good night." He rose and held out his hand. "Come," said he, "you are my only friend in these parts, and you must shake hands."

She brushed her hand upon her skirt, and offered it, blushing.

"God bless you, my dear," said he.

And then, when he was alone, he opened one of the windows, and stared down into the dark valley. A gentle wimpling of the river among stones ascended to his ear; the trees upon the other bank stood very black against the sky; farther away an owl was hooting. It was dreary and cold, and as he turned back to the hearth and the fine glow of fire, "Heavens!" said he to himself, "what an unfortunate destiny is mine!"

He went to bed, but sleep only visited his pillow in uneasy snatches. Outbreaks of loud speech came up the staircase; he heard the old stones of the castle crack in the frosty night with sharp reverberations, and the bed complained under his tossings. Lastly, far on into the morning, he awakened from a doze to hear, very far off, in the extreme and breathless quiet, a wailing flourish on the horn. The down mail was drawing near to the "Green Dragon." He sat up in bed; the sound was tragical by distance, and the modulation appealed to his ear like human speech. It seemed to call upon him with a dreary insistence—to call him far away, to address him personally, and to have a meaning that he failed to seize. It was thus, at least, in this nodding castle, in a cold, miry woodland, and so far from men and society, that the traffic on the Great North Road spoke to him in the intervals of slumber.

CHAPTER III

JONATHAN HOLDAWAY

NANCE descended the tower stair, pausing at every step. She was in no hurry to confront her uncle with bad news, and she must dwell a little longer on the rich note of Mr. Archer's voice, the charm of his kind words, and the beauty of his manner and person. But, once at the stair-foot, she threw aside the spell and recovered her sensible and workaday self.

Jonathan was seated in the middle of the settle, a mug of ale beside him, in the attitude of one prepared for trouble ; but he did not speak, and suffered her to fetch her supper and eat of it, with a very excellent appetite, in silence. When she had done, she, too, drew a tankard of home-brewed, and came and planted herself in front of him upon the settle.

" Well ? " said Jonathan.

" My Lord has run away," said Nance.

" What ? " cried the old man.

" Abroad," she continued. " Run away from creditors. He said he had not a stiver, but he was drunk enough. He said you might live on in the castle, and Mr. Archer would pay you ; but you was to look for no more wages, since he would be glad of them himself."

Jonathan's face contracted ; the flush of a black, bilious anger mounted to the roots of his hair ; he gave an inarticulate cry, leapt upon his feet, and began rapidly pacing the stone floor. At first he kept his hands behind his back in a tight knot ; then he began to gesticulate as he turned.

" This man—this lord," he shouted, " who is he ? He was born with a gold spoon in his mouth, and I with a dirty straw. He rolled in his coach when he was a baby. I have dug and toiled and laboured since I was that high— that high." And he shouted again. "I'm bent and broke, and full of pains. D'ye think I don't know the taste of sweat? Many's the gallon I've drunk of it—ay, in the midwinter, toiling like a slave. All through, what has my life been? Bend, bend, bend my old creaking back till it would ache like breaking; wade about in the foul mire, never a dry stitch; empty belly, sore hands, hat off to my Lord Redface; kicks and ha'pence; and now, here, at the hind end, when I'm worn to my poor bones, a kick and done with it." He walked a little while in silence, and then, extending his hand, "Now, you Nance Hold- away," said he, "you come of my blood, and you're a good girl. When that man was a boy I used to carry his gun for him. I carried the gun all day on my two feet, and many a stitch I had, and chewed a bullet for. He rode upon a horse, with feathers in his hat, but it was him that had the shots and took the game home. Did I complain? Not I. I knew my station. What did I ask, but just the chance to live and die honest? Nance Holdaway, don't let them deny it to me—don't let them do it. I've been poor as Job, and honest as the day, but now, my girl, you mark these words of mine, I'm getting tired of it."

"I wouldn't say such words, at least," said Nance.

"You wouldn't?" said the old man, grimly. "Well, and did I when I was your age? Wait till your back's broke, and your hands tremble, and your eyes fail, and you're weary of the battle, and ask no more but to lie down in your bed and give the ghost up like an honest man; and then let there up and come some insolent, ungodly fellow—ah! if I had him in these hands! 'Where's my money that you gambled?' I should say. 'Where's my money that you drank and diced?' 'Thief!' is what I would say; 'thief!'" he roared, "'thief!'"

"Mr. Archer will hear you, if you don't take care," said Nance; "and I would be ashamed, for one, that he should hear a brave, old, honest hard-working man like Jonathan Holdaway talk nonsense like a boy."

"D'ye think I mind for Mr. Archer?" he cried shrilly, with a clack of laughter; and then he came close up to her, stooped down with his two palms upon his knees, and looked her in the eyes, with a strange hard expression, something like a smile. "Do I mind for God, my girl?" he said; "that's what it's come to be now, do I mind for God?"

"Uncle Jonathan," she said, getting up and taking him by the arm; "you sit down again, where you were sitting. There, sit still; I'll have no more of this; you'll do yourself a mischief. Come, take a drink of this good ale, and I'll warm a tankard for you. La, we'll pull through, you'll see. I'm young, as you say, and it's my turn to carry the bundle; and don't you worry your bile, or we'll have sickness, too, as well as sorrow."

"D'ye think that I'd forgotten you?" said Jonathan, with something like a groan; and thereupon his teeth clicked to, and he sat silent with the tankard in his hand and staring straight before him.

"Why," says Nance, setting on the ale to mull, "men are always children, they say, however old; and if ever I heard a thing like this, to set to and make yourself sick, just when the money's failing! Keep a good heart up; you haven't kept a good heart these seventy years, nigh hand, to break down about a pound or two. Here's this Mr. Archer come to lodge, that you disliked so much. Well, now you see it was a clear providence. Come, let's think upon our mercies. And here is the ale mulling lovely; smell of it; I'll take a drop myself, it smells so sweet. And, Uncle Jonathan, you let me say one word. You've lost more than money before now; you lost my aunt, and bore it like a man. Bear this."

His face once more contracted; his fist doubled, and shot forth into the air, and trembled. "Let them look out!" he shouted. "Here, I warn all men; I've done with this foul kennel of knaves. Let them look out."

"Hush, hush ! for pity's sake," cried Nance.

And then all of a sudden he dropped his face into his hands, and broke out with a great hiccoughing dry sob that was horrible to hear. "O," he cried, "my God, if my son hadn't left me, if my Dick was here ! " and the sobs shook him ; Nance sitting still and watching him, with distress. "O, if he were here to help his father ! " he went on again. "If I had a son like other fathers, he would save me now, when all is breaking down ; O, he would save me ! Ay, but where is he ? Raking taverns, a thief perhaps. My curse be on him ! " he added, rising again into wrath.

"Hush ! " cried Nance, springing to her feet : "your boy, your dead wife's boy—Aunt Susan's baby, that she loved — would you curse him ? O, God forbid ! "

The energy of her address surprised him from his mood. He looked upon her, tearless and confused. "Let me go to my bed," he said at last, and he rose and, shaking as with ague, but quite silent, lighted his candle, and left the kitchen.

Poor Nance ! the pleasant current of her dreams was all diverted. She beheld a golden city, where she aspired to dwell ; she had spoken with a deity, and had told herself that she might rise to be his equal ; and now the earthly ligaments that bound her down had been straitened. She was like a tree looking skyward, her roots were in the ground. It seemed to her a thing so coarse, so rustic, to be thus concerned about a loss in money ; when Mr. Archer, fallen from the sky-level of counts and nobles, faced his changed destiny with so immovable a courage. To weary of honesty ; that, at least, no one could do, but even to name it was already a disgrace ; and she beheld in fancy her uncle, and the young lad, all laced and feathered, hand upon hip, bestriding his small horse. The opposition seemed to perpetuate itself from generation to generation ; one side still doomed to the clumsy and the servile, the other born to beauty.

She thought of the golden zones in which gentlemen

were bred, and figured with so excellent a grace ; zones in which wisdom and smooth words, white linen and slim hands, were the mark of the desired inhabitants ; where low temptations were unknown, and honesty no virtue, but a thing as natural as breathing.

CHAPTER IV

MINGLING THREADS

IT was nearly seven before Mr. Archer left his apartment. On the landing he found another door beside his own, opening on a roofless corridor, and presently he was walking on the top of the ruins. On one hand he could look down a good depth into the green courtyard; on the other his eye roved along the downward course of the river, the wet woods all smoking, the shadows long and blue, the mists golden and rosy in the sun, here and there the water flashing across an obstacle. His heart expanded and softened to a grateful melancholy, and with his eye fixed upon the distance, and no thought of present danger, he continued to stroll along the elevated and treacherous promenade.

A terror-stricken cry rose to him from the courtyard. He looked down, and saw in a glimpse Nance standing below with hands clasped in horror and his own foot trembling on the margin of a gulf. He recoiled and leant against a pillar, quaking from head to foot, and covering his face with his hands; and Nance had time to run round by the stair and rejoin him where he stood before he had changed a line of his position.

" Ah ! " he cried, and clutched her wrist; " don't leave me. The place rocks; I have no head for altitudes."

" Sit down against that pillar," said Nance. " Don't you be afraid; I won't leave you; and don't look up or down : look straight at me. How white you are ! "

" The gulf," he said, and closed his eyes again and shuddered.

" Why," said Nance, " what a poor climber you must be ! That was where my cousin Dick used to get out of the castle after Uncle Jonathan had shut the gate. I've been down there myself with him helping me. I wouldn't try with you," she said, and laughed merrily.

The sound of her laughter was sincere and musical, and perhaps its beauty barbed the offence to Mr. Archer. The blood came into his face with a quick jet, and then left it paler than before. " It is a physical weakness," he said harshly, " and very droll, no doubt, but one that I can conquer on necessity. See, I am still shaking. Well, I advance to the battlements and look down. Show me your cousin's path."

" He would go sure-foot along that little ledge," said Nance, pointing as she spoke ; " then out through the breach and down by yonder buttress. It is easier coming back, of course, because you see where you are going. From the buttress-foot a sheep-walk goes along the scarp —see, you can follow it from here in the dry grass. And now, sir," she added, with a touch of womanly pity, " I would come away from here if I were you, for indeed you are not fit."

Sure enough, Mr. Archer's pallor and agitation had continued to increase ; his cheeks were deathly, his clenched fingers trembled pitifully. " The weakness is physical," he sighed, and had nearly fallen. Nance led him from the spot, and he was no sooner back in the tower stair, than he fell heavily against the wall and put his arm across his eyes. A cup of brandy had to be brought him before he could descend to breakfast ; and the perfection of Nance's dream was for the first time troubled.

Jonathan was waiting for them at table, with yellow, blood-shot eyes and a peculiar dusky complexion. He hardly waited till they found their seats, before, raising one hand, and stooping with his mouth above his plate, he put up a prayer for a blessing on the food and a spirit of gratitude in the eaters, and thereupon, and without more civility, fell to. But it was notable that he was no less speedily satisfied than he had been greedy to begin. He pushed his plate away and drummed upon the table. " These are silly prayers," said he, " that they teach us.

Eat and be thankful, that's no such wonder. Speak to me of starving—there's the touch. You're a man, they tell me, Mr. Archer, that has met with some reverses?"

"I have met with many," replied Mr. Archer.

"Ha!" said Jonathan, "none reckons but the last. Now, see; I tried to make this girl here understand me."

"Uncle," said Nance, "what should Mr. Archer care for your concerns? He hath troubles of his own, and came to be at peace, I think."

"I tried to make her understand me," repeated Jonathan, doggedly; "and now I'll try you. Do you think this world is fair?"

"Fair and false!" quoth Mr. Archer.

The old man laughed immoderately. "Good," said he; "very good. But what I mean is this: do you know what it is to get up early and go to bed late, and never take so much as a holiday but four; and one of these your own marriage day, and the other three the funerals of folk you loved, and all that, to have a quiet old age in shelter, and bread for your old belly, and a bed to lay your crazy bones upon, with a clear conscience?"

"Sir," said Mr. Archer, with an inclination of his head, "you portray a very brave existence."

"Well," continued Jonathan, "and in the end thieves deceive you, thieves rob and rook you, thieves turn you out in your old age and send you begging. What have you got for all your honesty? A fine return! You that might have stole scores of pounds, there you are out in the rain with your rheumatics!"

Mr. Archer had forgotten to eat; with his hand upon his chin he was studying the old man's countenance. "And you conclude?" he asked.

"Conclude!" cried Jonathan. "I conclude I'll be upsides with them."

"Ay," said the other, "we are all tempted to revenge."

"You have lost money?" asked Jonathan.

"A great estate," said Archer, quietly.

"See now!" says Jonathan, "and where is it?"

"Nay, I sometimes think that every one has had his

o

share of it but me," was the reply. "All England hath paid his taxes with my patrimony; I was a sheep that left my wool on every brier."

"And you sit down under that?" cried the old man. "Come now, Mr. Archer, you and me belong to different stations; and I know mine—no man better—but since we have both been rooked, and are both sore with it, why, here's my hand with a very good heart, and I ask for yours, and no offence, I hope."

"There is surely no offence, my friend," returned Mr. Archer, as they shook hands across the table; "for, believe me, my sympathies are quite acquired to you. This life is an arena where we fight with beasts; and, indeed," he added, sighing, "I sometimes marvel why we go down to it unarmed."

In the meanwhile, a creaking of ungreased axles had been heard descending through the wood; and presently after the door opened, and the tall hostler entered the kitchen carrying one end of Mr. Archer's trunks. The other was carried by an aged beggar man of that district, known and welcome for some twenty miles about under the name of "Old Cumberland." Each was soon perched upon a settle, with a cup of ale; and the hostler, who valued himself upon his affability, began to entertain the company, still with half an eye on Nance, to whom in gallant terms he expressly dedicated every sip of ale. First he told of the trouble they had to get his Lordship started in the chaise; and how he had dropped a rouleau of gold on the threshold, and the passage and door-step had been strewn with guinea-pieces. At this old Jonathan looked at Mr. Archer. Next the visitor turned to news of a more thrilling character: how the down mail had been stopped again near Grantham by three men on horseback—a white and two bays; how they had handkerchiefs on their faces; how Tom the guard's blunderbuss missed fire, but he swore he had winged one of them with a pistol; and how they had got clean away with seventy pounds in money, some valuable papers, and a watch or two.

"Brave, brave!" cried Jonathan, in ecstasy. "Seventy pounds! O, it's brave!"

"Well, I don't see the great bravery," observed the hostler, misapprehending him. "Three men, and you may call that three to one. I'll call it brave when some one stops the mail single-handed; that's a risk."

"And why should they hesitate?" inquired Mr. Archer. "The poor souls who are fallen to such a way of life, pray, what have they to lose? If they get the money, well; but if a ball should put them from their troubles, why, so better."

"Well, sir," said the hostler, "I believe you'll find they won't agree with you. They count on a good fling, you see; or who would risk it?—And here's my best respects to you, Miss Nance."

"And I forgot the part of cowardice," resumed Mr. Archer. "All men fear."

"O, surely not!" cried Nance.

"All men," reiterated Mr. Archer.

"Ay, that's a true word," observed Old Cumberland, "and a thief, anyway, for it's a coward's trade."

"But these fellows, now," said Jonathan, with a curious, appealing manner—"these fellows with their seventy pounds! Perhaps, Mr. Archer, they were no true thieves after all, but just people who had been robbed and tried to get their own again. What was that you said, about all England and the taxes? One takes, another gives; why, that's almost fair. If I've been rooked and robbed, and the coat taken off my back, I call it almost fair to take another's."

"Ask Old Cumberland," observed the hostler, "you ask Old Cumberland, Miss Nance!" and he bestowed a wink upon his favoured fair one.

"Why that?" asked Jonathan.

"He had his coat taken, ay, and his shirt too," returned the hostler.

"Is that so?" cried Jonathan, eagerly. "Was you robbed too?"

" That was I," replied Cumberland, " with a warrant ! I was a well-to-do man when I was young."

" Ay ! See that ! " says Jonathan. " And you don't long for a revenge ? "

" Eh ! Not me ! " answered the beggar. " It's too long ago. But if you'll give me another mug of your good ale, my pretty lady, I won't say no to that."

" And shalt have ! And shalt have ! " cried Jonathan ; " or brandy even, if you like it better."

And as Cumberland did like it better, and the hostler chimed in, the party pledged each other in a dram of brandy before separating.

As for Nance, she slipped forth into the ruins, partly to avoid the hostler's gallantries, partly to lament over the defects of Mr. Archer. Plainly, he was no hero. She pitied him ; she began to feel a protecting interest mingle with and almost supersede her admiration, and was at the same time disappointed and yet drawn to him. She was, indeed, conscious of such unshaken fortitude in her own heart, that she was almost tempted by an occasion to be bold for two. She saw herself, in a brave attitude, shielding her imperfect hero from the world ; and she saw, like a piece of Heaven, his gratitude for her protection.

CHAPTER V

LIFE IN THE CASTLE

FROM that day forth the life of these three persons in the ruins ran very smoothly. Mr. Archer now sat by the fire with a book, and now passed whole days abroad, returning late, dead weary. His manner was a mask; but it was half transparent; through the even tenor of his gravity and courtesy profound revolutions of feeling were betrayed, seasons of numb despair, of restlessness, of aching temper. For days he would say nothing beyond his usual courtesies and solemn compliments; and then, all of a sudden, some fine evening beside the kitchen fire, he would fall into a vein of elegant gossip, tell of strange and interesting events, the secrets of families, brave deeds of war, the miraculous discovery of crime, the visitations of the dead. Nance and her uncle would sit till the small hours with eyes wide open: Jonathan applauding the unexpected incidents with many a slap of his big hand: Nance, perhaps, more pleased with the narrator's eloquence and wise reflections. And then, again, days would follow of abstraction, of listless humming, of frequent apologies and long hours of silence. Once only, and then after a week of unrelieved melancholy, he went over to the "Green Dragon," spent the afternoon with the landlord and a bowl of punch, and returned as on the first night, devious in step, but courteous and unperturbed of speech.

If he seemed more natural and more at his ease, it was when he found Nance alone; and laying by some of his reserve, talked before her rather than to her of his destiny, character, and hopes. To Nance these interviews were but a doubtful privilege. At times he would seem to take a pleasure in her presence, to consult her gravely, to hear and discuss her counsels; at times even, but these were rare and brief, he would talk of herself, praise the qualities that she possessed, touch indulgently on her defects, and lend her books to read and even examine her upon her reading; but far more often he would fall into a half-unconsciousness, put her a question and then answer it himself, drop into the veiled tone of voice of one soliloquising, and leave her at last as though he had forgotten her existence. It was odd, too, that in all this random converse not a fact of his past life, and scarce a name, should ever cross his lips. A profound reserve kept watch upon his most unguarded moments. He spoke continually of himself, indeed, but still in enigmas; the veiled prophet of egoism.

The base of Nance's feelings for Mr. Archer was admiration as for a superior being; and with this, his treatment, consciously or not, accorded happily. When he forgot her, she took the blame upon herself. His formal politeness was so exquisite that this essential brutality stood excused. His compliments, besides, were always grave and rational; he would offer reason for his praise, convict her of merit, and thus disarm suspicion. Nay, and the very hours when he forgot and remembered her alternately could by the ardent fallacies of youth be read in the light of an attention. She might be far from his confidence; but still she was nearer it than any one. He might ignore her presence, but yet he sought it.

Moreover, she, upon her side, was conscious of one point of superiority. Beside this rather dismal, rather effeminate man, who recoiled from a worm, who grew giddy on the castle wall, who bore so helplessly the weight of his misfortunes, she felt herself a head and shoulders taller in cheerful and sterling courage. She could walk, head in air, along the most precarious rafter; her hand feared neither the grossness nor the harshness of life's web, but was thrust cheerfully, if need were, into the brier bush, and could take hold of any crawling horror. Ruin was mining the walls of her cottage, as already it had mined and subverted Mr. Archer's palace. Well, she faced it with a bright countenance and a busy hand. She had got some washing, some rough seamstress work from the "Green Dragon," and from another neighbour ten miles across the moor. At this she cheerfully laboured, and from that height she could afford to pity the useless talents and poor attitude of Mr. Archer. It did not change her admiration, but it made it bearable. He was above her in all ways; but she was above him in one. She kept it to herself, and hugged it. When, like all young creatures, she made long stories to justify, to nourish, and to forecast the course of her affection, it was this private superiority that made all rosy, that cut the knot, and that, at last, in some great situation, fetched to her knees the dazzling but imperfect hero. With this pretty exercise she beguiled the hours of labour, and consoled herself for Mr. Archer's bearing. Pity was her weapon and her weakness. To accept the loved one's faults, although it has an air of freedom, is to kiss the chain, and this pity it was which, lying nearer to her heart, lent the one element of true emotion to a fanciful and merely brain-sick love.

Thus it fell out one day that she had gone to the "Green Dragon" and brought back thence a letter to Mr. Archer. He, upon seeing it, winced like a man under the knife: pain, shame, sorrow, and the most trenchant edge of mortification cut into his heart and wrung the steady composure of his face.

"Dear heart! have you bad news?" she cried.

But he only replied by a gesture and fled to his room, and when, later on, she ventured to refer to it, he stopped her on the threshold, as if with words prepared beforehand. "There are some pains," said he, "too acute for consolation, or I would bring them to my kind consoler. Let the memory of that letter, if you please, be buried." And then as she continued to gaze at him, being, in spite of herself, pained by his elaborate phrase, doubtfully sincere in word and matter: "Let it be enough," he added haughtily, "that if this matter wring my heart, it doth not touch my conscience. I am a man, I would have you to know, who suffers undeservedly."

He had never spoken so directly : never with so con-vincing an emotion ; and her heart thrilled for him. She could have taken his pains and died for them with joy.

Meanwhile she was left without support. Jonathan now swore by his lodger, and lived for him. He was a fine talker. He knew the finest sight of stories ; he was a man and a gentleman, take him for all in all, and a per-fect credit to Old England. Such were the old man's declared sentiments, and sure enough he clung to Mr. Archer's side, hung upon his utterance when he spoke, and watched him with unwearying interest when he was silent. And yet his feeling was not clear ; in the partial wreck of his mind, which was leaning to decay, some after-thought was strongly present. As he gazed in Mr. Archer's face a sudden brightness would kindle in his rheumy eyes, his eyebrows would lift as with a sudden thought, his mouth would open as though to speak, and close again in silence. Once or twice he even called Mr. Archer mysteriously forth into the dark courtyard, took him by the button, and laid a demonstrative finger on his chest ; but there his ideas or his courage failed him ; he would shufflingly excuse himself and return to his position by the fire without a word of explanation. " The good man was growing old," said Mr. Archer, with a suspicion of a shrug. But the good man had his idea, and even when he was alone the name of Mr. Archer fell from his lips continually in the course of mumbled and gesticulative conversation.

CHAPTER VI

THE BAD HALF-CROWN

HOWEVER early Nance arose, and she was no slug-
gard, the old man, who had begun to outlive the
earthly habit of slumber, would usually have been
up long before, the fire would be burning brightly, and
she would see him wandering among the ruins, lantern
in hand, and talking assiduously to himself. One day,
however, after he had returned late from the market
town, she found that she had stolen a march upon that
indefatigable early riser. The kitchen was all blackness.
She crossed the castle-yard to the wood-cellar, her steps
printing the thick hoar-frost. A scathing breeze blew out
of the north-east and slowly carried a regiment of black
and tattered clouds over the face of heaven, which was
already kindled with the wild light of morning, but where
she walked, in shelter of the ruins, the flame of her candle
burned steady. The extreme cold smote upon her conscience. She could not bear to think this bitter business
fell usually to the lot of one so old as Jonathan, and made
desperate resolutions to be earlier in the future.

The fire was a good blaze before he entered, limping
dismally into the kitchen. "Nance," said he, "I be all
knotted up with the rheumatics ; will you rub me a bit ? "
She came and rubbed him where and how he bade her.
"This is a cruel thing that old age should be rheumaticky,"
said he. "When I was young I stood my turn of the
teethache like a man ! for why ? because it couldn't last
for ever ; but these rheumatics come to live and die with
you. Your aunt was took before the time came ; never
had an ache to mention. Now I lie all night in my single
bed and the blood never warms in me ; this knee of mine

it seems like lighted up with the rheumatics; it seems as though you could see to sew by it; and all the strings of my old body ache, as if devils was pulling 'em. Thank you kindly; that's someways easier now, but an old man, my dear, has little to look for; it's pain, pain, pain to the end of the business, and I'll never be rightly warm again till I get under the sod," he said, and looked down at her with a face so aged and weary that she had nearly wept.

"I lay awake all night," he continued; "I do so mostly, and a long walk kills me. Eh, deary me, to think that life should run to such a puddle! And I remember long syne when I was strong, and the blood all hot and good about me, and I loved to run, too—deary me, to run! Well, that's all by. You'd better pray to be took early, Nance, and not live on till you get to be like me, and are robbed in your grey old age, your cold, shivering, dark old age, that's like a winter's morning;" and he bitterly shuddered, spreading his hands before the fire.

"Come now," said Nance, "the more you say the less you'll like it, Uncle Jonathan; but if I were you I would be proud for to have lived all your days honest and beloved, and come near the end with your good name: isn't that a fine thing to be proud of? Mr. Archer was telling me in some strange land they used to run races each with a lighted candle, and the art was to keep the candle burning. Well, now, I thought that was like life: a man's good conscience is the flame he gets to carry, and if he comes to the winning-post with that still burning, why, take it how you will, the man's a hero—even if he was low-born like you and me."

"Did Mr. Archer tell you that?" asked Jonathan.

"No, dear," said she, "that's my own thought about it. He told me of the race. But see, now," she continued, putting on the porridge, "you say old age is a hard season, but so is youth. You're half out of the battle, I would say; you loved my aunt and got her, and buried her, and some of these days soon you'll go to meet her; and take her my love and tell her I tried to take good care of you; for so I do, Uncle Jonathan."

Jonathan struck with his fist upon the settle. " D' ye think I want to die, ye vixen ! " he shouted. " I want to live ten hundred years."

This was a mystery beyond Nance's penetration, and she stared in wonder as she made the porridge.

" I want to live," he continued, " I want to live and to grow rich. I want to drive my carriage and to dice in hells and see the ring, I do. Is this a life that I lived ? I want to be a rake, d' ye understand ? I want to know what things are like. I don't want to die like a blind kitten, and me seventy-six."

" O fie ! " said Nance.

The old man thrust out his jaw at her, with the grimace of an irreverent schoolboy. Upon that aged face it seemed a blasphemy. Then he took out of his bosom a long leather purse, and emptying its contents on the settle, began to count and recount the pieces, ringing and examining each, and suddenly he leapt like a young man. " What ! " he screamed. " Bad ? O Lord ! I'm robbed again ! " And falling on his knees before the settle he began to pour forth the most dreadful curses on the head of his deceiver. His eyes were shut, for to him this vile solemnity was prayer. He held up the bad half-crown in his right hand, as though he were displaying it to Heaven ; and what increased the horror of the scene, the curses he invoked were those whose efficacy he had tasted—old age and poverty, rheumatism and an ungrateful son. Nance listened appalled ; then she sprang forward and dragged down his arm and laid her hand upon his mouth.

" Whist ! " she cried. " Whist ye, for God's sake ! O my man, whist ye ! If Heaven were to hear ; if poor Aunt Susan were to hear ! Think, she may be listening." And with the histrionism of strong emotion she pointed to a corner of the kitchen.

His eyes followed her finger. He looked there for a little, thinking, blinking ; then he got stiffly to his feet and resumed his place upon the settle, the bad piece still in his hand. So he sat for some time, looking upon the half-crown, and now wondering to himself on the injustice and partiality of the law, now computing again and again the nature of his loss. So he was still sitting when Mr. Archer entered the kitchen. At this a light came into his face, and after some seconds of rumination he despatched Nance upon an errand.

"Mr. Archer," said he, as soon as they were alone together, "would you give me a guinea-piece for silver?"

"Why, sir, I believe I can," said Mr. Archer.

And the exchange was just effected when Nance re-entered the apartment. The blood shot into her face. "What's to do here?" she asked rudely.

"Nothing, my deary," said old Jonathan, with a touch of whine.

"What's to do?" she said again.

"Your uncle was but changing me a piece of gold," returned Mr. Archer.

"Let me see what he hath given you, Mr. Archer," replied the girl. "I had a bad piece, and I fear it is mixed up among the good."

"Well, well," replied Mr. Archer, smiling, "I must take the merchant's risk of it. The money is now mixed."

"I know my piece," quoth Nance. "Come, let me see your silver, Mr. Archer. If I have to get it by a theft I'll see that money," she cried.

"Nay, child, if you put as much passion to be honest as the world to steal, I must give way, though I betray myself," said Mr. Archer. "There it is as I received it."

Nance quickly found the bad half-crown. "Give him another," she said, looking Jonathan in the face; and when that had been done, she walked over to the chimney and flung the guilty piece into the reddest of the fire. Its base constituents began immediately to run; even as she watched it the disc crumpled, and the lineaments of the King became confused. Jonathan, who had followed close behind, beheld these changes from over her shoulder, and his face darkened sorely.

" Now," said she, " come back to table, and to-day it is I that shall say grace, as I used to do in the old times, day about with Dick "; and covering her eyes with one hand, " O Lord," said she, with deep emotion, " make us thankful ; and, O Lord, deliver us from evil ! For the love of the poor souls that watch for us in Heaven, O deliver us from evil ! "

CHAPTER VII

THE BLEACHING-GREEN

THE year moved on to March; and March, though it blew bitter keen from the North Sea, yet blinked kindly between whiles on the river dell. The mire dried up in the closest covert; life ran in the bare branches, and the air of the afternoon would be suddenly sweet with the fragrance of new grass.

Above and below the castle the river crooked like the letter "S." The lower loop was to the left, and embraced the high and steep projection which was crowned by the ruins; the upper loop enclosed a lawny promontory fringed by thorn and willow. It was easy to reach it from the castle side, for the river ran in this part very quietly among innumerable boulders and over dam-like walls of rock. The place was all enclosed, the wind a stranger, the turf smooth and solid; so it was chosen by Nance to be her bleaching-green.

One day she brought a bucketful of linen, and had but begun to wring and lay them out when Mr. Archer stepped from the thicket on the far side, drew very deliberately near, and sat down in silence on the grass. Nance looked up to greet him with a smile, but finding her smile was not returned, she fell into embarrassment and stuck the more busily to her employment. Man or woman, the whole world looks well at any work to which they are accustomed; but the girl was ashamed of what she did. She was ashamed, besides, of the sun-bonnet that so well became her, and ashamed of her bare arms, which were her greatest beauty.

"Nausicaä," said Mr. Archer, at last, "I find you like Nausicaä."

"And who was she?" asked Nance, and laughed in spite of herself, an empty and embarrassed laugh, that sounded in Mr. Archer's ears, indeed, like music, but to her own like the last grossness of rusticity.

"She was a princess of the Grecian islands," he replied. "A king, being shipwrecked, found her washing by the shore. Certainly I, too, was shipwrecked," he continued, plucking at the grass. "There was never a more desperate castaway—to fall from polite life, fortune, a shrine of honour, a grateful conscience, duties willingly taken up and faithfully discharged; and to fall to this—idleness, poverty, inutility, remorse." He seemed to have forgotten her presence, but here he remembered her again. "Nance," said he, "would you have a man sit down and suffer or rise up and strive?"

"Nay," she said. "I would always rather see him doing."

"Ha!" said Mr. Archer, "but yet you speak from an imperfect knowledge. Conceive a man damned to a choice of only evil—misconduct upon either side, not a fault behind him, and yet naught before him but this choice of sins. How would you say then?"

"I would say that he was much deceived, Mr. Archer," returned Nance. "I would say there was a third choice, and that the right one."

"I tell you," said Mr. Archer, "the man I have in view hath two ways open, and no more. One to wait, like a poor mewling baby, till Fate save or ruin him; the other to take his troubles in his hand, and to perish or be saved at once. It is no point of morals; both are wrong. Either way this step-child of Providence must fall; which shall he choose, by doing, or not doing?"

"Fall, then, is what I would say," replied Nance. "Fall where you will, but do it! For O, Mr. Archer," she continued, stooping to her work, "you that are good and kind and so wise, it doth sometimes go against my heart to see you live on here like a sheep in a turnip-field! If you were braver——" and here she paused, conscience-smitten.

"Do I, indeed, lack courage?" inquired Mr. Archer of himself. "Courage, the footstool of the virtues, upon which they stand? Courage, that a poor private carrying a musket has to spare of; that does not fail a weasel or a rat; that is a brutish faculty? I to fail there, I wonder? But what is courage, then? The constancy to endure oneself or to see others suffer? The itch of ill-advised activity—mere shuttle-wittedness—or to be still and patient? To inquire of the significance of words is to rob ourselves of what we seem to know, and yet, of all things, certainly to stand still is the least heroic Nance," he said, "did you ever hear of *Hamlet?* "

"Never," said Nance.

" 'Tis an old play," returned Mr. Archer, "and frequently enacted. This while I have been talking Hamlet. You must know this Hamlet was a Prince among the Danes," and he told her the play in a very good style, here and there quoting a verse or two with solemn emphasis.

"It is strange," said Nance; "he was then a very poor creature?"

"That was what he could not tell," said Mr. Archer. "Look at me; am I as poor a creature?"

She looked, and what she saw was the familiar thought of all her hours; the tall figure very plainly habited in black, the spotless ruffles, the slim hands; the long, well-shapen, serious, shaven face, the wide and somewhat thin-lipped mouth, the dark eyes that were so full of depth and change and colour. He was gazing at her with his brows a little knit, his chin upon one hand and that elbow resting on his knee.

"Ye look a man!" she cried, "ay, and should be a great one! The more shame to you to lie here idle like a dog before the fire."

"My fair Holdaway," quoth Mr. Archer, "you are much set on action. I cannot dig, to beg I am ashamed." He continued, looking at her with a half-absent fixity: " 'Tis a strange thing, certainly, that in my years of fortune I should never taste happiness, and now when I am broke, enjoy so much of it, for was I ever happier than to-day ? Was the grass softer, the stream pleasanter in sound, the air milder, the heart more at peace ? Why should I not sink ? To dig—why, after all, it should be easy. To take a mate, too ? Love is of all grades since Jupiter ; love fails to none ; and children——" but here he passed his hand suddenly over his eyes. " O fool and coward, fool and coward ! " he said bitterly ; " can you forget your fetters ? You did not know that I was fettered, Nance ? " he asked again, addressing her. But Nance was somewhat sore. " I know you keep talking," she said, and, turning half away from him, began to wring out a sheet across her shoulder. " I wonder you are not wearied of your voice. When the hands lie abed the tongue takes a walk."

Mr. Archer laughed unpleasantly, rose and moved to the water's edge. In this part the body of the river poured across a little narrow fell, ran some ten feet very smoothly over a bed of pebbles, then getting wind, as it were, of another shelf of rock which barred the channel, began, by imperceptible degrees, to separate towards either shore in dancing currents, and to leave the middle clear and stagnant. The set towards either side was nearly equal ; about one half of the whole water plunged on the side of the castle, through a narrow gullet ; about one half ran lipping past the margin of the green and slipped across a babbling rapid.

" Here," said Mr. Archer, after he had looked for some time at the fine and shifting demarcation of these currents, " come here and see me try my fortune."

" I am not like a man," said Nance ; " I have no time to waste."

" Come here," he said again. " I ask you seriously, Nance. We are not always childish when we seem so."

She drew a little nearer.

" Now," said he, " you see these two channels—choose one."

" I'll choose the nearest, to save time," said Nance.

" Well, that shall be for action," returned Mr. Archer. " And since I wish to have the odds against me, not only

P

the other channel but yon stagnant water in the midst shall be for lying still. You see this?" he continued, pulling up a withered rush, "I break it in three. I shall put each separately at the top of the upper fall, and according as they go by your way or by the other I shall guide my life."

"This is very silly," said Nance, with a movement of her shoulders.

"I do not think it so," said Mr. Archer.

"And then," she resumed, "if you are to try your fortune, why not evenly?"

"Nay," returned Mr. Archer, with a smile, "no man can put complete reliance in blind Fate; he must still cog the dice."

By this time he had got upon the rock beside the upper fall, and, bidding her look out, dropped a piece of rush into the middle of the intake. The rusty fragment was sucked at once over the fall, came up again far on the right hand, leaned ever more and more in the same direction, and disappeared under the hanging grasses on the castle side.

"One," said Mr. Archer, "one for standing still."

But the next launch had a different fate, and after hanging for a while about the edge of the stagnant water, steadily approached the bleaching-green and danced down the rapid under Nance's eyes.

"One for me," she cried with some exultation; and then she observed that Mr. Archer had grown pale, and was kneeling on the rock, with his hand raised like a person petrified. "Why," said she, "you do not mind it; do you?"

"Does a man not mind a throw of dice by which a fortune hangs?" said Mr. Archer, rather hoarsely. "And this is more than fortune. Nance, if you have any kindness for my fate, put up a prayer before I launch the next one."

"A prayer," she cried, "about a game like this? I would not be so heathen."

"Well," said he, "then without," and he closed his

eyes and dropped the piece of rush. This time there was no doubt. It went for the rapid as straight as any arrow.

"Action, then!" said Mr. Archer, getting to his feet; "and then God forgive us," he added, almost to himself.

"God forgive us, indeed," cried Nance, "for wasting the good daylight! But come, Mr. Archer, if I see you look so serious I shall begin to think you was in earnest."

"Nay," he said, turning upon her suddenly, with a full smile; "but is not this good advice? I have consulted God and demigod; the nymph of the river, and what I far more admire and trust, my blue-eyed Minerva. Both have said the same. My own heart was telling it already. Action, then, be mine; and into the deep sea with all this paralysing casuistry. I am happy to-day for the first time."

CHAPTER VIII

THE MAIL-GUARD

SOMEWHERE about two in the morning a squall had burst upon the castle, a clap of screaming wind that made the towers rock, and a copious drift of rain that streamed from the windows. The wind soon blew itself out, but the day broke cloudy and dripping, and when the little party assembled at breakfast, their humours appeared to have changed with the change of weather. Nance had been brooding on the scene at the river-side, applying it in various ways to her particular aspirations, and the result, which was hardly to her mind, had taken the colour out of her cheeks. Mr. Archer, too, was somewhat absent ; his thoughts were of a mingled strain ; and even upon his usually impassive countenance there were betrayed successive depths of depression and starts of exultation, which the girl translated in terms of her own hopes and fears. But Jonathan was the most altered : he was strangely silent, hardly passing a word, and watched Mr. Archer with an eager and furtive eye. It seemed as if the idea that had so long hovered before him had now taken a more solid shape, and, while it still attracted, somewhat alarmed his imagination.

At this rate, conversation languished into a silence which was only broken by the gentle and ghostly noises of the rain on the stone roof and about all that field of ruins ; and they were all relieved when the note of a man whistling and the sound of approaching footsteps in the grassy court announced a visitor. It was the hostler from the " Green Dragon " bringing a letter for Mr. Archer. Nance saw her hero's face contract and then relax again at the sight of it ; and she thought that she knew why, for the sprawl-

ing, gross black characters of the address were easily
distinguishable from the fine writing on the former letter
that had so much disturbed him. He opened it and began
to read ; while the hostler sat down to table with a pot
of ale and proceeded to make himself agreeable after his
fashion.

"Fine doings down our way, Miss Nance," said he.
"I haven't been abed this blessed night."

Nance expressed a polite interest, but her eye was on
Mr. Archer, who was reading his letter with a face of
such extreme indifference that she was tempted to suspect
him of assumption.

"Yes," continued the hostler, "not been the like of it
this fifteen years : the North Mail stopped at the three
stones."

Jonathan's cup was at his lip, but at this moment he
choked with a great splutter ; and Mr. Archer, as if startled
by the noise, made so sudden a movement that one corner
of the sheet tore off and stayed between his finger and
thumb. It was some little time before the old man was
sufficiently recovered to beg the hostler to go on, and
he still kept coughing and crying and rubbing his eyes.
Mr. Archer, on his side, laid the letter down, and putting
his hands in his pocket, listened gravely to the tale.

"Yes," resumed Sam, "the North Mail was stopped
by a single horseman ; dash my wig, but I admire him !
There were four insides and two out, and poor Tom
Oglethorpe, the guard. Tom showed himself a man ; let
fly his blunderbuss at him ; had him covered, too, and
could swear to that ; but the Captain never let on, up with
a pistol and fetched poor Tom a bullet through the body.
Tom, he squelched upon the seat, all over blood. Up
comes the Captain to the window. 'Oblige me,' says he,
'with what you have.' Would you believe it ? not a man
says cheep !—not them ! 'Thy hands over thy head.'
Four watches, rings, snuff-boxes, seven-and-forty pounds
overhead in gold. One Dicksee, a grazier, tries it on :
gives him a guinea. 'Beg your pardon,' says the Captain,
'I think too highly of you to take it at your hand. I

will not take less than ten from such a gentleman.' This Dicksee had his money in his stocking, but there was the pistol at his eye. Down he goes, offs with his stocking, and there was thirty golden guineas. 'Now,' says the Captain, 'you've tried it on with me, but I scorns the advantage. Ten, I said,' he says, 'and ten I take.' So, dash my buttons, I call that man a man ! " cried Sam, in cordial admiration.

" Well, and then ? " says Mr. Archer.

" Then," resumed Sam, " that old fat fagot Engleton, him as held the ribbons and drew up like a lamb when he was told to, picks up his cattle, and drives off again. Down they came to the 'Dragon,' all singing like as if they was scalded, and poor Tom saying nothing. You would 'a' thought they had all lost the King's crown to hear them. Down gets this Dicksee. 'Postmaster,' he says, taking him by the arm, 'this is a most abominable thing,' he says. Down gets a Major Clayton, and gets the old man by the other arm. 'We've been robbed,' he cries, 'robbed ! ' Down gets the others, and all round the old man telling their story, and what they had lost, and how they was all as good as ruined ; till at last old Engleton says, says he, 'How about Oglethorpe ? ' says he. 'Ay,' says the others, 'how about the guard ? ' Well, with that we bousted him down, as white as a rag and all blooded like a sop. I thought he was dead. Well, he ain't dead ; but he's dying, I fancy."

" Did you say four watches ? " said Jonathan.

" Four, I think. I wish it had been forty," cried Sam. " Such a party of soured herrings I never did see—not a man among them bar poor Tom. But us that are the servants on the road have all the risk and none of the profit."

" And this brave fellow," asked Mr. Archer, very quietly, " this Oglethorpe—how is he now ? "

" Well, sir, with my respects, I take it he has a hole bang through him," said Sam. " The doctor hasn't been yet. He'd 'a' been bright and early if it had been a passenger. But, doctor or no, I'll make a good guess that

Tom won't see to-morrow. He'll die on a Sunday, will poor Tom ; and they do say that's fortunate."

"Did Tom see him that did it ? " asked Jonathan.

"Well, he saw him," replied Sam, "but not to swear by. Said he was a very tall man, and very big, and had a 'andkerchief about his face, and a very quick shot, and sat his horse like a thorough gentleman, as he is."

"A gentleman ! " cried Nance. "The dirty knave ! "

"Well, I calls a man like that a gentleman," returned the hostler ; "that's what I mean by a gentleman."

"You don't know much of them, then," said Nance. "A gentleman would scorn to stoop to such a thing. I call my uncle a better gentleman than any thief."

"And you would be right," said Mr. Archer.

"How many snuff-boxes did he get ? " asked Jonathan.

"O, dang me if I know," said Sam ; "I didn't take an inventory."

"I will go back with you, if you please," said Mr. Archer. "I should like to see poor Oglethorpe. He has behaved well."

"At your service, sir," said Sam, jumping to his feet. "I dare to say a gentleman like you would not forget a poor fellow like Tom—no, nor a plain man like me, sir, that went without his sleep to nurse him. And excuse me, sir," added Sam, "you won't forget about the letter, neither ? "

"Surely not," said Mr. Archer.

Oglethorpe lay in a low bed, one of several in a long garret of the inn. The rain soaked in places through the roof and fell in minute drops ; there was but one small window ; the beds were occupied by servants, the air of the garret was both close and chilly. Mr. Archer's heart sank at the threshold to see a man lying perhaps mortally hurt in so poor a sick-room, and as he drew near the low bed he took his hat off. The guard was a big, blowsy, innocent-looking soul with a thick lip and a broad nose, comically turned up ; his cheeks were crimson, and when Mr. Archer laid a finger on his brow he found him burning with fever.

" I fear you suffer much," he said, with a catch in his voice, as he sat down on the bedside.

" I suppose I do, sir," returned Oglethorpe ; " it is main sore."

" I am used to wounds and wounded men," returned the visitor. " I have been in the wars and nursed brave fellows before now ; and, if you will suffer me, I propose to stay beside you till the doctor comes."

" It is very good of you, sir, I am sure," said Oglethorpe. " The trouble is they won't none of them let me drink."

" If you will not tell the doctor," said Mr. Archer, " I will give you some water. They say it is bad for a green wound, but in the Low Countries we all drank water when we found the chance, and I could never perceive we were the worse for it."

" Been wounded yourself, sir, perhaps ? " called Oglethorpe.

" Twice," said Mr. Archer, " and was as proud of these hurts as any lady of her bracelets. 'Tis a fine thing to smart for one's duty ; even in the pangs of it there is contentment."

" Ah, well ! " replied the guard, " if you've been shot yourself, that explains. But as for contentment, why, sir, you see, it smarts, as you say. And then, I have a good wife, you see, and a bit of a brat—a little thing, so high."

" Don't move," said Mr. Archer.

" No, sir, I will not, and thank you kindly," said Oglethorpe. " At York they are. A very good lass is my wife—far too good for me. And the little rascal—well, I don't know how to say it, but he sort of comes round you. If I were to go, sir, it would be hard on my poor girl—main hard on her ! "

" Ay, you must feel bitter hardly to the rogue that laid you here," said Mr. Archer.

" Why, no, sir, more against Engleton and the passengers," replied the guard. " He played his hand, if you come to look at it ; and I wish he had shot worse, or me better. And yet I'll go to my grave but what I covered him," he cried. "It looks like witchcraft. I'll go to my grave but what he was drove full of slugs like a pepper-box."

"Quietly," said Mr. Archer, "you must not excite yourself. These deceptions are very usual in war; the eye, in a moment of alert, is hardly to be trusted, and when the smoke blows away you see the man you fired at, taking aim, it may be, at yourself. You should observe, too, that you were in the dark night, and somewhat dazzled by the lamps, and that the sudden stopping of the mail had jolted you. In such circumstances a man may miss, ay, even with a blunderbuss, and no blame attach to his marksmanship." . . .

EDITORIAL NOTE

By Sir Sidney Colvin

THE Editor is unable to furnish any information as to the intended plot of the story which breaks off thus abruptly. From very early days Mr. Stevenson had purposed to write (since circumstances did not allow him to enact) a romance of the highway. The purpose seems to have ripened after his recovery from the acute attack of illness which interrupted his work from about Christmas, 1883, to September, 1884. The chapters here printed were written at Bournemouth soon after the latter date ; but neither Mr. Henley nor I, though we remember many conversations with the writer on highway themes in general, can recall the origin or intended course of this particular story. Its plot can hardly be forecast from these opening chapters ; nor do the writer's own words, in a letter written at the time to Mr. Henley, take us much further, except in so far as they show that it was growing under his hands to be a more serious effort than he first contemplated. "The Great North Road," he writes, "which I thought to rattle off, like Treasure Island, for coin, has turned into my most ambitious design, and will take piles of writing and thinking ; so that is what my highwayman has turned to ! The ways of Providence are inscrutable ! Mr. Archer and Jonathan Holdaway are both grand premier parts of unusual difficulty, and Nance and the Sergeant—the first very delicate, and the second demanding great geniality. I quail before the gale, but so help me, it shall be done. It is highly picturesque, most dramatic, and if it can be made, as human as man. Besides, it is a true *story*, and not, like *Otto*, one half story and one half play." Soon after the date of this letter the author laid aside the tale in order to finish for press the second half of *More New Arabian Nights—The Dynamiter*, and never took it up again.

THE STORY OF A RECLUSE

Printed here for the first time in a popular edition.

THE STORY OF A RECLUSE

MY father was the Rev. John Kirkwood of Edinburgh, a man very well known for the rigour of his life and the tenor of his pulpit ministrations. I might have sometimes been tempted to bless Providence for this honourable origin, had not I been forced so much more often to deplore the harshness of my nurture. I have no children of my own, or none that I saw fit to educate, so perhaps speak at random; yet it appears my father may have been too strict. In the matter of pocket-money, he gave me a pittance, insufficient for his son's position, and when, upon one occasion, I took the liberty to protest, he brought me up with this home thrust of inquiry: "Should I give you more, Jamie, will you promise me it shall be spent as I should wish?" I did not answer quickly, but when I did, it was truly: "No," said I. He gave an impatient jostle of his shoulders, and turned his face to the study fire, as though to hide his feelings from his son. To-day, however, they are very clear to me; and I know how he was one part delighted with my candour, and three parts revolted by the cynicism of my confession. I went from the room ere he had answered in any form of speech; and I went, I must acknowledge, in despair. I was then two and twenty years of age, a medical student of the University, already somewhat involved with debt, and already more or less (although I can scarce tell how) used to costly dissipations. I had a few shillings in my pocket; in a billiard room in St. Andrews Street I had shortly quadrupled this amount at pyramids, and the billiard room being almost next door to a betting agency, I staked the amount on the hazard of a race. At about five in the afternoon of the next day, I was the possessor of some thirty pounds—six times as much as I had ever dreamed of spending. I was not a bad young man, although a little loose. I may have been merry and lazy; until that cursed night I had never known what it was to be overpowered with drink; so it is possible I was overpowered the more completely. I have never clearly been aware of where I went or what I did, or of how long a time elapsed till my wakening. The night was dry, dark, and cold; the lamps and the clean pavements and bright stars delighted me; I went before me with a baseless exultation in my soul, singing, dancing, wavering in my gait with the most airy inconsequence, and all at once at the corner of a street, which I can still dimly recall, the light of my reason went out and the thread of memory was broken.

I came to myself in bed, whether it was that night or the next I have never known, only the thirty pounds were gone! I had certainly slept some while, for I was sober; it was not yet day, for I was aware through my half-closed eyelids of the light of a gas jet; and I had undressed, for I lay in linen. Some little time, my mind hung upon the brink of consciousness; and then, with a start of recollection, recalling the beastly state to which I had reduced myself, and my father's straitlaced opinions and conspicuous position, I sat suddenly up in bed. As I did so, some sort of hamper tore apart about my waist; I looked down and saw, instead of my night-shirt, a woman's chemise copiously laced about the sleeves and bosom. I sprang to my feet, turned, and saw myself in a cheval glass. The thing fell but a little lower than my knees; it was of a smooth and soft fabric; the lace very fine, the sleeves half way to my elbow. The room was of a piece; the table well supplied with necessaries of the toilet; female dresses hanging upon nails; a wardrobe of some light varnished wood against the wall; a foot bath in the corner. It was not my night-shirt; it was not my room; and yet by its shape and the position of the window, I saw it exactly corresponded with mine; and that the house in which I found myself must be the counterpart of my father's. On the floor in a heap lay my clothes as I had taken them off ; on the table my pass-key, which I perfectly recognised. The same architect, employing the same locksmith, had built two identical houses and had them fitted with identical locks ; in some drunken aberration I had mistaken the door, stumbled into the wrong house, mounted to the wrong room and sottishly gone to sleep in the bed of some young lady. I hurried into my clothes, quaking, and opened the door.

So far it was as I supposed ; the stair, the very paint was of the same design as at my father's, only instead of the cloistral quiet which was perennial at home, there rose up to my ears the sound of empty laughter and unsteady voices. I bent over the rail, and looking down and listening, when a door opened below, the voices reached me clearer. I heard more than one cry " good night " ; and with a natural instinct, I whipped back into the room I had just left and closed the door behind me.

A light step drew rapidly nearer on the stair ; fear took hold of me, lest I should be detected, and I had scarce slipped behind the door, when it opened and there entered a girl of about my own age, in evening dress, black of hair, her shoulders naked, a rose in her bosom. She paused as she came in, and sighed ; with her back still turned to me, she closed the door, moved towards the glass, and looked for a while very seriously at her own image. Once more she sighed, and as if with a sudden impatience, unclasped her bodice.

Up to that moment, I had not so much as formed a thought ; but then it seemed to me I was bound to interfere. " I beg your pardon——" I began, and paused.

She turned and faced me without a word ; bewilderment, growing surprise, a sudden anger, followed one another on her countenance. " What on earth——" she said, and paused too.

" Madam," I said, " for the love of God, make no mistake. I am no thief, and I give you my word I am a gentleman. I do not know where I am ; I have been vilely drunken—that is my paltry confession. It seems

Q

that your house is built like mine, that my pass-key opens your lock, and that your room is similarly situate to mine. How or when I came here, the Lord knows; but I awakened in your bed five minutes since—and here I am. It is ruin to me if I am found; if you can help me out, you will save a fellow from a dreadful mess; if you can't—or won't—God help me."

"I have never seen you before," she said. "You are none of Manton's friends."

"I never even heard of Manton," said I. "I tell you I don't know where I am. I thought I was in —— Street, No. 15 — Rev. Dr. Kirkwood's, that is my father."

"You are streets away from that," she said; "you are in the Grange, at Manton Jamieson's. You are not fooling me?"

I said I was not. "And I have torn your night-shirt," cried I.

She picked it up, and suddenly laughed, her brow for the first time becoming cleared of suspicion. "Well," she said, "this is not like a thief. But how could you have got in such a state?"

"Oh!" replied I, "the great affair is not to get in such a state again."

"We must get you smuggled out," said she. "Can you get out of the window?"

I went over and looked; it was too high. "Not from this window," I replied, "it will have to be the door."

"The trouble is that Manton's friends—" she began, "they play roulette and sometimes stay late; and the sooner you are gone, the better. Manton must not see you."

"For God's sake not!" I cried.

"I was not thinking of you in the least," she said; "I was thinking of myself."

ADVENTURES OF HENRY SHOVEL

To Sir Sidney Colvin early in 1891, Stevenson wrote: "I have a strange kind of novel under construction; it begins about 1660 and ends 1830, or perhaps I may continue it to 1875 or so, with another life. One, two, three, four, five, six generations, perhaps seven, figure therein; two of my old stories, 'Delafield' and 'Shovel,' are incorporated; it is to be told in the third person, with some of the brevity of history, some of the detail of romance. *The Shovels of Newton French* will be the name. The idea is an old one; it was brought to birth by an accident, a friend in the islands who picked up *F. Jenkin,* read a part, and said: 'Do you know, that's a strange book? I like it; I don't believe the public will; but I like it.' He thought it was a novel! 'Very well,' said I, 'we'll see whether the public will like it or not; they shall have the chance!'"

And in May of the same year to Charles Baxter: "*Henry Shovel* has now turned into a work called *The Shovels of Newton French: including Memories of Henry Shovel, a Private in the Peninsular War,* which work is to begin in 1664 with the marriage of Skipper, afterwards Alderman Shovel of Bristol, Henry's great-great-grandfather, and end about 1832 with his own second marriage to the daughter of his runaway aunt. Will the public ever stand such an opus? Gude kens, but it tickles me. Two or three historical personages will just appear: Judge Jeffreys, Wellington, Colquhoun, Grant, and I think Townsend the runner. I know the public won't like it; let 'em lump it then; I mean to make it good; it will be more like a saga."

ADVENTURES OF HENRY SHOVEL

CHAPTER I

THE beginning of my sorrows was that my father died before I was born, and that my mother lived till I was twelve years old. The death of the one was no doubt a severe loss ; but I am undutiful enough to imagine the survival of the other my chief misfortune. Before she died (which she did all in a moment, sitting in her chair by the fireside in the front parlour) she had so spoiled and petted me that I was the prince of children ; and as her income died along with her, I was left in the world without a circumstance to recommend me. My faults were my own, no doubt, and born with me as large as life, but that was no healthful education which let me grow to my thirteenth year without ever having felt the smart of a blow or the mortification of a reprimand, and so ignorant of our affairs that I supposed myself the heir to an estate.

The day of the funeral, the parson, Dr. Bryant, had me into the front parlour and explained the truth to me with an affectation of kindness, much greater than he felt or than I required. For whatever my faults, I was no coward. Indeed I had so ingrained a belief in my own parts that I was not the least dismayed. I knew there were two classes of great men, those born to greatness and those who achieved it by their merits. I had supposed myself to belong to the first, which was the more dignified, I found I belonged to the second, which was the more adventurous, and it is possible that I was even pleased   I stood there in an attitude, bowed prettily to my informant, and asked him what course he would advise me to pursue.

"For I am well aware, sir," said I, with perfect condescension, "what a value should be set on your opinion."

He looked at me with surprising irritation in his eye, and seemed to struggle for speech. Then he explained that he had written to my only kinsman, the Reverend Diggory Shovel; that Mr. Shovel would no doubt either come or write for me; that he was a gentleman of considerable means, being both squire and parson of his parish; that he would no doubt take charge of my education from henceforth, and if I continued to please might ultimately leave me his estate. "But there," added the doctor, "is the difficulty; and I must really impress upon you, my dear Henry, that your present manner is very ill-designed to conciliate interest. You must really strive to conceal your self-sufficiency. You must imitate other and simpler children who continue to be so much less offensive to their elders." And although he called me his dear Henry (which had never been his practice) his voice trembled with irritation as he spoke.

My kinsman came two days later in a chaise and four, and put up at the inn, where Dr. Bryant dined with him the same night and the pair consumed a prodigious quantity of port; the rumour of this exploit, which ran round the town, came early to our house, and was the first word I had of my relative. Presently after, Dr. Bryant arrived, as white as a candle and very black about the eyes; his voice, too, was faint and his talk interrupted with deep sighs. He told me my kinsman was a good churchman and a generous, open-hearted gentleman, and meant well by me. "But," said he, "you must give your attention to pleasing him. He is a very different person from the dear lady whose loss we have to lament, or indeed," said he, sighing, "from myself. I feel sure he would not like what he would call a milksop. He is a gentleman of a very hearty disposition." And with that he put his hand to his head, and both I and my mother's maid (who was in the room with us) supposed he would have fainted.

"Dear heart alive," cried the maid, "I fear your reverence is unwell." "It is a qualm," said he faintly. "I was up late upon a sermon. If you have a glass of wine, Mrs. Winslow, I would thank you." "Were you writing a sermon with Mr. Shovel?" I inquired; but he only scowled at me and as soon as Mrs. Winslow had filled a glass, took it with a tremulous hand and carried it greedily to his lips.

We had left the street door open on Dr. Bryant's entrance; and profiting by this, my kinsman came straight into the house, a tall portly figure of a man, with a very cheerful, ruddy countenance, gustatory lips, and a bold humorous black eye, that seemed to mock at his canonicals. He had no sooner caught sight of the doctor with his glass to his mouth, than he brought his staff to his shoulder like a gun and merrily took aim at his brother churchman. "Ha! ha!" he cried, "at it again!" And then turning to me and looking me all over with a jolly expression, "Well, sir," said he, "and how do you like your cousin, the parson?" and he clapped me on the shoulder with his large hand.

I remember telling him seriously that I trusted I should never be found failing in respect for one of his age and cloth; whereupon he laughed aloud, tasted the wine, over which he made a wry face, and told Dr. Bryant he would certainly lose his health if he drank such tipple. "Now, what we had last night," said he, "would never hurt an infant. But this, my good sir, this is bottled infirmity—gout sticks to the glass; besides which, the nasty stuff is corked. You see me the man I am; I must attribute it (under Providence of course) to a very conscientious choice in wines."

"Indeed, sir," said poor Dr. Bryant, "I am no judge and have no strength of stomach to experiment with."

"All the more reason to be careful, sir," returned my uncle, with a formidable gravity, and he read his brother divine a lecture upon wines and cellarage, in the midst of which the post-chaise drove to the door. Even as my things were carried out, even while Winslow was weeping and kissing me farewell, the lecture was continued ; and the last word I heard uttered in my native place was the name of a wine merchant, on whom Dr. Bryant was assured he might rely " up to a moderate price."

We travelled all that day seeing more country than I had supposed the world to contain ; so that, when evening came, it found me full of wonder that we had not got to an end of little England. But my chief surprise was in my uncle's character. We had lived very retired ; I had always been treated like a very serious child ; my mother, Winslow, Dr. Bryant, and the red-haired graduate from Durham who had taught me lessons, the few Methodistical ladies who drank tea with us on an occasion, all either held or affected melancholy views of life, were all discouragers of mirth, and, in every detail of manner and belief, the just antipodes of Uncle Diggory. He laughed much, and he sought to make me laugh ; when we stopped for a meal, he would drink wine with me and gravely invite my opinion of the bottle ; he gave me to understand he was a card player and had been to balls ; he spoke continually of field sports, and while we were on the road, he would be always spying for hares and partridges, which he would cover with his stick out of the chaise window and affect to bring down. Of Methodism, to which my mother was exceedingly inclined and even Dr. Bryant was thought to have a leaning, he spoke with a gravity of displeasure that embarrassed me ; for the derision of the unthinking I had been prepared, but not for serious and seemingly grounded condemnation ; and when I treated him (like that odious little beast, the pious child) to a specimen of my own proficiency in matters of religion, he took my breath away by his reproof : " Child," said he, " I will suffer no profanity " ; and he assumed (as he said so) an awful gravity of manner ; in this, and indeed in most things, it was plain that I displeased him exceedingly ; he was continually repeating that he must make a man of me, that he would have to make a man of me from the beginning, and words to the like purpose, which cut me to the quick, and presumably as a foundation, he entertained me with tales of his own youth, of broken heads and windows, orchard robberies, and a host of riotous misdeeds, at the bare mention of which I knew not where to look. I was the more surprised to find my father figuring in these conflicts, since my mother had always drawn him as a saint on earth impatient for release, and a model of propriety beyond my powers of imitation.

It would be hard to exaggerate my pain and wonder; I could have thought I was in a post-chaise with the devil. And yet all the while he was taking a position in my respect by his cheerfulness, his huge stature—a thing that counts for much with children, his liberality with the post-boys and his fine, commanding manner in the inns. I remembered making a journey with my mother, and how humble and fussy she had been, and could not doubt but that after all my uncle was a very great gentleman and must be partly in the right. And this opinion was the more struck into my mind when we paid by the way a visit to the deanery of the diocese, and were welcomed with respect, and Mr. Shovel was listened to like a man of weight; for with all her Methodism my mother had taught me a great reverence for the Church.

I had been taught by silly women and a silly clergyman. I supposed there were but two camps in the world; one of the perfectly pious and respectable, one of the perfectly profane, mundane, and vicious; one mostly on its knees and singing hymns, the other on the highroad to the gallows and the bottomless pit. Yet here was my uncle, a wine bibber, a card player, a sporting parson, a contemner of Methodists, an amateur of boxing; and he could reprove me for profanity; and would roll out family prayers in the presence (or rather to the back views) of near a score of servants, with a reverent unction that surprised me; and his sermons were to the full as dreary (though not quite so long) as Dr. Bryant's; and though his views were not the same as the doctor's he was equally intolerant of contradiction, a thing which I had always understood to be the mark of persons in the right. To complete the impression, he lived in a very fine house,

with lawns up to the windows, cut hollies, a park and a
fruit wall thirty feet high ; he was a magistrate and pro-
digiously severe on poachers ; ruled his house and his
parish with an authority, partly feudal, partly ecclesiastical,
striking his great staff and shooting out his lip, so that
the stoutest quaked before him ; and against profane
swearing and what he called " gross immorality," he was
even puritanic in his rigour. " No man shall take the
name of God in vain in my house. Take off that coat,"
I heard him say to an unfortunate footman before I had
been two days at Singleton St. Mary's ; and it was his
constant boast that there should be no " baggages " in his
parish. There was no doubt about it ; this man was not
merely vicious or merely worldly, and (twist language as
you please) not the devil himself could accuse him of
profanity ; so here, at the age of twelve, my first education
broke calamitously down. I gave up Methodism for a
tissue of nonsense, and followed Uncle Diggory instead
of Dr. Bryant.

But here comes my next misfortune. My uncle thought
a great deal of himself ; he recalled his own fire-and-
brimstone boyhood as a pattern of manliness ; and as he
had no children of his own, and had never lived with young
people since he came to man's estate, he had no idea how
much he might dislike the smell of brimstone in another.
Consequently, it was his own boyhood that he set before
me for a model ; whatever he had done, that was what a
boy ought to do ; to poach, to break windows, to raise
riots, to get and give black eyes, to be the pest of a neighbourhood and the curse of a house, such appeared to me,
as I digested his conversation, the whole duty of a boy.
Virtues he must have to be sure ; he must fear nothing,
he must tell no tales, he must never do anything that was
" un-English, sir—un-English." It seemed a very genial
creed ; and though I spied difficulties, though I could
never make out (for instance) why poaching was a jovial
escapade for the rector in his boyhood and a rank offence
against the constitution in the least of his parishioners, or
why he should boast of robbing orchards when he was

young and yet condemn the practice so unsparingly from the bench, yet I was led very early to adopt so much of it as I could understand for my guiding principle in life. Of the danger of this course, I was early warned by Mrs. Shovel. "The Doctor," said she, "talks a great deal of nonsense ; he is a perfect child, my dear ; and though he is very fond of you (as I am sure we all are) you must have sense for both, or this will end badly." This was all true ; the doctor had early learned to delight in my society, as I am sure I always did in his ; but he had no sense, and I had none, and the thing ended as badly as it could. I will not trouble the reader with the intermediate steps ; how I shook off, along with my Methodism, my parcel of my former good behaviour, and retained nothing of my original character, beyond its self-sufficiency ; how I grew an adept in every kind of field sport and riotous mischief ; how complaints began to arise from the whole parish, rich and poor, gentle and simple ; how my uncle called me in question and how I, with insolent ill-taste, instanced his own example in the past. Even the dreadful scene that followed upon that, need not delay us ; nor the still sodden day when I was brought to the house in custody (with a neighbour's compliments) as a detected poacher. I scarce like to think of what my uncle suffered, and they were only wayside episodes, not stages, in my history ; for in spite of one and all, I was still kept at home and still (in the intervals) used and regarded with the kindest and friendliest indulgence. My stay at Singleton St. Mary's came to an end upon what might seem a slighter provocation ; but was one that touched my uncle in his self-respect.

There came upon a visit in an evil day for me, a certain thin, precise, prosy little dignitary of the Church, whose name I must not mention, as he is still alive and holds a conspicuous post. He was no such great man in the days of which I write, but he held himself in much honour already ; and for some reason, so did my uncle. All growing creatures must have detested him by nature ; a monkey must have plucked his cassock, and a squirrel gibbered at the man as he went by ; and to me, as he was anxious to please my uncle, he made himself tenfold detestable, for to me he insisted on unbending. Whenever he found me alone, he would hem and put me through my pacings ; at table, he would interrupt the talk, bid me turn it into Latin, and jeer at me for the result in what he supposed to be pleasing raillery. Our taste in humour was so different, that I determined at length to treat him to a specimen of mine. I knew he walked every morning in the kitchen garden, bemusing to himself and repeating long passages of Homer ; as I believed, in the hope that some might overhear and admire his erudition. I determined he should have some apples for his Greek ; and the loft being at that time well supplied with rotten ones, I conveyed a good sheetful of the worst to the roof of the lean-to shed behind the fruit wall. There, in a very impregnable post, I set myself at a very early hour to await the scholar, with one of my village aides-de-camp, Billy Jervis by name, the blacksmith's son, a fellow pretty well known in the neighbourhood by the sound of his voice as his father leathered him ; Billy and I made each a pile of apples on the cope ; we had each one ready in his hand ; and as soon as the door opened we let fly.

It was certainly a most unfortunate event. My own apple hit the dignitary fully in the bosom. Billy's, not aimed so truly, passed over his shoulder, and struck no less a person than Dr. Shovel, who was accompanying his guest. We were down from the cope in an instant, rolled anyhow down the lean-to roof and took to flight (as the play books have it) severally ; Billy towards the plantation, where he ran into the arms of an under-gardener ; I, to go round by the back of the house and up to my bedroom, where I changed my dress and came down again with the best affectation of indifference I could assume. I met the footman on the stairs ; he brought me th Doctor's compliments, and a request that I should stay in my room till I was sent for ; by which I saw very plainly I had been recognised upon the wall, and must make my account for trouble. I was so used to that situation that

I went back to my room, whistling. Two hours after, I was summoned to the study, where my uncle read me the most furious lecture I had ever received, dwelling, first of all, on the rottenness of the missiles. "A nasty trick, sir, called an exploit, a dirty, nasty trick; a thing, sir, no gentleman would stoop to. I had to wash, sir. I had to wash myself; I was covered with nastiness. I do not dwell," he continued, with more dignity, "on the insult offered to me in the person of my guest, a gentleman and a churchman," giving to that last word a radiancy of distinction, "because he has himself asked me to pass it over. I will now call him in; and you shall apologise to him yourself in terms befitting your nasty, beastly, vile outrage, and" (with a return to dignity) "the character of the gentleman you have insulted." And before I could find words he had opened a door and my enemy stood before me.

I was never ready at apologies, to be asked for such a thing has always filled me with a raging sense of man's injustice; and though I would crush this down for one I loved, and had often done so for my uncle, to do so for a man I hated was beyond me. He came in with a smile, showing his bad teeth, which made one of the grounds of my distaste, and holding out his hand. I had been behaving well of late; my uncle and I had been on excellent terms; he had promised to carry me along with him to London, in a week or so, when I should see the play and the Houses of Parliament. If all this was in the water, whose was the fault, and I put my hands behind my back and anger swelled within me.

"Henry," cried my uncle, with a voice of surprise and pain, that he had almost conquered my ill-will, ay, and would have done it, I believe, with that, the bare naming of me; had not the other cut in with his detested voice. I do not doubt he meant kindly, but the mere sound of his speech turned me cold.

"I will apologise to you, sir," said I, "for I am sorry you were struck; but as for him, I meant to and I am glad I did."

My uncle sprang upon me, caught me by the shoulders, and flung me on my knees. " I slavishly beg your pardon, in the sight of God Almighty," he dictated. " Repeat those words, repeat them on your knees. I slavishly beg your pardon."

" For God's sake, my dear Shovel," said the guest, " let him go no further. Consider my position in your home."

" Consider mine, sir," retorted my uncle. " A guest insulted ; a gentleman, a dignitary of the Church, a guest of mine insulted in my garden," he cried, making the possessive pronouns ring. " Your position is nothing ! I will have an apology, a slavish apology, or he leaves my home."

I was in such a pickle of rage and spite, and soreness, for my uncle had thrown me down with a great deal of violence, that I was long past the point of any concession. " I will leave your house, then," said I ; " much I care ! "

Dr. Shovel turned as white as a sheet, he continued to look upon me without speech, till I could have fairly roared for pardon ; only the presence of my enemy sealed my lips.

" Return to your room," said he at last. And the next day, without having seen the face of any one except my aunt, I was packed off in a post-chaise to Mr. Bryce's school.

CHAPTER II

MR. BRYCE kept school at Long Dumbleton Green between Long Dumbleton itself and Dumbleton Parva, in the next county to Singleton St. Mary's. The hamlet was not above half a dozen roofs ; the "Seven Stars" pothouse, the blacksmith's shop, a few cottages with lollipops in the windows to attract us schoolboys, and on the opposite side of the green, beyond the sawpit and the duckpond, a good red brick house in a walled garden, which was Bryce's. The country around was all hill and dale ; the hollows enclosed and leafy with woods and orchards ; the hill-tops open and heathy where asses and horses browsed in droves, and gipsies camped among the hazels. So that there was no lack of delightful excursions, or of those shadows of adventure in which schoolboys so much delight and which they love to magnify in the retrospect.

Mr. Bryce was a diminutive grey-faced creature, with a ridiculous Scotch accent (I have always disliked that nation) and a manner of the most painful embarrassment. There is no denying he was a good scholar ; but a kitten was as fit to manage schoolboys. When he carried us abroad on our half-holiday walks it was our favourite sport to scatter after the manner of the Chouans, of whom there was much talk in those days, to every point of the compass ; so that he stood in the midst, quite deserted, not knowing which to pursue, weakly calling upon all of us and bewailing his ridiculous position. Henceforth we did what we pleased about the heaths or the orchards ; and Mr. Bryce went slowly homeward by himself. Only it was an understanding that he should wait for us, and that we should rejoin him at the entrance to the village ; how this grew up, it would be hard to say, but the cause of it was plain enough, for the whole party of us, and her husband in the front rank, stood in awe of Mrs. Bryce. If it had come to that lady's ears, that we roamed the country at will, she would certainly have found some means to put a stop to it ; the fear of which made the boys punctual ; and she would no less certainly have taken Mr. Bryce to task, and the fear of that made him patient at the rendezvous. Often have I found him, seated in the ditch like a man asleep, or pacing up and down by the wayside and talking (the poor soul) and smiling to himself, with the rain pouring down his back and the wet squelching in his shoes ; pleased enough, no doubt, to get off so cheaply and to have a few hours without his sworn tormentors. His face fell as we began to collect again from our excursions, and when at last there was enough of us together, and we dared to meet the eye of Mrs. Bryce, and set forth along the green for the red house, of all these returned truants I believe it was the master that regretted his truancy most sorely.

The same common fear of Mrs. Bryce, the same tacit understanding between her husband and his scholars, ruled us in class time. It was a case of give and take, he, on his part, would pass over every sort of petty disrespect ; we, on ours, granted him a certain proportion of work ; if either side failed in the bargain, a slight heightening of the voice whether in master or scholar would call in Mrs. Bryce from her own room which was close by, and there was an end of pleasure for all parties. Her presence was a check upon the boys, who respected her to the ground ; to her husband, it was the deadliest humiliation. Before her, who knew his true weakness, and before the boys, who were as good as his accomplices, he must then play the part of the disciplinarian, hectoring and threatening with the feeblest assumption of severity, and all the while blushing and wincing at a look. Poor devil, my heart bleeds for him at the recollection.

I could scarce have been placed, I believe, at a worse school. I was clever at my tasks ; clever and strong in all field sports ; the best boxer and by far the richest boy, for my uncle kept me well supplied with money. Bryce feared me, indeed he feared us all, from the least to the greatest; but me in particular, for a dozen of reasons, the least although the first of which was that he owed my uncle money. The boys looked up to me, as the first in class and the most daring in mischief out of school. Even Mrs. Bryce showed me unusual favour; partly, no doubt, in honour of the debt; partly because of my own account, for I believe I had the manners of a gentleman. I was always civil to her, and even to her husband perhaps less odiously rude than most of my companions. All this created for me a situation of singular preponderance. My companions vied with each other to obtain my favour. When we forecast our life in the great world without, I was to be the general, they my lieutenants, or I the minister and they members of my cabinet. None presumed to be my equal, a thing strange to think of now-a-days. Bainbridge Nivan was gazetted Admiral last month; Davis is a Q.C. Humphrey has commanded at Madras; and here am I writing my confessions in a little, dingy house near Sadler's Wells, contented enough, I thank God, and at this moment happy in the act of recollection, and at all moments happy in my family; but a man the most unknown perhaps in London, looking back on a career the least dignified; his own name of Shovel quite unheard of, and that other name under which he passed some years of his unfortunate youth, remembered (if it is remembered at all) for the sake of one morning's parade near Salamanca, and one conspicuous and unmerited disgrace.

I went home, of course, for the holidays; always with renewed delight in my uncle's company; but if the truth is to be told, both he and I used to separate again with satisfaction. Mr. Bryce was tinctured, like many Scots, with radical principles; he inclined towards French opinions, he had a sneaking admiration for Napoleon, and had once dined with Dr. Priestly. I promise you I would not tolerate any of these sentiments in his presence; and under my rough assaults, and with the fear lest something should leak out and come to the ears of the boys' parents

R

(which would have been the ruin of his school) he would make great haste to withdraw them. But for all that some of it stuck to me; and as I loved to be in opposition and to prove my superior talents, I would treat my uncle over his wine to a defence of the French Revolution, just as I would treat Mr. Bryce on a school holiday to the praise of Pitt and Coburg. My uncle was hurt to the quick; he wondered where I could have picked them up, for I was not the lad to tell tales upon my schoolmaster; he rated and baited and thundered upon me; ague drove him to the bottle, wine influenced his indigestion; and night after night he would reproach me with my lack of natural affection and common dignity, instancing, again and again, my heartless speech to himself and calling me cold-hearted to my friends and faithless to my native land. I cannot but smile, in the midst of my regret, when I think how I would pick up the hard words with which my uncle belaboured me, and when my turn came round, discharge them upon Mr. Bryce. It was my glory that I should see both sides; I seemed to myself to be engaged in a most worthy enterprise, when I encountered each in turn, and trod upon their prejudices. Vain old fools, I called them; and promised myself that I would enlarge their minds; but the great point was to parade the ndependence of my own

I came back to Mr. Bryce's for my last term in the year 1810, much against my will. For I was then eighteen years of age, and looked to be three and twenty, had used a razor for some time, learned all that Mr. Bryce was fit to teach me, and most properly desired to go at once to Oxford. But my uncle was on so ill terms with me upon the French Revolution, that he took this means to pay me off. There was a new boy at Bryce's; a little, pretty, clever, mean, ear-wigging creature, such as abound in schools. I can read him very clearly, looking back; but the truth is he was an ingenious flatterer, carried tales cleverly, and knew how to set a value on his servility to me by insolence to all besides and Mr. Bryce in the first rank. He came of a very good family; one of his uncles

was a duke, another a general with Lord Wellesley in the
Peninsula, and this was one of the strings on which he
played. We were the only two gentlemen in the school,
he said ; his people would never have let him come to the
place, if they had known the class of boys he would have to
associate with ; and indeed it was certain he would never
return. I must come and stay with him : the duke let
him invite whom he pleased to Bainbridge ; and what did
I say ? Why should I not give up the Church (to which
I was then destined) and go upon his uncle's staff in
Portugal. I confess honestly this turned my head. The
creature had no design but on my pocket and the lollipops
in the cottage windows ; and even if he had really liked
and wished to serve me, he most pitifully lacked the
means ; for the duke detested both him and his father,
and the general was of the same mind. But I let him
talk me quite over, put me on a coldness with many of
my old friends, and take possession of my mind. You
will hear how this weakness was the means of my
destruction.

Like many adroit people, whether young or old, my
familiar had a plentiful lack of brains. He could never say
his task, and as he added to incompetence a degree of disrespect unusual even in that insubordinate school, I think
Mr. Bryce had grown positively to hate him. To add to
his other qualities, he was an arrant coward ; and when
he found himself fallen into such disfavour he would be
sometimes seized with paroxysms of fear. " I know he
will beat me," he cried sometimes ; and I, with the noblest
feeling, reassured him. " He dare not," I told him. " I
will protect you."

One morning, the schoolmaster called him up. " Brown,"
said he (let me call my flatterer Brown, for he still lives
and has curried his way into a station of some note),
" Brown, come here."

" Yes, Bricey," said Brown.

This potty impertinence reached the master's ear, and
he fell (as he rarely did) into a passion.

" What is that ye said ? What name is that I *hard* ? "

said he, jumping from his chair, with his Scotch pronunciation much increased.

" Nothing, sir," said Brown.

" I heard ye, sir. I will not *toalerate* this *disrespact*," cried Mr. Bryce. " I will not be made a Merry-Andrew of in my own *skill*. I will make an example of ye, Brown." And he took up his ruler.

Brown ran back, as frightened as a wench, and cried to me by name to protect him.

I rose at once and stepped forward, glowing with a consciousness of my nobility.

" Let that little fellow alone, sir," said I. " The school will not allow it." He looked at me for a moment; and then his whole life of shame seemed to turn sour upon his memory at once, anger conquered cowardice, and though I was a foot taller in height, and twice his strength, he shut his eyes and ran upon me with the ruler. I put the blow aside with one hand, and struck him with the other; he went down like a nine-pin; and at the same moment, the door opened and Mrs. Bryce appeared.

She looked round her, saw what had happened, and without so much as speaking to her husband, who scrambled to his feet again, " Henry Shovel," she said, " come here." And she led the way into her own room. I had no thought of disobeying: as soon as the man's wife had appeared upon the scene, I had an illumination; I saw what I had done was mean and cowardly. I would have given my hand to recall the cowardly blow; and it was with shame burning in my cheeks that I followed her.

" Shut the door, Henry, and sit down," she said, very quietly, taking at the same time her own seat and leaning her elbows on the table where her work lay scattered.

" Mrs. Bryce," I began.

But she put up her hand. " Let me speak," she said. " What harm has Mr. Bryce done to you ? "

" None, Mrs. Bryce, I assure you," I answered.

" Have you ever found him unjust or cruel ? I am sure you have not ; I will speak for him myself. When you came here first you were still only a boy ; he might have thrashed you, had he pleased, and you deserved it often, Henry Shovel, did you not?"

"Mrs. Bryce, I did," cried I. "I know all this; I know, I feel, all that you can say."

"I am going to say it, though," said Mrs. Bryce. "I will not speak to you about gratitude, for that is a sentiment that is of no value when once it has been asked for. But I think you have the feelings of a gentleman; and I am going to speak to these. Mr. Bryce is a poor man; a very poor man; for my sake and the children's, with a courage that I wonder at, he continues to keep this school. I should have thought a person of your age would take a generous pleasure in helping him. The other boys look up to you; do not deceive yourself, Henry Shovel, it is for your pocket money more than for your virtues; still you have that influence, and I ask you how is it used? Not for the boys' good; not for mine or Mr. Bryce's. No, you are still quite a child, you like to play the first part in small rebellions that you know—O fie, Henry!—that you know to be quite safe, and you let toadying children, fresh out of the nursery, lead you by the nose. Well, it has come to a fine pass to-day. The question is, if Mr. Bryce must not give up his school; we all knew how unfitted he was for such a business from the first; how is he to continue it after this cruel—this public affront? You never thought of that, I suppose?"

"I never did, Mrs. Bryce," I cried in agony.

"And there is another thing you never thought about," she continued. "You know how much Mr. Bryce has taken at your hands; it was doubtless partly because you were a clever pupil, and he found less drudgery in teaching, but, Henry, Henry, you have heard of our debt to your uncle. He has been a generous creditor, a generous friend to us; you thought you had something commanding in your nature; 'Old Bryce dare not touch me!' you have said, I doubt not, often and often. And it was true he dared not; but yet, my poor boy, you were only trading on our gratitude to Dr. Shovel."

"O Mrs. Bryce, spare me another word," I cried.

" I know you ought to send me away ; and if you do, I give you my word of honour Dr. Shovel shall hear the truth. If I ask you to let me stay, it is only that I may prove my gratitude ; let me go into the schoolroom, I will make the most ample apology, and I promise on my word of honour, I will help him from this day forward."

" Can I trust you, Henry ? " she asked very gravely and very doubtfully.

" Mrs. Bryce, you said I was a gentleman," I pleaded. " I mean you said you thought I was one. O let me prove that you were right ; give me one chance to prove it. Indeed and indeed, I do respect you ; indeed I see my error ; only give me the chance ! "

" Well, Henry," she said, " I will try you."

She went into the schoolroom, where all this while the most perfect silence had continued to reign, and where (as I afterwards heard) the sound of my supplications had been listened to with awe.

" Henry Shovel has asked to be allowed to apologise, my dear," said Mrs. Bryce. I heard the master scrambling up from his chair. " He wishes to apologise in public," resumed his wife. " Will you give him one chance more ? I have been thinking perhaps as you are so kind, you would allow him to ; at his age, it might do him a real injury if he were sent away."

Mr. Bryce's answer was inaudible ; but it was sure he could not run counter to his wife in public : and the next moment she returned and motioned me to go into the schoolroom. It was an odd scene that I came back to ; boys and master, all with book in hand, affecting earnest study, all in reality racked with suspense and curiosity ; and it was almost painful to see the eyes dart at me from every corner, as I showed my tear-stained face in the doorway.

" Mr. Bryce," I said, " I have always shown myself a most ungrateful pupil ; but how I came to forget myself as I did this morning, I really cannot explain. I wish to apologise slavishly " (my uncle's word coming into my mind) " for my misconduct ; and if you will pass it over and give me another chance, it shall be my business to see that you have no ground for complaint in the future."

"Very well," said Mr. Bryce, " I will give you another chance." But he did not look at me, and I could see he had not forgiven, as indeed he never did forgive, my blow.

From that day, I began to play a new part in the school ; on which I have not the heart to expatiate. For I did indeed mean honourably well and if I failed it was for a want of tact that I can hardly wonder at in one so young and vain. I patronised and protected Mr. Bryce with the most florid chivalry ; I cumbered him with aid, I loaded him with my support ; I can see now how he must have chafed under my obtrusive powers, how I must have belittled and humbled the poor man, already so small and so inured to disrespect ; but at the time, upon my soul, I thought I was playing the most noble part, and when the end fell on me, it took me dead aback. I presume Mr. Bryce went to his wife, and declared he could no more endure it ; but the inner history of this revolution is of course beyond my knowledge ; all I can tell is the manner of its coming to my ears.

But I must tell first an incident that had a marked effect on my career. It was the habit of the older boys, in winter time when the afternoons were dark, to steal over to the " Seven Stars " and drink mulled ale, or what they now call Tom and Jerry, in the kitchen : not for the love of the liquor, which was very ill compounded, but for the sake of seeming to be men. Our talk, in consequence, was always pitched in a very brave key ; we discussed politics, we talked of the great world, we debated Russian history ; we felt ourselves to shine before the landlord ; and he, of course, flattered us to the top of our bent, and used to pretend he got much pleasure from our talk. I was there one afternoon with Davis and another of the big boys whose name I have forgotten ; but I daresay Mr. Davis will not have forgotten the scene. I was talking very big, as usual ; and perhaps talked the bigger because there was a guest in the chimney corner, a dry, humorous, rosy-looking man, with town-made clothes. I spoke of Oxford with contempt; it was too late, I said, to go there; I should regard it as a waste of time. "I tell you, Davis," said I, "most men lose time now-a-days: they begin the world too old. Look at Pitt; he was prime minister at twenty-one. Look at the luck of the French; getting a young general like Boney; see how he smashed up the old Austrian fribbles! Then look at our man, Wellesley; do you think we should hold our own in Portugal, if he was one of the usual dry old bucks that they put at the head of armies when they ought to be in bed? All the dash and go of youth is foozled away in what they call their educational establishments." A great deal more to this effect I said; and said it all the louder, and adduced the more historical illustrations, as I perceived the old gentleman in the chimney to be very sedulously giving ear. At last, as I had hoped, he addressed me.

"Young gentleman," said he, "do I understand rightly that you are an admirer of Buonaparte?"

I told him I was; so it proved was he: and for this once, as he was a stranger and I desired to make good my footing with him, I abounded in the sense of my interlocutor: going far beyond Mr. Bryce in liberal sentiments. The stranger, who said his name was Mr. Clarges, professed himself delighted with my company and stimulated by the daring of my views.

"I was a good deal struck," he said at length, "with something that fell from your lips when you first came in: something about young men and education. I doubt its soundness," says he and shook his head. "Youth has fire, no question of that, but youth, my dear sir, lacks sense."

I assured him he was in error; poor men were thrown early on the world, I reminded him, and often got on better than the rich; I instanced once again my list of historical instances; and to clinch the matter, "If I had a little money of my own," said I, "do you suppose, sir, I would waste my time at school or college? I know all that is wanted now; I can read and write, and I know how to use and where to find books: that is the whole of education, Mr. Clarges. And if I had a little money, I would begin my life to-morrow."

"I have no doubt of that," said he, and then seemed to ruminate. "Look here," he said at length, "how much money would you want?"

"I could begin on fifty pounds," cried I contemptuously.

"Well, I will advance the money," said he, "and make it guineas."

"Sir?" said I.

"O! No offence, Mr. Shovel," said he, "I regard the thing as an investment. See, here is my card; you can't refuse to keep that in civility; and if ever you want to adventure on the world, come to that address, and I'll risk my fifty pounds on your success. Good evening to you, sir; or as our friends the French would say—*au revoir!*" And he trotted out of the room, leaving his card upon the table before me.

"Samuel Clarges. For an admirer of General B's. 8 Gerard Street, Soho," I read. "Well, he is a rum customer, is Mr. Samuel Clarges: but mind you, he is a man of pretty sound political opinions; and I'll keep his card for that."

It was a little before teatime, and I had just returned from a walk, when Mrs. Bryce called me into her room; I saw she looked constrained, and feared that something might be wrong. "Henry," she said, "I do believe you have been trying to do better. I am sorry to tell you, you have failed." I said nothing, but the blood came hotly into my face, and I looked her in the eyes. "Yes," she went on, looking down, "I am very sorry, but we shall have to part."

"Do you mean that I am expelled," I said: "for nothing?"

"I would not use the word expelled," she returned; "but you are to leave this school where indeed you have been too long. Mr. Bryce will write to Dr. Shovel, explaining the affair, and I may tell you he will recommend that you should be sent at once to the University."

I stared straight at her in silence, until I saw the colour

begin to come into her face. " You will excuse my appearance at tea, madam," said I, and turning on my heel, I
left the house.

Here was a predicament for a lad of my inordinate
vanity : my favours thrown in my face ; my kindness
met with unpardonable insult ; I, the great disputant, the
grim man, expelled from a child's school, and sent home
to my uncle in disgrace. It was more than I could bear :
I could not face that shameful return to Singleton ; I had
not the courage. I determined, striding to and fro on
the dark heath, that I should cast myself at once on the
world : I had no money, but then I had the card of Mr.
Clarges ; I could walk, I could beg my way to London ;
once there, I was in fortune's vestibule ; if Clarges were
true to his fantastic offer, I had fifty guineas to begin
upon ; if he proved false, I had my talents, I had my physical
strength ; if the worst came to the worst, I could enlist.
So it was to be, I decided, sabring the bushes with my
stick. I would show them I was a man ; I would rise in
spite of them, in spite of my enemies, of the Bryces, of my
uncle. For by this time, they all seemed enemies to me :
the Bryces who were the authors, my uncle who was so
soon to hear of my disgrace. I would have started, then
and there, upon the London road ; but it was plain I could
not start upon an empty belly, and to appear before the
Bryces or my schoolmates, was what my vanity forbade.
I must wait there until all were abed ; they would not
shut me out, I judged ; they would leave me some supper ;
or if they did not, I could forage for myself in the kitchen
quarters : and once my hunger stayed—eastward ho for
London and the new life !

Past eleven at night, I ventured back : the door was
open, a light was left on the master's desk, and beside the
light a note from Mrs. Bryce to say I should find supper
in her room. It was kindly worded, but I rolled it up and
trod upon it.

By a most unfortunate circumstance the cold salt beef
and beer was laid for me at one end of the lady's table ;
at the other she had been working at her weekly bills, and

among the litter of papers, I spied three sovereigns and some silver. Two of these sovereigns and the change I put into my pocket, leaving a note in their place in these words :

" Madam,

" You could hardly expect me to return to my family after what has passed ; and I have taken the liberty to borrow from you the sum of two pounds eight shillings and sixpence. If you choose to regard this as a theft, it will be of a piece with the other misconstructions I have had to suffer in this place ; but the sum, such as it is, I will return from my earliest earnings ; and I can only trust the loan will put yourself and Mr. Bryce to no inconvenience. I am, madam, your most obedient, humble servant, Henry Shovel."

This letter cost me many a blush in the days immediately succeeding ; and when not so long ago I had the chance to read it once more at Mrs. Bryce's home, when I was on a visit, I could not wonder enough at its sufficiency and silliness. But at the time, it seemed to me both elegant and businesslike ; a fine first step in my career of life. And when I had sealed and directed it, I set forth out of Mr. Bryce's home in a glow of corroborated vanity.

CHAPTER III

WHAT with corroborated vanity, two pound eight and six in my pocket, a fine, firm, frosty road running downhill and ringing aloud under my active feet, the cold pure air of the night and the downs, and the blessed sense of the world's doors standing at last unbarred in front of me, I made my first stage to Long Dumbleton in the most cheerful spirits. The darkness was close; the night exceeding still; only the stroke of my own feet on the crackle of ice on the pools by way of sound: nothing but the ghosts of hedgerows for the sight. And yet all the while I saw, far in front of me, bright pictures of the future and the distance: of thronged London streets, and myself already moving there; of the House of Parliament, and myself upon my feet, enrapturing hearers; of manœuvring, myself in the saddle at the head; of pagoda'd Indian cities, with the red-coat troops of England lying close about them, waiting my signal to attack; the general hard by upon a hillock, surrounded by his staff, and that general myself. A little way out of Long Dumbleton I heard the bells of a waggon ringing in the night, and presently the bright spot of a waggoner's lantern hove in view. I found when he came up to me he was bound for Haverstock (or, as we called it, Hav'stock) Abbas, where he was due by daylight. It occurred to me at once, it would be a good plan to strike across country and make for London in a fresh direction; so I covenanted with the waggoner to get a cast for a few shillings, and took my place by his side, where I was excellently entertained all the first part of the night by my own thoughts, the jingling of the bells upon the harness, and the whistling of the driver himself, who had a note like a blackbird and knew an extraordinary variety of tunes. About three in the morning it had grown bitter cold, and I was stricken out of a drowsy state by the stoppage of the team, and the voice of the waggoner asking me if I would have some gruel. This was at the door of a hedge ale-house, where it soon appeared my companion was both known and trusted; for the people of the place, when he had roused them, by knocking on a window and crying his name, threw out the key to him with scarce a word; and he and I made an entrance into the kitchen, lent of the fine clean pewter, made ourselves gruel, left our money on the table, handed back the key into the window, and set off again upon our way without having seen the face of man or woman. We were now well warmed and wakened; and from thence until we got to Haverstock, my waggoner taught me tunes, the pair of us whistling together in the dark with great enjoyment.

At Haverstock, I said farewell to him, and had some eggs and bacon and a pot of tea by lantern light in the ostlers' room of the posthouse, for the front quarters were still closed. What I particularly remember, the paper had come down some hours before; a poor, decayed man, a drunkard who had been a schoolmaster, was there to read the news aloud to the stablemen for a dram of brandy, according to a standing bargain, and the chief item for the day was the news of Marshal Morsenci's retreat from before the lines to Santarcu. I took it for a cheerful omen that the time of my setting forth on life should be thus signalised by a triumph for the arms of my country.

On the next up-coach, I found a seat, travelled all day with continued delight in the motion and the changing scene, and continued joyful anticipations of the future, and about eight o'clock at night found myself in London. I was so anxious about Mr. Clarges that I did not even wait to sup, but leaving my bundle at the cellars where the coach stopped, inquired my way at once to Soho, marvelling as I went at the bright lights and the endless hubbub of the streets. The name was on the door; I knocked, a maid came, and when I asked if Mr. Clarges was at home, inquired my name.

"If you will show him this card, which he gave me by way of introduction," said I, "I believe it will serve better than a name."

And sure enough I was almost immediately introduced to a room in which Mr. Clarges and another gentleman with a mulberry face sat taking their wine.

"Well, well," said my friend; "and so here is my young radical, eh? Come for your money, have ye?"

The blood came into my face and I could have bitten my tongue when I found we were not to be alone; it seemed to me unpardonable grossness to refer to our arrangement in the presence of a stranger; but I had taken the money from Mrs. Bryce, I had sold my future, and I felt I must stand the shot of any discourtesy till I had my debt repaid. It was well I had made up my mind to this at once; else I should scarce have had the patience to support what followed, for Mr. Clarges told the mulberry-faced gentleman what had passed at Dumbleton with every detail of my schoolboy vanity and ostentation, and the mulberry-faced gentleman laughed until he must hold his sides. All the while both would glance at me, where I stood before them, for I was never asked to sit down, and at my glance they would burst out with fresh laughter.

"And so," said the stranger, wiping his eyes, "you took Sam for a philanthropist?"

"Not in the smallest, sir," said I, "I took him to be a whimsical person; there is no doubt he made that offer in derision; that was his jest, and no doubt a very good one at the time. For all that, the offer was made; here I am for the money; and that is my jest, and, I flatter myself, quite as good as his. Laugh on both sides, sir, and oblige me"; and with that, having plucked up my courage at the sound of my voice, I took a chair.

The man with the mulberry face was hugely amused. "No, really, Sammy," said he, "this is too much. O truly, this is too much." And he laughed again and again. "Here is a jest will cost you fifty guineas—O lud, O lud —and I have all the fun for nothing. I have not laughed so much this year." And he wiped his eyes again.

I wish I could have dared to join him in his laughter, but I was inwardly so tremulous with wrath that I feared I might betray myself. Yet I was bound I must prove myself unabashed ; and so now it occurred to me to pull my chair in to the table like a person quite at home.

" You might wait till you are asked," said Mr. Clarges, with an angry look.

" I must remind you," said I, " that I am here in your house by your own invitation ; I leave you to judge if you have set me an example of civility."

" No, really, Sammy," cried the laugher, in an ecstasy, "—no, really, I'll be damned if ever I heard the beat of this. You've caught a Tartar, Sam ; by jiggers, caught a Tartar. Now, sir," he said to me, " let me have the pleasure of a glass of wine—a glass of wine with you. I never knew Sammy so put down."

I could see Mr. Clarges was one of those who like a jest to be one-sided ; he was now pretty tired of the laughter he had been the first to provoke ; and to make an end of it, pulled out his cheque book and began to fill me up an order for fifty-two pound one.

" Order of whom ?" said he.

" Henry Shovel, if you please," said I.

" There," said he, " take it and go to the devil in your own way. It won't take you long."

I took the glass of wine which the other had poured out for me without the smallest hurry, conversing in the meanwhile of different matters ; then I rose, shook hands with the laughing gentleman, and bowing to Mr. Clarges, " I have your address, sir," said I, " and at my earliest convenience I shall repay this trifling advance."

As I went out the stout gentleman was still uproariously mirthful, but it did my heart good to see Mr. Clarges with his face upon one side. " I have put you down," thought I ; " and I have your money too ; which is now my battle horse to win the world upon." And that putting me in mind that I had now something considerable to lose, I stopped in the passage of the house, put my cheque in my pocket book, and buttoned that into an inner pocket

of my waistcoat. And then whistling and swinging my
stick I set forth on my return to the cellars.

Next day, I went first of all to the bank where I changed
my cheque, against one twenty, two tens and the rest in
gold ; thence about the streets to London Bridge, to the
Tower, and to St. Paul's, where I might see Nelson's
grave. There I met an ancient mariner who had been on
the quarter-deck of the *Victory* when the hero fell ; he was
so well gotten up and had his lesson so perfectly it cost
me a pint or two of ale before I had marked him out for
an impostor. This incident had a double effect : it increased my suspiciousness on the one hand, and my self-
confidence on the other ; so that I was more than ever
persuaded both that London was a den of thieves and I
was perfectly able to defend myself.

In this frame of mind, I returned to my inn for dinner,
and then under the arch I passed a very handsome, slender,
and elegantly dressed girl of perhaps my own age or a
little older, who gave me such a full flash of her dark eyes
that I could not but conclude she had been struck with
my appearance. I made not much account of this at the
time, though you may be sure I was not displeased ; but
when I came out into the court after my meal, and found
her there in the company of another elegant young lady,
and got another speaking stare, which sent a little thrill
through me, and had quite convinced myself that they
were both a trifle too elegant to be hanging round the
courtyard of an inn, I conceived it was due to my manhood to accost them. This I did with the most sickening
affectation of ease ; and found the new one very come-on,
but my first acquaintance rather inclined to silence, only
making play at me between times with her eyes. The
affable young lady told me they were new from the country,
which I directly disbelieved, and were staying in the inn
with their brother, who was a captain in the army. She
told me besides they were to have some friends at supper
that same evening ; and she dare sayed, since I was a
stranger like themselves, the brother would be glad to
invite me. " We did not come to London," said she,

" to be mewed up and I daresay no more did you." I was not the least deceived in the character of my acquaintances ; indeed, in my then humour, if I had met with the Dean of Westminster, I should probably have suspected him of a design upon my pocket ; but I had perfect confidence in myself ; had no fear of the supper party ; and when the silent girl, as they turned to leave me, stole her hand for the least instant on to my sleeve and with another full look at me whispered me to " Do come," I even made up my mind, if the invitation should be given to me, that I would accept it.

A man of the hotel was standing by. " You're in luck, sir," said he, with a wink. " That's a fine-looking piece, that dark-eyed one."

" If you'll take my advice," said another, " you'll keep clear of their supper. The captain was there when you were asking for the bank."

This warning settled me. " Thank you," said I drily, " I know the world pretty well."

About half an hour later there was a knock at the door of my room, and the captain appeared. He was a plausible enough looking fellow ; if there was any fault to be found with him, he was a shade too military in his manner, and suggested a corporal more closely than a captain : but he was profuse of fine words, treated me like a man of the world, confessed that this sort of invitation was an unusual sort of thing, and added openly enough, " We can drop the acquaintance on either side without offence, I hope. A meeting in an inn is like one on shipboard." These arts were quite thrown away upon me ; I diagnosed the man for an adventurer, just as I had known the girls were baggages ; and I accepted his supper with my eyes open.

Of course, and for excellent reasons, I regret the whole business ; but what I regretted, ay, and still regret with a perfect fury of penitence, was one particular oversight : I could still beat myself when I recall it. For in place of despatching the money I had stolen to Mrs. Bryce, what must I do, but go forth and waste my last hours of

s

opportunity strolling in the streets ? Very fine people I saw, and a very fine cane (like a true schoolboy) I took the occasion of buying with seven shillings of my money. It is true that I was not quite idle, for I visited a coffee house and read all the papers, spying for some chance of employment. There was nothing in my way, and this chilled me ; so that I returned to the inn seven shillings poorer, and about as many degrees lower in hope. But the dark eyes still ran in my mind, and I found my way at once, though it was still before the appointed time, to Captain Marcus's rooms.

They were two, one opening off another ; the first laid for supper, the other with a card table set out. The company consisted of the captain, his two sisters, and a certain Major Dicksee who could only have been a major in so far as it was a long time since he had been a minor and whom I was glad to see devote himself to the more lively of the girls. Indeed, the dark-eyed sister seemed to be surrendered to me ; and I soon found that she was a great fool, with not one word to say for herself, except to thank me burthensomely, for having come, and no idea of making herself agreeable beyond those same bold and languishing looks, by which she had first attracted me, and which, I feel sure, she must have been taught to deliver by some one with more sense. For all that she was very pretty, she seemed really to like me, and she reassured me by warning me not to take a hand at cards.

" Thanks," said I, " I never play with strangers."

" That's quite right," she said. " Then we can stay in here together."

And so when the other three went into the next apartment to play cards, a special bowl of punch was left in the supper room for me ; I have no doubt it was special in every sense, for I do not remember drinking much of it, till I woke up past noon of the next day, in my own room, whither, I presume, I had been carried by the Captain and the Major. I now found myself in possession of a most intolerable headache, my shirt, trousers, and shoes and my new cane, which, in a derision, they had thrust down the back of my neck. The rest of my clothes, my bundle and my money had all disappeared with the Marcuses. I had nothing to send to Mrs. Bryce, nothing to pay my bill with in the inn. Yet at the moment I was careless of these troubles ; what weighed upon me, then, was the shame of issuing forth in my shirt sleeves and bareheaded, and the fear (above all things) of encountering the man whose good advice I had neglected. I was sitting on my bedside, my burning face in my hands, and crushed by these concerns, when the door opened and the chambermaid came in.

" I beg your pardon, sir," said she. " I am sure I thought you was gone out long ago." And then suddenly : " But dear me, sir, what in the world has come to your bundle and your clothes ? " I could not answer ; I kept my face covered. " Ah," she resumed, " a pretty fool they've made of you, and serve you properly right too : a boy of your time of life going trolloping about with such dirty hussies. I'd be ashamed of myself if I was you ! And what are you going to do now, I should like to know ? You'll have to write to your friends, I suppose. A fine show-up ! You'll see with clear eyes the next time they let you come to London by yourself."

Now that my humiliation was fully disclosed to one person of that inn, I determined she should be the only one, lifted my face from my hands, saw she was a plain-looking soul, not so young as she had been, but no severer for that ; laid my whole miserable case before her, told her I had no friends, no hope, no wish but to get clear of that inn without derision ; and begged and pleaded with her to help me, telling her she had a sweet face, and kind eyes that gave me hope she would never refuse me, and even taking her hand in my eagerness.

" La, sir," said she, looking pretty well pleased and a little flushed, " there's no call to make such a matter. I am sure I am very sorry for you, though I cannot say but what it serves you right. But to be sure, it would be a pity if you was to go to prison for your bill."

So to make a long story short, she smuggled me down

the back stairs and let me out of the servants' entrance, advising me, as I shot out into the streets of London, to go home as fast as my feet could carry me. Years after, I found she had the amount of my bill stopped out of her wages ; but though I had inquiries made I never could find her, so there is a debt I shall owe to my dying day. Her name by the inn books was Emily Cartwright : I set it down here in gratitude. . . . [I return from the bank to put away my money ; then see the girl, so back to my room to wait and get the invitation, then out to coffee house where I see the old naval officer accused. " I declare to God I have bled for England." Tried to show his wound. Admiral Berkeley ; Admiral Keats. His kissing my hand when I had reassured him. Hunger, sir, hunger. Altogether 8 and twenty shillings.]

THE OWL

To Sir Sidney Colvin in May, 1893, Stevenson writes: "I might likely have some more stories soon: *The Owl, Death in the Pot, The Sleeper Awakened;* all these are possible. *The Owl* might be half as long; *The Sleeper Awakened,* ditto; *Death in the Pot* a deal shorter, I believe. Then there's *The Go-Between,* which is not impossible altogether. *The Owl, The Sleeper Awakened,* and *The Go-Between* end reasonably well; *Death in the Pot* is an ungodly massacre. O, well, *The Owl* only ends well in so far as some lovers come together, and nobody is killed at the moment, but you know they are all doomed, they are Chouan fellows."

The Owl was to be a Breton story of the Revolution; *Death in the Pot,* a tale of the Sta. Lucia mountains in California; the scene of *The Go-Between* was laid in the Pacific Islands; of *The Sleeper Awakened* we know nothing.

THE OWL

CHAPTER I

HE had no sooner quenched the light than all thought of sleep fled from him and he turned instead to the window of the room. Of the danger of his situation, repeated experiences had made him careless ; it served but as a relish to those extraordinary joys which he came so far, and risked so much, to taste and to renew. Once again he had seen her and she had smiled on him ; once again he was to sleep under the same roof with all that he held precious. On the impenetrable inky ground of night and forest, his eyes recreated the lamplit supper table and the speaking looks and gestures of his mistress ; through the profound silence, his ears still followed the melody of her voice.

How long he had stood there, looking upon dreams and marrying the past and future, himself could not have guessed ; when there arose, out of that gross blackness in which the castle, the garden, the inclosing forest and the whole face of night and nature were confounded, the sudden hooting of an owl. In the ears of one placed as he was, a republican officer sleeping under a disguise in the house of Croqueloup, no sound could be more ominous. To tell the true owl from the false that then hooted night by night in all the skirts of Brittany, was beyond the fineness of man's hearing. It might be the innocent bird, the hunter of mice ; as it might be the challenging pickets of that intangible army that lay infused through all the forests of the west, that spread army men's feet like water and slew like a pervading pestilence, that broke forth of a sudden in the night with outcries and the flames of conflagration and (the blow dealt) was gone again before the morning. Not even the bravest, and this man was brave, could think upon such enemies in such a place, and not be chilled. The current of his thoughts was changed ; he remembered his homeward journey of the morrow between hedge and ditch and through a land of spies ; he remembered it were well he should be early asleep and early afoot again ; and fully dressed as he was, he turned from the window and cast himself upon the bed.

With the change of attitude, a sleeping sentry in his memory awoke. His papers, which might at any moment prove to be his life, had been left upon a table in the dining-room corner ; he could see the place, he could recall the very gesture with which he had cast them down, the very look with which Renée had welcomed and caressed him as he did so ; even in the dark, in that well-known house, he thought it but a little matter to reach and to regain them ; and to leave them where they were would be an act of madness. The Baron de Croqueloup was himself suspected ; his life and his daughter's liberty had often hung already by a hair ; none knew it better than his guest who had secretly protected them so often, who came so often to their house daring a double danger, who was equally surprised to escape murder on his journey and arrest at his return. And if such was the character of the master, what could be looked for of the servants, dwelling between moor and forest, in a land where every tree stump was an ambush, rustic, devout and savage, the kinsmen and compatriots of the rebels ? Before the day came, before these untrusty lackeys should begin to move about the house, it was plain these papers must be recovered.

He groped his way to the door and down the low-browed stairs. The house of Croqueloup was ancient and of an antique stability ; the solid planking sustained his tread without a rumour ; and when he paused to listen, only the buzzing of his own ears rewarded his attention. So he came noiseless to the door, opened it without creak, entered the dining room, and came of a sudden to a startled pause. He could not have told why; there was no name in his vocabulary for the mute advertisement that thus arrested him, and held him, on the threshold, in the ineffable darkness, spell-bound and straining his senses. The sounds of his own breath and heart, the very rustle of his shirt, swelled great upon his hearing; and it seemed that he grew slowly conscious of other and similar noises—horribly small, hatefully near at hand, like that we hear in fever. "I am not alone," he thought; "some one is near me, almost within touch." Nameless fear grew upon him till he could bear the strain no longer, and with the desperation of a suicide, he flung out both hands before him briskly.

In the same instant, he was clutched at arm's length with another man, and the pair thrilled together in the brute darkness of the chamber with a similar alarm.

"Who are you?" he gasped.

His unseen assailant uttered in the same breath what was either an ejaculation in a foreign tongue, or perhaps a pass-word in some gibberish.

"Who are you? what is it?" repeated the republican.

"And I believe I know that voice," said the stranger. "So we meet at last, and in the dark," he continued, releasing his grasp. "I have long looked forward to this pleasure—how am I to call you? Count des Escherolles? or Citizen Clané?"

"You know me?" said the republican, still struggling for some shadow of that self-command which the other had regained so lightly.

"You and your business here," was the reply. "There are few things unknown to me in Brittany, and none in the place of Croqueloup. Yes, I know your business here, Captain Clané, and I compliment you on your taste —except in names and politics."

"Aha, but I begin to place you now, too," said the man addressed as Captain Clané and the count; "and unless I am the more mistaken, you, too, have a new name since last we met. They call you the Owl, I fancy. I preferred the old."

" And I prefer the new ; we clash in many things," was the reply. " But it is dull work talking in the dark ; and I have a curiosity—a great curiosity—to see you."

" I have good reason to share it," said the other ; " our cursed resemblance came near costing me my life."

" And yet oddly enough," replied the Owl, " it is not the resemblance, it is the difference, that troubles me." And he was to be heard in the darkness working with a tinder box.

His tone throughout the interview had been displeasing, almost hateful ; but in that last speech some undercurrent of strong feeling had clanged out, had startled and alarmed his hearer. The two men were kinsmen and old schoolfellows ; but in those truculent days and savage places, the ties of blood and the memories of a common boyhood counted for nothing. To the renegade aristocrat, to the disguised republican officer, far from any help of his own party, in the midst of that ill-reputed forest, any man might be counted a danger ; and perhaps this man above all—often-hunted and ubiquitous bearer of royalist despatches, the famed spy, he whose nocturnal activity and diurnal disappearance had earned him years ago the nickname of the Owl. It is certain that he thought so ; at that inscrutable inflexion of his cousin's voice, his hand passed swiftly and fiercely to his pistol ; and it was in a painful anxiety that he awaited the lighting of the lamp. The Owl was deft—he had learned and practised in his wandering career inscrutable dexterities—and the flame had scarce caught before he faced the count and looked him over.

" You can take your hand out of your pocket," he observed. " I will not hurt you. I give you my word of honour, if you remember what that means."

The count flushed hotly and crossed his hands upon his bosom.

" There is a mirror here," said the Owl. " We shall see better in the glass. We can compare better. If you will be good ? " And he led the way, lamp in hand, to the far end of the apartment.

They made a strange pair. The count was disguised indeed, but his disguise was comely ; and though he wore civilian clothes, he carried them off like a soldier and a dandy. Clean-shaven, close-cropped and brown-necked, he stood squaring his shoulders and poising his head, all the more haughty for his recent terror and present peril. The appearance of the Owl, on the other hand, was sylvan and ominous like his nickname. He was dressed like a peasant, with the great hat, the wide breeches, and the wooden shoes ; his clothes were stained with the mire of the wayside and torn by the briars of the forest ; his hair streamed on his shoulders long as a woman's. He held the lamp high, and himself stooped below it, bending forward and studying his cousin with what seemed a passionate intensity of interest ; his mouth was set, his hand trembled, and the light shook in his grasp, and the shadows on the faces wavered and changed.

The nature of his scrutiny, and the emotion that plainly lay behind and prompted it, escaped the deepest penetration of the Count Clané des Escherolles ; but he resented, he was troubled by it ; the blood came in his face, as it might into a maiden's ; and he turned upon his heel.

"I can see no such great resemblance," said he.

"Nor I so great a difference," said the Owl.

Both were right ; under the trenchant opposition of dress and demeanour, it was certainly possible to discriminate what is called a family likeness, one of those likenesses that come and go, that now strikes us with sudden wonder and that anon we stare and study for in vain. The height, the set of the figure, and certain movements familiar to both were even identical. Each besides had the same prominent chin and nose, the latter finely chiselled and of a very arrogant design ; each the same dark eyes sloping somewhat downward towards each other like the wing of a bird in flight. It was conceivable they might, upon an occasion, be confused apart ; when they were seen together, in those incongruous habits and under the influence of sentiments so different, the likeness was difficult to identify.

The count continued to walk away from the mirror towards the door, scarce with a set purpose; only to put space between himself and one who had grown bothersome.

"M. le comte Clané des Escherolles," said the Owl, slightly raising his voice. "I direct your attention to the fact that I am about to sup. I have covered eight leagues since I broke my fast."

The count turned, and observed for the first time that the tablecloth had been laid again since he retired and spread with meat and wine. The sight gave him a pang; Ariane must have known of it and had not told him; and the sense of exclusion rankled in him deep.

"Ah! you were expected!" he said.

"Even so, my cousin," replied the Owl, taking his place. "Will you join me?"

"I thank you. I have supped already," said the count.

The Owl looked up at him with a sudden expression that was at once menacing and imperious. "And yet I will ask you to sit down with me," he said.

There was a moment's hesitation; but it was plainly the better part to temporise, and the count drew in a chair and took a seat; at the same time he leaned his elbow on the table and his head upon his hand, so as to conceal some portion of his face.

The Owl took off his great hat, muttered a prayer and covered himself.

"You were not so devout of old," observed the count.

"A fashion," returned the other. "It is a fashion in our camp, and a gentleman must always be in the mode. But it is quite harmless and not catching."

He took a deep draught of wine and began to eat with a business-like voracity; it seemed he had forgot the presence of his kinsman, when he suddenly pointed at him with his knife.

"To think that I once loved that man!" said he.

The count started. "Chevalier," said he, "I am here at your desire. I have to request you to refrain from sneering."

"You are not a great reader of the heart : there was no sneer in that," replied the Owl. "But there was much bitterness ; because it is quite true that I once loved you. My God, and admired him, too ! " he added. "And now here you are, afraid to be alone with me ! "

"I am not easily frightened," said the count, "or I should not be here."

"Yet I should be vastly concerned to meet you in the streets of your garrison, and I am often there—oftener than you dream for," said the Owl. "Suppose we did—for the sake of conversation—what would you do ? "

The count flushed and paled. "My duty," he replied.

"It is very well said. But to do it is another thing," said the other. "Denys, do you love me still ? Do you think that I still love you ? "

"I am in no humour for conundrums," said the count.

"Am I to congratulate you, then ? This love affair has been a long while nursing ; is it ripe ? I am curious—I have a great interest in your love affair."

"And I deny your right to be informed," said the other.

"Well, I shall ask Aimée," said the Owl.

The count ground his teeth. "I am not very sure, M. de Quimpoli," said he, "but I believe you seek to thrust on me a quarrel."

"Far from that," replied the Owl. "I am about to suggest to you the propriety of your immediate departure from this house."

"Now ? In the dark ? I am very much obliged to you."

"You may very well be, for the advice is excellent," said the Owl.

"And why do you give it me ? " asked the count. "You do not love me ; you have had ado to keep your hatred covered."

"No, but I love Aimée," replied the other.

"Ah, and that is what has been wrong with you all night ! "

"That is what has been wrong with me all night," returned the Owl.

" And for the same reason I refuse it, then ! " said the count, rising. " I shall sleep here, as I was invited, under the banner of Aimée's father. And with that I wish you a good evening."

[After he was gone from the room, the Owl sat a while motionless ; then filled his glass and drank. His face was dark and troubled.

And with that, thrilling with irritation, he left the room, mounted the stair, and once more threw himself in the dark upon his bed, this time certainly not to sleep. Rather indeed he passed what then remained of darkness in perfectly impotent endeavours to judge the character of his cousin, the motive with which he had advised him, and the question of his own folly or wisdom in questioning that advice.]

The cousin sat but a little while at the table. He rose and set forth in turn in the dark house, came to a door, and knocked upon it in a particular manner.

" Who is there ? " said a voice from within.

" It is I, Alain," he replied. " I must speak with you."

A moment after the door was opened, and a girl in her nightdress and roughly muffled in a cloak, appeared before him. She was in no way discomposed ; in that time and house nocturnal summonses were things of course.

" Ariane," said the young man, " I have to put a question to you which it is very needful you shall answer truthfully. Is it as I suppose, or am I deceiving myself ? Do you love—" he paused a little at the name—" Monsieur des Escherolles ? "

She replied with perfect simplicity, " I do."

" It is a very bad business," said he. " There is no sense in it. It will end, it must end, in misery for you both."

" I am afraid of it," said Ariane.

" And yet you go on—with your eyes open you go on ? " asked the Owl.

" With my eyes open, Alain," said the girl.

" Well ! Then tell me how to save him. I cannot.

I have warned the man and he will not believe me. This house is no place for him to-night."

"Why, what do you mean? To-night? What is there to-night?"

"I do not know. I do not speak from certainty, but I believe the Good Apostle will be here to-morrow. As I came in to-night, the Owls were very lively in the forest. Trust me, I know their voices. It was some one closing in on Croqueloup, and you will have company to breakfast."

"It is in the teeth of all my information," said Ariane. "Jean-Baptiste is not gone from here six hours; he told a different story. You must be wrong. He has never before gone without warning us."

"What I fear is something sudden," said the Owl. "As I came by Letoits St. Antoine, I heard shots fired. Some of ours had been taken. It was some one considerable, for the hounds cheered consumedly. Half a league farther on and I began to suspect I was on the outskirts of a movement. The Owls began to cry; and on the top of the moor beyond the sandy stones, I am sure I saw men moving."

The girl was very pale. "Alain," she said, "this is only guess-work."

"It is more than guess-work, it is instinct. I have led this damned life so long that I feel things in my bones—feel them before they happen, as the rheumatism comes before the rain."

She shook her head. "But my information is explicit," said she. "It outweighs all instincts. Food was prepared for them eight leagues to the westward; there can nothing have occurred to change a settled plan. And besides—if there were any hope in it! But to send him off in the dark along that road, it is but a forlorn hope at the best; it is almost certain death, you know it, you cannot deny it——"

"It is a great risk," said Alain. "I can never deny that. And yet if I were in your place, he should not stay here for one moment. I cannot prove to you that I am right, and yet I know it. I *know* it, Ariane! Keep him here and to-morrow, by the break of day, you will see him in the hands of the Good Apostle."

She shuddered in spite of herself, for the leader named was one of the most savage in that most savage war. "I am sure you mean right, I will always trust you, Alain."

CANNONMILLS

Printed here for the first time in a popular edition.

CANNONMILLS

I

THE SPRING WIND IS POSTMAN

THE Spring comes upon that city with the horrors of invasion. It lies far north on the battleground of heat and cold ; those who dwell there are marchmen, they live in the borders where the war begins first and lasts longest. It stands high besides, with a sight upon the one hand of the cold seas, on the other of snowy mountains. The winds blow about it bringing rain and hail, blowing hot and icy. The soil cracks underfoot with ice, and slacks again into a slough. So it is with the bodies of the sensitive. As in some dungeon of the Holy Office, by lantern light, among cowled heads, people of yore were tortured, and an impassive secretary took down their groans, so the spirit of youth is here stretched upon a rack of agonies and pleasures, and he is aware of a heavenly recorder keeping the tally of his cries.

The first hero of this sketch woke on a Spring morning in his father's house in Inverleith Row to the knowledge of a voluminous despair. It was built together out of many ; consciousness of the approach of that day of judgment, an examination ; the desire to live thwarted by a thousand barriers ; eagerness of that semblance of living which was alone permitted him ; hero of the last night's hectic and unlovely pleasure, already discovered, already reported, which was yet in the transaction : below all, and perhaps chief of all, the physical distress of the equinox, the rude extremes and violences of the season tearing in

his nerves.   He covered his eyes from the light and groped
in his mind for any grain of consolation.   There was none.
All within was dark, bleak, and discomfortable as a winter
storm ; the heavy thoughts lay piled in his bosom like a
heap of wounded that he could hear groaning as they
died.   " Can I live to forty and go on waking like this ? "
he thought, and recoiled from the prospect.   A thought
of suicide trickled in his mind, and was instantly discarded.
Even out of the bottom of despair, his young hands grasped
too fervently the bars of hope's altar.

The crash of a gong sounded in the house, and he
sprang from bed.   A wonder of sunlight received him.
The day had cleared away barbarous clouds, unbeautiful,
cheerless ; it had arrived again in a glory of gold and sun
with which the east still smiled, and the trees in the garden
were animated by a gladsome wind ; Hope leaped in his
bosom like a giant Enceladus ; despair fell upon it once
again.   Only in youth, that has not yet known and tasted,
can the desire of possible happiness thus shape the tene-
ment of man ; only in youth could such a revelation pass
and be contained, such a pang of hope come and be thus
crushed, and awake no more comment than a groan.
The next moment the sufferer was splashing in his tub.

Meanwhile, below, the family was getting to breakfast.
Mr. Fordyce was in the armchair with the *Scotsman ;*
Mrs. Fordyce was busied with the tea and eggs, Miss
Fordyce and Miss Adamson were . . . .

MR. BASKERVILLE AND HIS WARD

This fragment is printed here for
the first time in a popular edition.

MR. BASKERVILLE

MR. BASKERVILLE AND HIS WARD

CHAPTER I

MR. BASKERVILLE of Singleton St. Mary's was a gentleman of excellent repute in the county, very well to do in land, a magistrate, talked of for the county member and on the eve of marriage with a beautiful lady, an heiress; and until this report of his cruelty ran suddenly abroad, there had been never a word to say against him. He was a sharp man with his servants, some of whom he had recently dismissed; and these were no doubt the authors of the rumour. But, for his misfortune, Mr. Baskerville was on no very good terms with Archdeacon Porter the rector of Singleton Abbas, a man with much weight by reason of his cloth, his learning, and his virtues. The Archdeacon and Mr. Baskerville had sat together on the bench; and as they were both men who had the art of disagreeing, they had come more than once to disobliging words. The doctor was very much the Anglican ecclesiastic, not very great on charity; prone rather to believe evil and then very indignant; no saint, but a bold, hot-headed generous man of the world; and when Beale brought him the first wind of Mr. Baskerville's inhumanity, he flushed scarlet.

" I will protect this child," he said, and no doubt that thought was in his mind, but the part that really tickled him was to punish Mr. Baskerville. " Chastisement is very fit; but this smells of murder; I believe Baskerville is the child's heir. It must be looked into narrowly. I will see to this, Mr. Beale."

Accordingly, he made some business towards Singleton

St. Mary's when he knew Mr. Baskerville was to be abroad ; and hung about the entrance, both going and coming till, on the second occasion, sure enough he saw Robin Rutledge in the gravel path and beckoned him. The boy came with a very furtive, startled manner ; he had a dodging way with him, as he spoke, like one used to sudden blows ; he was exceeding pale besides and undergrown, like one stinted in his meat.

" Do not be afraid of me, Mr. Rutledge," said the Archdeacon, " I am an ecclesiastic ; I desire to speak with you in strict confidence. There is a bruit in the county that Mr. Baskerville mishandles you."

" I don't know," said Robin.

" It is reported he beats you with an inhuman, great staff, and with the buckle of a belt," the clergyman continued. " If you had any wounds upon your person, it would be better I should see them ; I shall then protect you with the more authority."

Robin seemed to muse, and his eye kept ferreting upon all sides as if in quest of danger.

" Is there any that can overhear us ? " asked Dr. Porter, who had no wish to be observed in this employment.

" I do not know," said Robin.

" Do you understand," said the Doctor, " that I am here on a very strange step, entirely from humanity, entirely with an eye to your protection ? "

" No," said Robin. " I do not." And he blew in his hands, for it was cold weather.

" This boy is an idiot ! " cried the Doctor.

" No, I am not an idiot," said Robin ; " you lose your breath upon me ; I will tell no tales." And he retreated a little from the Archdeacon, with a strange look of dishonest, shifty doggedness, that would have disheartened the most patient.

That was not the clergyman's character : the blood flew to his brow, and he rode off at no very reverend pace, cursing the lad heartily. But the interview was not without results. Robin could think of nothing else, for though he would not trust himself a hairbreadth, he bore no love to Mr. Baskerville and this talk of deliverance affected him profoundly. He left his task, in consequence, unlearned ; was handsomely beaten, which still more confused him ; and pretty soon after was taken in a falsehood, which was indeed the boy's great defect and Mr. Baskerville's particular abhorrence. For this he was thrashed once more and sent to the gable room for a week, a prisoner on bread and water.

Meanwhile the archdeacon, from being very angry with the boy, passed on to be all the angrier with Mr. Baskerville. The story kept growing in the countryside, until the houses rang with it. Some busybody looked into the will of Robin's father ; Mr. Beale and the archdeacon gave tongue like old hounds ; the Jacobites followed in a mass, for Mr. Baskerville was a Whig, and the elections were at hand ; and four days after, which was market day in Singleton Abbas, that unhappy gentleman rode into town without a thought of misfortune, and found every eye avoid him and every hand slip into a pocket on his approach.

Though he had never courted popularity, he was a man who loved respect, and had been used to it. His marriage was near, so were the elections ; he saw himself threatened at once in everything that he valued ; and what was the most painful to support, he had not a guess at what should be the cause of his disfavour. It was in vain that he angled to bring some one to book ; either his own anger made him maladroit, or the whole county acted together on a common plan, and one after another slipped between his fingers. The poor man was near beside himself by the time he came on Dr. Porter in front of the " Red Lion." There were many bystanders, but they made a ring about the two chief actors, so that it was in the most public manner that the Archdeacon disregarded his salute. Mr. Baskerville turned and caught him by the sleeve.

" I think you omitted to bow to me," said he.

" And so I did," says Dr. Porter, " and have offered myself purposely to have this explanation because, as my cloth protects me, you cannot affect to turn this off into a brawl. It is wished you should feel the displeasure of the county."

"I stand here a very blameless man," cries Mr. Baskerville. "This is some intrigue; it is political; I knew you was of that party."

"You will find all parties in one against you, you abominable man!" the archdeacon broke out. "But look to it! it will not be borne; there are eyes on your behaviour, Mr. Baskerville. Lay another finger on young Rutledge, and you see if you have any to defend you!"

Mr. Baskerville's conscience was so clear, that he was at first struck silent by surprise, and then vastly relieved, to hear the matter was no worse.

"I will chastise my family as I think fit," said he, "and as I believe you do yourself," which was a good retort, for the doctor was irascible. "I am the boy's guardian," he added.

"Not only that, I think," says Dr. Porter shrewdly.

"What do you mean by that?" cried Mr. Baskerville, a little shaken, for he saw something ugly was intended and could not guess what it should be.

"I thought you was his heir, too," says the Doctor. "O, sir, your schemes are pierced! You may pray God you have not gone too far; for if the boy dies, here is the whole county ready to cry murder on you! If he dies, you hang for it; so you are fairly warned."

Mr. Baskerville was so struck to the heart by this speech, by its falsity—for nothing could be falser, and its sweeping and fatal consequence to his own character, that he forgot for the moment the sacred office of the accuser and lifted up his whip. Dr. Porter stood his ground, like a man delighted; and from the ring of bystanders (among whom there were many of the most considerable persons in the county) there broke out such a storm of hisses that the arm of the aggressor fell to his side.

"You don't strike me?" says the archdeacon.

"This is an old grudge with you, Dr. Porter," said Mr. Baskerville. "But you can rest easy now; you have killed your man."

And he walked into the "Red Lion," called for his horse,

drank a shillingsworth of brandy in the time it was saddling, and rode out by the back way just as the dusk was falling. Sometimes he rode hard ; sometimes he let the reins fall on his horse's neck, and sank into mere obstruction of mind ; sometimes he spoke furiously with himself ; but so great was the crash of all his hopes and ambitions and so deadly the malice of this calumny that he came to his own door an angrier man than when he left the inn. He came near falling when he dismounted ; and then, spiriting up again, caught the groom by the collar.

"Is this any of your doing ? " he yelled. "Have you been telling tales ? "

"Lord love you ! " said the groom, and before he could get out more, his master had unhanded him again and strode into the house.

There was no light in the hall, for he was not expected home till bedtime, and he stood and leaned against the table thinking. What did it all mean ? He had always hated this white-faced, idle, lying urchin, to be sure ; but he had done his duty by him sternly. Too sternly ? He wondered, and thought not—the child was of so ill a disposition. And now he was ruined ! He cast down his riding whip upon the floor with violence, and turned and went upstairs.

The gable room, where Robin was in durance, occupied one end of the upper storey ; its ceiling was uneven, for it was close under the roof, and it got its light from a single window in a gable ; whence the name. Books were kept there, for Mr. Baskerville was a ripe scholar, and well fitted in everything but patience to be Robin's master. There was an old secretary in a corner, where Mr. Baskerville did some of his affairs ; a pallet bed had been put in, since it was chosen to be Robin's prison-house ; and there was a lamp, which the boy tended for himself.

When Mr. Baskerville unlocked the door and entered, the lamp was already lighted, and by its dim rays he saw a scene of great disorder. Books had been pulled down from the shelves by the hundred, and were scattered on the floor in some odd sort of disposition, here in strings, there piled on one another. In the midst of this, Robin sat, looking mighty white and frightened and making believe to study in his Carderius. Mr. Baskerville had an old maid's horror of disorder, and a saint's impatience of falsehood, whether spoken or acted ; this was a scene that appealed to what was worst in the man, through what was best ; and the very look of the boy was now hateful to him.

"Put that book down," he said in a clapping tone. "You cannot deceive me ; you have not looked in it since I was gone. What does this mean ? " and he waved his hands at the books.

Robin said nothing ; he looked at Mr. Baskerville with eyes of obstinacy and terror.

"Will you not answer, sir ? " said Mr. Baskerville.

And again Robin said nothing, only his eyes wavered

The guardian sat down ; he was conscious of something in himself that cowed him ; conscious of the depth of the hatred that he bore the boy, and a kind of unmanly greed he had to punish him. He fought this down in silence.

"You will never try to please me," he said at last ; " it is past hope ; you take a pleasure to provoke me. But to-night, whatever you do or have done, you shall go scot-free. I only wish to ask you a question. Now, Robin, for the sake of God, be truthful. Will you, indeed ? If I promise you shall not be punished ? "

"Yes," said Robin.

"What did you say to Archdeacon Porter ? " asked the guardian.

"I never spoke to him," said Robin.

Mr. Baskerville rose and walked about the floor ; he wiped his brow.

"*Robin*," said he, " *I saw you*. How often am I to tell you not to lie ? It is the pitifullest vice ; and you lie so openly ! Will you not be truthful once ? I cannot—I warn you of that—I cannot endure a lie ; I will not take one, do you hear me ? Do you hear me, sir ? "

"Yes," said Robin.

Mr. Baskerville walked about again, till he was a little the master of himself. "And now," says he, " what passed at this interview ? Remember that I know what passed ; I know the gist of it ; I want but the words."

Robin cast about in his mind what he should say. He had no idea of telling the truth ; that was never his custom ; but he stood in a cruel fear of his guardian, and was bent on pleasing him at any cost.

" He said I was an idiot," said he at last.

Could this be true ? thought Mr. Baskerville ; it was at least his own opinion. " What else ? " said he.

" He desired his compliments to you," said Robin.

" I believe that is a lie," said Mr. Baskerville. " Take care, what did he ask you ? That is what I want."

Robin racked his wits for an answer ; he searched his master's eye for any hint of what was wanted, but there was nothing there to read except the glow of anger. He pulled his fingers and made up his mind.

" He asked when you was to be married," said he.

Mr. Baskerville, affronted with a fresh lie that struck him like a taunt, lost all control. He gave a voiceless cry, and sprang upon Robin. The boy on his part heard mischief in that strange sound ; he had the passive, slavish courage in a very high degree ; he could set his teeth and stick to a manifest misstatement under any extremity of correction ; and he was so used to the rod that he could scarce be said to mind it. What now woke in him was a fear beyond the fear of stripes ; he felt that Mr. Baskerville was being mastered by his passion ; he thought he read murder in his eye ; shrank in upon himself with a squeal like a weasel's, and snatching the hand of his assailant, bit it to the bone.

The pain and the surprise were so extreme that Mr. Baskerville turned as white as a sheet and stood transfixed, staring at his bloody fingers. Then he became aware that the boy had crouched in a corner and was howling with terror at what he had done, so that the house rang with it ; and the fear of further scandal seized on the unhappy man. He went hastily from the room, and locked it behind him ; and to his unspeakable relief, the cries immediately ceased. Yet he stood awhile by the door and hearkened ; and he was still so listening, when the butler and one of the maids came tumbling upstairs, and found him there with a white and clouded countenance, and his blood dripping on the floor. He turned to them at once, indeed, and bid them go down and leave the boy alone ; but his voice shook like a fiddle string.

" Here," he said, " bring me a rag, Sally. See, the little beast has bit my finger ! " and he muttered oaths to himself as he followed them downstairs. " Mind," he added, when they were got down as far as to the hall, " not one of you goes near the gable room to-night ! He who does shall leave my service. Let him starve, let the thankless —— starve," and he called the boy by an opprobrious name.

All this told heavily against him the next day, when Robin was found to have disappeared.